Adolphe d' Ennery

A Martyr

Or, a victim of the divorce law. A novel

Adolphe d' Ennery

A Martyr
Or, a victim of the divorce law. A novel

ISBN/EAN: 9783337028299

Printed in Europe, USA, Canada, Australia, Japan

Cover: Foto ©Andreas Hilbeck / pixelio.de

More available books at **www.hansebooks.com**

A MARTYR;

OR,

A VICTIM OF THE DIVORCE LAW.

A Novel.

BY

ADOLPHE d'ENNERY.

Translated from the French, by Aristide Filiatreault.

Toronto:

ROSE PUBLISHING COMPANY.

1886.

TO THE READER.

In translating this work, of one of the most popular writers of the day, my aim has been chiefly to bring before the readers a class of novel which is not usually translated into English. Heretofore, with few exceptions, the translators of French novels seem to have chosen only the works of fiction of such authors as Zola and his disciples, which, I am happy to state, are being relegated into the obscurity from which they should never have issued. There was in their favor only the attraction of novelty; but the good sense of the public soon rejected those *pornographic* writings. The only reason that can be assigned for their existence is the boast which some of those writers openly made, to plunge so far into obscenity that none would dare to follow them. In the minds of a great many people a French novel is something highly " spiced ;" and it has led to the remark I have often been met with, that in French literature of this kind—novel-writing—there is nothing but immorality, to put it in a mild form, depicted. The reader who will peruse this work in the hope of finding such condiments will be sadly mistaken,

M. Adolphe d'Ennery, the author of this work, is a dramatic writer of fame, and his dramas are played in the great theatres of France by great artists. When asked to write a novel, he refused at first, pleading *incompetency;* but he was prevailed upon at last, and the result has been "A MARTYR," a *chef-d'œuvre.* With his acknowledged dramatic talents, it is no wonder that the work should abound with stirring scenes of the greatest effect; and from the first page to the last the reader is kept in a state of thrilling excitement. And throughout the entire work, not one word—not one thought—but is calculated to depict the nobler feelings and instincts of human nature, written in elevated and flowery language.

The only thing I am conscious of is, that I have been unable to do full justice to the work, and that my version will be deficient in force. As extenuating circumstance, I plead inexperience (this being the first translation of the kind I have ever attempted), and I hope the reader will be indulgent enough to forgive me in favor of my good intentions. At first the translation was not meant to be published, having been done as a pastime; but I was induced to have it printed by some literary friends, who, I am afraid, were partial to its merits. Be that as it may, it is in your hands now, and I claim a welcome for it, if not for my sake, for the sake of the author.

My sincere thanks are due to Mr. Charles Dedrickson, of the editorial staff of the Toronto *Mail,* for his valuable hints, and corrections of idioms. His thorough knowledge of French enabled him to grasp the exact meaning of the author, and to give the corresponding meaning in the English language, with which he is no less familiar.

With the hope of having done something to help you, dear reader, to while away an hour in intellectual enjoyment, and at the same time to confirm you in the idea that there is still some good left in human nature, I leave my work to your kind appreciation, being comforted with the precept that, "*il sera pardonné beaucoup à celui qui a beaucoup péché.*"

ARISTIDE FILIATREAULT.

A MARTYR.

PROLOGUE.

I.

THE story which we are commencing will soon develop itself on the Parisian ocean, so full of storms and tempests; but to know its origin the reader will have to go hundreds, even thousands, of leagues away.

Let us proceed first to Italy, to Naples. A noisy mob crowded the sidewalks, and in that crowd could be seen a marvellous creature walking by herself, disdaining to answer the provocations of the merchants and the more interested ones of the young men. She was twenty years old at the most, although she looked older. Her costume was very modest, even poor: a linen dress and a net of imitation lace. But under the linen, almost transparent with wear, the body of a goddess moulded itself. It was supple, nervous, of almost provocating perfection, which owed nothing of its delicacy to the use of the corset. And through the broken meshes of the net, her rich black hair fell upon her neck and forehead, throwing a shadow on the flame of her eyes. She was well known on Toledo street, where she was then, looking with envy in the windows of the jewellers and merchants; and every minute she was familiarly saluted with, 'Good-day, Gorgon!' This popularity left her indifferent. She hardly ever answered the greetings she received. She had turned into the street leading to the royal castle of Capodimonte, at the gates of the city. But she soon left the main street and took to the little lanes which form a sort of spider's web at the foot of the hill. She stopped in front of the shop of a melon merchant, and looked around to see if anybody had observed her. The lane was deserted. She took three or four coppers, which constituted her whole fortune, out of her pocket, and bought one of these water-melons in which, as they say in Naples, there is both drinking and washing water. With this acquisition she turned into a small lane and entered an old house which seemed to stand up only by a miracle. Arrived at the second story, she pushed a door open. Gorgon was at home. This apartment consisted of a room with a small closet or rather a bed-recess, and was at the same

A

time the parlor, the dining-room, the bed-room, and the kitchen.
The whole was quite in accord with the occupant.   In the midst of
sordid poverty, besides two or three broken chairs, on a pallet
whose only mattress was never shaken and whose sheets were never
washed, were to be seen flashing tinsels, white and rose-colored
satin shoes, gilded lace, short petticoats all tumbled up, garlands
of artificial flowers, all faded.   In short, all the paraphernalia of a
ballet girl.   One thing only contrasted with the general effect of
that mean furniture and those scattered rags.   It was a wooden
table laden with papers, briefs, pens and ink.   If all the rest belonged to her, this table certainly did not.   To get acquainted with
its owner, the reader must follow Gorgon, who opened the door of
the recess with her knee.

' Peppo ! ' she said.

A stifled grunt was the answer.   The young girl remained on the
threshold of the room.   She could hardly go in, anyway, for a dirty
mattress spread on the floor, covered the whole of this den.   She
crossed her arms, and with indignation, roused the lazy fellow.

' Peppo ! ' she repeated, ' get up.   It is already ten o'clock.'

' Eh ?   What ?   What's the matter ? ' asked Peppo, ' is the house
on fire ? '

' I wish it was, and that it would burn you until the day of judgment,' said Gorgon.   ' Is it not a shame ?   Ten o'clock ; and you
should be at your office at nine ! '

' Bah ! ' said Peppo, rubbing his eyes, ' I do enough for the money
I receive.   Sixty francs per month !   The salary will not ruin the
municipality.'

' Sixty francs per month is not much money, but it is enough to
exist upon,' said the young girl with a nervous laugh, ' and if you
should lose that situation, what would become of us ? '

' You would return to dancing.   The ballet corps of San Carlo
will always be glad to have you.'

' Yes, but I will not have it.'

During this time Peppo was getting up.   He was dressing, unmind-
ful of the young girl's presence.   Evidently these two splendid
beings did not embarrass each other.   We said these two splendid
beings.   Peppo was, in fact, as handsome as Gorgon was beautiful.
Being brother and sister they were very much like each other, mo-
rally and physically.

' So, then,' said Peppo, ' it is decided, you quit the theatre ?   Per
Baccho !   What stupidity !   A beautiful girl like you !   You have
too much virtue, my dear ! '

Gorgon shrugged her shoulders.

' It is not virtue,' she said disdainfully.   ' Only, all that rabble of
the theatres disgusts me.   If I am to make a fortune with my beauty,
it must be by other means.   Otherwise I prefer my poverty.

As the reader can judge by their conversation, Peppo and Gorgon, were not over scrupulous. It must be said, to their credit, that they were born and had been raised in the most deplorable conditions. Their mother, a ballet girl, had not kept that purity of manners which is usually observed by the women of her class in Italy. She had had all kinds of adventures, and her greatest profit had been the birth of a son and a daughter, at an interval of five years' time. She called her son Peppo, which means Joseph, simply because he was born on the day of the feast of that saint. As to her daughter's name, there was more poetry in its origin. The greatest success of the dancer had been the creation of a ballet called 'Medusa.' As everybody knows, Medusa is one of the three fabulous Gorgons. It was under this mythological costume that the dancer made the conquest of a gallant captain. She was only paying a debt of gratitude to love when she gave to the beautiful girl we have just presented to the reader the name of the character she had filled a year before her birth. When she died Peppo was ten years old, and Gorgon five. Instead of calling public charity to their assistance, the little bohemians set their wits to work to glean a living on the streets, like birds fallen from their nests. At fifteen years of age Gorgon made a *début* at San Carlo, the finest and the largest of theatres after La Scala. Born on the boards, so to speak, the maiden knew a little of dancing from seeing and imitating others. But as she had never made any serious studies, she never advanced beyond the rank of a ballet girl, and it was due to her beauty that she ever reached that title. The vanity, or rather the just pride, of this ambitious girl was not to be kept down in such a mean situation of life. If she were to fall she wanted to do it gloriously and get wealthy on the start. The occasion did not present itself at San Carlo, and she preferred to quit the theatre rather than submit to the humiliating familiarities of her companions. It was eighteen months since Gorgon had taken that resolution, and as she was not earning anything, Peppo had to utilize the few talents he possessed to eke out a precarious living for both. The greatest of these talents was calligraphy. During his leisure time he had perfected himself in that art, and he could do nothing better than draw from it the resources he and his sister needed so badly.

In Italy municipal servants are poorly paid, and there are almost always vacant situations in the civil service. Peppo took one of these situations, because he could get nothing better, and became clerk of the records.

He finished his toilet that morning and commenced his breakfast, eating a large slice of the melon. While eating, he was listening to her complaints. The promenade she had taken in front of the brilliant stores of Toledo street, had awakened in her mind a covetousness always ready to burst. Her misery appeared more unen-

durable because fortune seemed to directly defy her. Between her
and the millions heaped up in the windows under the most alluring
forms of modern luxury, there was only the thickness of a transparent glass, and she would say to herself that her beauty and her
ambition would be, when she liked, two diamonds hard enough to
cut the glass and allow her to lay hands on all the treasures which
actually tempted her uselessly. Once that resolution taken, she
was sure of success. She was saying all this to her brother with a
great volubility of language, expressive gestures, and with an auda-
cious rebellion of voice and looks. These projects did not scandalize
Peppo ; still he made a few objections, for the sake of appearances.
She stopped him.

'Do not play such a comedy,' she said, brusquely. 'However,
listen. If it annoys you that I should undertake to make our fortune, I give you eight days to do it in.'

Peppo did not return an answer. With a miserable pittance of
sixty francs per month, what could he do in eight days' time ? He
merely shrugged his shoulders and opened the door, intending to go
to his office. On the landing he ran against a little old man who
had the strangest aspect one could imagine.

'Ah !' he said, ' our neighbor, the Duke de San Lucca. Come
in, your excellency. Perhaps Gorgon has a slice of melon left for
you.'

And he went away, leaving the old man there. In spite of his
miserable aspect and ragged clothes, the man Peppo had just
left was a nobleman, and actually a duke. He was even a duke
of very illustrious ancestry. The family to which he belonged
claimed to be descended from St. Luke, the evangelist. Be that
as it may, his excellency, the Duke de San Lucca had filled
the highest positions in the gift of the court of the Two Sici-
lies. When Garibaldi entered Naples, on the 7th of Septem-
ber, 1860, the duke was doing service in the king's household,
and he followed that sovereign in his flight. On the 13th of
February, 1861, when Gaöte was surrendered, the duke was the
last to leave the citadel. The fall of the Bourbons was a fatal blow
to the old gentleman in every respect. The courtier of the old
régime could have, like one of his nephews, trimmed his sail to the
new breeze, but he was stubborn and brave, and he would not cap-
itulate with his conscience. On the contrary, he clothed himself in
his ruin as the ancient philosophers in their tattered robes. ' Revolution has made me a beggar,' he declared. ' Then beggar I am,
and beggar I shall remain.' And to affirm his resolution, he looked
for the most miserable lodging that could be found in Naples.
Chance brought him to the door of a half-demolished house, at the
foot of the suburb of Capodimonte. He rented on the second story
a room, the possession of which he had to fight for against the com-

bined efforts of the sun, the rain, and the wind. Then he sold a golden snuff-box, which he had found in a pocket of his coat, and with the proceeds he bought a splendid brass plate, which he nailed on the door. On this plate the engraver had inscribed the two following lines, very short, but very significant :

HIS EXCELLENCY THE DUKE DE SAN LUCCA,

Beggar.

Not satisfied with thus exposing his new profession, the old man practised it with ostentation. The first day he appeared on the public place, soliciting alms, he had elegant clothes, almost new. The pedestrians took great delight in this gratuitous recreation, and in a few minutes the duke had gathered twenty sous. When he had that sum, M. de San Lucca made a graceful bow, declared that his day's work was done and that he would be at the same place on the next day. The next day he was there, and also the following days. When he possessed one franc, which was all he wanted, he returned to his miserable room. Curiosity, however, had given way to indifference, and sometimes he had to beg for many hours before he could gather his pittance. After a time his clothes became nothing but rags, and looked more like a harlequin's dress than any other known raiment. His poor excellency led this life for seventeen years. We termed him an old man on the day when for the first time the duke asked for charity. Seventeen years later, he was no more an old man ; he was Methusalah in person. He was only eighty years old, but he looked double that age. His little body was dried up and shrivelled. During the last years of his mendicity, the poor old man had experienced some very hard times. He became sick and he could not collect his daily receipts. Several times he would have died of hunger and fever, if Providence had not brought to the room next to his the two young and beautiful children we are already acquainted with. Gorgon and her brother loved this old man, and had, so to speak, adopted him. However poor they were, they were always ready to share their miserable dinner with his ruined excellency. They had shown him respect and what was still better they had given him affection. That was the reason why, without blinding himself as to the morality of his young protectors, the duke had for them a paternal affection. Such was the character who entered Gorgon's room on the day our tale commences. At the first glance, the duke perceived that some grave discussion had just taken place between his neighbors, and he interrogated Gorgon. The pretty girl did not hesitate in the least to acquaint him with her revolts and her projects. M. de San Lucca was of an age not to be astonished at anything. So he showed no surprise whatever on hearing the confession thus made to him.

'Eh! eh! *Gorgonetta mia,*' he said patting her cheek with his bony fingers. 'We have enough of this eating of mad cow!'

'Even if there were cow flesh!' answered the marvellous creature with humor, 'I would not care if it were mad or not. But what is to be done, your excellency? It is hard, when one has teeth like a mouse, to have nothing to put between them.'

'*Corpo di Baccho!*' the gentleman swore, gallantly, 'in fact, your teeth are sharp enough to crunch diamonds. But it is a sin, all the same, to think that those beautiful eyes, that splendid hair, and that fine figure shall become the prey of some cad of this petty King of Savoy, who has thrown the snow of his shoes on the flames of our old Vesuvius! You deserve a better fate than that, goddess that you are!'

Gorgon shrugged her shoulders and said:

'What can I do?'

However, she had appreciated the compliment, which had soothed her a little.

'It would ve very amusing,' thought the duke aloud.

'What?' Gorgon asked.

'Nothing. An idea which had entered my head.

The old man stopped, with a queer smile.

'Well, tell me your idea.'

The duke did not hesitate long. Hovever, he gave her only half of his idea.

'Do you see,' he said, 'there is a thing which frightens me for you in the battle you are about to engage in.'

'What?'

'The point you start from is too low. The way to the summit of fortune will be long. You have nothing to throw in the balance; no name, no family.'

'They call me Gorgon!' said the beautiful girl with pride.

'Undoubtedly! A surname! less than nothing! you are the daughter of a whim and of a fancy, that's all. Have you been even baptized?'

'My mother used to burn tapers before the madonna every evening of first representation. She would not have let me live like a slut.'

'Very well, but that is not a very great treat to offer to your lover who is to be. You must win your stripes in the gay world one by one; and you will wear out your youth before you reach the golden epaulets.'

'I know it well,' answered Gorgon, biting her lips with rage. 'But, once more, how could I help it?'

'If,' answered the duke, 'you had a great situation to sacrifice, you would enter into the career of gallantry at the first onset, like those sons of a family who obtained the rank of colonel while still young, before this confounded revolution. Ah! *Diavolo!* if you only had a great name to call your beautiful face by!'

'Yes, but I have not,' quietly answered the young girl. 'Why speak of things which cannot exist?'

'How do you know?' asked the duke, fixing his piercing eyes on Gorgon.

'What do you mean, your excellency? I do not understand you.'

The old man got up and stood before his companion, almost as gallantly as when he was a courtier of the king, and with one arm around his tattered hat,

'Gorgon,' he said, bowing deeply, 'I am only a beggar like you, and I am over eighty years old, but I am Marquis de Corriolo, Count de Castello, and Duke de San Lucca. Would it please you to be countess, duchess and marchioness? Would it please you to be my wife?'

Gorgon had thought at first, because of the solemn attitude of her host, that he was joking, but she understood by his accent that he was in earnest. Almost stunned, with the blood rushing to her head, she got up in her turn.

'Your excellency,' she said, with her voice altered, 'You would not laugh at a poor girl who has never done you any harm. So, I think you are speaking in earnest. But I am not the woman to take what you offer without knowing why. Tell me why you want to make me a duchess, and I shall then decide whether I ought to accept or refuse.'

There was an immense pride in this demand of a nameless girl who was valuing her co-operation in an obscure bargain. The duke at first would not answer her question, except by non-committal.

'Plague of your pride,' he said, smiling. 'You are beautiful, Gorgonetta, as no woman has ever been. You have been generous and good to the ruined old beggar. And you are astonished that the old beggar should reward, with the only thing he possesses, that is to say his name, the beauty and kindness with which you have made his last days happy!'

'You have no other reason to offer?'

'No other.'

'Then I refuse,' she said, proudly.

The spectacle was very curious. On the one hand the astonished duke was trying to guess the motive of Gorgon's refusal, and on the other she could not understand the reason of so unexpected an offer. These old friends, so sincerely devoted to each other, were now like two adversaries. M. de San Lucca was the first to regain his coolness. He took the young girl's hand and kissed it reverently. Then he sat down and invited her to follow his example.

'Tell me,' he said, lightly, 'why you refuse my proposal?'

'Tell me first why you make it?'

' Well, then; since you wish it, know, then, Gorgon, that this
marriage would be the logical and natural consequence of the life I
have led for the past twenty years. Like all old men, I have become very indifferent to men and things. I would not do any more
harm to a revolutionist than to a fly. But there are some who are
not included in this indifference, and on whom I should like to
play a good joke before I die. These are my own parents, who wear
my name, and who, having enjoyed the benefits and favors of the
dethroned family, have sacrificed gratitude to their ambition and their
cupidity. I blush to see at the court of the new king a duke and a
duchess de San Lucca, grand-children of the brother I have lost. I
am ashamed of their cowardice and baseness. My greatest pleasure
would be to humiliate them as they have humiliated me. This intention has guided my life thus far. I have displayed my misery
to the world, and I have shown a noble duke de San Lucca, begging
in the streets, at the door of the palace of his relatives, who have
become traitors. To-day I find the means of doing even more, and
I improve the occasion. There is, I have already told you, a duchess
of my name at the new court of Italy. Well, I wish that another duchess, bearing my name also, should go and scandalize that
name, and cover it with another kind of shame. In the theatres,
at the Corso, everywhere the crowd sees, judges and peers, I wish
to see two duchesses de San Lucca face to face, and the people hesitating which of the two is the more unworthy of the title, the one who
makes a trade of her beauty or the one who traffics with the fideli-
ty of her ancestors. Go, Gorgon, take boldly the name that I
offer you, with which to enter on that new life. Make it the step-
ping-stone of your fortune. You cannot soil it enough, to my desire,
since I hold it as the most contemptible of all Italy ! '

The duke underwent a change while speaking these words. At
first he had conceived this project of marriage as if actuated by his
fondness for joking. But little by little the light comedy had
turned to heavy drama, and the noble old parent had assumed the
tone and manners of a hero of tragedy. He almost rose to the sublime of the art in his imprecations against the parents whom he
despised. Only his anger overreached its object and made the
proud girl understand too well the indignity of the *rôle* she was
asked to assume. A less noble woman would have accepted the
bargain. Gorgon, who was proud even in her weaknesses and her
vices, still refused.

' Seek another to accomplish your project,' she said, boldly. ' I
am not the tool you are in need of.'

' But—'

' If I were wearing your name,' she said, with intense feeling, ' do
you know what I would do with it ? I would use it to elevate, not
to lower myself. I would perhaps strike with it, but I would not

trail it in the mud. Keep your name for yourself, your excellency ; since that is the use you want me to make of it, it would no longer be worthy of me. The lost woman which I shall become will deserve some excuse, being only Gorgon. She will only return where she came from. She will be what her mother **was.** But if she were the Duchess de San Lucca, she would be infamous and worthless ; nay, she would be sacrilegious ! '

Her vehemence subdued the old man. In spite of himself he compared his own conduct with that of this adventuress, the daughter of an adventuress, whose every word struck him, a duke, the son of a duke, and he understood that even in the most depraved souls there are sometimes found sublime principles. **The** girl who stood before him was going to plunge without a blush into an infamous life, and still one word was enough to arouse generous sentiments in her heart. As Gorgon, she would wallow without remorse in the mire, but suddenly become duchess de San Lucca, she would conquer the world instead of serving it. In his admiration, he felt ashamed, and he humbled himself.

'Gorgon,' he said, softly, 'Gorgon, you have just accomplished a miracle, and I thank you. You have caused me to return to my senses and made me understand, in a single moment, the error of my whole life.'

Then he folded the young girl in his arms and kissed her as if she had been his daughter. He left her and went to his own room, **where** he threw himself on his miserable bed, his mind deeply engrossed, and his body aching.

Let us leave him, a prey to the bitter regrets of his solitude, making the painful examination of his conscience, to which he had condemned himself at this late hour of his life, and let us return to Gorgon. Already the flame which had been flashing for a moment in that magnificent statue was extinguished. One would have said that nothing unexpected had crossed her projects of **corruption.** On the contrary, she returned to them with avidity, her soul serene and tranquil. As she did not expect that during the eight days she had accorded to her brother, Peppo would realize the fortune **she** coveted, she was getting ready for the fray.

Her modest wardrobe was spread over the mattress. It was chiefly with the remains of her old costumes that Gorgon tried to make a dress which would be pretty nearly worthy of her beauty. She made a bundle of **what** could not be utilized and took it to a second-hand dealer, who agreed to give her twenty francs. It was certainly very little, but she had not possessed such a sum for a long time, and the contact of the gold piece caused her a shiver. She **had** been in only a few minutes when Peppo arrived in his turn.

' Why ! already ? ' cried the young girl. ' The bell has not struck

three yet.   Ah ! *cattivo*, you should not rob the government in such
a shameful way.'

The chief of the bureau of records did not answer.   He merely
pushed the door and locked it, as if afraid that somebody would
come in :

' What's the matter ? ' asked Gorgon, astonished at this unusual
display of precaution, ' One would think you are afraid of robbers.'

' Perhaps,' simply answered Peppo, who was very pale, depositing on the table a pocket-book filled with papers.

' Ah ! *poveri !* I would pity them.   What could they take here ?
However ! here ! Peppo ! look !   Here are twenty francs I brought
here a minute ago.'

' And I,' said the young man in a subdued tone, putting his hand
on his pocket-book, ' I bring you twenty millions in my turn.'

' Twenty millions !'

Gorgon repeated these two words in a shriek.   All her covetousness and her appetites for pleasure and luxuries came to her
lips.   She wanted to tell Peppo all she was going to have.   Something like the bark of a dog in pursuit of its prey died in her throat.

' Twenty millions ! twenty millions !' she repeated again and
again, shuddering.   ' Show them to me, let me see them.   I want
to know what twenty millions are like !'

' Shut up !' said Peppo, seizing her abruptly by the arm, to prevent her falling into hysterics.   ' Do you want to bring all the
people in the street up here ?'

' Show them to me,' she said in a lower tone.   ' Are the twenty
millions in that pocket-book ?'

She tore the bundle open, taking the papers which it contained
and scattering them about.

' Where is the money ? ' she said, in a strangled voice.

As she found only old papers, almost illegible, or files of judicial
documents, she took fright and thought her brother was making
fun of her.

' Ah !' she said grinding her teeth, ' Have a care !   If you have
deceived me, I think I shall kill you !'

She fell exhausted on a chair.   Peppo availed himself of her
momentary weakness and drew near to her.

' Listen,' he said, in a low voice almost in her ear.   ' The twenty
millions are there, but like gold, they are buried deep under the
earth.   They are there, only we must dig deeply to take them.

Gorgon shook herself as if awakening from a dream.

' Come,' she said.   ' I do not understand.   Explain yourself.'

The young man commenced a long recital, lengthened involuntarily by Gorgon asking a thousand questions and making him repeat
the same things twenty times over.

Three months before the day when our readers have seen Peppo getting up so lazily in his den, an important communication had been addressed to the chief of the bureau of municipal records, at Naples. The chief of the bureau, that is to say Peppo himself, had received the communication, **and** had attended to it. It was to the following effect :

A business man of Paris had written to the municipal authorities at Naples, to acquaint them with the fact that he had been called on to liquidate the estate of a wealthy banker who had died recently. This banker, whose name was Giacomo Palmeri, had left **a** will in which he had established his origin very clearly, and by which he also disposed of his immense wealth. Giacomo Palmeri belonged to a poor Neapolitan family, and at twenty years of **age he** was the only representative of the family **with a** younger brother, whose name was Antonio Palmeri. Tired **of** eking out a miserable existence, Giacomo and Antonio resolved to expatriate themselves and tempt fortune in far-off countries. **At first** they decided to conquer the golden fleece together, but they soon dissolved partnership. They could not agree on the choice of the country where they were most likely to win their fortune. Giacomo wanted to remain in Europe, while Antonio contended for going **to** Asia or America, he did not exactly care which. To settle the dispute they resolved to cast lots, and to this effect they put in a hat a number of small pieces of paper, on each one of which was written the name of a city or country. After these preparations the drawing of the lottery commenced. Antonio put his hand in the hat for his brother and took out the word *France*. **Giacomo did** the same thing for Antonio, and brought out the words *British India*.

Giacomo Palmeri had gone to Paris where he amassed an **immense** fortune in the banking business, and he had given himself **up so** entirely to questions of finance, that nothing else could interest or seduce him. He had never had enough leisure to marry, **so** that, used up by incessant labors and by the excitement incidental to the Bourse and the Bank, he fell sick one fine day and never got better. By his will he left his whole fortune to this brother, and in the case of his death, to his widow and orphans.

Such were the circumstances under which an official letter has been received by the municipal authorities of Naples. Although he saw nothing but an increase of labor in this adventure, Peppo **took** a lively interest in the study of this document of the Parisian business man. Having acknowledged the receipt of the epistle, he wrote directly **to the** Italian consul at Calcutta asking him to send him all the information and documents he could gather on the subject. Having written a letter to the consul, signed with his own name, **by** power from the mayor, he thought no more of the matter.

These events had taken place three months before we commenced
our tale, and since then nothing had transpired to recall their remembrance to Peppo's mind, except a letter from the agent in Paris
asking him how far the researches had been successful. Peppo had
written that the answer of the consul would be transmitted as soon
as received. Such was the tale, or rather the story, which Peppo
narrated to his sister. From time to time Gorgon would interrupt
him with a violent harshness of language.

'But the twenty millions!' she would ask. 'Where are the
twenty millions you have promised me?'

Peppo did not allow himself to be diverted from the logic of
his narrative. He continued it as if he were making an official re-
port. One would have thought that he delighted in exciting the
anxious curiosity of the young girl.

'The twenty millions!' he said at last, tired of playing with the
fever and anguish of Gorgon. 'Have patience! we are getting to
them!'

Peppo had good reasons to ask his sister to have patience; hers
was nearly exhausted.

'Go on! go on!' she said.

'Well,' continued the young man, 'the answer of the Italian
consul at Calcutta arrived this morning, and it contained the papers
that you see there.'

'What do these papers say?'

'First you must know that the functions of the Italian consulate
at Calcutta are exercised by an English trader, as is the case in
nearly all the countries in which we are represented.'

'Then these papers that you have brought are written in English?'

'No, in the present case the documents and the letter are written
in good Italian. The signature of the consul alone betrays an
English hand.'

'But these documents, this letter, what do they say? Have you
sworn to make me die?'

'Have patience! I tell you. The letter says that Antonio Palmeri and his wife indeed lived in Calcutta together, and that they
were married in the offices of the consulate. They had also two
children, Annibal and Claudia, whose births have been duly regis-
tered. The letter adds that the poor devils are no more in this
world.'

'Who! Antonio and his wife?'

'Antonio, his wife and their two children! The four of them
died within a few hours' time from an epidemic of cholera.'

'That's horrible!'

'Not at all! that's charming!'

'How?'

' This enormous envelope which I have brought from the office, and which has been sent directly to my addres, as you see, this envelope, I say, contains :

' 1st, The certificate of marriage of Antonio Palmeri with Nissa Alessandri ; 2nd, The certificate of the birth of Annibal Palmeri, and that of Claudia Palmeri ; 3rd, The certificate of death of the father and mother ; 4th, The certificate of death of each of the two children. In all seven documents absolutely regular, and as authentic as they can be.'

' Then the twenty millions will be given to the state, since the natural heirs are dead ?'

' Certainly, unless we stop them on their way.'

Gorgon looked at her brother, asking herself if he had not become crazy.

' Explain what you mean,' she muttered.

' It is the simplest thing in the world, like all ideas of genius. You shall see. Let us suppose that the children of Antonio Palmeri and Nissa Alexandri are not dead, and that, consequently, the certificate of their decease are not among the deeds that are there ; let us suppose that they come to the bureau of records and claim these deeds which prove their identity and the decease of their father and mother, let us suppose that, armed with those deeds, they insist upon their right to be put in possession of the estate of Giacomo Palmeri, what would happen ?'

' It would happen that they would get the twenty millions ; there is no doubt of that. Unluckily for them, the children of Antonio Palmeri are dead !'

' However, let us further suppose that I, Peppo, am Annibal Palmeri, and that you, Gorgon, are Claudia Palmeri, my sister. Who can contradict us, after all ?'

' All Naples know who we are !'

' All Naples, yes! but all Paris, no ! And at Paris, where the estate is to be transferred to the heirs, nobody knows, or even has any doubts of our existence.'

' Come ! let us see ! ' said Gorgon, trying to put a little order in the chaos in which this project had thrown her mind, ' If I understand you rightly, your plan is to substitute ourselves for the children of Palmeri, and to inherit in their place ?'

' Yes, simply.'

' But that's a robbery ?'

' Oh ! ' said the municipal employé, disdainfully, ' it is a robbery, if you wish to call it so. It injures nobody, for in case the heirs of Giacomo cannot be found, the state will inherit in their place. And you know very well that to rob the state is to rob nobody.'

Gorgon's moral principles were not serious enough to rectify what was so dishonest and subversive in this allegation of her brother.

On the contrary. This taken for granted, Peppo's reasoning did not tickle her conscience at all. It was a strange anomaly on her part. A few minutes before, the proud girl had been indignant at the proposition of the Duke de San Lucca ; the action he wanted her to commit was not in itself a crime, it was only low. And sooner than be guilty of that baseness, she had refused, she, the nameless child, one of the noblest ducal crowns of Italy. Whilst now she did not think that it was a criminal action in the highest degree, to steal a fortune which did not belong to her. We have said it was a strange anomaly, and still, understanding the character of the woman, it was easily explained. Only one point was obscure in Gorgon's mind, or rather only one fear made her doubtful of the successful issue of this gigantic project.

'Come now,' said her brother, ' I can see by your face, that you are not yet satisfied.'

'No. I have a misgiving yet. Let us suppose that we have done all you have said. We have taken all the papers of the Palmeri ; we have gone to France ; then the gentleman who has the care of the estate will perhaps say : " The papers, very well. These are the necessary papers. But it is not proven that they belong to you. You might have found them, or perhaps stolen them." And then there would be an enquiry, and instead of inheriting twenty millions, we should be put, Peppo and Gorgon as heretofore, for a few years in a prison.'

Peppo had a benevolent smile.

' Artless child ! ' he said, 'you have not enough confidence in your brother.'

' Then you do not believe in the danger which I have just pointed out.'

' Very little. But still as that danger exists, I have managed so as to set it aside.'

' How did you do that ? '

' Look ! What do you call these two pieces of paper ? '

' These are passports. That is to say blanks which would be passports if they were filled in and if they bore the signature of the prefect. But they are worthless, since they are neither filled nor signed.'

' Well,' modestly answered Peppo, ' in a minute I can give them all the virtues which they lack. Follow me in the little work I am going to undertake.'

And sitting down at the table, Peppo, the clever calligrapher, commenced to manufacture passports in which their description was given very accurately, under the names of Annibal and Claudia Palmeri. When he had only the signature of the prefect to affix at the foot of the two forged passports, the municipal employé took out of his pocket a ministerial paper on which was the signature he wanted for a model. With prodigious ability Peppo copied the name and the flourish of the prefect.

'There!' said he to his sister, What do you think of this?'

'Oh!' cried the young girl, 'it is splendid!'

And in fact, in comparing the two signatures, it was impossible to tell the forged from the true one.

'And now,' asked Gorgon, 'what shall we do?'

'We will take, with these two passports, all the papers which have been sent from Calcutta, excepting, however, the certificates of our decease, which will make a bonfire in honor of our new fortune. Give me a match.'

A minute later, a pinch of ashes was all that remained of the compromising documents.

'And then, then?' insisted Gorgon.

'Then? I shall write to the French business man, in my own handwriting, and in my capacity as chief of the bureau of records, to acquaint him with the early arrival in Paris of M. Annibal and Mlle. Claudia Palmeri, provided with all the documents establishing their identity.

'And we leave?'

'In eight days, if you wish! and then the twenty millions and the name of the Palmeri will be ours.'

In spite of the magical horizons thrown open before her by the project, Gorgon was still hesitating. The last words of her brother caused her to pout disdainfully.

'Oh!' she said, 'the millions of the Palmeri, well and good! But their name!'

'It is not to your taste! Faith, I am satisfied with it. Everybody cannot have the name and the title of the Duke de San Lucca!'

'How do you know?' abruptly said the young girl.

Peppo looked at his sister with curiosity.

'Well,' said Gorgon, 'what's the matter? Is there anything very astonishing in what I am telling you? Do you think a woman like me is not worthy of a ducal crown?'

'Oh!' he said gallantly,' you deserve the crown of an empress. The only difficulty in the way is to find the duke or the emperor who will consent to offer it to you.'

'That's what the Duke de San Lucca has done, no later than two hours ago.'

'Oh! the worthy man! and I hope you jumped at his offer.'

'No, I have refused!'

'You have refused! Then you are more foolish than I thought you were!'

And saying these words, he was almost threatening his sister with his fist. But all at once he became calmer.

'In fact,' he said, 'it is as well that you have refused. With the twenty millions we are going to have, a title more or less does not make much difference. Decidedly everything is for the best in the best of all possible worlds.'

'I have refused,' said Gorgon, 'but I have changed my mind, and I am going to tell the Duke de San Lucca that I accept his offer of marriage.'

'You have changed your mind again? And why this tomfoolery?'

'You shall know. Listen.'

In her turn the beautiful girl narrated to Peppo the interview she had had with the duke, and why she had repulsed his proposal.

'But now,' she continued, 'these reasons do not exist ; the title I declined, because I would not drag it in the mire, I now desire that I may give it more lustre than it ever had.'

Peppo was thinking.

'Provided,' he said, 'that our old comrade does not change his mind in his turn.'

Gorgon had a smile of superb confidence.

'Come with me,' she said 'and you will see.'

They crossed the landing and after having uselessly knocked, entered the room of their neighbor. M. de San Lucca was lying on his pallet, with his eyes wide open.

'There is a queer look about him,' said Peppo in a low voice. 'I have seen people on the point of death, and they looked like him.'

Gorgon put her hand softly on the shoulders of the old man.

'Ah ! it is you, little one,' he said painfully, 'I am very glad to see you, and also your brother.'

He made an effort, and raised himself up, leaning on his arm.

'I was telling you a minute ago,' he said, 'that my days were numbered. Now I feel that they have been turned into hours. If you had accepted my offer, Gorgon, you would soon be a widow.'

'Your excellency,' said the young woman, without trying to give her old friend false hopes, 'I have come to ask you now for what I refused ; if I have come to ask you to make me your wife, what will you say?'

The duke looked at her interrogatively. She continued.

'A great secret has just been revealed to me,' she said, sitting down on the bed. 'I have a family, and I am wealthy, enormously wealthy. If you consent to give me your name, there shall be as you said, two duchesses de San Lucca, and I swear to you that nobody will hesitate in deciding which of the two does more honor to this great name and to the title which follows it.'

The old man looked at her attentively.

'I have neither the strength nor the desire to interrogate you, Gorgon,' he said. 'The San Luccas of olden times never withdrew what they have once said or offered. You shall be my wife since you call upon me to redeem my promise. Only we must hurry up. Magistrates have the right, I believe, to celebrate marriages in extremis, outside of ordinary rules. Let Peppo go to a magistrate and tell him that a dying man requires his services. Go, Peppo, go.'

The young man started rapidly. Gorgon, who had remained alone with the old friend of King Francis II., wanted to explain the reasons which had made her accept his proposition after she had refused it once.

'No,' said the duke. Do not wear out uselessly the few drops of oil still remaining in the lamp. I want to know nothing. When one is at the point of death, things that are human become perfectly indifferent.

Then there was a solemn silence, broken only by the breathing of the dying man. Peppo came back at last, bringing with him a magistrate and a priest. Four witnesses picked up in the streets accompanied them. The ceremony was performed in the prescribed forms. On the certificate of his marriage, the duke was able to affix his signature. When it was Gorgon's turn to sign, she boldly wrote: Claudia Palmeri.

The magistrate asked her if she had any legal documents establishing her civil status, and she showed him the very deeds sent by the consul from Calcutta. The noble genealogical parchments of the Duke de San Lucca and the plebeian deeds of the new Claudia Palmeri were then put together and handed to the young bride.

A few minutes after M. de San Lucca died with his head resting on the arm of the courageous young girl, who was not frightened by the spectacle of death. As long as he could see, he kept his eyes fixed on her beautiful face where pity and gratitude were depicted. It was a splendid farewell to life, and her radiant beauty cheered his soul when the last shadows of death fell on his eyes wide open.

According to her brother's instructions, Gorgon spread the news around the neighborhood that she intended to return to the theatrical career ; money had been needed to pay the expenses of the funeral of the duke de San Lucca, and there was more wanted to undertake the trip to France. Without entering into details, let me say that Peppo's cleverness soon remedied that. He forged a cheque and the 1,000 francs required were at their disposal.

The hour of starting at length arrived. As the train commenced to move, Gorgon opened the window and looked on Naples for the last time.

'The cradle has been beautiful,' she said, in a low voice, with more emotion than she thought herself susceptible of. 'Farewell ! Naples !'

B

'Good morning, Fortune?' cried Pepp�, snapping his fingers.

At these words Gorgon became herself again.

'We have twenty millions, and I am a duchess,' she said. 'The world is mine!'

Now let us transport ourselves to Pondichéry, the capital of the French possessions in India. As we retraced the events of three years before the beginning of our tale in Naples, so we will go back about two years in Pondichéry. Only this time we shall not take our readers to the slums of the society. On the contrary, we will find our heroes in the highest ranks and amongst the most eminent. Entering the palace of the governor of the colony, we will go through the business offices, to pass into the apartments reserved for the family of the Count de Moray, the governor-general, and let us enter the room of a young girl about fifteen years old, Mlle. Paulette de Moray, the daughter of the governor-general. The child is lying in an arm-chair, clad in a morning robe of white muslin. But the whiteness of her clothing and of the hangings of her virginal chamber are nothing in comparison with the paleness of her face. Only a few days before, Mlle. de Moray was on the point of death. To-day Dr. Roblin hopes she is saved. Her long illness has left startling traces, but there is now no immediate danger to be feared, and for the first time in many weeks, the count and the countess remain with their daughter without having to assume an air of tranquillity. Happiness is beaming in their looks, and their eyes meet in burning thanks to God.

The governor-general, the Count Roger de Moray, is a man in the prime of life. He has hardly turned forty and does not look that age. His wife is thirty-two, and would look much younger if in reality her features did not bear the traces of the anxiety and anguish she has been subjected to during her daughter's sickness. Near M. and Mme. de Moray, there is a woman familiarly called Aunt Basilique. She is the eldest sister of the Count de Moray. Aunt Basilique would never marry, so as to be at liberty to follow her brother to the distant countries to which he may be called by the noble profession he has embraced. Aunt Basilique is forty-five years old and looks more. Her delicate nature has resisted only by a miracle the fatigues of her voluntary exile. As we entered the room of Mlle. de Moray, the doctor was coming out of it. Whilst he stated that the sick child had entered the period of convalescence, he also declared that great care must be taken to prevent a relapse.

'Very soon,' the countess had said, 'we will ask for leave of absence, and we will go to Europe for six months. The native air will do more good to our daughter than all your science, however precious it may have been until now.'

'Take good care not to do that!' cried Dr. Roblin. 'Nothing is more fatal to persons who have caught our Indian fevers than to leave the country before they are entirely cured. They take with them the germs of the disease which becomes incurable. It is in the place itself where it was caught that it must be lost.'

'Then we are condemned to remain here?'

'For six months at least. Perhaps a year.'

And M. Roblin withdrew. Since the beginning of his daughter's sickness the count had naturally somewhat neglected his official functions, relying, and with reason, on the devotedness of his employés. He had been more especially seconded by his deputy, M. Gaston de Vallières, a charming young man whom he had admitted into the intimacy of his family. But now that his mind was more easy, he would take occasion to attend the ceremony of the celebration of the feast of agriculture, which happens once a year. M. de Moray gave orders to have an escort ready to follow him, and left with Maltar, his *dobachi*, that is to say his steward, his factotum. Maltar had all the best qualities of the Indian servants, and by a happy chance he had none of their faults. Much devoted to his masters, he fairly adored the countess and her daughter. When the governor-general arrived with his escort, the *fête* was at its height, and to show his respect for the ancient religion of the Indian population, M. de Moray remained exposed to the heat of the burning sun all through the ceremony. Maltar told him it would be imprudent to remain any longer, and he himself gave the order, almost in spite of the count, to return to the city. Arrived at Pondichéry M. de Moray found his daughter still better than when he had left her. The evening was spent in pleasant conversation, and they retired early for fear the child would get tired ; and he himself was worn out with fatigue. He was feeling a sensation of intense cold, and at times it seemed to him as if tongues of fire were burning through his veins. He was restless and agitated all night. A sort of ceaseless delirium filled his brain. Next morning when Maltar, the *dobachi* entered his master's room, he was terrified. M. de Moray's face was aglow, and he spoke in a low and irritable voice. He was complaining of sufferings which he could not explain. The Hindoo servant could not mistake the symptoms of the disease. He had seen so many Europeans attacked by the terrible Indian fever that he could not doubt. Very recently, perhaps three months before, he had been the first to notice the same precursory signs on the daughter which he now observed on the father. Notwithstanding the assurance of the count, Maltar ran to the doctor's and acquainted him with what he had seen. M. Roblin hastened to the palace, and one look convinced him that if the count was not yet attacked by the disease, he would infallibly catch it before long. The doctor called on the countess who hurried up to receive him, thinking he had come earlier than usual merely to see her daughter.

'You are up very early,' she said to the doctor, smiling. 'Well, to reward your zeal, I will give you good news of Paulette. The dear child has slept more soundly than she has done for a long time, and even at this moment she is still asleep.'

'I have not come to speak to you of Miss Paulette,' answered the doctor, gravely.

'Of whom, then?' cried the countess, turning pale.

Seeing the emotion exhibited by Mme. de Moray, even before she knew anything, the doctor hesitated. He was going to inflict a terrible blow. However, there was not a minute to be lost. The good man resolved to cut to the quick.

'I have come to speak of M. de Moray,' he answered.

'Of my husband.'

'Yes, the count is unwell this morning.'

'Has he sent for you?'

'No, but Maltar was anxious about his health, and came for me.'

'What is the matter?'

'Nothing serious as yet.'

'Oh, God be blessed!' cried the countess, 'you have cruelly frightened me, doctor.'

'Less than I should have,' said Mr. Roblin, shaking his head, sadly, 'since you change so rapidly from anxiety to tranquillity. It is true M. de Moray's sickness has not declared itself, yet, but——'

'But what? In heaven's name tell me all!'

'But the symptoms are such that it is impossible to mistake their import; any moment the disease may declare itself and be almost beyond cure.'

'And that disease?'

'Is the same from which your daughter has just escaped.'

Mme. de Moray raised a cry of anguish.

'Ah!' she cried. 'That fever! That horrible fever which kills the strongest!'

'Alas! the strongest are the ones it kills, because it is fed from the forces it breaks. By what has happened in the case of your daughter, you have seen that the children escape its deadly effects. But men in the prime of their age and vigorous, like M. de Moray ——'

'Those are condemned, are they not? Is not that what you mean?'

The doctor did not answer.

'Ah!' she cried, wringing her hands in despair, and falling on a chair, 'all is lost. I understand you too well!'

A sob came up to her throat and nearly choked her. The doctor could have quieted her anxiety, by telling her of the hopes he entertained, because he thought an immediate departure from the colony would cure the count, but he wanted to frighten the unhappy woman so that she would not raise any objections to the grave obstacles which were in the way. The doctor had foreseen these obstacles. We will acquaint the reader with them in a few words.

'Listen,' he said, after the first burst of her natural despair. 'No. Perhaps all is not lost.

The countess did not dare to question him. But with intense anxiety she was trying to read on the face of her friend the chances of salvation he might allude to.

'So long as the fever has not developed itself, there is hope. But to obtain that result you must take your husband far away from the dangerous climateric influences surrounding him.'

'That is to say ?'

'He must leave the colony.'

'When ?'

'This very day. The mail steamer leaves this morning. If M. de Moray does not leave to-day, he will have to wait for the next steamer, that is to say fifteen long days, fifteen mortal days, to speak more correctly.'

'Leave, you say ? But where will he go !'

'To France ?'

'But M. de Moray will never give his consent.'

'We will do without it. We will force his will by putting him to sleep. Alas ! dear madam, the plan which I propose is very bold, and both of us will be assuming a very weighty responsibility. If you are willing to take your share of it, I shall gladly accept mine.'

'I will do anything to save my husband.'

'Well, M. de Moray is in a state of excitement which causes him to drink very often ; I can throw into his glass an opiate which will make him sleep soundly. This opiate, renewed with prudence, will keep him for a few days in such a state of mental weakness that he will not know the place he will be in, nor will he be astonished at not finding himself here any longer.'

'So, you want to send my husband on board the steamer ?'

'Unknown to himself, yes.'

'Very well.' said the countess. 'Do just as you say, doctor. As for me, an hour will be sufficient to notify M. de Vallières, my husband's deputy, to take charge of the administration, and to awaken Paulette.'

'M. de Moray's life is condemned, if he remains in Pondichéry,' the doctor said, unfeelingly, 'but Miss Paulette's life is as surely sacrificed, if she goes away.'

The countess looked at the doctor with amazement. What she understood him to say seemed so horrible to her, that she could not believe it.

'Come, now,' she said with the look of a maniac, 'I did not hear you properly. You say that my husband must go ?'

'In three-quarters of an hour, now, because time unfortunately
flies rapidly !'
'And you say that my daughter must remain ?'
'Yes, for several months yet.'
'Very well, and what am I to do? I cannot let my husband
go without me, since he is already in danger of death. And I cannot leave my daughter, because she is also in danger of death. You
see very well that your plan is not feasible.

Time was pressing. To obtain a solution at once, the doctor
took upon himself a heavier responsibility than he had yet assumed.

'I answer for the life of Miss Paulette,' he said, 'whatever may
happen.'

'Even if I desert her ! Even if I break her heart by leaving her
to the care of mercenary hands ! Even should she doubt my tenderness and my love, in the state of prostration she is in !'

During the painful conflict, a new character had entered the
room. Having been notified of the doctor's arrival, Aunt Basilique
had come down to enquire into the cause of this unusual visit ;
although she arrived at the end of their conversation, she had heard
enough to understand the terrible questions which were being agitated. In the generosity of her heart, she at once resolved to
sacrifice herself. As Mme. de Moray was rebelling against the
thought of leaving her daughter to the care of mercenary hands,
Aunt Basilique advanced.

'Laura,' she said with authority, 'You can leave without anxiety
with the one whose chances of life depend on your care and your
love. I, the sister of your husband, shall remain with your
daughter.'

'Ah, aunty !' cried the countess, turning round and throwing
herself into the arms which were opened to receive her, ' you also
wish that I should leave my daughter.'

'What I wish is this : in the doubt in which your heart is
struggling, you must go where duty calls you, and you must listen
only to your duty.'

And taking the direction of the events, the devoted woman addressed herself first to M. Roblin.

'Doctor,' she said, 'attend to my brother, and make the terrible
experiment which your science and your wisdom suggest.'

While speaking, Aunt Basilique had rung the bell, and a servant
soon appeared

'Call M. de Vallières,' she said. 'He must come at once.'
Then turning to Mme. de Moray.

'Laura,' she said softly, ' you have only one short half hour to
prepare yourself and see your child. But, if you take my advice
you will not disturb her sleep ; as you have not even time to invent

a pretence for your departure, **and the** emotions caused by such **a** farewell might be fatal to her.'

' You want me to go away without seeing my daughter, without kissing her! But that is downright cruelty. You must understand that what you **ask is** impossible ! '

' Come, then, to **her for** an instant, since you **must** see her, but once again, do not tell her you are going ; do not awaken her ! '

' But some day she will have to be told——'

' **When you** shall have gone with your husband, I will prepare **your daughter,** by degrees, to the idea of this necessary separation. **She will know the** whole truth only when she is strong enough **to** bear **its revelation.'**

The **counsels** of Aunt Basilique **were wise** and Mme. de Moray had to **heed them.** Whilst her maid was preparing the toilet articles **necessary for** such a long voyage, the countess supported by her sister-in-**law** entered Paulette's room. The chaste young girl was sleeping, **and** her rest was quiet and deep enough to allow Mme. de Moray, who was smothering **her sobs,** to go near her couch without disturbing her. The poor woman would have given many years of her life to be allowed to pour out all her love in a single kiss. But she readily understood that Paulette would certainly awake at this usual caress, and she merely kissed the sheet which wrapped her sleeping child, the while bathing it with her silent tears. Aunt Basilique shortened this painful scene as much as possible, as she was afraid the courage and prudence of the poor mother, who **had been** so heroical until then, would fail at the last moment.

' Come,' **she** said, **in a low voice.**

And she dragged her **away. It was only** when she was far from her daughter's room that she burst into a passion **of** despair. The crisis was short, however. The countess was a woman with a stout heart and the sacred duty which was imposed upon her required all her attention.

The captain consented to delay **the** steamer for a short time, and half an hour after, M. **de** Moray was on board with his wife and Maltar.

' Then, doctor,' asked M. de Vallières, on returning from the steamer, ' your opinion is that —— '

' M. de Moray would have died within a month if he had remained here.'

' While now ? '

' He has some chance **of** escaping the disease.'

' Much ? '

' I would not say that, but certainly his prospects are improved.'

' May God hear you ! I am **so** attached to M. de Moray.'

'And Miss Paulette is so charming!' added the doctor.
The young man blushed.
'What do you mean?' he asked.
The doctor smiled good-humoredly.
'Nothing,' he said. 'Nothing but what is quite natural and proper. Miss Paulette is a charming young lady and you are a charming young man. Everything brings you together : age, fortune, social position. What more is needed to explain the nature of your sentiments towards her?'
'What! doctor, you have found out ——'
'There was no need to be a sorcerer to guess that. Your anxiety, your emotion during that painful sickness of three months have told me your secret. Upon my word, I believe that if the governor-general had remained in Pondichéry another year, you would have had a particular favor to ask him.'
'It is true,' said the young man, dolefully. 'While now that he is gone ——'
'Well, now that he is gone you will have to speak to Miss Paulette herself. Do you complain, and will it be so painful to hear a pretty and sweet girl like her tell you that your sentiments do not displease her.'
'What do you say?' cried the young man, with excitement. 'Do you really think I can hope?'
'Hush!' said the doctor, 'we have arrived at Government house, and I must go and see if my patient has awakened.'
Aunt Basilique went to meet him.
'Well,' she asked, 'how did you manage the embarking?'
'Very well!'
'And my brother?'
'He was put on board under the best possible conditions. Have confidence. But is there anything new here?'
'Nothing yet. I preferred awaiting your return before revealing anything to Paulette. However carefully I might do it ; an accident may happen.'
'Miss Paulette is awakened?'
'Yes, she was astonished at not seeing her mother by her bedside as usual. I evaded her anxiety.'
'I shall go and prepare her to hear the truth. Ah! tell me is she up?'
'She is resting in an arm-chair.'
'Then M. de Vallières can come with us. Allow me to call him.'
'What for?'
'In a difficult situation, many will do more than one,' answered the doctor evasively.
A few moments later, Aunt Basilique, the deputy-governor, and the doctor entered the large room which had been assigned to

Paulette. She was astonished to see M. de Vallières so early, although she had received him almost as intimately as a relative during the course of her long illness, but it always had been at a later hour and in the presence of her father and mother. In spite of the pleasure she felt at seeing him, a premonition of trouble filled her heart.

' M. Gaston ! ' she said, rising a little, What chance has brought you here ? '

' It is not M. Gaston who pays you his respects,' answered the young man, trying to smile, ' it is the governor-general *ad interim* who is now before you.'

' The governor-general *ad interim?* Where, then, is my father ? Where is my mother ? ' she said, with increasing anxiety, addressing Aunt Basilique.

The latter assumed a look of unconcern.

' Oh ! your mother,' she said, ' you will not see her to-day.'

' Not to-day ? '

' Neither to-morrow, perhaps ! '

' Where is she ? Where are they both ? '

The doctor intervened in his turn.

' Miss Paulette,' he said, ' I am the guilty one, and you must blame me. Do you see, your dear father neglected his duties while you were sick, and much of his business fell behind hands. For example, do you remember the projected excursion in the district of Bahour ? '

' Yes, I recollect. Well ? '

' Well, the excursion had been postponed on your account. Grave interests were at stake. Then, as you are about three-fourths cured, I have given the signal of departure. The governor-general started this morning.'

' Without bidding me good-bye ? Oh ! '

' It was to avoid the emotion of a farewell that I stood guard at the door when he wanted to come and kiss you this morning, with the countess.'

' My mother ! Has my mother gone also ? '

' Certainly, I have just told you so.'

The good doctor had not said it, and he knew it well. But when one has bad news to impart, he does the best he can. The young girl was well enough now to have recovered all the lucidity of her mind. She understood that the doctor was not telling the truth.

' Nayre,' she called abruptly.

One of the two Indian girls who were in the room, rose and came to her.

' Nayre,' said Paulette, trying to speak calmly, ' do you know where my mother is ? '

The little Indian girl, who was the favorite servant of Mlle. de Moray, had not been instructed as to what to tell,

'The countess has gone,' she answered. 'Gone to France with M. de Moray.'

'Gone! Both gone! Gone to France!' cried Paulette, rising suddenly from the chair, where she was resting. 'That is not possible!'

They tried to make her sit down, but she repulsed the friends who were surrounding her.

'No,' she said, 'leave me alone; I want to see.'

Mme. de Moray's room was adjoining her daughter's. Paulette went there, alone, refusing all help.

'I want to see,' she repeated, 'I want to see!'

She opened the door and the disorder she observed in the room confirmed the terrible news she had just received.

'Ah!' she cried with anguish. 'Gone! they are really gone! They have abandoned me!'

Her strength failed her. She nearly fell down. Aunt Basilique was rushing to her help, when the doctor arrested her, and it was M. de Vallières who caught the poor child in his arms and laid her on the divan.

'Now,' said the good doctor, 'the dear child must know everything, and M. de Vallières will undertake the task. He will find language more persuasive and more consoling than we could employ to tell her all.'

And the young man commenced the recital of the events we have just narrated.

. . . .

During this time the steamer which bore M. and Mme. de Moray was sailing at full speed towards France. Peppo and Gorgon, starting from Naples, were also going there, and from the meeting of these four persons will spring all the evils, all the sufferings of the poor MARTYR, who makes the subject of this story.

END OF THE PROLOGUE.

Part First.

WE have promised our reader to take him to Paris, let us fulfil this promise, and make him acquainted with a new character, Admiral Firmin de la Marche.

Two years ago, that is to say at the time this story was being enacted, the admiral was, unquestionably, the greatest figure of the French navy, where types of honor and bravery were, however, to be found very often. He was seventy-eight years old, and his career had been filled with brilliant actions. Since his youth, since his boyhood, rather, each one of his years has been marked by some resounding feat of arms, in warring against men and against the elements. Mme. Firmin de la Marche was a few years younger than her husband; she was still beautiful and her crown of white hair inspired veneration in all those who approached her. She belonged to a very ancient family, and had many relations in the old and proud nobility of France. Better known personally than the admiral himself, having resided in Paris almost continuously, Mme. de la Marche was acknowledged the leader of the religious and benevolent people of the gay city. The most striking feature of her character, in the midst of the brilliant existence she had led, was the constant sadness noticed in her face. Whatever effort she made to hide to the world the deep melancholy which was affecting her, no one could help observing with astonishment the spells of prostration to which she abandoned herself, often unconsciously. M. and Mme. de la Marche had but one child, named Laura, whom they had given to the Count de Moray. It was not without sorrow that Mme. de la Marche had consented to the union which separated her from Laura, who was then only eighteen years old. The admiral had had occasion to appreciate the brilliant and solid qualities of M. de Moray, and took his demand into serious consideration, when, as he was on the point of leaving to assume the post of Governor of Senegal, he had asked the hand of Laura. This union, which presented very important advantages, had to be accepted or rejected at once. As M. de Moray was just as acceptable to the daughter as to her parents, he soon possessed the treasure he coveted. A few days after his marriage he left with his young bride for the colonies. She followed him everywhere, and during one of these long and perilous exiles, she was delivered of Paulette, the dear girl we have seen so ill in Pondichéry. By good luck M. de la Marche had a very large fortune, as also had the Count de Moray. With the intention of helping his son-in-law to do honor to the high positions he occupied which require heavy expenses to be kept up with becoming display, the admiral had given a very large dowry to Laura. He had curtailed his own allowance on this occasion, so that Laura could bring to her husband a little more than six hundred thousand francs, which was nearly as much as he possessed himself. Be that as it may, the marriage of Laura must have had a great deal to do with the usual sadness of Mme. de la Marche. The almost continual estrangement of these two women so closely united by a deep love for each other, explained the gloomy sadness of the mother, one might even say of the grandmother, for although Mme. de la Marche had seen her grand-daughter but very seldom, still she loved her with excessive tenderness. Paulette had been brought over to France only once or twice since her birth. Her last sojourn had been the longest ; she had lived for one year in an old mansion of the family, on de Varennes street, which M. de Moray would never sell, though he rented part of it, and used the remainder for his own family, whenever he was absent on leave for a few months from his post of duty.

. . . .

One day the admiral had entered the room of Mme. de la Marche. 'My dear Noémie,' he said, 'I have just received a despatch. Guess who it comes from ? '

'Since you ask me that question, it is because it comes from Laura, is it not ? '

'You find out everything. And where does it come from ? '

'Naturally from Pondichéry. But, my God ! you make me anxious. Has anything happened ? Paulette was sick at the last letter we received. Is it ?——'

'Don't be uneasy. The despatch is not from Pondichéry. However, it was sent by your daughter. As to Paulette, she is better. But, here, I am very clumsy in my explanation. I should have handed you the despatch at once.'

Mme. de la Marche seized on the telegram, which was from Aden, and read thus :

'We have left Pondichéry suddenly, through a serious illness threatening Roger. All imminent danger is over to-day. Paulette, who is convalescent, has remained in Pondichéry with Aunt Basilique. Shall arrive in Marseilles on 20th June. Will be very happy to see you again.

'LAURA.'

It is not necessary to add that Mme. de la Marche resolved to go to Marseilles on the 19th. The admiral had thought of going also, but the exigencies of the service kept him in Paris at the last mo-

ment. So Mme. de la Marche found herself alone on the wharf
when the governor-general of Pondichéry and his wife disembarked
from the magnificent steamer. Laura threw herself in her mother's
arms, and remained a few moments on her breast, her eyes
bathed with **sweet** tears, which made her forget **the** bitterness of
those she had shed since her departure from the **Indian** coast. At
last Mme. **de la** Marche disengaged herself and greeted her son-in-
law, **who** was waiting, he also much agitated, leaning **on** Maltar's
arm. The good and noble woman was much pained by the sight **of**
M. de Moray. She could not recognize the man she had known **so**
strong and vigorous. It was not that he had grown very **old since**
his last trip to France. It was not either that he had lost **anything**
of his real beauty. On the **contrary**, perhaps his sufferings had improved his appearance by refining him, **as it** were. The brutal
fever which had struck him down, and which was still lasting, without, happily, the danger of the pernicious effects it would have had
in India, this brutal fever, **we** say, gave to his whole being a strange
aspect. Its **flame** was shining in the **count's** looks with burning
glimmer. The complexion of his face, **which had** become very dull,
would have excited the envy of a Creole woman. It was the beauty
of a sick man, to be sure, but it was very striking. Mme. de la
Marche was much impressed, and felt pity and sadness.

'My poor child,' she said, 'how you must have suffered!'

However, they proceeded to the hotel, where rooms had been
set apart for them. While Maltar, the faithful Indian, helped his
master to go **to** bed and take a little rest, Mme. de Moray and her
mother remained alone.

'My father! speak to me **of** my father!' said **Laura, almost on**
her knees at her mother's feet, 'is he always full **of health, strong,**
and great, in mind as well as body?'

'Yes, always,' answered Mme. **de la Marche.** 'I need not tell
you with what impatience he **is awaiting our return to Paris.** But
it is not of him **we must speak,** it is of Paulette, your daughter, *our*
daughter.'

New tears rushed to the eyes of the Countess de Moray.

'**Paulette!**' she said, 'you must imagine, my dear mother, what
was my **despair at** leaving her. How is it that I did not become insane when **I was** forced to go away suddenly without even kissing
her? Doubtless God wished to keep me for the cruel combat in
which I had to fight for the life of my husband, with the cabin of a
ship for a battlefield, during **a** voyage which I shall never forget, **I**
assure you.'

'You left India **without kissing your** daughter!' cried **Mme. de
la Marche.**

'I **had to**; our departure was decided on, and accomplished in
less than an hour, Roger's life being at stake. In an hour I would

not have had the time to prepare my daughter to the horrible necessity of our separation.   She would have insisted on coming with
us, and in the state of weakness she was in, it would have been a
crime to consent to such a thing.   And God only knows if I would
have had the strength to resist her entreaties to the end.'

'And you do not know, naturally, how she bore the discovery of
your departure, when she was told of it ?'

'We found despatches at all the stations where the steamer stopped, at Colombo, Aden, Suez.   Even here, before we landed, the
pilot boat met the steamer and brought us a new despatch.'

And what did these despatches contain ? '

'Good and consoling tidings, such as this :   "Great sorrow but
great courage ; the convalescence follows its regular course ; I am
happy to learn that my father is out of all danger." '

' You were able to telegraph yourself to give Paulette news of her
father ? '

' Yes, at Colombo and at Eden.'

' And this good news, which was expected with such impatience,
you were able to send.   Roger felt better when you started.'

' I was only feigning hope.   For two weeks, I thought my husband would die.'

Mme. de la Marche looked at her daughter with compassion.
How she must have suffered.   During this conversation, M. de
Moray had taken an hour's rest.   On awakening, he asked for his
wife, who entered her room with his mother.

' Well,' he said, smiling, and rising with a painful effort, ' now
that I am strong and well, we will decide on the time of our departure for Paris.'

' Oh !' answered Laura, ' that is too quick.   You know what I
have told you, Roger ? '

' What was it ? '

' The promise I made to good Dr. Roblin before our departure.
These were his last words :   " Let your first care be, on landing, to
send Dr. Chasserant these few lines I have written in haste, which
will acquaint him with the situation.   Chasserant knows the nature
of M. de Moray's illness, because he made a long sojourn in India,
at Chandernagor, before he went to Marseilles, and he can speak
with authority on such matters, and whatever he may command you
must obey."   I gave Dr. Roblin the promise he asked.   I gave it
in your name as well as in my own, and we shall keep it together.'

' Then you have notified M. Chasserant ? ' asked M. de Moray,
annoyed by the delay, but still grateful to his wife for the tenderness she exhibited towards him.

' And he replied that he would be here within an hour.   The
hour is almost over, and probably he is here now.'

(Maltar had entered, bringing a card on a salver.)

'It is the doctor,' said the countess, after looking at the card. 'Tell him to come in, Maltar.'

Mme. de la Marche looked at the Indian, while he was going on his errand. His face of red-brown hue, which had intelligence and cunning depicted on his features, astonished her. Maltar came back with the doctor, and on a sign of approbation from the countess, who understood his desire to be present at the consultation, he remained in the room. After having examined his patient with careful attention, and interrogated him at length, M. Chasserant wrote a detailed prescription, in which was indicated the treatment to be followed, and which he declared necessary.

'I thank you, doctor,' said M. de Moray, 'and when will you allow me to start ?'

'Start ? Where to ?'

'To Paris.'

'Oh ! we do not agree.'

'How is that ?' said the count, visibly annoyed.

'You are not in a fit condition to defy the climate of the north of France.'

'The north—the north !'

'Pardon me. Paris is altogether the north. It is even the north pole for a man like you, used to the Indian climate. In any circumstance it is dangerous for those who have lived in the colonies where you have passed most of your life, not to remain a long while on the shores of the Mediterranean; it would be still more dangerous for you, who have just escaped the fever. So, in the present case, I do not advise, I command, and I intrust the execution of my orders to the affection of all those who surround you, and chiefly to Mme. de Moray.'

The count was sorely disappointed.

'And how long will I be exiled ?' he asked.

'I cannot tell you exactly. A month or two, perhaps.'

'Perhaps six,' said M. de Moray, with impatience.

'No, because in that case you would have to remain all next winter in the south, which would certainly be wiser. Anyway, we will see then.'

'Well, since there is no help for it, let us remain in Marseilles.'

'Not so. Marseilles would hardly be better than Paris. The climate is too severe. The *mistral* would try you too much.'

'Then, where do you send me ?'

'Wherever you may like to go. There are plenty of good places. Hyères, Nice, Manton, or what would be still better, Cannes. Now, I am thinking of a point where few people go as yet, but which, however, is visited by people of the best society. And you will find there very comfortable quarters, which are not to be despised, if you are to remain there a certain time.'

'And that place?'

'Is the Cape of Antibes.'

'Antibes, do you say? But Antibes is not a city prepared for the accommodation of strangers.'

'I do not mean Antibes itself, but the Cape of Antibes. You will find there very nice villas. Perhaps you may rent one. However, I would advise you to stop at the hotel. It is an immense palace where you will find all the modern conveniences and comforts.'

'Do you think we will find room there?' asked the countess.

'You certainly will at this season of the year. If you had arrived one month earlier the case would have been different. But at the end of the season the great affluence of people has necessarily diminished.'

'So much the better. When shall we go, doctor?'

'As soon as possible, since M. de Moray is able to undertake the voyage.'

'Then we shall go to-morrow.'

The consultation was ended, and the doctor went away. The next day, M. and Mme. de Moray took the ten o'clock express to Antibes itself. From there a carriage took them to the Hotel of the Cape, distant about one league from the station. The travellers found everything such as the doctor had described, and they were very glad to have obeyed him blindly.

Laura and Roger had not come alone to the cape. Mme. de la Marche, after hesitating a little, had decided to accompany them. It was painful for her to remain away from her husband, even for one month, but she could not leave her children so quickly, after their long and painful separation.

The exigencies of our tale have obliged us to delay the attention of our readers longer than we had expected on mere questions of health. But we had to explain the reasons which forced the heroes of this drama, either in Italy or India, to start for France at a given hour. That's what we have done. We had also to explain the motives which prevented M. and Mme. de Moray from coming directly to Paris, and forced them to remain for two months on the Mediterranean coast. Knowing that they were to remain some time at the hotel, the count and his wife, as also Mme. de la Marche, made themselves as comfortable as possible. They occupied splendid rooms on the first floor, and from their windows the view was beautiful. In the gardens which surrounded the hotel, and in the field which extended as far as the sea, the orange and lemon trees intermingled their flowers and their perfumes, whilst the palm trees, like fans artistically cut, waved gracefully in the breezes from the sea. All this marvellous prospect was animated by the occupants of the hotel. Women and children increased

the attraction of the scene by the music of their laughter and the
charm of their beauty and their elegance. In the evening all the guests
were united at the dinner table, and after dinner they all found themselves in the elegant drawing-rooms, sparkling with lights, full
of flowers, and resounding with music.   Concerts and balls succeeded each other in the animation of pleasure, and were almost
princely in their display, the society residing at the cape being
recruited from all the aristocracies in the world,—aristocracies
of birth, of art, of fortune, and of beauty.   Everybody spoke
French, but this charming French spiced by a foreign accent.

    We are of those who believe in Providence more than in chance.
So we will hold Providence responsible for the meetings which
awaited M. and Mme. de Moray at the cape.

    At the public table, on the very first days of their arrival, they
found themselves seated beside a woman whose elegance, perhaps a
little too luxurious, and whose beauty attracted the attention of
everybody.   This woman was accompanied by a man, who at first
Laura and Roger thought her husband, but on enquiry M. de
Moray found out that they were Italians, brother and sister ; that
the man was called Annibal Palmeri, and the woman was a young
and wealthy widow, the Duchess de San Lucca.

    Our readers, who have seen Gorgon and Peppo leave Naples in
such a pitiful equipment, will perhaps not be sorry to know how
they find them to-day at the Cape of Antibes, surrounded with all
the prestige which follows a great name and an immense fortune.
It was about one year since the two Bohemians had left Naples for
France.   They had about five hundred francs left out of the thousand they had procured, God knows how, on the day they started.
They stopped at a small hotel, next door to the house occupied by
the judiciary administrator, M. Renouard.   An hour after their
arrival, they called on him, and made themselves known.

    The reader will remember that the chief of the record office of
Naples had officially notified the business man of Paris of the early
arrival in that city of the children of Antonio Palmeri, nephew and
niece of the deceased.   Peppo and Gorgon spoke French well
enough to be understood in that language (one can learn a little of
everything in the streets of Naples), and they soon came to an
agreement with M. Renouard, who made no difficulty in putting
them in possession of the estate, all their papers being regular, and
their identity established beyond question by the famous passports
forged by Peppo. To put them in possession of the estate, we have
said ; this expression has to be rectified because the will of the
testator declared Annibal the only heir of the whole fortune.

    ' What does that mean ? ' asked Gorgon.

    ' The chief of the record office at Naples, a very worthy man,
who enjoys an excellent reputation,' added Peppo, speaking thus

C

impudently of himself in those eulogistic terms, 'the chief of the
record office has told us that you had asked him to give him certain
information——'

'On the surviving heirs of the late Palmeri : that is quite correct,' answered M. Renouard, 'but it is also quite correct that the
testator, who had amassed that immense fortune by dint of hard
work, did not want it divided, lessened, and finally reduced to the
proportions of an ordinary fortune.'

'Ten millions is nice,' observed the Neapolitan.

'Yes,' said M. Renouard, laughing, 'but twenty millions, is
more than nice, it is very nice—and M. Giacomo Palmeri, who
gloried in this fortune, which was the work of his life, did not wish
it to be mutilated by dividing it in halves. So that he decided that
the twenty millions would belong exclusively to his brother
Antonio, if he were still alive, or to his nephew Annibal, in case
your father had ceased to live, and finally to his niece Claudia, in
case you were dead.'

'Then, from what you have said, Antonio Palmeri, our father,
being dead, the whole fortune belongs to me alone,' cried Annibal
joyfully.

'To you alone ; on condition, adds the testator, that you will
give a handsome wedding portion to your sister.'

'Everything is for the best,' said Claudia, smiling calmly.

And as Peppo looked at her with surprise.

'We shall agree very well together,' she said, 'the tie of——
fraternity which binds us is more powerful than all the wills in the
world.'

'A thousand times more powerful,' hastily answered Peppo, who
had understood that the word : fraternity, accented as it had been
by Gorgon, meant complicity.

'Between us two, there is only one will,' said Claudia.

'Only one,' assented Peppo.

'And that will is mine,' thought Gorgon.

Peppo humbly bowed his head, and both left the office. Success
being assured, Peppo proposed to his sister to rent fine rooms, but
she opposed his project.

'No,' she said ; 'no lodgings. We do not exactly know what our
situation will be. The first thing wanted is a wardrobe which will
give us an aristocratic air. We will move from this inn, which re-
calls to my mind the *locanda* of the suburb of Capodimonte, to the
Grand-Hotel. I am told that all strangers of distinction stop there.
So our place is there.'

Once installed at Gorgon's desire, they started in search of the
famous wardrobe they needed. With money one can do many
things in Paris in twenty-four hours. Our adventurers did not
spare money, and the result was simply immense. They could be

seen the next evening in one of the boxes of the Varieties, for which they had paid twenty-five pounds to a theatrical agent, to see Mme. Judic in a new play.

Women, it has often been said, have a prodigious facility of adaptation. In any situation they may be thrown by chance, they seem to be in their place. Intuition in their case takes the place of education, at least if seen at a distance. So the curiosity of the theatre-goers was at a loss to exactly define the new star which was just appearing on the Parisian horizon.

'A woman of the *demi-monde?* No. It is not possible,' said a few. 'We would know her.'

'A great lady! Impossible!' said others. 'There are, however elegant that splendid woman is, errors of orthography in her dress. She wears too much jewellery for the theatre!'

'Don't you see she is a stranger,' said others.

'Stranger, yes; but that does not tell us her social condition.'

Gorgon felt she was the objective point of all the glasses leveled towards the box she occupied with Peppo, but she boldly supported the ordeal. Her superior intelligence made her almost understand the nature of the conversation going on below. The disdainful gestures of the men and their smiles convinced her that their observations were not of a flattering nature. Her vanity was offended, and at times she had a foolish desire to cry out to all those people who were staring at her.

'I am not the one you take me for, apes that you are! I am the Duchess de San Lucca, the greatest and the richest heiress of Italy!'

And truly, so sincere was her pride that in speaking thus, she thought she was speaking the truth. In forty-eight hours she had forgotten that her name was Gorgon, and that but a few months before she was a ballet girl at the theatre San Carlo, in Naples. On the other hand Peppo understood nothing. He seemed to be intoxicated by the pleasure of exciting so much curiosity. He leaned forward on the front of the box, so that he could be seen to better advantage. Gorgon forced him to retire in the shade, and even went away on his account, before the spectacle was over. A second attempt, made under similar circumstances, did not succeed better than the first Gorgon was intelligent, we have often said. She soon found she had made a mistake, and resolved to follow another road.

'Three more evenings like this one,' she said to her brother, 'and we will become impossible in Paris. I am quite willing that we should enjoy ourselves, but we must do it with less noise. If you are willing, as I am, to gain a high place in society, we must manage with more cleverness.'

This conversation took place on the very day M. Renouard gave
to the pretended Annibal and Claudia Palmeri the titles and bonds
of all sorts, which constituted a fortune almost princely.   Intoxicated by this triumph due to his ability, the Neapolitan formed the
project of dazzling and conquering Paris. He put on the airs and
assumed the attitude of the gladiator who defies the gaping crowd.
Gorgon shrugged her shoulders.

'I have been thinking a good deal these last few days,' she said,
'and I begin to see my way clear. We are acting like clowns, that's
all.   With all our millions we will reach nothing, unless we can get
hold of some family who will take charge of us. The question is
to find that family.'

'There are plenty of people in Paris who will be only too glad
to pilot us,' said Peppo, striking his pockets full of gold.

'Yes,' answered his sister with contempt, 'they will pilot us
like the guides, who will show you all that can be seen for five
francs, but they will not introduce us in any of the drawing
rooms where the admission is free.   They are not the people we
want.   We must find genuine representatives of the true nobility.'

'Well,' said the young man, philosophically, 'you can manage
those things according to your own ideas.   Provided I have a
good house and a good table, pretty women, and fast horses, I
am perfectly happy.'

Gorgon looked at him with contempt. The baseness of his
character humiliated her.

'And he calls himself my brother!' she said.

'Well,' said the Neapolitan, 'we have had the same mother,
I think.'

'The same mother, yes, but perhaps that is all,' muttered the
pretty girl, caring but little about the offensive doubt she was
casting on the memory of the ex-dancer, who had died in a hos-
pital one winter's night.

Be that as it may they suddenly modified their manner of living.
They bought a house near the plain Montceau, in the name of the
Duchess de San Lucca, and they moved into it as soon as a fashionable upholsterer had furnished it. As the new millionaires had given
him full powers, and he happened to have good taste, their installation was all that could be desired. From the stables, filled with
fine horses, and the cellars, full of good wine, to the drawing rooms,
provided with furniture of the old style and the gallery, hung
with masterpieces, everything was perfect.

'The cage is pretty,' said Gorgon to her brother.   'Now the
birds must learn to sing.'

And masters of all kinds were called in to give lessons to these
strangers, who confessed without shame their desire to learn the

manners of the Parisian aristocracy. Peppo did not like the school-
ing he had to submit to, but he resigned himself to it, thus acknowledging the superiority of his sister. In the evening he would frequent the public places until the hour he could go into one of those
low clubs whose doors are always wide open to those who have
plenty of money. In those doubtful clubs where he was received
with open arms, Annibal Palmeri had made the acquaintance of a
few gentlemen attracted there by the love of gambling. One night,
after coming out of the club, Annibal had entered a restaurant in
the company of the Marquis de Roquevaire. The marquis, **who** was
about thirty years old, belonged to one of the best families **of** the
St. Germain suburb. Being very sceptical, he was not particular
about his social relations, so long as those relations were only casual
meetings, at the theatres, at the club, or even in the *boudoirs* of
gallantry. But he was merciless when there was any attempt to
force open the doors of true society by the upstarts who from all
quarters of the world are continually alighting in Paris. Peppo,
taking advantage of **their** familiarity, confessed himself to the
marquis, and told him **of** the difficulties his sister and he himself
found in gaining an *entrée* into society.

'And my sister is the widow of the Duke de San Lucca!' **he**
added.

The marquis was frank.

'My dear sir,' he said, since you **want to know** the truth, I will
tell it to you. You understand that people like the duchess and
yourself do not pass unnoticed. The name you bear, the fortune
you have inherited from old Palmeri, and chiefly the beauty of your
sister have drawn enough attention to you during the past month
to cause enquiries to be made. You are well known, and certainly
you are very honorable ; but then, such as you are, you were wrong
in trying to enter too suddenly into our world. You would have
succeeded better by taking a circuitous path.'

'But how ?'

'For example, by mixing **with** the high cosmopolitan society
which **is** not so exacting as ours, and where we recruit every now
and then.'

'And where **will** we find that high cosmopolitan society ?'

'Oh ! almost everywhere, chiefly in bathing places. In summer
at Dieppe or Trouville ; in winter at Nice or some other point on
the Mediterranean coast. If you take my advice, my dear sir, you
will spend the remainder of the season at Monaco.'

Next day, at breakfast, Peppo told his sister the conversation he
had had the night before with M. de Roquevaire. Gorgon was
thoughtful for a moment.

'The advice is good,' she said, 'and we must follow it. By the
way where does your marquis live ?'

'I don't know. Why do you ask?'

'Because.'

And without further explanation the duchess wrote a few lines rapidly.

'Here,' she said, 'give this to your friend, in the gambling hell where you meet him.'

One should have heard the tone with which she pronounced those two words: *your friend!* A friend! this great lord one could meet only in disreputable society, and whose address was not known! In truth, was it worth while to play such a terrible game not to be further advanced after a struggle of six months' duration!

Peppo did not understand the heart-broken irony of the remark.

'My friend! my friend!' he said, 'not so much as all that. The marquis is a very good fellow, and he is even the only one who has given us good advice, because this is good advice, is it not?'

'Excellent!'

'And what do you write to my friend?'

'I ask him to come and see me.'

'Ah! bah! look here! Would you? —— '

Gorgon looked at him with contempt.

'Here,' she said, 'you will never be anything but a *facchino!* If I wanted the marquis for a husband, or even for a lover, would I write to him?'

'Come, calm yourself! I was only joking. It appears we must not trifle with the virtue of the Duchess de San Lucca!'

'With her virtue,' cynically answered Gorgon, 'as much as you like. With her pride, never! Remember this once for all.'

The letter which Annibal Palmeri gave the same evening to his friend was very short. Three or four lines only, by which the Duchess de San Lucca asked the Marquis de Roquevaire to be so kind as to call on her the next day, at five o'clock. At the hour appointed the marquis called on the duchess, puzzled as to what she had to communicate to him.

'Here I am, duchess,' he said, as he entered, 'to your orders.'

'We will see directly,' answered Gorgon, motioning him to sit down.

And she approached the question squarely. Her brother had told her the conversation they had at the restaurant and had repeated the advice he had received.

'M. Palmeri has been very indiscreet,' said the marquis embarrassed. 'There are certain things which are said between men, and which must not be repeated to a woman.'

'Do not regret my brother's treachery,' said the beautiful Claudia plainly. 'It has given me the proof that in you I have a——.'

'An admirer,' said M. de Roquevaire, not knowing what the

duchess wanted, and placing himself voluntarily on the ground of commonplace gallantry.

The duchess bit her lips.

'I was going to say a friend,' she replied, 'but since you did not see fit to use that word, I shall simply say a protector.'

'Oh!' answered M. de Roquevaire, 'the word is too humble not to be full of pride. Come, tell me what I can do for you, and whatever it may be I shall do it with pleasure.'

'You can be very useful to me. I have decided to pass the winter in the south.'

'Well, you are right,' frankly said the marquis. 'It is really a pleasure to counsel a woman who listens to advice. Where will you go?'

'To Monaco, since it is your opinion.'

'Well, I was wrong. Go through Monaco. Do not remain there. Try the stations of the coast-line, one after the other. When you have found the psychological sojourn, if you will allow the expression, pitch your tent.'

'But by what signs shall I recognize that pshychological sojourn?'

'Oh, I leave that to your acuteness,' said the young man, laughing.

'I shall do the best I can. Oh! will you do me another favor. You are surely acquainted with some of the most influential members of this foreign colony through which you advise me to pass before entering into your world, which is rigorously sealed, and into which I have the ambition to enter, only because the door is closed. There, at least, could you introduce me?'

The marquis was looking at the beautiful young woman, and he could not help feeling a secret sympathy with her ambition. The beauty of the duchess, dazzling as it was, was only an accessory to the real admiration she inspired him with.

'You are a real woman!' he said, kissing her hand.

'And I want to become a real duchess,' she replied, withdrawing her hand, where the kiss lingered too long.

'The devil take me if I don't help you,' cried the young man, smiling, 'so you will have the letters. You will have to do the rest, remembering that every road, as the proverb says, leads to Rome.'

'No, not to Rome,' said the duchess, as he was taking leave. 'To Paris.'

The plan so quickly conceived was as rapidly executed. A few days after, the duchess left Paris for the south with her brother, and within a month she had visited all the principal stations of the coast. However, she pleased herself nowhere. At Mauton, there were too many invalids, Nice was too windy, Cannes too wet;

Hyères and St. Raphael did not please her for other causes. One day chance brought her to the Cape of Antibes, and, as she found the country delightful, she at once resolved to live there.

At the cape, as everywhere else, the letters of the marquis had produced their effect. As they were addressed to a Russian prince, to the son of a lord, and to a grand cousin of Queen Isabella of Bourbon, the beautiful Neapolitan soon found herself the reigning leader of a small court, which soon augmented, as even the most elegant women of the colony sought the acquaintance of a duchess so young, so beautiful, and so wealthy. Soon Gorgon had no other occupation than to limit the ever increasing number of her admirers. In her turn she showed herself hard to please.

During the few winter months she passed at the hotel of the cape, where she lived in the rooms occupied the year before by a royal princess of England, she saw before and around her all the most aristocratic idlers of Europe. And still there was a shadow overhanging this magnificent tableau. There was no French society there. All those people who had come to the cape for a few days did not belong to the society in which she had resolved to enter at any cost. It is because the French people, those at least she wanted to conquer, have not the cosmopolitan habits of other nations.

Time was passing away and the season was drawing to an end. The Duchess de San Lucca, totally discouraged, was thinking of going away. She had already announced her intention to her brother, who was thrown into despair at the thought of leaving. Annibal found himself, at the cape, the happiest of men. Carried into the orbit of his sister, like a faithful satellite, he had shared her pleasures and her successes. He had also had a few good fortunes of which he was very proud.

'Where will we find a better place than this one ?' he asked. 'A splendid country ! beautiful women ! What more do you want, my dear ? '

Gorgon did not deign to answer, except to tell him that since he amused himself so much, he had better take advantage of it during the few remaining days.

'We shall go in three days,' she had said, in a tone which did not admit of a reply.

This conversation had taken place on the very day of the arrival at the hotel of the Count and Countess de Moray and of Mme. de la Marche. The noise made in the rooms next to hers, which were being prepared for them, attracted her attention, and she instructed her maid to enquire who these travellers were. M. de Moray's name did not afford her any information. The count, having passed the greater part of his life in the colonies, was a stranger to her. It was not so when she learned that Mme. de Moray was the daughter of Mme. de la Marche, and that the latter had come with the count and countess. The fame of the admiral's wife was such **that** no one could possibly ignore it. We have already said so, the **name** she bore was universally known, and the duchess had heard it often.

The beautiful Neapolitan was startled by the news brought by the maid. Was it at the very moment that she was going to give up the fight, that heaven put such a great chance **of** victory within her reach? The Admiral Firmin de la Marche ! **The** Count and Countess de Moray ! What did she care now for a queen's relative, for lords, or for princes of the Caucasus or of Transylvania ? She would have given the whole of them *en bloc* to be certain **of** making a casual acquaintance with those French people, **who-** occupied such a large place in the history and honor of their **country.** She felt **a** great emotion in going down **to** dinner that **evening.** But the travellers dined in their own room, and it was **a bitter disap-**pointment.

If the inhabitants of the Hotel **of the Cape dined** together in full dress, they always breakfasted in **morning** costume, at different tables. They had the advantage of having **more** independence to settle the occupation of the day. Breakfast, however, was **al-**ways over at one o'clock, and it was usual, **on** leaving the dining-rooms, to go into the large garden which surrounded the hotel. They used even to ride and drive around the country surrounding the hotel, and those who did not feel inclined to go, looked on at the preparations for the departure from the verandah where they remained some time, deriving pleasure from the amusement of the others. Usually the duchess was the first to give **the** signal to all the promenaders, and she was always accompanied by a large es-cort, noisy and full of merriment. The day after we have seen her so disappointed at not meeting the strangers at dinner, she broke her daily habits, to the great astonishment of all.

'Amuse yourselves without me,' she answered **her** companions. 'I am a little tired and I will take **a rest.**'

Annibal offered to remain with **her,** but she declined his pro-posal in a disdainful tone. A little **vexed at** the reception accorded to his amiable attention, Palmeri did not insist and merely answered : 'Just as you wish, my dear !'

Instead of going to her room after the departure of the excur-sionists, Gorgon remained a moment in the garden, walking through the deserted alleys. She was thinking. Her thoughts were not of a very agreeable nature, if we are to judge of them by her actions. She was striking the gravel of the walk with the end of her um-brella as if in anger. It was because she felt ashamed at her in-ability. To her own eyes she appeared miserable. To have so many **trumps in** her hand, and not to have scored a triumph ! It was **pitiable.**

Even the attempt she had decided to make, on the advice of M. de Roquevaire, did not reach a soil where the roots of the wealth and nobility she had just acquired could expand freely. And what annoyed her more than anything was the discovery that she was not proof against her own discouragements. She had arrived at a crisis, she well knew, when obstacles, instead of giving more energy kill whatever may be left. The incidents of the previous day had unnerved her. So her good humor, her pleasures, her joys depended on the whim of a few travellers, whether they sat at the same table with her or not. Truly, it was enough to cause one to be angry with one's self. She was walking, as we have said, anxious and thinking only of her own troubles, when turning into a side avenue she almost ran against somebody coming in the opposite direction and who had barely time to step aside to allow her to pass. The unexpected motion recalled her attention, and her astonished look, like that of a person who is suddenly awakened from a deep slumber, rested on the living obstacle which had nearly caused her to stumble. It was a man whose sight produced in her an emotion she had never experienced before. That noble face on which honor and rectitude were clearly depicted, where the authority of command dwelt in spite of the appearances of sufferings which it bore, that face struck her more deeply than any other she had ever seen. Who was that man? She did not know. Nobody had named or indicated him to her—and still she recognized him. He was, she would have wagered her life, the gentleman who had arrived the day before; a man who was great by his own achievements, and perhaps greater by the ties which united him to the family of an illustrious soldier. It was the Count de Moray; it was the son-in-law of the Admiral Firmin de la Marche.

Their eyes met, attracted by a sort of magnetism. The searching look of Roger de Moray fixed itself on the half wild stare of the Duchess de San Lucca. The stoppage caused by their meeting lasted but an instant, but that instant was enough to embarrass and even cause them both some emotion. The Count de Moray, at first motionless for a few seconds, stood aside to give more room to the fair promenader, and slowly raised his hat. It was not the commonplace and courteous bow which every well-bred man owes to a woman whom he meets face to face. It was, the unconscious and almost religious feeling which causes one to uncover his head when he sees a work of art, or when he passes before a temple. The duchess regaining her composure smiled, inclined herself slightly and passed on. A few steps further, at the curve of the path, she turned around. M. de Moray was still standing in the same place, in the same immobility, as if transformed into a statue, looking at her and not even thinking of following her. Their eyes met for the last time. But then their glances were no more those of two strangers who had astonished each other a few minutes before, they were the glances of two companions who meet after a long absence. An instantaneous compact of alliance had just been concluded between them. When they were separated by clumps of palm-trees, Gorgon regained her coolness and became again the duchess she had ceased to be for a moment. She soon found herself in front of the hotel, and sat down in the shade of the verandah, very thoughtful. She was then almost alone, having before her the finest panorama in the world, which she was contemplating inattentively.

An old lady whose features, bonnet and dress denoted her nationality at first sight, was seated beside her. This lady, called Lady Helton, who was the widow of a superior officer in the English navy, tried to relieve her own idleness by engaging with the duchess in a common-place conversation, which we must acknowledge she was not in the humor of keeping up. Just at the moment the beautiful Neapolitan intended to go to her room to escape the prattle which conflicted with her unappeased emotion, without affording any distraction, two unknown women came and sat down at a short distance on the same terrace.

'Ah!' cried Lady Helton, looking at these two women through her eye-glass, 'in truth, it is she. Oh! I am very happy! Indeed!'

And rising hastily she went and shook hands with the elder of the two.

'Oh! dear Mme. de la Marche,' she said with a pronounced English accent, 'how happy I am to see you!'

Mme. de la Marche, for it was she, accompanied by her daughter, at once recognized Lady Helton, whom she had met very often in Paris, and especially at the brilliant receptions of the English embassy. Graciously acknowledging her welcome, she introduced Mme. de Moray to Lady Helton.

'I am so happy to meet you here,' said Mme. de la Marche, with her habitual sad smile, which suited so well the dignity of her features. 'I was afraid that the sojourn at the cape would be a little lonely for my daughter and her husband. I shall beg of you to introduce them to your relations.'

'Oh!' said Lady Helton, 'I will make you acquainted at once with a charming woman who will make your stay here more agreeable than I could do it myself.'

Without waiting an answer to her proposition, the widow of the British sailor turned round. Two or three chairs only separated the little group from Gorgon.

'My dear duchess,' said Lady Helton, 'allow me to present to you the wife of one of the most illustrious of French sailors, Mme. Firmin de la Marche, and her daughter, Mme. de Moray, the wife of the governor-general of Pondichéry.'

Then addressing herself to her new companion.

'Mme. the Duchess de San Lucca,' she said, 'one of the greatest names of Italy.'

The three women bowed to each other graciously. The duchess was the youngest of the three. Moreover she was almost at home in this hotel which she had inhabited for several months, and of which she had almost made a palace ; so she got up and went to Mme. de la Marche. In that moment she felt a great joy. It was in the hope of this meeting that she had given up her daily promenade. Chance had gratified her wish.

The interview was cordial in every way. Very happy at this good fortune, which on the first day introduced a charming relation to her daughter and her son-in-law, Mme. Firmin de la Marche departed from the usual austerity of her manner ; as to Mme. de Moray, while she was forced to render homage to the beauty and grace of the duchess, she did not feel attracted towards her with the same force which impelled her mother. It was a feeling she could not explain and which she tried to resist, because she found it unjust. The beautiful Neapolitan, with the ease and grace of the most accomplished woman, made the new comers acquainted with the charms of the country where they had met for the first time.

'Look, Mme. de Moray,' she said, showing her a large green nest rising in the midst of the gulf, 'that is the island of Ste. Marguerite. How beautiful it is ! It is my favorite promenade. Every week a little steamer comes for me. We will go some day, taking our provisions with us, and we will breakfast under the pines.'

As she was saying these words, a man appeared on the terrace.

'Ah !' said Mme. de la Marche, 'here is a companion who will accept your invitation with great pleasure. Allow me to introduce M. de Moray.

Then turning towards her son-in-law.

'Mme. de San Lucca, Roger,' she continued. 'The duchess, my dear child, is, it appears, the queen of the Cape of Antibes. Do not fail to pay her your respects. Ah ! I also introduce you to Lady Helton.'

M. de Moray had left the countess and her mother, after dinner, with the intention of going as far as the beach, and he had promised to return in half an hour. It was during this short promenade that the unexpected meeting we have described above had taken place. In returning to the hotel he was still much pre-occupied with the vision which had appeared to him. He was so much absorbed in his thoughts that in coming near his wife and Mme. de la Marche, he had not noticed that those ladies were not alone. It was only at the moment he was presented to the duchess that he recognized her. A violent emotion shook him to the bottom of his heart. But happily it was not noticed. He bowed without saying a word. We have just said that his emotion was not noticed, the reader will readily guess that we except **Gorgon**. The trouble of the count could not remain unnoticed by **her**, who was the direct cause of it. She herself felt for a moment the **physical** fever to which **she had** been subjected a quarter of **an hour before.** But, better prepared than the count for this interview, she controlled herself more easily, and she extended her hand to him in a most natural way, without betraying any embarrassment. However, neither the count nor the duchess said they had already met in the garden walk hidden from view by the clumps of palm-trees. It was a secret which they kept, and which created a tie of complicity between them. M. de Moray was grateful to Mme. de San Lucca for her silence. He found in it a sort of mysterious appeal for another meeting, which thereafter would not be provoked by chance. All the natural forces of his being, hardly escaped yet from the mortal Indian fever, were allured by that woman, unknown to him less than an hour before. He was contemplating her voluptuous beauty from which were flashing out towards him currents of magnetic attractions. He admired her and she provoked in him a mad desire.

The conversation had become general and the time passed very rapidly. The large clock of **the** hotel struck **four.** The countess rose.

' We must go up to **our room for** a little while,' **she said.** ' Are you coming, Roger ? '

' No,' answered M. de Moray. ' The weather **is so** beautiful. I shall rejoin you in a moment.'

Mme. Firmin de la Marche and her daughter retired, accompanied by Lady Helton. M. de Moray remained alone with the Duchess de San Lucca. Both were silent, but **not** embarrassed. It was a silence made of unspoken demands and **answers. Gorgon was** the first to break it.

' Why did you stay ? ' she simply asked in her rich voice.

' How could I go ? ' answered M. de Moray, making designs on the sand with his walking-stick, so as **to** avoid looking at her too directly. ' Yes, how could I go without first thanking you ? '

' Thanking me ! ' said the duchess with astonishment. ' **For** what ? **Because** I have told you that the little cluster of white houses, up there, on the mountain, is called Grasse, or because I have told you that there would be a ball **this** evening in the reception rooms of the hotel ? '

' No ; you are well aware that it is not for that.'

He raised his **head** and let his eyes speak at the same time **as** his lips.

' **I** have to thank you,' he said with a languid slowness, ' for **being so** beautiful, and for doubling by your radiant beauty the **splendor** of the **nature which** surrounds us.'

Gorgon did not interrupt him. It was her turn to be silent, to lower her eyes, and to breathe with difficulty, her fair bosom heaving under the gauze which barely covered it. M. de Moray continued.

'Look,' he said, extending his arm, 'look at those mountains, those forests, those seas, and those glaciers. The grandest things God has created are there, under our eyes. But all those splendors were slumbering in an eternal quietness but a few minutes ago, before I saw you. Now, it seems to me that all these things,—the dazzling snows, the blue waves, the pines and the green oaks, the porphyry rocks, are full of life and sing to you a hymn of adoration, saying : "It is you who are the most beautiful, and we admire you ! " And I, the unknown of yesterday, the weak and feeble man ; I, who feel so little beside those immensities, but whose heart conceives the purity of the snow, the storms of the waves, and the burning winds of the mountains which bend the heads of the oaks, I thank you in my turn for being the sovereign beauty which fills my eyes and intoxicates my soul ! '

In love talk it is the voice which very often gives to the words their charm and persuasion. Coming from anybody else, and spoken with the accent of a poet with long hair, this anthem of passion would have made the Duchess de San Lucca smile. But Gorgon was moved by a delicious feeling, thanks to the deep intonation of the voice she was hearing for the first time, and which vibrated with increasing intensity, as each word fell from his lips. She never gave a thought to the character she had assumed. She never asked herself what a true Duchess de San Lucca would do, if a man she did not know an hour before had offended her in such a manner, or had offered such homage. She abandoned herself wholly to the ravishing emotion she had never experienced before, having never loved, and all her reason was lost in a delicious weakness.

Anything else they might have said would have only lessened the effect, shared by both, of these hasty avowals. They felt this to be so, and separated On rising Gorgon offered her hand to her new friend, without speaking. M. de Moray took it and pressed it for a moment in his own. This was, so to speak, the betrothal of their love. After this they retired, feeling that the hour just passed would be decisive in their lives. Neither knew what engagement they had contracted towards each other. But they were well aware that such flames cannot be stirred up without provoking, some day, terrible conflagrations.

While the duchess had retired to her room to take a little rest, Roger descended into the garden. He was not in a state to appear before his wife without betraying himself, and took another walk to quiet his nerves. Mme. de Moray was at her window, looking on the beauties of nature, which had awakened such passion in the soul of her husband. She saw the count walking down the path, and she joyfully called her mother to her side.

'Look at Roger, mother,' she said. 'Who could believe he is the same man I have seen only a week ago struggling in agony? God has performed an unhoped-for miracle in restoring him to health.'

'Yes,' answered Mme. de la Marche, 'God has done it all. But it was by means of your tenderness that He accomplished the prodigy. Dear child, the love of your husband will reward you amply for the life you have saved!'

'I depend upon it,' said the countess, 'Roger owes me that love if it were only to reward the sacrifice I made in leaving my daughter.'

A little later the excursionists returned to the hotel, and Annibal Palmeri went up to his sister's room.

'Well,' he said, 'were you lonesome, little sister?'

'No,' she said, 'reassure yourself.'

As the dinner hour was at hand she began to dress. Was it merely the result of chance, or was it by means of a clever negotiation between Annibal Palmeri, acting under the orders of his sister, and the waiters, we are not in a position to say, but one thing is certain : two hours after, at the dinner table, Mme. de la Marche, her daughter, and her son-in-law were near neighbors of the Duchess de San Lucca.

The latter, after making imperious recommendations to her brother, had presented him to her new friends. At table M. de Moray and Annibal were seated side by side. The ice having been broken by a formal introduction, the two men chatted a long time over the dinner table. M. de Moray was even gay in his conversation, and for the first time in many months, that is to say since the day that Paulette had caught the terrible Indian fever, a smile lit his face. The countess noticed the transformation and she was sincerely happy, and in the gratitude she felt towards her companions, she tried to combat an instinctive sentiment, which prompted her to repulse their advances. In fact, a mysterious intuition was telling her to mistrust, for the sake of her happiness, the beauty, and the artifices of this Italian who was possessed of such irresistible powers of seduction. During the dinner and in the evening she, by powerful efforts, restrained herself, thinking it would be unjust to repulse without any serious motive, offers of intimacy by which the mental welfare of the being to whom she had consecrated a life of devotedness and love would be strengthened. She had noticed the impression the Duchess de San Lucca had produced on the mind of her husband, and she was frightened at the beginning of the interview which had taken place during the day on the terrace. But, later she was reassured when she saw her husband walking alone in the garden, and returning to her more loving than he had been for a long time.

The reader will remember that M. de Moray sincerely recipro-cated the saintly and pure love of his wife. He admired Laura, and he loved her. So, in spite of the fever which was burning his veins on that day, and which was to return in future every time the duchess would come near him, he felt himself protected against completely falling by the powerful roots of a constant and undivid-ed attachment of eighteen years. The few days which followed brought to the Count de Moray the same emotions, even keener, if possible. But we repeat it, however provoking were the advances of the countess, he firmly fought against them. After the surprise of the first interview, he was more reserved in his relations with her. He managed so as to avoid meeting her alone, taking care to always place between himself and Claudia, as a shield, the presence of his wife. This conduct on his part inspired the Neapolitan with sentiments of revolt. She did not understand how the count; ex-periencing beside her certain emotions, the particular nature of which could not remain unknown to him, entrenched himself in such an austere reserve. She felt wounded in her womanly pride, and perhaps still more in the sincerity of a passion in which, thanks to her early education and principles, she found nothing reprehensi-ble. Once this rebellion awakened, she resolved to spare nothing to triumph over what she termed the stupid silliness of an honest man. Only she understood that she would gain nothing by openly attacking that fortress of virtue, and she thought of misleading the vigilance of her adversary in love. The plan was well conceived, and was destined to obtain an entire success, as the reader will see. For the time being, Annibal, who was not an idiot, amused himself at this comedy. Gorgon did not put herself out on account of Peppo, and the more she resigned herself to momentary prudence with others, the greater anger she displayed when alone with her brother.

' *Per Baccho!* ' said the Italian, one evening that his sister and himself were alone in their room and Claudia appeared still more nervous than usual, 'do you know that I never saw you in such a state ? You must be madly in love, my dear ! '

' In love,' answered Gorgon, looking daggers at him, ' perhaps so ! It is quite possible ! But at least there is one thing I am quite sure of, and that is, I hate them ! '

' Who ? ' asked Annibal, stupefied.

' All of them ! Even the one whom you say I love, and who hides himself like a frightened child behind the petticoats of his wife, after having shown me, on the first day we met, the purpled horizons of a foolish passion. Yes, I hate him. 1 hate him for his cowardice after his boldness, and I cannot forgive the offence of his

willing coldness after having forgiven his thoughtless enthusiasm.
But one I hate more than him, is that woman to whom I am sacrificed, and who seems to defy me from the height of her legitimate
rights ! Here ! I have often told you that I abhorred all these great
lords whose family pride closes their doors to me ; well, I detest
her more than all the others, this great lady who closes to me the
heart of that man, and who, to prevent me from entering it, has
only to erect the phantom of her twenty years of marriage ! '

Palmeri had listened to this outburst with amazement. To tell
the truth, he found his sister insatiable. Zounds ! there were
enough other men ! However, as he had a solid affection for Gorgon,
he took pity on her.

' Come,' he said, with the tone of one speaking to an angry child,
' do you want me to help you ? '

' Eh ! what can you do for me,' she said, shrugging her shoulders.

' More than you think ! Have patience, little sister ! With time,
one may do a great many things.'

' Time !' cried Gorgon. ' Have I time ? Did they not tell us of
their early departure ? In fifteen days they will be in Paris, and
once there, good-bye ! we will not even see them !'

' Once there,' said the Neapolitan, in a tone of modest triumph,
' do you know what I have prepared to please you, I whom you seem
to despise, and who only think of helping you ? '

' What is it ?' asked Gorgon, with avidity.

' Well, once there, we will all live together, the Count and the
Countess de Moray, the old admiral and his noble wife, and, lastly,
we two, Annibal Palmeri and her excellency the Duchess de San
Lucca. What do you think of that, little sister ? '

Gorgon thought this was a stupid joke of Peppo's. Her only answer was a look of anger. However, Annibal insisted.

' Why, don't you believe me ? We will all live together like a
troup of little patriarchs, unless you refuse to join us.'

' Then that story is true ?' asked Gorgon, with anxiety, shaking
his arm.

' What a grip,' said Palmeri, disengaging himself. ' If ever you
take hold of your lover in that manner, he will not leave you in a
hurry. Well, yes, that is true ! How many times must I repeat
it ? '

' Then, explain yourself.'

' It is very simple,' answered Annibal, lighting a cigar, ' you
know that I am on the most intimate terms with this excellent
Count de Moray.'

' Yes.'

' As he has not to avoid me the same reasons which make him run
away from you, and that I am, so to speak, something of yourself,

D

he is quite crazy after me. Of course I pretended to think his
friendship very sincere, but it was only make-believe on my part.'

'Go on ! Go on !' she interrupted, impatiently.

'Then, we promenade together a good part of the day, and while
walking, we chat. In the course of these conversations the count
has spoken to me of a thousand and one things, and amongst others
of the fear he entertains of remaining definitely in Paris, on account of
his health. It appears that it would be very dangerous for him to
return to India. So he will stay in Paris for a long time, perhaps
for ever, and he will occupy an old residence belonging to his family
on de Várennes street.'

'I have heard speak of that house, by Mme. de Moray in
fact.'

'Well, as it appears this mansion is very large, the admiral
Firmin de la Marche and his venerable wife will occupy the ground
floor of one of the wings, while the count and his wife will lodge
in the first story of the same wing. So there remains another wing
and the main body of the house.'

'And then ?'

'Then I asked the count who lived in this second and more important part of the old house, and he told me that it was vacant,
the legation of Roumania having just moved out of it. I forgot
to tell you that this was said in the presence of the old lady,
whose majestic bearing always intimidates me. At the news of
the removal of the legation, news which had only arrived that
very morning, and which she had not heard of, the austere dow-
ager expressed her regret, telling her son-in-law that it was a
serious matter, as the rent was very high, and a new lodger difficult to find.'

'Then, then ?' repeated Gorgon, while her brother was relight-
ing his cigar, which had gone out.

'Hold on ! There—that's it—. Then I don't know what prompted me to invent an adventure exactly similar, except that it is
the contrary, and to say that the proprietor of the house we live
in had given us notice.'

'Why did you say that ?'

'I don't know. A whim. And just see how well I was inspired.
Mme. de la Marche then said : " Well, M. Palmeri, here is a good
opportunity to satisfy everybody. If our old suburb does not seem
too gloomy for the Duchess de San Lucca, rent the apartments
rendered vacant by the departure of the legation, and let us live
like good neighbors in Paris as we do at the Cape of Antibes.'

'She made that proposition ?' said Gorgon, who could not believe
her own ears."'

'As I am telling you.'

'And what did the count say ?' asked the beautiful Claudia.

' What could he say, except confirm his mother-in-law's proposal ? Just think of it, lover and proprietor at the **same** time. The least thing he could do was to offer me a lease of three, six, or nine years, at the respective wishes of all parties, and that's just what he has done, and with eagerness I would have you believe.'

Although speaking in a playful mood, **Palmeri was in** earnest. His sister did not doubt it now, but she was **troubled.** She could never find a better combination for the success of her projects. The intimacy which would certainly be established between **them,** thanks to **their near** neighborhood, would throw wide open **the** portals of **that** world, which **the** pride of the upstart made **her** desirous of entering. **And on the** other hand **it** seemed impossible to her that, through this familiarity, M. de Moray would not come out of his stoical and absurd reserve. Only one thing caused her some anxiety, and that was **the consent of** Mme. de Moray **to** the execution of this project.

' And she ? ' asked Gorgon, **abruptly.**

' Who ? '

' Mme. de Moray, what did she say ? '

' At first she could not say anything, because she was not present. But as I was telling Mme. de la Marche that I would speak to you about the project, the count declared that he would refer the matter to his wife, who is part owner of the mansion with him, and that in any case he would not take such **a** determination without consulting her.'

' But did you not tell me he had accepted at first ? '

' Indeed he did ! and with enthusiasm. But after reflection he asked me not to say a word about the matter until **he** had **spoken** to the countess.'

' And you have stupidly obeyed him ? '

' For the following reason. Suppose that Mme. de Moray would not dare to encounter the neighborhood **of** a woman **so** dangerous to the rest of her husband, which would only be very legitimate, what was the use of causing **you the** annoyance of a deception ? '

' You thought, then, that **I would** accept ? '

' Absolutely.'

' Well, you were right,' said Gorgon, resolutely. ' Not only do I accept, but this project must succeed, and it will, even if we have to put such a price **on** the location as will vanquish all difficulties.'

' It is useless **to do that.**'

' Why ! '

' The count took me apart this evening, while you were dancing, and **he told** me that the countess is willing to accept us as tenants, provided, however, that it is our intention to become such.'

' **Yes,** it is our intention,' said Gorgon with a wicked smile, ' and **on this, as it is** two o'clock in the morning, go to bed. I will think **of this before going to sleep.**'

They shook hands and separated. The beautiful Claudia was a long time in getting to sleep, and she had enough leisure to think of this new combination and to deduce all the consequences which might arise out of it. Next morning, after breakfast, as everybody was on the terrace of the hotel as usual, the duchess went straight to Mme. de Moray.

'Countess,' she said, 'my brother has told me last night of a project to which you have given your consent. Before taking a determination myself, I should like to know if the project has received your assent without reserve.'

We have said very often that with all her faults and her vices, Gorgon had an eminent quality, bravery. She would have scorned to wage war against Mme. de Moray without first warning her. The countess would have had only one word to say, like this, for instance : 'I yield to the will or to the desire of my husband,' and it is probable that Gorgon would have been satisfied with such a victory without going any further. But Mme. de Moray did not make that answer. She looked at the duchess frankly, and said :

'Why should I not wish you to come and live beside us, almost with us ? What would I have to fear from your presence ?'

To Mme. de Moray's mind, this question signified exactly this :

'I have discovered that my husband has not remained insensible to the power of your beauty. But I confide the rest and the joy of my life to your friendship and your honor. Can I depend on them ?'

To Gorgon's mind, on the contrary, this question : 'What would I have to fear?' meant a challenge. She understood that the countess looked on her as an unworthy adversary, over whom she would easily triumph. And it was in that spirit that she accepted the challenge. As the countess was tendering her hand when they separated she shook it in a way which meant a declaration of war. Fifteen days after, they all left the Cape of Antibes together on the same day, and a few days later, the Duchess de San Lucca and her brother were installed in the house on de Varennes street.

II.

It was with a sentiment of triumphant pride that Gorgon left her residence on the plaine Montceau to go and dwell in the ancient habitation of the Count de Moray. The relations created at the cape being given, and the conditions on which her installation had been accepted, this removal was equivalent to taking possession. Now, she was sure of conquering that world which had so persistently remained closed to her. The doors of the highest Parisian society would be thrown wide open on her passage, when she would advance, leaning on the arm of Mme. de la Marche, that most powerful impersonation of honor. She was sure, also, of overcoming the resistance which his sense of duty interposed between the **love** of M. de Moray and herself; the day would come when his **elevated** conjugal honesty, which had mastered his passion after **the surprise** of their first meeting, would succumb.

In the midst of all these agitations Annibal Palmeri **lived in a** sort of philosophical serenity which was exasperating **to his sister.** In spite of his early and vicious surroundings, to which he owed some vulgarity of tone and manners, this *lazzarone*, transplanted to Parisian soil, had got a hold on Admiral de la Marche. Even his artless familiarity had privileges of language which would not have been tolerated in others. The adventurer was never disrespectful, however, and at times he felt for the noble sailor a very sincere admiration, which he acknowledged. He even spoke of the sailor's career with almost poetic exaggeration. One day after breakfast, at which he and his sister were guests, as it happened **very** often, he expressed himself with enthusiasm.

'Yes, Admiral,' he cried, with his Italian animation, accompanied with extravagant gestures, 'I have always had a great admiration for your noble calling. *Per Baccho!* To have an entire fleet under your orders. To command men and fight the elements. It is splendid.'

M. **de** la Marche smiled, but with a feeling of sadness.

'**Bah! my dear** M. Palmeri, like every other medal, the sailor's **medal has a reverse.**'

'You say that!'

'I say that and I also believe in it. Do you see, whatever may be the devotedness one bears to his country, there are hours of discouragement when he asks himself if the glory he has won is not paid for too dearly.'

This was said in the presence of all our personages. Mme. de la Marche alone had retired to her room, wearied, probably, by the noise that surrounded her, and which troubled her accustomed melancholy. Mme. de Moray was chatting with her husband and the Duchess de San Lucca, of indifferent things probably, for she heard the remark of the Admiral. She was astonished at an assertion giving such a flat denial to the whole life of her illustrious father, and she turned around to interrogate him.

'You want to know,' she asked, 'if your glory **has not** been paid for too dearly. What do you mean by that?'

'Alas! my poor Laura,' said the admiral, 'however brilliant it may be, the exile of the sailor on board his vessel is nevertheless a real exile, with all the sorrows comprised in that word.'

' I do not understand at all,' said Palmeri, artlessly.

' I will tell you, my child,' said M. de la Marche, still addressing his daughter, 'although you have lived far away from us since
your marriage, you cannot have forgotten that you have seen, when
still a young girl, the commencement of the sad melancholy of your
mother ? '

The countess nodded affirmatively.   M. de Moray intervened.

' I have often remarked the great sadness you speak of, Admiral.
But the deep respect I have for you and for the mother of my wife
always prevented me from enquiring about it.   What is wanting to
the happiness of Mme. de la Marche ?   Has she not a glorious husband ? a daughter whom she adores ? '

' And who adores her,' interrupted Mme. de Moray.

Gorgon herself was attracted by this conversation, and she enquired in her turn with a sort of involuntary bitterness.

' Has she not everything that is wanting in so many others, a
name which cannot be assailed, a situation above all suspicion ? '

' And chiefly,' continued Mme. de Moray, 'a reputation for benevolence and virtue sufficient to protect her against the basest jealousies.'

' All that is true,' answered the admiral, and he continued, with
a thoughtful accent, as if making a review of his past life, and almost speaking to himself, ' what a light-hearted young girl she was,
in days gone by, when a simple lieutenant, I asked her father for
her hand , and later, what a cheerful young bride during the first
years of our married life !   After the short cruises I used to make
then, she was so happy at each of my returns, that the announcement of a new departure found me strong to support it.   During the
first years, I made only short expeditions.   One day I had to take
the command of a frigate which was sent to Madagascar, where, as
everybody knows, our interests are not yet well defined.   The
mission which was confided to me was difficult of accomplishment,
and I returned only after three years.   I had left a consolation to
the wife I was abandoning to serve my country.   I had left you to
your mother, my beloved Laura !   And still, when I returned, the
half widowhood which the sailor's wife undergoes had done its
work of sadness and mourning.   The length of our separation and
the anxieties it had brought to her heart had been the cause of a
dangerous illness.   It was a cruel surprise for me to find her so different from what she was on the eve of my departure.   Time and a
firm will have arrested the progress of this moral ruin which was
wrecking my happiness.   But the effects already produced at the
time of my arrival still exist , and when everything seems to unite
to ensure to the companion of my life the serenity of heart, which
her virtues entitle her to, I must witness, powerless to avert it, the
sadness which you have all remarked.'

On these words the admiral broke down. Everybody felt that **a** deep sorrow had attacked the great love he bore to his wife, a love made of thirty-five years of devotedness and veneration. They all respected his emotion and very soon retired. Annibal, in shaking hands with the admiral, excused himself for having involuntarily awakened such sad memories.

' They were not asleep,' answered the admiral, trying to smile, ' they were only silent. Perhaps I am obliged to you for having given me the occasion to speak of them. My heart will be comforted for some time, I hope.'

Mme. de Moray had always been struck by the troubled **state of** her mother's mind, but she had never dared to ask for an explanation which was not offered, and it was the first time her father had spoken so freely in her presence about her mother. At the onset of the conversation she had **hoped** that it would throw some light on the causes of the austere severity which had saddened her youth, but she soon found out that the admiral did not know any more than herself. The admiral attributed the illness of Mme. de la Marche to the sadness of long separations, but this reason did not satisfy her.

' There is certainly,' she thought, ' something my father does not know, and it is a secret my mother keeps to herself alone. Why has not she more confidence in me ? Why does she not reveal the mystery which weighs on her life ? It seems to me that my tenderness is deep enough to bring to her suffering heart the consolations it yearns for. Well, let us have patience. Perhaps an occasion will present itself when I shall be able to restore to her the rest she has lost. God knows I would willingly give my life for her.'

The occasion, as the reader will see, was soon to present itself. Since her arrival in Paris, Mme. de Moray lived in great intimacy with her mother ; she had made herself as indispensable in her life as she could, trying to alleviate the weight of her occupatio**ns**. She was her secretary for the numerous charities which solicited her patronage. It was the countess who opened the letters of Mme. de la Marche, and who answered, without even consulting her, except in important cases, the demands which were addressed to her.

On the day, after the conversation we have just narrated, she went to her work as was her new habit, and took the letters arrived by the morning mail. At the third envelope she opened, a violent emotion seized her. Laura read that letter several times, trying to think that she had not understood its meaning, and hoping that in weighing its terms she would succeed in changing its import. But whatever she tried, its clearness and brutality left no room to equivocation. Although it **is** somewhat lengthy, **we** will reproduce it in its integrity. The letter read thus :

'To Mme. Firmin de la Marche,—

'A man whose name is unknown to you, but who has undoubted
rights to your benevolence, claims a moments' interview. That man
is myself. And that name you do not know is mine. I call myself
Robert Burel. But in spite of this vulgar name, I am the son of a
baron. The son of M. de Corpsdieu. This little phrase of itself
must tell you many things. I think that you will not desire much
to see such a man as I am coming into your house to revive the
associations which the name of M. de Corpsdieu will certainly recall to your memory. So be kind enough to come and see me, No.
20, *Court of the Dragoon*, in a house of mean appearance where I
lodge, in the last room of the last story. The Court of the Dragoon
is only a few steps from de Varennes street. Yes, decidedly, I
think that you would rather come and see me than receive me in
your mansion, where, perhaps, it would be difficult to explain my
presence to the Admiral de la Marche. Be that as it may, one day
or other, whether you come to me, or I go to you, there is one
thing you may be certain of : it is that your reputation of virtue
and your honor depends upon the reception you will extend to this
letter from your most humble and most obedient,

'ROBERT BUREL.'

The letter was evidently an attempt to blackmail her mother ; it
was odious ; it was infamous ; there was nothing serious in it, and
silence and contempt would be the best answer to it. Such was
the first thought of Mme. de Moray ; but when she had recovered
from her astonishment, she commenced to reflect on its contents.
There was only one thing to do ; tear up the impure sheet, throw
it into the fire, and pay no attention to it. But however resolved
Laura might have been to carry this into effect, as she was about to
tear the letter she changed her mind. Since Providence had permitted her to open this cursed envelope, it was because Providence
had chosen her to find out the mystery of this infamy, and to hide
the secret of it from her mother. Yes, she would go herself to this
rendez-vous ; she would see this Robert Burel ; she would ask him
the explanation of his threats ; she would crush him under the
weight of her indignation ; she would force him to blush, to tremble, perhaps.

This resolution once taken, she was not long in executing her project. Without speaking to anybody, without even calling her maid,
she hastily dressed herself and went out. The street of the Dragoon is only a few steps from de Varennes street. A few minutes
after, Laura arrived there, and entered into the Court of the Dragoon itself. She went straight before her until she reached the
number indicated. The house, older and darker than the others,

had six stories. She started to climb the stairs without stopping, suffocated to some extent by the rapidity of her ascension, but still more so by the foul smells emanating from every hole and corner. More than once she nearly fainted. However, in spite of her repulsion, she went up until she reached the last story, where she found a long passage with doors opening right and left ; **she** followed this passage to the last door. Before entering her courage failed her for a moment. Her heart was beating as if it was going **to** break. She thought she had been foolish to come, and chiefly to come alone ; that a trap was set behind those rotten boards. ' If I should run away ?' she said to herself. But she was ashamed of her instinctive terror. What could she fear ? And even admitting that there **was a** hidden danger, was it not her duty to face it in place of her **mother ?** The key was in the door. She did not open, but knocked. **A voice** answered :

' Come in !'

One last hesitation ; one last **effort of her** will. Abruptly, the courageous woman turned the key, pushed the door open, and entered. She found herself in a small **room,** furnished only with a broken chair, an iron bedstead, **whose mattress had** not been shaken **nor the** clothes washed for a long **time,** and a rough table. Light was obtained from a sky-light cut through the ceiling. Laura at first could distinguish nothing, but her eyes becoming accustomed to the obscurity, she soon noticed a man standing in front of her. He had evidently just got up, for his hair was in disorder ; he was looking **at** her with astonishment. After the first moment of embarrassment on the part of both of them, the young man opened the conversation.

' To whom have I **the honor to speak ?** ' he said, **contemplating** with curiosity the noble **woman who was** bringing into **this** miserable room the perfume of her virtue, and the radiant brilliancy **of** her beauty.

Laura did not answer directly.

' M. Robert Burel ? ' she said in her turn.

' It is myself,' said the young man. ' Take the trouble **to** sit down, madam.'

And he advanced the only chair which **was** in the **room.** She would have preferred to refuse it, but since she had come, she thought it was better not to wound his feelings, so she sat down. She was very much astonished. The man standing before her did not answer to the idea she had formed of him. In spite **of** his worn-out clothes, and the paleness of his face, which was certainly **due** to the misery and anguish of poverty, the wretch had the appearance and manners of a man of the world. His voice was sorrowful and full **of** bitterness. But his language **was** correct, and his intonation naturally distinguished.

'So, then, you are truly Robert Burel?' asked Laura again, not noticing, in her trouble and her astonishment, that she had already asked the question.

'I have had the honor to tell you so a moment ago,' said the young man, smiling. 'But you, madam, have not told me who you are.'

And yielding to an old habit of courtesy, he continued with less rudeness,

'But I know, in return, who you are not. Your age and your beauty cannot belong to the person —— to a person I was expecting.'

'You mean Mme. de la Marche,' Laura said with emphasis.

'Herself,' answered the young man, bowing coldly. 'So, however flattering your visit may be, I am obliged to repeat my question for the third time : To whom have I the honor to speak, and how is it that Mme. de la Marche has seen fit to send you in her place. It is to her interest not to mix a stranger in the subjects I intended to discuss with her.'

'Mme. de la Marche does not know of this visit, and I hope she will never see the letter you have written, and which I have opened. I am the Countess de Moray, the daughter of Mme. de la Marche.'

'Then,' said the young man astonished, 'you are my sister.'

On hearing these words : 'You are my sister !' Laura thought the man was crazy. But instead of being frightened she felt a great joy. Everything was explained now. The man who had written that threatening, almost disgraceful letter, was a poor wretch devoid of reason. However, she wanted to know how far his insanity extended, and she spoke to him softly, and humoring his whim.

'Ah!' she said, 'I am your sister. I did not know. Now, Monsieur Burel, will you explain to me how it happens that I am your sister. Imagine that my father and mother have forgotten to tell me that I had a brother !'

Robert looked at her with astonishment, although he was a man not to be surprised at little things. At first he thought Mme. de Moray was mocking him, and spoke with irony. But he soon discovered the truth in noticing a tender pity in her eyes.

'Ah!' he said in his turn, 'you believe that I am a lunatic, or that I am drunk. You are mistaken. It is a long time since there has been enough wine in this room to make me tipsy, and I have not suffered enough yet to shatter my reason. Believe me, madam, I have told you the truth, and I am truly your brother.'

Laura felt that the unfortunate man, if he was crazy, spoke in earnest, and believed what he asserted. But his pretension was so absurd that she did not think it was necessary to hear any more. She rose to go, saying :

' If you really believe what you are saying, sir, it is not to me, it is not even to my mother that you must speak. Address yourself to Admiral de la Marche, that is to say, your father. He will answer you.'

She thought to end the adventure with **these words**. At least, she was confiding the honor of her mother to a man whose situation and authority would promptly deal with this **groundless pretension**.

' I beg your pardon,' said Robert, motioning her by a gesture to sit down again. ' I see that you do not understand clearly, **and in** your interest as **well** as in the interest of your mother, I beg **of you** not to be too hasty. I have told you that I was your brother, **but** I did not say that I had the honor to be the son of the admiral ;~ and perhaps you will think, now that you are **better acquainted** with the situation, that it is useless to tell him **of the ties which** bind us to each other, outside of his knowledge.'

Only then Mme. de Moray understood the full meaning of **the** pretensions of the man. He called himself **the** son of Mme. **de la** Marche, and not that of her husband, a son conceived in shame and in crime. Her blood rushed to her face, and **she felt** a choking sensation in her throat.

' Ah !' she cried, **as soon as** she could speak ; ' you accuse my mother, that is to say, a saint ; she whose name is synominous with honor and virtue ; the worthy companion of the most respected man the world knows ! It is a cowardly and infamous act ! You are not a lunatic, sir, you are a bandit !'

Robert Burel had listened to her insults without interruption. In spite of himself, he admired the great love, and **the** deep veneration of the daughter defending her mother. However, **he** was not **a** man to be dominated by such sentiments, and he continued :

' I am sorry that you have opened the letter I sent to your mother. If she had come, instead of you, this painful scene would not have taken place. Trust me, give me back the letter you have intercepted. I shall put it under a new envelope, addressed to Mme. de la Marche. She will read it and she will **come,** and you may be sure that she will not rebel as you think **you have a** right to do in her name.'

For a moment Mme. de Moray felt inclined to follow **this** advice. Not that she believed that her mother was guilty, but because she thought that with one word the noble woman would justify herself. But she also thought that this accusation, although baseless and slanderous, would wound her deeply, and since she was engaged in **it, it** was better that she should go **on to** the end. She looked at **Burel**. The man was about thirty years old, although excesses of all kinds, poverty and the deceptions of life made him look much older. Although marked with the stigma of misery and vice, one

could easily distinguish the degenerated offspring of a pure race.
Laura even thought she could see a distant resemblance to the
handsome face of her mother. She was startled.

'Come,' she said then, 'I want to know what you have to say.
Tell me all.'

Robert looked at her in his turn, hesitating to engage in a contest
with a sister, whom he did not know fifteen minutes before, whilst,
if it had been Mme. de la Marche, he would have had only to mention his name, or rather the name which was in his letter, and
which was his father's.

'You wish it?' he asked.

'I wish it.'

'Very well. Blame only yourself if the secret I am going to reveal makes you suffer in your respect for her who is truly my
mother as she is yours.'

Laura was startled. In spite of herself, the firmness of the young
man's voice shook her faith.

'My story is very simple,' commenced Robert, 'and whatever
prejudice you may have against me, you will very soon acknowledge
that I deserve your pity more than your hatred. I am truly the
son of M. de Corpsdieu and of Mme. de la Marche, and if you want
proofs, I shall place under your eyes letters from your mother which
attest it.

And he gave her the letters. In these Mme. de la Marche revealed with a heart-rending sincerity, the painful secret of her
life. The first, dated July 25th, without any indication of the year,
read thus:

'*To M. de Corpsdieu,—* .

'An evil! a terrible evil! It wanted that to force me to write,
to induce me to be the first to break the silence I had claimed and
obtained from you. Suppose, invent the most terrible punishment
God could reserve for the guilty wife. You understand, do you
not? It is almost two years since my husband is away, thousands
of leagues from France, and in seven months I will be a mother!

'I write to-day because I do not know if I will have the strength
to do so in a few days. Still I must recommend to your care the
child I cannot keep. You will be notified by the doctor. Be in
waiting in the forest where we used to meet; you will receive the
child and take him away.' .

The last letter was dated seven months later.

12th February.

'It will be this night. I am already suffering. The doctor will
take this letter to you. Wait at the place appointed. This letter
will probably be the last *souvenir* you will have from me, for perhaps God will have the kindness to call me to him!'

When she had finished, big tears escaped from Mme. de **Moray's eyes.**

'Oh ! my mother !' she muttered, **'I understand** now the reason why your features always bear the stamp **of** sorrow! It is the remorse which follows you ! '

However, she raised her head.

' It is true,' she said in broken accents ; ' Mme. de la Marche has forgotten her duty, and a son was born to her from her guilty love with M. de Corpsdieu, but where are the proofs that you are really that son. How am I to know that you have not stolen this terrible secret and that you make an infamous **use of it** without **being the** one you pretend to be ?'

' Wait a minute,' answered the young man, who had regained **all** his coolness after the embarrassment of the first moment. ' Let me go on with my story. The child was brought by the doctor to M. de Corpsdieu who was waiting at a small door of your mother's park. Before delivering his light burden, the doctor hesitated a little. "I have nothing to fear from you," he said. "The life of this child will be sacred to you ?" A word and a gesture re-assurred him. M. de Corpsdieu then started in the night. Towards noon he arrived at a small farm which belonged to him, distant about twelve leagues. He had heard, by chance, that the farmer's wife had just been confined. M. de Corpsdieu pretended to have found the child on the highway. He made his declaration to the mayor **of the** commune, and gave the child the name of Robert. Here **is** a legal copy of this declaration. See, father and mother unknown. The name of Burel belongs to my adopted parents. I have always borne it without having any right to it.

' A few weeks after M. de la Marche arrived in France, and found his wife in such a poor state of health, bodily **and** mentally, that he made her quit, in less than an hour, the wild country she had lived in during the past three years. M. **de** Corpsdieu, also very unhappy, tried to forget, and for that purpose he commenced to travel. When I was old enough he took me with him, and to-day there are very few countries in the world I have not visited. However, the health of M. de Corpsdieu was greatly impaired by the fatigues he had undergone, and one day, conscious of his approaching end, he thought he would tell me of the ties which united us. In truth, this revelation **did not** astonish me, for I expected it every day.

' Still, in telling me the history of his life, M. de Corpsdieu had **made a reserve :** he had obstinately refused to divulge the name of my mother. As I was pressing him to let me know it, more out of curiosity than out of love for the woman who had given me birth in adultery, and who, after all, had placed a little late the duties of a wife above the duties of a mother, M. **de** Corpsdieu answered :

' " Do **not** insist any more, Robert, I shall not tell you that name.

The secret of the woman who has loved me, even if it was only one hour, must die with me !"

'And still,' said Mme. de Moray, with bitterness, 'you know that name, and to-day you want to make it an instrument of threats and of ——'

She hesitated. Robert laughed.

'Why do you stop ?' he asked. 'An instrument of blackmail. Very well ; I will not dispute about words. But before you give way to surprise and accuse me let me finish.'

'Shortly after this conversation M. de Corpsdieu died, leaving me all his fortune by his will. To the will was annexed a letter in which my father accused himself of having allowed my passions to take too much empire over me, and lastly, he expressed the fear, that in case of ruin and reverses, I would not have enough strength to fight against adverse fortune.

'"On the day you find yourself ruined," he said, at the end of his letter, "go and see the notary who has given you this letter, and if he thinks your position sufficiently desperate, he will hand you a little box. In this box you will find the name of your mother, and convincing proofs that you are truly her son. Perhaps she will be able to help you, in her turn, in your hour of distress. It is a liberty which I have not the painful courage to spare her at the moment death is on me, and when I fear for you the dangers of wealth too easily acquired."

'You see ;' quietly said Robert, addressing Mme. de Moray, 'that I make an open confession, as I had intended making it to Mme. de la Marche, without disguising what I am or what I am not, worth. One thing is certain, the predictions of my father were realized to the letter. I squandered a part of my fortune, I managed the remainder very badly, and I tried to recoup myself at the gaming table until, about six months ago, I found myself totally ruined. Since that time, I tried everything, and succeeded in nothing. In despair, I intended to shoot myself with this pistol, which is the last remnant of my past splendor, and which I would not have sold for my last piece of bread, when I remembered the letter annexed to the will of my father. "But I am forgetting that I have a mother !" I cried, and I went to the notary's. Faithful to the mission he had received from my father, he gave me the box which M. de Corpsdieu had entrusted to his care, and which he supposed contained a reserve of money prudently put aside. In the box I found the letters of your mother, of my mother I can say now, which I have just shown you. They are signed only with one initial letter, but the note annexed to them bears the following words :

'"The letters herewith annexed have been written by Mme. Firmin de la Marche. The child therein mentioned, born from her, and belonging to me, bears the name of Robert Burel. At the moment I am writing these lines, knowing that I am near my end, I swear on my eternal salvation they contain the whole truth, and that Robert Burel is truly my son, and the son of Mme. de la Marche. Signed, BARON DE CORPSDIEU."

'I must confess that I was amazed on reading this declaration. I did not know Mme. de la Marche any more than I know her to-day. I have never seen her. But she has such a high reputation for honor and virtue that I had to read the affirmations of my father several times before I could believe them. Now that the secret of my birth was known to me, I was almost as much embarrassed as before. What was the use of my mother's name to me since she was not free and could not come to my help efficaciously ?'

' You never had a mother, and now that you discovered one, you did not feel your heart inundated with joy ?' cried Laura. ' In your place I would have seen my mother within an hour. I should have placed myself mysteriously in her passage, and I would have elevated my heart towards God with feelings of thanks and gratitude ! '

Robert Burel looked at her with an air of deep stupefaction. Evidently he had not understood at first. But he soon recovered his composure.

' Ah ! yes,' he said. ' I see what you mean ; elevated sentiment, is it not ? My mother ! I have a mother ! Saved ! I am saved ! Well, no, I confess it, I did not think of that at all when I learnt my mother's name ! And, if we are so different from each other with regard to filial love, it is because both of us have, in the same person, you, an angelic mother, worthy of all your tenderness, and I, a guilty mother, unnatural, and who deserves, if not hatred, at least indifference on my part.'

' Then a mother might not be loved,' cried Laura, with an accent of revolt.

' Would you love your mother,' cried Robert, brutally, ' if you had never known her, and if she had abandoned you completely ? For it is true ! I have been abandoned by her. I might have been thrown into some orphan asylum, condemned to misery, to suffering, and she would have known nothing of it. The pauper to whom she gives alms in the street might have been me, and she might have refused me help, not knowing who I was.'

' You complain because she has abandoned you,' cried Laura. ' But just think of this, she was married ! What could she do ? '

' She should not have brought me into the world,' coolly answered Robert, ' and when she had done so, she should have had the courage to suffer the consequences of her fault, instead of throwing her responsibility on the innocent. But why this discussion between us ? You will not persuade me any more than I shall convince

you. Each of us is in his *rôle*, and we are both right, according to
the standpoint in which we are respectively placed.'

'Very well,' said Laura, 'but you have an objective view in
demanding an interview from Mme. de la Marche. Let me know
what you expect from her, and if it be possible, I will try and satisfy you.'

'Whether it be possible or not,' coolly answered Robert, 'it will
have to be done. So I will let you know what I would have said
to Mme. de la Marche. I have imprudently wasted my life ; I have
no resources, I am deserted by all those whom I have obliged, or
who have simply been my companions of pleasure ; I have only one
ambition, one dream, to leave this country, where I hate every
thing and every person, and go into a new world to start life anew.
But I will not make such an attempt exhausted and vanquished on
the start for want of resources. I will not wear out the few years
of manhood and the spark of energy still left in me, in conquering
degree by degree the elements of the fortune for which I am going
to fight. I want arms and ammunition before I engage in the
struggle for life.'

'I understand, said Mme. de Moray, who saw with joy a means
of avoiding the living peril threatening the honor of her mother.
'You want money?'

There was, however, an involuntary accent of contempt in her
exclamation. Robert Burel noticed it, and smiled.

'Money!' he said, 'yes, money! Did not your mother give you
money when you were married ? And still how many things did you
get which I had not : consideration, a family, the love of all those
surrounding you. To all this your mother has added the benefit of
a dowry. By what right would she refuse one to me, who has received nothing of all this of which you are so largely possessed ?'

'Further discussion is useless,' said Laura, with pride. 'We are
making a bargain now. What are your exigencies ?'

Robert hesitated a little.

'What dowry did you receive when you were married ?' he
asked.

'I could not say exactly ; eight hundred thousand francs, I believe.'

'Well,' said the young man, slowly, and weighing his words,
'my exigencies, to borrow your own term, will not be extravagant.
Let your mother give me the eighth part only of what she has
given you, and I will never trouble her again.'

This figure startled Mme. de Moray.

'One hundred thousand francs !' she cried. 'Where do you suppose I could get that sum ?'

'I do not ask it from you, but from your mother.'

'Do you think that she could dispose of such a large sum
any more than I can, even if I told her of your demand ?'

'This is not a demand, it is a bargain. My departure and my silence depend on that sum.'

'But once more what you ask is impossible. Women, as you are well aware, do not dispose of their fortune.'

'It is the duty of Mme. de la·Marche to do impossiblities. In giving me birth she has contracted a debt towards me, and if she attempts to forfeit it, I will reveal it to the whole world.'

'You would not do that!' cried Mme. de Moray, '**you would** not betray your mother's secret!'

'Upon my life, I swear that I **would** do it,' answered Robert, **with** quiet firmness.

The unhappy young woman **felt as if strangled by a will and** force that nothing could conquer.

'I would willingly give you millions **if** I could!' she muttered. 'I will try to find the sum you are asking. I will—I will——'

'You, or your mother; it is immaterial.'

'Oh! it will be I,' said Laura, trembling. 'Can you suppose I would have the courage to reveal to my mother that I possess· her secret. Once more, it will be I. I will look, I will try; I have jewels; I will sell them, I will pawn them.'

'There is another means. If you do not want to speak of this to your mother, tell your husband. M. **de** Moray is very wealthy, I am told. He will give you the money.'

Laura rebelled at the proposition.

'Tell my husband,' she cried. 'What kind of a conscience have you to admit that even to my husband, chiefly to my husband, I would reveal this secret. I would rather die than cause him to lose the respect he bears to the old **age** of my beloved mother. Yes, die! a hundred times!'

'As you will,' said Robert, with carelessness. '**Take** whatever **means** you see fit, provided you succeed. **When** will you give me **this** money? I give you forty-eight hours.'

'But it is impossible!'

'It is your business **to make** it possible. The **day after to-mor-** row, at the same time, **I shall** await you here.'

'Here!' protested Laura. 'No, not here. I could not resign myself to re-enter this room, where I have learned such frightful things.'

'Another place is the same to me. Where then?'

'Well, I do not exactly know. Why not at the church of Saint-Germain-des-Prés, where I usually go?'

'Very well, the day after to-morrow, at the same hour. It is understood.'

'Yes, but——'

'What?'

E

'When I shall have given you the money, if I succeed in getting
it, how can I tell that the same danger will not exist.'

'If I gave you my word, you would not believe in it. I can only
offer one thing. In exchange for the bank-notes you will remit me,
I will give you the letters of your mother and the declaration of my
father. I assure you that in making this bargain I have not exceeded my just rights. But if, after you have given me that sum,
I attempt to do the same thing again, I would look upon myself as
a mean scoundrel, and I swear to you I am not one. Look at me
full in the face, and judge if you are to believe me ?'

Granting his demand, Laura looked in his eyes, and however
painful their interview had been, she could not help but feel a
softer emotion. Under the stigma of excesses of all kinds could be
seen a noble and handsome face. Laura had already noticed the
resemblance between Robert and her mother. She was still more
struck by it in this solemn moment. Who knows what the man
would have become if he had not been condemned by his birth to
a life of adventures. There were certainly strong extenuating circumstances in his favor.

'Yes,' she said, 'I believe you, and I will attempt the impossible to help you to start life anew ; and I sincerely wish that you
will find happiness.'

Her voice trembled in saying these last words. Robert noticed
it.

'Here !' he said in a more anxious tone, 'I am really very glad
that you have seen my letter and that you have come. It seems to
me that I call you sister more willingly than I would have said
mother.'

He extended her his hand. Laura took it without hesitation.

'The day after to-morrow, four o'clock, at St. Germain-des-
Prés,' she said.

'The day after to-morrow.'

Laura went away much troubled, so much so that she was nearly
run over by a carriage. In less than five minutes after, she was in
her room. She forbade entrance to everybody and recalled to her
mind the events of the past few months. Certainly she had known,
in less than a year, many sorrows. Her heart had been struck in
its tenderest place as a mother and as a wife. She had nearly lost at
one blow, the two beings to whom she had consecrated her whole
life, her daughter, her beloved Paulette, and Roger, her husband.
And when she had endured these cruel trials, she thought they were
the extreme limit of suffering, but the unexpected wound she had
received that day was more horrible than all the others. Her
mother, her venerated mother, had been sacrificed on the altar she
had erected to her in her heart ! Be it said to her praise, so great was
the affection she felt towards that mother, even guilty, that it did

not shake either **her** love or her respect. She pitied her, that's all. Troubled as she was, she could not appear before her family without betraying herself, so she excused herself and did not come down to dinner, and she soon felt so ill that she went to bed, asking not **to be** disturbed in her sleep. The reader can easily guess the nature **of such** a slumber ; a vigil, torpid **and** full of threatening dreams !

The next day she got up very early, however. She had **a** struggle to **engage** in, a terrible struggle, to find one hundred thousand francs in forty-eight hours ; and nearly twenty had already **gone** by. She went out and took a carriage which brought her to one **of** the greatest jewellers of Paris, M. Smith. All her jewels had been bought in his stores, her wedding **ornaments,** and the presents made by her husband on different occasions. M. Smith had also reset some expensive family diamonds given to her by her mother. By a happy chance, although it was hardly ten o'clock, M. Smith had arrived. Mme. de Moray asked to speak to him in private, and she followed him into his office. There she made him **ac**quainted, with much embarrassment, with the object of her visit. For some reason she would not give, she wanted a considerable sum of money, unknown to her husband. She must have one hundred thousand francs, this very day. She had brought him in payment her finest jewels. Would he be kind enough to replace the real stones by imitations, so that the substitution could not not be suspected ? Very much astonished at this demand, M. Smith answered that the jewels represented certainly a greater value than the sum she wanted. But he was not in a position to give it at such a short notice. He had **just bought** for **cash a** large amount **of** goods, and he did not like **to borrow.** He **would** be able to accommodate her in four or five days. However, **if Mme.** de Moray found herself in a very pressing need of money, **he might——.** Laura did not dare to insist.

'No,' she said, 'in four days. Only will **you be kind enough to** give me a word stating that the sum will **be at my disposal at that** date. It will be sufficient, I think.'

The jeweller gave her what she asked, and, **more** reassured, **she** entered the house in time for breakfast. It seemed to the poor woman as if God was seconding her efforts to save her mother. On that day and during the beginning of the next she felt relatively better, and her parents, her husband, the Duchess de San Lucca and Annibal Palmeri, who were now living in close intimacy **were** very glad to see that her indisposition had not been serious. **In the** afternoon she went out to make her usual visits ; as the count was asking her why she did not drive, she said she wanted to walk, and she started on foot. At four o'clock she entered the church. In the darkness of the nave, she at first **could see nothing.** But very soon her eyes became used to the dim light provided by a few candles, and she noticed a man leaning against a pillar near the entrance. She went up to him. It was Robert.

'I was beginning to think you were not coming,' he said in a low tone, 'and I was preparing to go to your mansion.'

'You would not have done that,' she answered, trembling at the thought.

'But I would,' he said with his usual carelessness, and speaking louder than the solemnity of the holy place allowed.

Laura placed her hand upon his arm to remind him that he should lower his voice.

'Well,' he said, heeding her mute observation, 'you have the money?'

'No, I have not, but——'

'You have not!' repeated the young man, 'and still, you promised. Ah! you have done wrong to deceive me. But it will be of no use, I can assure you. What I have not done two days ago, I shall do to-morrow, or rather this evening. Before an hour, I will have seen your mother.'

'I beg of you,' said the unhappy woman, 'not to speak so loud. I have not deceived you, and here is the proof.'

Then taking from her pocket the note given her by the jeweller, she proved conclusively the reality of the efforts she had made.

'You can see,' she added with anxiety, 'that I am not deceiving you. M. Smith declares that I have entrusted him with a certain number of jewels on which he will give me the sum of one hundred thousand francs. That was yesterday morning. The date is written above the signature. Then in three days I shall have the money. In truth it is not too much to ask from you!'

In the midst of her supplications, she was despairing, because he was hesitating; at last he made a sign of assent.

'Very well,' he said, 'in three days. But it is the very last delay. Here, in three days, at the same hour. If you are not here then, I shall go to your mother's and whatever may happen, I will give to whoever is entitled to them the letters which prove her dishonor!'

'Ah!' said Laura, 'the ransom you exact for my mother's fault is cruel, and you know too well what means to employ to obtain the payment of it. But I am in your hands, and there is no use in repeating these words because nothing can touch your heart.'

She went away rapidly, and Robert in his turn, left the church a few moments after. When she was home, Mme. de Moray felt calmer. She had, in spite of all, once more averted the dangers threatening the honor of her mother, and, chiefly, the rest and happiness of her father. In acting as she did, it seems to her that she was paying to her beloved parents the debt of gratitude she had contracted towards them since her birth, and which was made of devotedness and love. At the family gathering on that evening, her mind was calmer and her heart softer than it had been during the last few days. The serenity of the whole family was a proof of that, and Laura gave the example of a gaiety which astonished them all. As Mme. de la Marche was enquiring, with a sad smile, the only one which at times flitted across her features, what made her so happy, she felt that she must divert the astonishment which her bearing might provoke.

' Oh ! dear mother !' she said, ' just think ! I have received this morning, as you are aware, a letter from my daughter, a letter so sweet and tender. In the same letter Aunt Basilique has written a few words, saying that, although still very weak, my beloved Paulette is progressing towards a cure. In three or four months at the most, now, I am certain, I will see my daughter again.'

III.

A few intimate friends had dined on that evening with Mme. de la Marche. Amongst them were the Duchess de San Lucca and her brother. At eleven o'clock, after tea, everybody retired. The reader will remember that the duchess occupied the first story of the mansion, which she had fitted up in gorgeous style. Usually she would retire alone and bid good-night to her brother on the landing. Annibal used to go out to spend the night in some gambling hell, or in one of his familiar *boudoirs*. On that evening as he was offering to shake hands, as was his wont, she stopped him.

' No,' she said, ' come up with me.'

' But somebody is waiting for me.'

' They will wait, that's all. Come up, I tell you, I must speak to you.'

In this household of adventurers, the sister was the reigning power. Her brother submitted and went up. The duchess rapidly undressed herself, put on a rich dressing gown covered with lace, and sent her maid away, telling her to bid M. Palmeri, who was waiting in the next room, to come in.

' Sit down there,' said Gorgon abruptly to Peppo, when they were alone.

And she showed him an arm-chair near the chimney. She remained standing or walked to and fro, as she used to do when she was much agitated.

' Oh ! oh !' said Peppo sneering.' ' It appears there is something up this evening. Little sister is like a lioness in her cage. And a

pretty cage it is, too,' he continued looking around him ; ' you have
made this old den beautiful.   It is splendid here, and one can wait,
without weariness, the end of the days he has to live.'

'You are mistaken,' abruptly said Gorgon, stopping in front of
him.   'As beautiful as it may be, it is nevertheless a cage, and the
lioness will leave it to-morrow.'

' Eh ! ' cried Peppo.   ' What are you saying ? '

' I am saying what I mean,' she said harshly, re-commencing her
walk which she had interupted for a moment.   ' It is to tell you of
my resolution, that I have asked you to come up with me this evening.   Yes,' she continued, abandoning herself to the enervating
influences she had been trying to conceal all the evening, so as not
to make a show of herself.   ' I have enough of this fight.   I give it
up, and I have resolved to go.'

' Come, come, you are getting crazy ! '

' I would become so if I continued this stupid struggle any longer.
I have had enough of it. I tell you, and I declare myself vanquished.

The young man put his hands to his head with a gesture of comic
despair.

' Santa Madonna,' he said.   ' I'll be hanged if I understand.   Explain yourself.'

' Listen, since you want to know my reasons.   And perhaps it
will soothe my nerves to tell them.   You know why we left our
house on de Villiers street, and why we came to live here.'

' Undoubtedly, since I conceived the idea and furnished the
means ; you were in despair at the Cape of Antibes, because you had
not succeeded in getting intimate with some great Parisian family.
To satisfy your whim, because I swear to you that I care not for
these noble relations, I have managed our entrance into this den
of nobility.   On the day I revealed my clever combination, you
wildly embraced me; is it not the same thing now ? '

' The reason of the joy which I manifested then was the one you
advance.   But you must remember there was another.'

' Ah ! yes, I remember,' said the Neapolitan, laughing.   ' You
had some sort of a fancy for the handsome governor-general of Pondichéry.'

' Say that I was mad after him.   Say that I loved him with passion the very minute I saw him.   I never loved like that before,
although I had received declarations of love, in the streets of
Naples, from the proudest and noblest, without feeling my heart
beat any faster, without pleasure and without trouble.   Say that
my love for M. de Moray has increased ever since ; that to-day it
possesses my whole being ; that it is the master of all my thoughts
and my actions.   And whatever you may say, tell yourself that
you are as much beneath the truth as the crawling worm is beneath the shining star ! '

' *Per Baccho !*' cried the young man with enthusiasm, ' you are quite a literary character, *sorella mia*, one can see that you frequent the theatre on Tuesdays. Reminiscences of Victor Hugo. Nothing else ? '

' Do not laugh ! you cad ! do not joke ! You see very well that I am not playing a comedy, from the tone in which I speak. I have there,' and she struck her breast, ' a true passion. And he that loves truly is worth all the poets in the world ! '

' 1 beg your pardon, Mme. the duchess, I will not laugh any more. Then you want to go because you love M. de Moray ; and he is insensible to your flame, the impertinent fellow ! '

' You are stupid ! ' cried Gorgon. ' The passion I have for M. de Moray is reciprocated by him. The same fever burns both of us ! '

There was an accent of gratified ambition in this exclamation. The pride of the beautiful girl, if not her love, must have been largely gratified to make her speak thus.

' Then I understand less and less,' confessed Peppo, with humility. ' You are loved and you love ; that is perfect happiness. For, without prying into your secrets, my chaste sister ! 1 do not suppose you love in a platonic way ? '

' I, no ! ' boldly answered Gorgon. ' But he ! '

' You don't say so ? '

' It is even so, I assure you. And if you do not believe me, it is because you do not know as well as I do the idiots we call honest people. You do not know, either, the imperious sentiment which they call honor ! '

' But I beg your pardon,' answered the adventurer, simply. ' I have heard a good deal about it.'

Gorgon shrugged her shoulders.

' Whether you know this splendid sentiment or not, one thing is certain, these people are the heroes and victims of it. M. de Moray loves me. He confessed his love to me on the first day we met, in a moment of surprise and abandonment. But since that day he has sealed his lips, and he would be smothered sooner than open them if a word of love was to fall from his heart.'

' Hum ! such a virtue is too beautiful to be sincere. I would be tempted to believe that he does not love you any more.'

' To convince me of that he must conceal the trouble in his eyes when he looks at me, tho emotion in his voice when he speaks to me, the trembling of his nerves when he is obliged to touch my hand when we meet or when we leave each other. Oh ! I assure you, he loves me ; or, if you prefer another word, he finds me beautiful and he desires me. But duty, but the respect he has for that woman whom I hate, because she is his wife and has a right to love and be loved, lastly, this absurd honor, which I told you about, all these things combined, build a wall between us which I am not powerful enough to demolish. This night I have played my last card, and I have lost. Whilst you were all conversing together, I said a few words to Roger privately ; I have thrown my love to him in a cry of distress. He was standing before me, burnt himself by a flame which I guessed, which I saw, and which I felt in some sort. His eyes fell on mine, and they seemed to ask for mercy. He said nothing, however. "But why do not you answer at least one word ?" I cried, tormented by his silence. For one moment I thought I had subdued his brutish obstinacy ; his lips opened but closed again, locked by his inflexible will.'

'And then ?' asked Peppo, carried away by the violence of his sister.

'Then, he bowed deeply, respectfully, and walked away. And while I was trying to get over my emotion, I heard him, who had joined his wife and Mme. de la Marche, rejoice with them at the good news they had received that very day from Pondichéry. His voice was still trembling, and I am sure that his emotion has been caused by my words. But these abhorred women could not understand that, and they undoubtedly imagined that his emotion arose from paternal love. Happily that odious evening was nearing its end. We retired, and I have been able to tell you of my anger and of my powerlessness.'

Having uttered these words, Gorgon fell exhausted into an armchair beside her brother. In truth, she was to be pitied. The passion she felt was culpable, even criminal. But it was sincere, and on that account Gorgon deserved some pity. Annibal, who until then had answered in a chaffing tone, was dominated by the invincible force of true sentiment.

'Poor little sister !' he said, taking the hand of his accomplice, 'I assure you that I am very sorry. Come, do you want me to help you ?'

'And what can you do ?' she asked disconsolately.

'If I made you marry the man you love,' asked Palmeri, 'what would you say ?'

The beautiful girl looked at her brother with a ferocity which would have made any other tremble.

'Ah !' she said, 'you are joking yet. Have a care, Peppo ; it is a dangerous game, which I do not advise you to play.'

'Look at me,' said the Neapolitan quietly. 'Do I look like a man who is joking ? Ungrateful girl that you are !'

In spite of all there was an accent of brotherly friendship in this reproach. Gorgon understood it and excused herself.

'Pardon me,' she said. 'But I am truly so unhappy ! And what you tell me is so impossible !'

'Why, impossible ?'

'Because he is already married.'

'What odds? His wife may disappear.'

'Kill her! You would do that! Is it indeed true that you would do that for **me**?'

Certainly at that moment, Gorgon would have put without remorse a dagger into her brother's hand. But the serene tranquillity of Peppo appeased her suddenly.

'Ah!' she said with bitterness, 'we are mad. Neither you **nor** I, whatever little scruples we may have, would think of doing such a thing.'

'But I don't think of that,' quickly answered Annibal. '*Diavolo!* Kill people! No! No! We could not do that, especially when there are other means at hand to gain the end in view.'

Gorgon saw that her brother had a well defined project. And, however **absurd it** might be in its impossibility, she wanted to know it.

'Come! Speak!' she said. 'What is your **plan**?'

'The only practical one—a divorce!'

'A divorce?'

'**Yes!** You know that we are not in Italy here; we inhabit a country where divorce flourishes. Indeed, it is said that one-half of France is in the act of obtaining a divorce from the other half,' he added, laughing.

'The divorce! that's true!' answered Gorgon. '**That's one** way.'

But after thinking.

'That is even more absurd than anything we have thought of as yet,' she said. 'For a divorce, two things are wanted. At first a determined cause, and then the consent of him who could invoke such a cause before the justice. And unhappily nothing of the kind exists in our case. The Countess de Moray, that woman whom **I** detest so deeply, is above all reproach. I am forced to acknowledge that! And her husband has no other cause of hatred against her than the love he feels for me, if he should consent to listen to the voice **of his** own love. It is **a** dream, I tell you. A dream which cannot be realized!'

'Well, **if I** could give **you** proof to the contrary, what would you give me?'

'Oh! heavens! Anything you may wish! The fortune of **a** Rotschild, **if** you could steal it like the other!'

'*Per Baccho!* not so loud!' said Palmeri, looking around him with fright. '**One** can never tell but there is **some** eavesdropper!'

He opened all the doors, and made sure that nobody had heard **the** imprudent remark of his sister.

'Nobody,' **he** said, returning. 'We are lucky. But **I pray you,**

my dear, no more of these imprudences ! You make me tremble !
The fortune of a Rotschild, you say ? No, little sister, mine is
sufficient. But perhaps some day I will ask you, if I succeed in
this undertaking ——'

'What ? Fix your price. It is accepted in advance !'

'I cannot tell you now. I do not know myself. But whatever
it may be, you swear ?'

'I swear !' she said 'on Gorgon's faith ! Now tell me the mad
hope you have in the possibility of a divorce.'

'Well, my dear, nothing is simpler,' commenced the Neapolitan.
'Mme. de Moray, that woman whose virtue you acknowledge with
such disinterestedness, Mme. de Moray has a lover.'

'A lover !'

'As I am telling you.'

'You are mad ! Unhappily she is the purest, the most innocent,
and the most irreproachable of women. Mme. de Moray loves her
husband and has no lover, and I am sure of that.'

'And I affirm the contrary.'

'If it were so, however !' muttered Gorgon. 'With her calmness, with her serenity, with her appearance of crushing virtue.
Ah ! if it were so, I think I would admire that woman, because, in
truth, it would be splendid.'

'My dear,' philosophically answered Peppo, 'I have heard somebody who knew say that when honest women become rogues, they
are more so than others.'

'Have you got proofs ?' asked Gorgon, anxiously.

'Do you think I would speak of such a thing if I did not have
proofs ?'

Proofs ! Although her brother had promised them, the splendid
girl, carried away by passion, could not believe it. Indeed, it
would be too much to expect ; she did not yet know what advantage she would derive from the discovery. But to satisfy her jealousy and her hatred, the certitude that the golden statue, which
crushed her with her lying chastity, had feet of clay, was sufficient.
And as Annibal was observing on her face the many impressions
caused by his words, she urged him.

'Why don't you speak,' she said, with passion. 'Don't you see
I am boiling ? So you say that the Countess de Moray has a
lover ?'

'When I say she has a lover, I do not exactly mean that.'

Gorgon trembled at this, but she was soon reassured. Her brother continued :

'I should have said she has had a lover. And the love story
actually carried on is an old intrigue nearing its end.'

'Explain yourself clearly,' insisted the young woman, with impatience.

'You will understand. It is as clear as crystal. Four days ago
I was walking the street about half-past three, not knowing exactly
where to go, when a woman, who was walking very fast, jostled me
on her way. My attention was arrested for a few seconds, and although I saw only her back, I thought I knew her. I followed her
and soon discovered that this elegant lady was Mme. de Moray.'

'Where was she going?'

'That's the question I asked myself; and she must have been
much preoccupied to have thus jostled me without perceiving it.
Where was she going, and what was the cause of her preoccupation?
Such was the double mystery I resolved to clear. There was only
one way to obtain that result; it was to follow the good lady, and
I did so very cleverly, so as not to awaken her suspicions, if by
chance she would turn around. In a very short time she turned into
Dragoon street.

'What is that street?' asked Gorgon.

'A street of mean appearance which your excellency has certainly
not crossed in your quality of noble duchess, and which would not be
out of place in the suburbs where we lived when we were in Naples.
But it is not the street, it is the court one must see. This court is
a sort of city where workingmen dwell. Mme. de Moray walked up
to the dirtiest of these ugly houses. A thought came to my mind,
and I called myself an idiot. There was only one cause which could
bring the noble countess to such a place. It was for charity's sake.
Very certainly the daughter of the admiral was paying a benevolent
visit to some of the paupers who besiege her door day and night. I
was moved, upon my word, and I reproached myself for having cast
suspicions on a virtue which did not disdain to carry her offerings
to the poor in their own homes. So, as a punishment, I resolved
to wait until she would come out again. "When she will appear,"
I said to myself, "I will go to her, tell her that I have followed her,
and I will give her a few pounds to increase the budget of her
charities."'

'So, you are charitable?' asked Gorgon, ironically.

'Why not?' quietly said the Neapolitan.' 'As opportunity offers.
And you must admit that the occasion was tempting, since it would
attract the good graces of a woman who after all has not much love
for us. So I waited. I have told you it was half-past three when
I commenced my duty as sentry; at six o'clock I was still on duty.'

'Stupid fool!' you had not noticed the countess coming out, or
she had gone by some other way.'

'That's just what I thought myself; however I stayed there
with patience, and was rewarded with success, for at a quarter past
six Mme. de Moray appeared.'

'And what did you say to her, then?'

'Nothing. I had changed my plan. Certainly this charitable lady was not on an errand to a pauper. One does not remain three hours in a hovel for the purpose of leaving alms. So there must be something else. As soon as I saw her, I felt sure that I was not mistaken. The eyes of the countess were red and heavy, and she evidently had shed many tears in the course of her long visit. I started after her, saw that she was nearly killed by a carriage, which, in her troubled state of mind, she had not noticed, and finally I saw her enter this house.'

'When did you say it happened?' asked Gorgon.

'Four days ago.'

'But, if I am not mistaken, that was the day the countess was unwell, and did not come down to dinner.'

'Exactly, and it was prudent on her part to do so, because her state of mind would have excited the curiosity of all those honest people.'

'Why did you not tell me of your discovery?'

'You know that I like to tell you of these things when I am sure of success. I have my self-pride, zounds! You can easily guess that I resolved to find out the mystery at once, and that I commenced to spy the countess in earnest. The very next morning Mme. de Moray, with a satchel in her hand, took a carriage and went to Smith's, the jeweller you know of?'

'What? to buy jewels? In the morning?'

'It was rather the contrary, as you will see in a moment. From my own carriage, in which I was hidden, I saw her come out of the store empty-handed; she re-entered the carriage and went back to the house. She looked well pleased on coming out of the store and I concluded that she had fully succeeded in whatever she had undertaken. But then I was somewhat mistaken, as you will see. She did not go out again on that day. The next day, in the afternoon, that is to say this very day, she started out again and I followed her, like a silly detective, expecting to see her return to the Court of the Dragon. She did not lead me there, however, and as the clock struck four, we were entering, one following the other, about twenty steps apart, the church of St Germain-des-Prés. Do you know St. Germain-des-Prés? It is a very fine church.'

'What odds is that to me?'

'Or to me! But what is very interesting on account of the object I had in view is that it is always so gloomy in that fine church that one can see nothing on first entering it. Thanks to this darkness I was enabled to reach a pillar, against which a young man was leaning, and where the countess joined him, after a moment's hesitation.'

'A young man? And this young man is her lover? And you heard what they said?'

'Without losing one word, thanks chiefly to the animation and bad humor of the fellow, who was not at all particular, never dreaming for a moment that some one quite near him was listening to everything he said. I heard enough to form an idea of the conversation which must have taken place two days before in the house of the Court of the Dragoon. This young man has in his possession love letters which establish beyond doubt, it seems, the dishonor of the noble family which has taken us by the hand, and as he appears to be in rather poor circumstances, he has conceived the idea of making money out of that correspondence, and he asked the countess the pretty sum of a hundred thousand francs for her epistles. Twenty-five thousand francs apiece. You see that it is not for nothing.'

'One hundred thousand francs ! And Mme. de Moray has given them ? '

'No. Only, as she had promised to give them, this handsome young man, for I am forced to say that he looks very well, in spite of the misery he must have endured, this handsome young man, I say, became very angry, and uttered, in a low voice, I know not what terrible threats, which threw the lady into a great state of terror.'

'But that fellow is a scoundrel !' said Gorgon, in spite of herself.

'Certainly, but a scoundrel to whom you will owe some gratitude. So, he was swearing and making a scene in the church, and I don't know how it would have ended, if the countess had not succeeded in calming him by showing him a declaration of Smith, the jeweller, attesting that Mme. de Moray had placed jewels in his possession, which were to be sold, and on which he would give her at a certain date, which is the day after to-morrow, a sum of one hundred thousand francs. In consequence, the countess was asking for a delay of forty-eight hours, promising to return to the same place to give him the money. After much trouble, she gained that point and went away.'

'How she must hate that man now, after having loved him so much !' thought Gorgon aloud.

'Well, I think you are mistaken. Certainly, Mme. de Moray has nothing to thank her lover for, and still I have noticed in her voice, as if in spite of herself, intonations of sympathy, almost of tenderness.'

'It is strange,' said the beautiful girl pensively. 'But we women are so singular in our fancies, that, after all, it might be possible.'

'Well, little sister,' asked Amnibal on rising to retire, 'what do you think of my story ?'

'I think,' said Gorgon, starting up, 'I think that if it is a true story, before three months are over, I shall have traded my crown of duchess for the crown of a countess, and that in my turn I shall be Mme. de Moray.'

This conversation, which we have shortened, lasted a good part of the night. It was after two o'clock in the morning when the adventurer left his sister, not before reminding her that whatever she might do, she had promised him to grant the first favor he would ask her. Gorgon had tried to find out what would be the price claimed by her brother in exchange for the information he had just given her, but he had obstinately refused to answer, saying that the project he was meditating was neither ripe nor sufficiently defined in his own mind.

Left alone at last, Gorgon went to bed and tried to sleep. But the unexpected revelation, made to her so abruptly, occupied her mind and did not allow her to sleep until morning. This woman, who less than any other had the right to be severe, was shocked at the thought that Mme. de Moray had failed in her duty to her husband.

'That's what they are, then, those great ladies of the fashionable world!' she thought. 'They lie, they deceive, like all the rest, and still they have not the excuse that a woman such as I am could advance.'

However, there is between women, even when they are jealous of each other, a sort of freemasonry. And there was in the heart of Gorgon, a native pride which made her look with repulsion at the use of a secret accusation, however justified it seemed to her.

'Eh! what odds!' she said aloud, sitting up on the bed where she was tossing, a prey to all the hesitations of her love and her conscience. 'What do I care if it be good or bad? I know only one thing, that I love even to dying, and that everything must give way to my love. I shall attempt then to satisfy my passion, everything I shall be able to do without injuring that unfortunate wretch. But if I fail, and if I have no other means, I shall ruin her, without remorse. So much the worse for her; let her guard and defend herself.'

Fatigue at last put an end to this feverish vigil, and at the hour at which those who have to work for their daily bread rise, Gorgon went to sleep. She never awoke until noon. It took her a few moments to recall all the emotions which had agitated her through the night.

'Oh!' she thought all at once, 'this is the day I shall fight a decisive battle.'

Recovering all her coolness, as a duellist on the morning of an engagement, she called for a light breakfast which she ate in bed, after which she got up and proceeded to put on a morning dress which showed her to the best advantage. She then examined herself for a long time in a large mirror. She had a sense of pride at finding herself so beautiful. The fatigues of the night just past gave to her eyes a flame still more intense than usual, and a duller milky paleness to her complexion. She well deserved her old name of *Gorgon*, that daughter of the goddess Ceto, whose look alone killed men, or, according to Pindar, petrified and changed then into rocks. She was indeed the dangerous creature whose love was to reverse the laws of nature, and who, scorned by chance, would put a heart of stone into the breast of him who refused to love her. Now that the moment of the struggle was approaching, she felt calm and resolute, and gave the order to go and beg of M. de Moray to come and see her. She had to speak to him.

The count hesitated at first and was tempted not to go. **It would** be the first time he would find himself alone with her since their arrival in Paris, for he had avoided until then all the occasions of a meeting, the perils of which he knew too well. However, he answered that he would go directly. It was one of two things. Either the interview asked by Mme. de San Lucca would be occupied in speaking of indifferent subjects, and that it would be ridiculous on his part to refuse to go ; or else, its hidden effect was to attempt a new effort against the loyal rigor of his resolution, and in this case it was better to put an end to it at once. The crisis would be dangerous and the struggle painful, because he would have to fight against himself as much as against a woman strangely fascinating. But he felt strong enough to come triumphantly out of the ordeal in the noble stubbornness of his duty. So he came. On seeing him the duchess bade him sit down. They were alone. For a moment they were silent. Both felt their hearts beating as if about to break. The adventuress was not a woman to risk the attack on the chances of a common-place **conversation** ; so she **went to** the assault with superb bravery.

'You must think,' she said, ' that if I have asked you to come and see me, it is to put an end to **a** situation which is as galling to me and to my pride, as it is painful to your patience. We cannot, you and I, indefinitely remain near each other like timid children. What has passed between us has been a humiliating accident for **both,** and I do not wish, any more than you do, to be exposed to it **a second time.** Our fate must be decided; we must separate for-ever.'

However resolute **he was to** keep his faith to his wife, M. de Moray was startled at the alternative offered to him. This **woman** who intoxicated him, who had become the very essence of the secret agitation which enervated all his faculties in delicious suffering; she was contemplating going away. He had not thought of that eventuality. For a moment it seemed to him as if the earth was whirling around him; the blood rushed to his head; his hands became icy cold. However, he got over this momentary weakness, and recovering his powerful will, he merely answered thus:

'Your departure, Madam, which you announce, will give me much pain. Mme. de Moray also will feel much regret ; and it is in her name, as well as in my own, that I give you the assurance of our sorrow.'

He had spoken slowly, coolly, lingering on purpose on the words : 'Mme. de Moray.' He then rose to retire. The duchess shrugged her shoulders disdainfully.

'Wait a minute,' she said. 'I am only commencing what I have to tell you.'

The count sat down again. In spite of the firmness of his resolution, he was happy to be condemned to stay longer. Since she was going away and he would see her no more, why not drink deeply of the boiling spring of love ! The duchess was speaking with an involuntary disorder of language. Evidently she was sustaining a severe struggle with herself. There were words coming to her lips she did not wish to say, at least not yet.

'Do not speak of Mme. de Moray,' she said ; 'do not make me think of that woman who detests me because she knows that I love you and that I hate her !'

'Because you know she loves me !' stoically interrupted the count.

The Neapolitan almost cried out : 'You are lying ! or rather she is lying ! she does not love you !' but she refrained. It was not yet time.

'Do I know why I hate her ?' she asked, abruptly. 'It doesn't matter, anyway. What I want to know from you is the reason why you are so mercilessly silent when I humiliate myself to the point of begging your love ? Why will you not love me ? Am I not free ?'

'Yes,' said M. de Moray, whose voice had regained all its firmness, 'you are free, but I am not. And the avowal you demand would be at the same time an offence to you, and a treachery towards her whose name you do not want pronounced in your presence !'

'A treachery ! an offence !' she cried with a ringing laugh. 'In truth you have a queer way of calling things. It is an offence, it is a treachery, according to you, to avow one's love ! Not so ! To love, and nothing but to love is all ! To say it is nothing ! And besides, if saying it is something, what do you not tell me, every moment, by all the voices of your being, by your devouring eyes, by your trembling hands, by your burning breath ? Your lips only are closed, or rather they lie, and their lie is a word more eloquent than all the others.'

M. de Moray was clinging to his conscience, and would not consent to be conquered.

'If my eyes, my hands, and my lips, all my faculties, even my breath betray a passion I disavow, my soul controls it, and it

would blush with shame if I consented to the monstrous division
which keeps to the honored wife the faithfulness of my heart !'

It was too much for Gorgon. She revolted at last.

'So,' she asked, abruptly, 'it is because the wife is chaste and
faithful that the man who adores me, whatever he may pretend to
the contrary, will not say to me : I love you !'

'Yes, that is the reason.'

'Ah ! do not repeat a second time what you have just said, for
your own sake, and chiefly for hers.'

'What mean these words ?'

'Nothing !' said the duchess, already regretting her threat.
'Nothing. They mean nothing.'

'Ah ! take care !' said the count, recovering his coolness, which
he had lost for a moment. 'You are on the point of doing something unworthy of such a woman as you are, to speak ill of an
honest woman !'

The temptation was really too great.

'An honest woman !' she said, with a sneer, which penetrated to
the heart of M. de Moray. 'Let us speak of that ! After all,' she
continued, 'the battles of love are like all other battles ; and every
one has the right to use the weapons he is possessed of. Well,
since it is so, I raise my head and I tell you that if your heart must
belong to the more worthy, I claim it and I take it !'

The count made a gesture of cold anger. In this moment all his
passion had vanished. He did not know whether he loved the
woman who was before him or not. He knew only one thing : A
human being, whoever she was, had just insulted the woman who
bore his name.

'Are you aware,' he cried, 'that in the words you have just pronounced, there is an odious accusation and an odious calumny
directed against the Countess de Moray ?'

'An accusation, perhaps. A calumny, no,' said the duchess, with
spirit. 'You have already the proof that I am not one who lies.'

'Then you will explain yourself, and you will tell me——'

'What ?'

'All ! all that you know, or rather that you pretend to know !'

The count was standing, as was also his adversary. For now one
would have said they were two mortal enemies face to face. The
man had seized the woman's arm, and was clenching it as if he
would break it.

'Speak ! why don't you speak ?' cried Roger.

The duchess disengaged herself violently, regaining her freedom
with all her plebeian strength.

'Well, no !' she said, losing her senses ; 'I will say nothing, for
if I spoke you would kill her !'

F

No avowal, if it had been voluntary, could be a more terrible
accusation. And still it was true, the anger of the count had opened
Gorgon's eyes. Until then she had thought that the discovery of
the fault of the countess would only provoke a judiciary separation,
a divorce between the couple. But now she understood that the
effect was far beyond her anticipation, and that the life itself of the
guilty one was at stake. Be that as it may, nothing could be more
terribly accusing than her cry of distress, and M. de Moray felt it.
All his being was moved in a fit of rage and despair at the same
time.

'I would kill her !——' he cried, stepping backwards, astounded
and roaring. 'You say I would——. But it is because it is true that
she is false——. She betrays me ! she dishonors my name !'

And the laugh of a maniac came from his throat.

'Ah ! ah ! ah !' he cried, 'Laura ! my wife ! An angel of modesty, of honor and virtue. She ! the wife who has given me her
whole life ! who has followed me through all my perils ! who has
shared all my tears and all my joys ! She ! the mother whose love
is inexhaustible, whose devotion is limitless ! she ! who is adored,
yes, adored by her husband and her daughter ! Ah ! the stupid
invention, and how good of you to have invented that ; because, in
truth I know not if I have ever loved you, you who have tried to
wound me so deeply !'

Gorgon was agitated by divers sentiments. She was ashamed of
her denunciation. She had pity on the despair she had provoked.
But she was also wounded by being suspected of having told a lie
so low and cowardly. However, her good instincts overcame her
evil ones. She resigned herself.

'Very well !' she said. 'I have lied to try your love. I have
calumniated the innocent to find out what punishment you would
mete out to the guilty. And chiefly, I wanted to probe to the bottom of your heart to know what space in it would be left for me, if
ever, per chance, the place occupied by Mme. de Moray became
vacant. I know what I wanted to know. You can go now. We
shall never see each other again !'

And here her voice failed. Her new attitude frightened the count
more than her accusation. He felt struck to the heart a second
time.

'There must be some truth in this infamy !' he thought.

And he wanted to know at all hazards. Only, having failed by
anger and despair, he tried other means.

'You have wounded me deeply,' he said trying to show a calmness which he was far from feeling. 'But I forgive you on account
of the frankness you have shown. As you have said, in love everything is fair. Well ! I will answer with equal frankness. You
wished to know what would happen if the place occupid in my heart

by Mme. de Moray became vacant. I will tell you. I am one of those men who do not admit of treachery, either for or against them. You are a witness that I wished to keep towards her who is my wife, my whole faith. But if ever she should become unworthy of it, there would remain for her, neither a regret, nor even a remembrance, in the heart she would have broken. And as I am also one of those men who cannot live without sharing with a woman all their thoughts and all their affections, a second one would infallibly exercise over me the empire, which the first would have voluntarily renounced. This other one to whom I would devote myself, and to whom I would belong, I need not name to you, who four months ago took possession, against my will, of all the sensations and of all the aspirations of my being!'

M. de Moray had drawn near the duchess while speaking. His voice, so rough and hoarse a little before, had taken inflections full of softness to convince her. Was he saying the truth? Was he playing a comedy in order to find out the secrets she would not yield to his threats? Gorgon did not know. She was still hesitating.

'You told me,' she said with an interrogative smile, 'that you would kill her if you should ever learn that she had betrayed you?'

'No!' said the count. 'I would merely drive her out of my house. She would not deserve a nobler anger on my part.'

Chance had brought them during this conversation near a window of the room overlooking the yard. The bell of the hall door was rung, and a man entered. It was M. Smith, the jeweller. A saint might have resisted the temptation thus offered by chance; Gorgon, who was far from being a saint, succumbed to it.

'Well,' she said, 'if you want to know the truth, enquire of that man. He can tell it to you.'

Then M. de Moray, yielding to a thoughtless feeling, opened the window.

'M. Smith!' he cried.

The jeweller raised his head and recognized the count. He bowed.

'Please come up,' continued M. de Moray. 'I have a few words to say to you.'

Then he rang, after closing the window, and told the servant who answered the bell to ask the gentleman to step into the next room, after which he turned to the beautiful Italian and asked coolly:

'Pray explain how the terrible secret you refuse to divulge is in the possession of that man?'

Carried away by the rapidity of events, Gorgon had gone so far now that it was impossible to draw back. She understood that she must tell all.

'M. Smith,' she answered, 'brings one hundred thousand francs
to your wife who has engaged her diamonds to redeem from her
lover the letters she has had the imprudence to write.'

The count did not even shudder, this time. He had assumed
the impassibility of a judge. He bowed.

'Madam,' he said, 'you have just pronounced a sentence. That
of my wife, if you have told the truth. That of your brother if you
have lied. If the honor of Mme. de Moray is proof against the
accusation you have borne against her, I shall kill M. Annibal
Palmeri to-morrow. Now I exact that you will not contradict one
single word of what I am going to say to this witness on whom depends the discovery of the truth.'

And going towards the next room, the count opened the door and
called the jeweller.

'Please come in, M. Smith,' he said.

'You desire to speak to me, M. de Moray?' asked that man,
taking the seat indicated.

'Yes, M. Smith, I wanted to tell you —— to speak of ——'

In spite of his coolness, he felt that his own voice had a strange
accent, and as he did not want to awaken the suspicions of the one
who was to decide the fate of his life, he tried to justify the state
of his mind.

'You must notice, M. Smith, that I feel a little emotion. The
reason is that the moment you arrived, madam was telling me of a
great secret with which you are mixed up.'

'A great secret with which I am mixed up?'

'Yes. But I have forgotten to present you to the Duchess de
San Lucca,' said the jeweller.

'I have the honor of being acquainted with Mme. de San Lucca.'

'Ah! then I have only to tell you what this secret is. The
duchess, who is the friend and the confidente of Mme. de Moray in
her good works, was telling me just now that the countess, to pro-
vide for the necessities of her inexhaustible charity, has entrusted
to your care a part of her family jewels, in exchange or as a guarantee for the loan of an important sum of money, one hundred
thousand francs! Madame de San Lucca, in the interest of her
friend, has told me of it. She thought I would be happy to asso-
ciate myself with the work of charity the countess was too discreet
to speak of, and she told me everything. You see that I know all,
and that you have no reason for reserve if I ask you to enter into a
little plot with me.'

'While very, very happy to be a party to the plot you are meditating,' said the jeweller, quite pleased, 'I must tell you that what
the duchess has told you is quite true. Mme. de Moray has effec-
tively asked me for one hundred thousand francs, which I was to
give her to-morrow; but the returns I was expecting failed me at

the last moment, and I was coming to ask your wife for another delay of a few days.'

These words confirmed the reality of the loan attempted by Mme. de Moray, and the count had no doubt but it was for the reason advanced by the Duchess de San Lucca. He felt something like the stroke of a dagger at his heart, but he had enough strength not to betray himself.

'Ah !' he said, even affecting to smile with approbation, 'you are not in a position to give her that sum. Well, no matter, it changes nothing in the combination I was going to propose. On the contrary it gives me an idea which will facilitate the execution of the plot I was speaking of. What is important is that nothing should disturb the execution of the charitable projects of the countess, and you will see that it is the simplest thing in the world. You have the jewels of Mme. de Moray at your store, no doubt ; will you be so kind as to go and get them ?'

'Pardon me, sir,' said M. Smith. 'I have them with me. I thought I should take them with me in case Mme. de Moray, not receiving the money at the date appointed, should change her mind, or should prefer to address herself to some other jeweller.'

'Then everything is for the best. Here is what we will do. You will give me the jewels, in exchange for the money which you will remit to my wife ; it is well understood that you will not tell her where it comes from. In this way she will be satisfied, and the diamonds will not go out of the house.'

'Depend on me,' said the jeweller, and he retired.

M. de Moray was anxious to find himself, if not alone, at least delivered from the presence of a stranger before whom he was obliged to feign a perfect quietness of mind, and M. Smith was hardly out of the room when the count abandoned himself to a paroxysm of despair. He was walking like a maniac about the room, breaking the furniture, and striking the walls with his clenched fist.

'So, it is true !' he was crying. 'She was betraying me ! Oh ! the wretch ! the infamous woman ! And while I was stifling at the bottom of my heart a violent passion, an indomitable love, even going as far as to deny that love, for I have denied it, while I was lying through idiotic virtue, she was lying through criminal depravity !'

It was hardly a human being who was thus bruising himself uttering these exclamations and roaring with rage, he was like a wild beast maddened with anger, which breaks its head against the walls of its narrow prison. Gorgon was frightened.

'For pity's sake,' she said, 'calm yourself !'

The sound of her voice changed the direction of his mind. To useless anger, to powerless despair, succeeded a burning desire for revenge.

' 'Very well,' he said. 'I am calm. One word only. What is the name of her accomplice ?'

'His name ? I do not know it.'

'Is it true ? Take care that you do not lie ! You have gone so far now, that no consideration of prudence or pity can prevent you from telling me all ! That name. Tell me his name.'

'I swear that I do not know it.'

'I will find out. And where will she remit the money to this trader in female virtue ?'

'I can tell you that. To-morrow at four o'clock, they are to meet in the church of Saint-Germain-des-Prés. He will bring the letters, and she will take the money to him.'

'And it is in a church that this monstrous bargain is to be accomplished ! Ah ! my God ! is it because you were so indulgent to the woman taken in adultery, that this woman has chosen your house to meet her lover. Ah ! the wretches ! the wretches !'

And he sobbed bitterly. With his head in his hands he remained quiet for a moment. Then forcing himself to be calmer, he added :

'To-morrow ! I will say nothing until then, hiding in the innermost of my soul the secret of my shame, and my anger ! But to-morrow ! ah ! to-morrow ! I will spy each one of her steps, I will see her, in hypocritical piety cross the threshold of the church. I will witness the interchange of the letters and of the money, and I will have the courage to hide myself and be silent, because I will be in the house of God. But when both are outside. Then with determination I will vindicate my honor !'

'And what will you do ?' asked Gorgon. 'Remember you have sworn to spare her life !'

'I have sworn for the woman, but not for the lover. I will drive her out of my house, and I will kill the man !'

'And when your revenge is satisfied,' said Gorgon with a start of joy, 'you will remember that I love you !'

Shortly after, the count went down to see the jeweller, and handed him the money. Of course, M. de Moray had not such a sum in his house, so he gave a cheque.

'Since your wife is to be ignorant of your intentions,' said the jeweller, 'I will go to the bank at once, and take notes which I will remit to Mme. de Moray to-morrow morning, unless I bring them here within an hour or so.'

'It is an excellent idea,' answered the count. 'Moreover, my wife will perhaps be happy to have the money earlier. In spite of the assurance you have given her, she might be anxious.'

'Very well, it is understood. I will come back during the day.'

And M. Smith went away, after having promised M. de Moray to keep their interview secret. After he was left alone, Roger opened the case containing the jewels.

'Here they are, these jewels!' he said with a heart-rending sigh,
'these jewels a thousand times more precious by the memories they
recall than by their value, which is enormous. They have been
worn before this worthless woman by her parents and mine. Family
jewels consecrated by the foreheads and shoulders of honest
women! Jewels given by my love on our wedding-day! And Laura
was pledging them to-day to pay the ransom of her lost honor! I
hold them in my hand! They bear witness to my shame and to
her crime! Yes, by them I have the proof of my dishonor! And
still,' he continued, his heart softening in spite of himself, 'there
is a doubt in my soul! All the past revives before my eyes! All
my recollections of happiness are awakened in my memory! It
seems to me that at this moment I hear my daughter's voice crying :] "It is not true, father, it is not true! She loves us both too
much to have done what she is accused of!" Ah! these proofs! if
they were only false!'

The unhappy man was tossed between contending sentiments,
wishing to hope against hope, and crushed by the terrible evidence
of the crime.

'Our daughter!' he thought. 'It is nevertheless true that she
must have forgotten that we have a daughter to become guilty!
and she loved so tenderly our Paulette we were obliged to leave
behind us almost dying! How is it that the recollection of her
daughter did not prevent her from falling! Presently, when I am
calmer, when I am able to speak without betraying myself by the
trembling of my voice, I will go near her, I will speak to her of our
beloved Paulette, then, I will see if, having forgotten her husband,
she could also forget her child.'

The poor man, thus lost in a stupid contemplation of his sorrow,
did not notice the time flying. And chance had it that at the same
time Mme. de Moray thought also more than usual of the dear absent one. As she was lost in these sad thoughts, Maltar, the Indian servant, brought her a piece of paper, on which was written the
name of a visitor who wished to speak to her. It was the name of
Robert Burel. This unexpected visit startled her like a threat of evil.

'Introduce this person, Maltar,' she said, with a deep emotion,
'and let nobody in until after his departure.'

IV.

Introduced by the Indian, who went away at once, Robert Burel
bowed respectfully. He was in a room of the first story which was
used as an office by Mme. de Moray and her mother, and which
formed part of the count's apartment. All their works of charity
were planned in that room. The mother and daughter had access

to it from their respective apartments, by different doors, and they
used to spend the greater part of the day together in it. On that day,
fortunately, Mme. de la Marche was not in, having been called outside by some family duties ; Laura was thankful that she was thus
permitted to receive this unexpected visitor without being obliged
to give explanations to her mother. However, Robert's arrival
threw her into deep trouble. She did not invite him to sit down.

'How did you dare to come ?' asked Laura, with agitation. 'I
was to meet you to-morrow afternoon, at four o'clock, to give you
the money, and you swore not to show yourself in my husband's
house ! But, in truth, I do not understand that you are here, when
you see the terrible anxiety your presence throws me into. Don't
you hear me ? Don't you understand me ?'

'I beg your pardon,' said Robert, 'I see, I hear, I understand
and I remain.'

He spoke with coolness, as would have done an indifferent visitor
treating of commonplace questions. And as if to better affirm his
resolution, he took a chair and sat down.

'Just think !' she said, moaning, 'my husband might come !
—'

'Your husband ? Well, what does that matter ? Neither of us
has anything to fear on his part. I am not your lover, I suppose !'

'And if he should ask me who you are, what would I answer ?'

'If he was ill-mannered enough to want to know absolutely under
what title I have come here, it would be very easy to give him the
proof that there is nothing in my visit which would be likely to
offend him.'

'Very easy, you say ? How ? Except by telling the truth !'

'Undoubtedly !'

'And consequently,' Laura continued, with anguish, 'by tar-
nishing the reputation of the most respected of women ! In throwing upon my mother the responsibility of an accusation which would
implicate me ! In revealing the mystery of a fault redeemed by
life-long remorse ! in tearing the heart of the noble old man who is
my father ! No, no, know it now ! I would rather a thousand
times be accused of a crime I had not committed than to divulge
the fault of my mother ! Yes, by God who hears me, I would
rather that the whole world would accuse you of being my lover
than to avow that you are my brother !'

'It is a sublime devotion,' answered Robert, smiling, ' but I hope
you will not have to give any proof of it. If anybody should come,
it would be easy to invent some excuse. The mission of charity
you fulfil so well leaves your door open to the unknown. Moreover,
it depends on you to shorten the length of my presence in this

house, if you think it presents such a grave danger. Only let me tell you the reason why I came.'

'Speak quickly, then.'

'Listen. When I saw you for the first time, I told you that I intended to try my fortune in a foreign land, far away, in America. At that time I had formed a project, the execution of which depended upon the receipt of the sum of money I have asked you for. When we agreed upon the amount and upon the date it would be remitted, I took some engagements myself, and I was sorely disappointed when you told me yesterday you wanted a delay of forty-eight hours, because I had promised to pay that money this morning to the parties I had made arrangements with. However, I had resigned myself, and at noon to-day, instead of depositing my share, I had to ask for a delay of two days, which was refused. Others more expeditious were ready to take my place. In short, all I could obtain was a delay of twenty-four hours, and to-morrow at noon, I must have the money, or all my hopes of fortune fall to the ground.'

'But you know very well that I have not got the money now. I will have it only to-morrow.'

'Yes, to-morrow morning, I know, and it is exactly for that reason that I have come. Instead of waiting until the evening to put me in possession of that money, bring it to me as soon as you have it yourself, and I will be in time to take advantage of the benefits which are offered to me.'

'Very well, to-morrow morning, then, at ——'

At the very moment Mme. de Moray was saying these words, the door opened. It was Maltar.

'My mistress will forgive me if I came without being called,' said the Indian, 'but it is for an important matter. M. Smith is here. He has come to give something to madam, but on being told that she was engaged, he did not wish to disturb her. He has only asked me to hand this parcel to madam.'

'Ah !'

'It is something that he was to bring only to-morrow morning, but he has thought it would be more agreeable to madam if she got it earlier.'

Mme. de Moray seized a voluminous parcel which Maltar was handing her. On touching it she felt that it was a bundle of bank-notes. Her features expressed a deep joy, and Robert understood the cause of it. He was himself violently shaken. Nothing more stood between him and fortune. He was almost tempted to seize the parcel which Laura still held in her hand and run away with it. But the presence of the Indian would not allow of this.

'Tell M. Smith that I am very thankful to him,' said Mme. de Moray to the Indian, 'I will go and see him to-morrow.'

And as Maltar was not going, the Countess added :

'What are you waiting for, Maltar ?'

'Madam,' he answered, 'Mme. de la Marche has just returned. She is in the antichamber talking with M. Smith, and she is coming.'

'Ah ! said Laura, starting up.

And she deposited on the table the envelope containing the bank notes.

'Ah ! ' thought Robert on his part, without feeling any emotion, 'then I am to see my mother. I am not sorry to find out how a mother is made.'

The only sentiment he felt was curiosity, but it was strong enough to engage all his attention, and he did not at once claim from Mme. de Moray the parcel brought by M. Smith. Mme. de la Marche entered at last.

'I was disengaged sooner than I expected,' she said, 'and I come ——'

She stopped on noticing the presence of a stranger.

'Ah ?' she went on, addressing her daughter, ' you are not alone. I will leave you then and will return shortly.'

She crossed the room to reach the door which led directly to her apartment, and in doing so came nearer to the group formed by her daughter and by Robert. He had risen and bowed respectfully. Mme. de la Marche answered his salutation by an inclination of the head, and on looking at him, she stopped without thinking. An embarrassing silence weighed on these three persons. Mme. de Moray was the first to break it.

'M. Robert Burel,' she stammered, presenting the stranger. 'Mme. Firmin de la Marche, my mother,' she continued, addressing the young man.

Robert bowed a second time, impressed by the severe beauty of this high lady, whose crown of white hair looked like the silver nimbus of a saint.

'I do not think I have met this gentleman here before,' said Mme. de la Marche, who noticed the embarrassment of her daughter, without, however, attaching any importance to it.

'In fact, mother,' said the countess, still more troubled, 'it is the first time that——'

'It is the first time, also, Madam,' said the young man, 'that I am in your presence. I did not expect this great honor, and I am, I must admit, moved a little.'

And Robert's voice had not its usual firmness. He felt an agitation quite new to him, and which he could not explain.

'And why this emotion, sir ?' asked Mme. de la Marche, with a kindly smile.

Laura, who was quite near Robert, said in a low voice :

'Take care, in heaven's name ! '

Without pretending to have heard **this** recommendation, Robert answered Mme. de la Marche, but with a little bitterness this time :

'The great consideration which surrounds you, Madam, and the high reputation for benevolence which you enjoy are sufficient to justify——'

'Do not praise me so much, sir,' said Mme. de la Marche. '**One** never **does** all the good one should do.'

'Then, Madam,' said the young man, 'your daughter is a noble exception. Good and charitable **on** her **own** account, she is **actu-ally** accomplishing **a work** of **redress** which was incumbent **upon** another.'

'In truth !' said Mme. de la Marche. 'It is well, Laura ! Please tell me that, **sir**, because my daughter willingly conceals the good she does.'

'Madam, it is——'

The countess quickly interrupted **him**.

'No, no, it **is** useless. Do not tell my mother, I pray you, sir.'

It was a strange situation, and well calculated to trouble the mind of Mme. de Moray. The poor woman was trembling at the fear that one imprudent word would cause her mother to suspect the truth. And she was the more afraid that Robert seemed to take a singular pleasure in prolonging this dangerous conversation. Mme. de la Marche insisted.

'And I, sir,' she cried, 'pray you to tell me the object **of** your **visit.** Since it is an act of charity **on** the part of my daughter, I have a desire to know.'

Robert bowed.

'I will obey you, Madam.'

And turning towards the countess :

'Fear nothing, Madam,' he said, '**I** will say **of your generous** action only what need be told.'

And then to Mme. de la Marche,

'It is, Madam, a mother who has abandoned her child.'

'Her child !' cried Mme. de la Marche.

'Sir !' muttered Laura, with an accent of supplication.

'Yes, Madam,' continued the young man. 'Her child ! **a—**daughter—yes—it is *a daughter.*'

He insisted on the word *daughter,* so as to divert the suspicions which Mme. de la Marche might conceive.

'Then, it is a daughter,' continued Robert, 'who has grown up, deprived of a mother's love and tenderness, who has lived in isolation and tears. And if it has been given to me to know Mme. de Moray, it is because she was lending a helping hand **to** this unfortunate. She **was** trying to raise her depressed **courage, to** soothe

the bitterness of her soul, and to replace, as much as she could, the unnatural mother who——'

Mme. de la Marche stopped him abruptly. There was a cry of revolt on her lips, when she said the following words :

'The unnatural mother, say you ? The word is very cruel, and it is perhaps, a very unjust accusation which you bring. Ah ! believe me, sir, pity the mothers who are obliged to abandon their children, still more than you pity the children forsaken by them. You do not know as I do——'

Her voice broke down. But she made an effort and went on.

'Ah ! you cannot know as well as I do, I, who have learned by the sight of the miseries which surround me, you do not know all that is horrible for a woman in the thought that her child will cease to belong to her ; that she must renounce the supreme joy of drying his first tears, of spying his first smile ? She will not receive a kiss from his lips ! She will never see him ; never ! Do you hear this word ? *Never !* And what is still more horrible is that she will be ignorant of what will become of the child ! She will not even know if he has succumbed ; or if he is not, admitting that he has survived, a prey to misery, to suffering ! Ah ! sir, this spectacle is so terrible that the mother whom you accuse, very lightly, perhaps, would undoubtedly have been less to be pitied if she had had the cruel consolation of seeing her child die before her eyes.'

'Oh ! mother !' cried Mme de Moray, 'do not say it would be less horrible ! Just think in your turn ! To see her child die !'

'Yes,' Mme. de la Marche went on, as crushed by her recollections. 'It must be an inconceivable sorrow ! But still the mother who is condemned to it has the consolation to know that her child is in God's heaven, a pure angel, mowed down before he knew the name of sin ! But this other child whom the poor mother has been forced to abandon, and whose fate she is ignorant of. What despairs he gives birth to ! Of what burning tears he is the cause ! At night she thinks she sees him, miserable and despairing, running after every woman he meets, and calling : "Mother ! Mother !" "He suffers," she says to herself, " he calls me to his help," and she can do nothing ! Nothing ! And she suffers with his sufferings, and she cries when he weeps'

Mme. de la Marche, who was standing, nearly fainted in pronouncing these words. It was because she was painting a living picture of her own sorrow. Happily Mme. de Moray caught her in her arms.

'Oh, mother ! mother !' she cried, sobbing bitterly.

Robert remained motionless, transformed, little by little ; while his mother was speaking, he had felt his icy indifference melting, and the bitterness of his rancor mellowing. He had been mistaken, he had misjudged. Where he had believed there was only forgetfulness, there was a mysterious wound, always bleeding. Tears, good real tears, came to his eyes, and for one moment he was tempted to throw himself at the feet of his mother, and to cry out :

'Re-assure yourself, at least, on account of the life of your child, my mother ! The being you have been obliged to abandon, and of whose fate you are ignorant, is living ; he is here, near you ; and all he asks is to love you, to dry your tears !'

He checked himself, however, not willing to run the chance to increase, by an avowal, the sorrow which he now desired to lessen.

'Ah !' he simply asked, 'these mothers whose sorrows you have portrayed so eloquently, how can they live ?'

Mme. de la Marche raised her head.

'I have known some who have died of despair,' she said.

And she added, trembling.

'And I know one who would kill herself if her shame were known !'

It flashed like an inspiration upon Robert that he had done well to restrain himself a moment before.

'She would kill herself ?' he cried, addressing Mme. de la Marche, but answering his own thoughts as much as her words. 'Ah ! if it is truly so, I have pronounced an unjust judgement and spoken cruel words ! If I was acquainted with the woman I spoke about, in calling her unnatural, if I could speak to her, as I speak to you, now, I would say : "I repent, pardon me, Madam, pardon me."'

Carried away by the strange and thrilling situation which placed him, the forsaken child, in presence of his despairing mother, Robert instinctively bent the knee before Mme. de la Marche.

'Pardon me !' he repeated again, as if he had personally offended her.

His motion brought her to herself.

'Calm yourself, sir,' she said, motioning him to rise, 'and please repeat all I have told you to this deserted child whose cause you were pleading a moment ago. Perhaps she is tempted, as you were tempted yourself, to accuse her mother. Teach her to pity her !'

'I will do so Madam,' answered Robert, who has mastered his emotion, 'and your words, reported by me, will be engraved on her heart !'

Mme. de la Marche was entering her apartment, when she stopped again and took a bracelet from her arm.

'If the child you speak of is poor,' she said, 'and she certainly is since you implore my daughter's help, Mme. de Moray will see to her wants. But I desire she should have a *souvenir* of the scene she has been the cause of between us. Ask her to accept this simple jewel in memory of a mother !'

'The child will keep the jewel always, Madam,' he said.   'I
promise in her name, and I thank you for her.'

Then bending over the hand which was tendering the bracelet,
he deposited on it a kiss, in which he put all his new tenderness,
and he seized the thin golden circlet and hid it in his breast.

'Farewell, sir,' said Mme. de la Marche.

And she retired.   She had hardly closed the door, when in her
turn, Mme. de Moray gave her hand to Robert.

'Well?' she said.   'Well, brother?'

'Ah!' answered the young man, whose eyes filled with tears,
how I wished to throw myself in her arms, and call her mother!
Ah? wretch! wretch that I am!   I who have cursed her during so
many years!'

The countess was the first to regain her composure.   She first
tried to soothe her brother's agitation, and then she thought of
hastening his departure.

'Now, Robert,' she said, 'let us lose no time.   Thank God!
my efforts have succeeded sooner than I expected.   The money I
promised you is there.   Take these banknotes which, I sincerely
hope, will give you happiness.'

Saying these words she handed him the envelope brought by the
jeweller.

'Why don't you take them!' she repeated, seeing that her brother
hesitated.

Robert Burel then took out of his pocket another envelope, very
thin, but far more precious than the first, since it contained the
secret of the fault of Mme. de la Marche.

'Take this in your turn,' he said handing the grievous correspondence to Mme. de Moray.   'These are the letters of my ——
of our mother!'

And he rejected the bank notes with a noble gesture.

'It was a shameful bargain I was making.   Keep this money,
Laura; I shall not take it.   I do not want to sell my mother's letters, now that I have seen her and that I have understood her sorrows.'

'Take them, Robert,' said the countess, with emotion.   'Take
them, not as the price of a bargain, but as a gift, almost a restitu-
tion of a sister, —— of a sister who loves you dearly now!'

'Oh! Laura!' cried the young man with transport, 'I, too, I
love you with all my soul!'

He seized and held her to his breast, and was kissing her with
passion.   The door opened.   The Count de Moray entered, pale as
death.   At the noise of the door which had been opened and closed
with violence, the countess disengaged herself promptly from her
brother's arms.

'Oh !' she cried with terror, and losing all coolness, ' my husband ! all is lost."

' Her husband !' muttered Robert, drawing backwards.

M. de Moray advanced slowly. He affected to be very calm, and he addressed his wife, handing her at the same time the jewel case she knew so well.

' Madam,' he said coolly, but with an altered voice, ' do you recognize this ?'

' My diamonds !' answered the unhappy woman, terrified.

' Yes, your diamonds, which you pledged in order to remit a large sum to —— to this gentleman, who was to give you a certain correspondence in exchange. Since I have given the money and redeemed the jewels, it is only just that I should have the correspondence; give me those letters.'

'Those letters ! you want those letters ?'

' I want them.'

The envelope containing the correspondence had been deposited on the table beside the bundle of bank notes. An imprudent look of the countess designated them to her husband, who advanced to get possession of them. Robert noticed this motion and rushed on the envelope which he seized.

' You shall not have these letters, sir,' he cried. ' They belonged to me, and I take back my property, and you can keep your own. The money is there.'

' I shall not have them ?' cried M. de Moray threatening.

' No !'

The two men looked each other in the face, ready to engage in a struggle. Laura threw herself between them.

' Roger !' she supplicated, ' what do you suspect ?'

' You dare ask such a question,' answered M. de Moray. On entering this room I find you in the arms of a man. I claim some letters for which you give an almost princely ransom, and you refuse to give them up. And you have the audacity after that, to ask me what I suspect. In truth, you are mad.'

' Yes ! it is true !' cried Laura distracted. ' I understand ; these jewels in your hands; this money you have given. This unknown, this stranger you find with me, and lastly these letters which I refuse to give up ; yes, I understand the horrible suspicions you have the right to conceive. Appearances are terribly against me. More than appearances, if you wish, proofs. But do you not say to yourself that your suspicions are unjust, these signs misleading, these proofs deceitful ?'

M. de Moray gave a heart-rending laugh.

' It is so,' he cried. ' It had to come to this. My jealousy is absurd. You are the most virtuous of women. Come, it is enough. Those letters, I say. I must have those letters.'

'Do not give them up, Robert,' cried the countess.

And she added in a lower tone, so that her brother alone could hear her words.

'She has said that she would kill herself if her secret was discovered. Do not give up these letters.'

The young man stood motionless, but firmly resolved to defend the secret of his mother, even at the peril of his life.

'If these letters are the only weapons I mean to use against Mme. de Moray,' said the count, more and more threateningly, 'there are others which I can employ against you, sir; take care!'

And he pulled a revolver out of his pocket. Robert merely smiled.

'If it had been possible to do what you ask, sir,' he said, 'I would have anticipated your threats. Now they put one more obstacle between us?'

M. de Moray was trembling with anger.

'Don't you read in my eyes,' he cried, 'the rage and the merciless hatred which fill my heart? Don't you understand the terrible struggle I am fighting against myself? Don't you see that if you delay one minute longer, I will kill you?'

Laura made another attempt to calm his anger.

'Roger!' she cried, falling on her knees, 'in heaven's name! in our child's name! listen to me! Believe me, Roger! If I did what you ask it would be a terrible, horrible action! It would be more than a cowardice; it would be a crime!'

'These letters! sir, these letters!' repeated the count, disdaining to answer the prayers and tears of Laura, who was kissing his knees. 'Give them to me, if you do not want me to take them from you; if you do not want me to kill you!'

He had raised his arm in the transport of his rage, and was going to fire, when Laura threw herself between the two adversaries. She was distracted with terror and despair.

'No! no!' she cried raising her imploring hands. 'Do not commit an unpardonable crime! Do not strike an innocent man! Since you must know, I will tell you all! I will tell you all!'

'The letters first,' answered M. de Moray, 'I will listen to your pretended justification only after having read them.'

'Yes, yes, you will read them, but a single word will convince you better than all the letters: Know it then? he whom you accuse of being my accomplice, is——.

Just at this moment the door was opened with violence. It was the admiral and his wife entering the room precipitately. The noise of this violent discussion, which had almost degenerated into a fight, had crossed the doors and the walls. They had heard, if not the words, at least the sounds of a quarrel which head reached the extreme limits of rage.

' What is the matter ? What is the matter ? ' both asked at the same time.

The appearance of the new comers fell like a thunderbolt between Laura and Robert. At the sight of her mother, the avowal that Mme. de Moray was going to make froze on her lips. The admiral repeated the question he had addressed on entering the room, but to which he had not yet received a reply.

' Once more, what is the matter ? '

' What is the matter ? ' cried M. de Moray. ' I will tell you. The matter is that I am deceived, dishonored ! The matter is that I have just surprised your daughter in the arms of her lover ! '

' Her lover ! ' repeated the admiral.

' It is impossible ! it is false ! ' cried Mme. de la Marche.

' The matter is,' M. de Moray continued, mercilessly, ' that instead of taking my revenge of that treachery, as I had a right to, I asked the wretches to give me the correspondence where I shall find the undeniable proof of their guilt ! '

' Then ? ' asked the admiral, panting.

' Then they refused to deliver up these letters ; but we will take them now, and you will read them yourself, after which you will pass sentence on your daughter and her accomplice ! '

' Read them ! he ? ' said Robert.

At these words Laura uttered a shriek of terror. The thought that her father would discover the secret of her he had loved and venerated for half a century, renewed her energy.

' Never ! ' she cried, stepping backwards and getting nearer to Robert. ' Never !—— You will not have them !—— '

' No ! no ! Never ! ' repeated Robert in his turn, his eyes constantly fixed on the beloved features of that mother he had learned to love only one short hour since, and for whom he was willing to sacrifice his life.

' But you will give them up, wretch ! ' cried the count, arrived at the paroxysm of rage. ' I will force you to deliver them up ! '

' Take them out of these flames, then ! ' answered the young man.

And he threw the envelope so eagerly fought for in the midst of a blazing fire. M. de Moray literally roared. He rushed towards the chimney to gather the papers which he thought contained the proof of his dishonor. But Robert pushed him away with force, so as to give the fire time to accomplish its work, and stood with his back to the chimney, with his arms crossed. A shot was heard.

' Die then ! ' cried M. de Moray.

Laura uttered a heart-rending shriek of despair. Robert never said a word. He had been struck, however, and he tottered. He had taken a step forward and was holding himself by the back of an arm-chair with one hand ; with the other he pressed his breast.

G

However, not a drop of blood flowed from the wound, which had closed after the passage of the bullet, and he experienced a choking sensation almost instantaneously.

'Sir,' said the unhappy man, 'I was without weapons, and you have killed me! It is a murder!'

He could say no more and fell forward, with his face on the floor. He was still breathing, however. Laura then went and knelt near the body which would soon be a corpse, and bending near enough to cause those present to think that she was giving a last kiss to her dying lover, in the very presence of her revengeful husband, she said in his ear:

'Brother, what do you command? What do you expect from me?'

The approach of death gives, sometimes, a rapid lucidity to the thoughts of the dying, as it gives to their last desires the authority of almost divine will. Robert felt all the courage and resolution there was in the spontaneity of the motion which had brought Laura to his side, and which would not fail to be taken, in the eyes of all, as the avowal of the fault she had not committed. He answered in a low voice:

'Let nobody ever know the truth! she would die! —— and —— one is enough! Never avow anything! —— except to him you love —— to your husband —— by whom I am struck! ——'

'Yes, only to him!' said Laura. 'To him alone!

Having received this promise, the unhappy man let fall his head, which he had raised for a moment, as if he had been waiting for these words to die. A last convulsion shook his frame, a last gulp of blood came to his lips, then a sigh, and then nothing. His dead eyes, wide open, seemed constantly fixed on the accomplice of his sublime devotion, as if to impose an eternal silence. It was this fixed stare which made Laura understand that all was ended. She threw herself backwards with terror.

'Dead!' she cried, 'he is dead!'

'Now,' said M. de Moray, 'I am waiting for you to pronounce those words which, better than the burnt letters, were to justify your conduct in my eyes. Speak then!'

'That I should speak!' answered Laura, looking around her wonderingly, 'That I should speak!'

'Yes,' said Mme. de la Marche, 'tell the whole truth!'

'I order you to do so!' thundered the admiral.

'And I implore you, my child,' said Mme. de la Marche.

'Be silent, mother, be silent!' muttered Laura, 'you know not what you ask, you do not even suspect the tortures you make me suffer.'

The poor woman was undergoing a terrible torment; a nervous trembling was agitating her body, her eyes were haggard, her voice

was short and shrill ; blood was rushing to her brain and she heard
a tolling of funeral bells in her ears. She felt that her reason was
leaving her.

' Will you speak, at last ? ' said M. de Moray.

Laura looked at him without saying a word. **He seized her by**
the arm.

' What **do** you want me to tell you ? ' she answered.

' The contents of the letters which have been burnt ? **Why** did
you want to redeem them at the price of one hundred thousand
francs ? and lastly, who was that man ? '

' Answer ! Justify yourself, **my beloved** daughter ! ' **said Mme.**
de la Marche, sobbing.

' Yes, love me well ! ' **said the unfortunate** woman, ' **love me**
always ! '

And she added, in a firm voice :

' You may torture me, Roger ; you may even kill me ! I will
say nothing now.'

' Because nothing could justify you ! ' cried the husband in **a**
thundering voice. ' That man was your lover, and I throw you
out of my house ! '

' And I—I curse you,' cried her father.

To pronounce this condemnation the old man had extended his
arms and raised his head in a gesture of supreme justice. He was
at the same time the judge and the executioner. This last ordeal
was more than Laura could bear. A cry of despair escaped from
her breast ; she put her hands convulsively to her forehead and
kept them there for a long time. When she let them fall **a com-**
plete transformation had taken place in her. Her face had become
impassive all at once. She was smiling, but her smile was strange,
unconscious, and her voice, sweet and calm, was repeating without
trouble, without emotion, and as if **she** had been proud **of the**
avowal : ' He was my **lover** ! ' The unhappy woman was mad.

During the terrible **scene** which had just taken place, every blow
struck on her heart had had a **fatal** echo in her brain. Each rending
of her heart had caused deep trouble in her mind and had filled it
with such darkness that the poor victim could no more distinguish
what was **true** from what was imaginary, so that now Laura thought
she **was really** guilty. **So** she was insane, but her madness extended **only to** one particular thing,—the accusation, which had
weighed **so** cruelly upon her, and on which her honor and dearest
affections had been wrecked, had appeared to be just and deserved ;
but this excepted, she was rational. This madness is a very common phenomenon ; it is called reasoning madness, the most difficult
to ascertain, because the patient sustains the dreams of his disturbed mind with all the logic of the soundest intelligence. Laura
knew the history of the fall of her mother, and in her mind this

history had become her own ; this fall was personal to herself.
When the judge was called in to find out the cause of the murder
of Robert, she appeared before him in the attitude of a culprit, as
if crushed under the weight of her dishonor.

'You admit,' said the magistrate, 'that criminal relations have
existed between you and the man who has been killed by your husband ? '

'I admit it,' was her answer.

That was all she would say. The recollection of the scene had
just crossed her mind. They had spoken of the victim, and the
terrible scene of the murder appeared to her in its entirety. She
saw herself in an attitude of prayer, at the knees of her husband,
ready to speak, when all at once, her father and mother had appeared. Then a pistol shot, and she also saw Robert ; and heard
him saying in her ear : 'Do not confide our secret to anybody except to him whose hand has struck me ! ' Once his mission accomplished, the judge told her she could go to her home. She retired
to her room, and threw herself on her bed, broken in body and
soul. From that day until the date M. de Moray was called to
answer the charge of murder, Laura remained almost constantly
alone. Her father and mother had left the mansion, the austere
principles of honor of the admiral not allowing his wife to kiss her
daughter for the last time before leaving. The countess was abandoned to the care of a chambermaid. The only friend who remained to her was very humble. It was Maltar, the Indian. The
poor servant felt for Mme. and Mlle. de Moray the attachment of
the dog to his master. It was on account of his devotedness to
Paulette that he was chosen as mediator between Laura and her
husband in an important question which it was urgent to settle.
The reader will easily guess the matter was about the unfortunate
young girl left by her parents in Pondichéry. Paulette was now
occupying all Laura's thoughts. She was asking herself with
despair :

'How can I hide my shame and sorrow from her ! Alas ! it is
impossible. If I could only hold her in my arms at the moment
she will hear the terrible revelation of the crime I have committed !
With my tears and my kisses I could try to alleviate her sorrow. I
could, with caresses, make her forget that I have been guilty. But
thousands of leagues separate us. Letters will reveal this secret to
the weak child. Alas ! will not the blow be too hard, and will she
not succumb when she learns that hereafter she must despise her
mother ! '

This thought was, to the unhappy woman, a source of heart-
rending which all mothers will understand. Happily, Maltar
was charged by M. de Moray himself to appease her maternal terror.
Not through pity for his criminal wife, but through pity for his

daughter, the angel of innocence **and** virtue, the count felt anxieties similar to those which Laura was feeling. He understood, as she did, the impossibility of revealing the fatal secret to his daughter, at least for the present ; and he also knew that a single imprudent word would put her very existence in jeopardy. Still, it was impossible that she should return to France, without being informed of these sad events.

It was under these conditions that Maltar was instructed **by M.** de Moray to transmit his wishes to Laura. They would keep on writing to Paulette as if nothing unusual had happened in their life. Each one would write in turn by each mail. However, they would not try to act a comedy. It would not be bad that Paulette should notice a tone of sadness in their double correspondence ; **an** unexplained sadness, almost vague. Nothing more. In the meantime M. de Moray would write secretly to his sister, to Aunt Basilique, who had care of the poor deserted child. He would acquaint her with their painful situation, and by each mail, he would tell her the incidents which would be the fatal sequel to it. Aunt Basilique would judge herself what would be the proper time to reveal the truth to Paulette without endangering her life. This combination was the **best** they could adopt in their disaster. Both knew the intelligent devotedness of Aunt Basilique, and that none could unveil the mystery which was to be sealed to Paulette for the time being with so much prudence.

The Indian had faithfully carried the message of his master to Mme. de Moray ; she had listened without interupting him, accepting everything, resigned to everything. Maltar went away with **a** heavy heart. He continued to respect and love Mme. de Moray. He pitied her and wept for her, saying to himself that in spite of all the proofs and all the avowals, a woman so good could not be guilty.

We will be brief now, and will simply say a few words of Gorgon. Once only Roger and the duchess found themselves together. It **was** an official interview, in which nobody could suspect the mutual passion which had seized them at one time. Gorgon could afford to be patient now. The future was hers.

Although we have not expressly said so, our readers will easily understand that M. de Moray was to be called upon to render an account of his acts to the justice of men. The murderer of Robert Burel must be subjected to common law, even when everything tended to prove that he had acted under the excitement recognized by law to be an admissible excuse. M. de Moray having intentionally killed a man, had to account for his action. The result could not be doubtful. The murderer was acquitted. The very next day M. de Moray took an action for divorce against his wife and a judgment pronounced the dissolution of his marriage. Laura had not attempted to defend herself. Twenty-four hours after, she

who had no longer the right to call herself Countess de Moray, received the order to leave the old mansion. The brutal process of
law which chased her out of the abode in which all her tender memories were gathered, was the last drop of bitterness which filled the
chalice to the brim. Once more she bowed her head and submitted
when she was obliged to leave, without hope of entering it again,
the house in which she had passed the happiest years of her life.

    .   .   .   .

Now the Count de Moray was free and the noble and saintly
MARTYR was going to pursue, still more painfully, the march she had
commenced on the road to her calvary.

 END OF THE FIRST PART.

Part Second.

I.

FIVE months have elapsed since the last events we have narrated. We are now at the beginning of the year 1885. The reader has seen at the end of the first part of this true story, that three months had been sufficient to M. de Moray to obtain a judgment of divorce. This rapidity of procedure is unexampled, and can only be explained by the peculiar circumstances in which it was presented to the judges. After the delivery of the judgment, and after the performance of the ceremony of divorce at the mayor's office, Mme. de Moray had left de Varennes street, and had rented a small apartment on François I. street. We said Mme. de Moray. It is through the force of habit that we still give her that name, for she had no right to it any longer ; she had renounced it with cruel sorrow. When she signed her lease, it was the first time in many years that she had given her maiden name. But now she had not the right to take another, and it was with tears in her eyes and with a trembling hand that she had written: Laura de la Marche. Her modest apartment was on the third story and she occupied it alone with a servant. She could easily have lived according to her old habits of comfort. The dissolution of her marriage had broken the community of fortune existing between her and M. de Moray, and had put each of them in possession of their dowry. However, this fortune which she had to take back, amounting to nearly one million, was crushing her. She resolved to give it to the poor. They, at least, would not seek the source of the help they would receive.

Laura, since her divorce, had not dared to go to see the father and mother whom she venerated and adored. Her letters had remained without answer. Even some had been returned to her un-opened. It had been a horrible heart-breaking, when, in the envelope, she had found the pages in which she was imploring the pardon of a fault she had not committed, but of which she thought herself really guilty, since the terrible scene which had overthrown her reason, and had been the cause of her brother's death. She felt crushed by the disdainful silence of her parents. She was not only suffering from her own sorrow, she also felt her mother's, because she knew very well that the heart of Mme. de la Marche was panting to bring her some consolation. It was certainly the inflexible will of the head of the family which kept her silent.

' Ah !' she said one day, tired and discouraged, ' I cannot live thus any longer. I must see both of them, even if they drive me out after ! '

So one morning she had dragged herself to the house where her parents lived, in the neighborhood of the Trocadero. She had rung at the door, and, as a stranger would have done, she had told the servant who had answered to notify Mme. de la Marche that a person wished to speak to her. The unhappy woman did not dare to say : Tell my mother that her daughter wishes to speak to her. *A person.* She had used this humble word which the poor knew so well. Unhappily, however changed and unlike herself she was, the servant had recognized her. And as his master had given the strictest orders, in the expectation that Laura would come and see her mother, the man did not dare to carry her message. He remained on the doorstep, to prevent the entrance of his master's daughter.

' Madam,' he said, much troubled, ' Madam, will excuse me but I cannot do what madam is asking ; I would be dismissed.'

' I beg of you !' Laura supplicated, humiliating herself before that servant she had very often treated with generosity. ' I beg of you ! '

She had not the strength to pronounce another word. Her legs bent under her. She almost fell on the doorstep.

' Alas ! madam, compose yourself !' said the servant, feeling deep emotion himself. ' You know very well that I cannot !'

' It is true !' muttered poor Laura, ' and I must not ask you to do what is forbidden. But my father has not told you, at least, to repulse me from the steps of these stairs. Then, please let me stay here, for charity's sake !'

And as the door had been closed against her, she sat down on the stone to wait until her father or her mother should come out. She remained in her position for nearly an hour. During this long time several persons passed by her, either going up or coming down ; they would turn around and look with amazement at the desolate attitude of that woman in deep mourning. At last the servant who had already spoken to her, reopened the door and approached her.

' Madam !' said the good fellow, in a trembling voice, ' madam, you must go. Do you see ! Although it is very strictly forbidden, when I noticed that you were there, I went and told M. de la Marche. He was not alone when I entered the room. Madam was at his side, sitting silently in an arm-chair, as she is in the habit of doing now since—since many months. Then at the risk of raising my master's anger, I told him what had happened, and——'

He hesitated to continue.

' And ?' said Laura, with beating heart.

'And M. de la Marche did not **interrupt** me, and when I had done, "I do not know the person you speak of," he said, "We will not go out until she has left the house."'

A sob came to Laura's throat. The servant continued :

'Then Mme. de la Marche looked at her husband with eyes that would have softened a gaoler, and joined her hands in a gesture of supplication without daring to speak. "Go and do as I told you!" my master said, harshly. I left the room and waited **some** time in the hall, hoping to be recalled. But it has been useless. I only heard through the door murmurs and sounds of prayer, and violent bursts of anger. A moment after Mme. de la Marche crossed the hall with agitated features. A violent scene had undoubtedly taken place. I believe that if you do not go away from here misfortune will fall upon your mother, who is already unhappy, **as it** can be plainly seen.'

Laura mechanically rose, and **went** away, having thanked the servant ; she returned **home** exhausted. When she arrived her servant met her.

'Madam,' she said, a man has been waiting for you for the past hour. He has a very queer costume. He says madam knows him.'

Laura pushed the door open and uttered a shriek. It was Maltar. Maltar! What recollections this name awakened in her! Memories sweet and painful at the same time.

'You!' cried Laura, 'you, Maltar, in my house!'

There was almost an accent of joy in the tone in which she pronounced these words. It seemed to her that the faithful servant of M. de Moray could not be in her house unless sent by her husband himself. The Indian probably understood her thoughts, for he at once undeceived her, in order that the dream having lasted but a short time the awakening would be less painful. He came near Laura, and bending his knee, he took her hand and kissed it respectfully.

'Mistress,' he said softly, 'Maltar has come secretly, without saying anything to anybody. Mistress will forgive Maltar, who loves her always?'

'Ah!' muttered Laura, '**what was I thinking of? Was** that possible?'

And motioning **to the Indian** to rise, she **showed him a seat. He** refused it.

Oh! mistress!' **he** said.

And he sat on the floor, Indian style, on his heels.

'Like this,' he said, 'as in India.'

The name of the country where her daughter was, thinking of her having no knowledge of her unhappiness, caused her tears to flow.

'As in India!' she repeated, 'as in olden times!'

And she went on, after a moment of **silence** :

'Thank you, Maltar, I am grateful that you have come, because it proves to me that there is at least one being in the world who has not abandoned me. Thank you!'

She was repeating her thanks, her soul full of gratitude. Oh! the unhappy and the poor! If we only knew how a little thing consoles and helps them.

'Come,' she continued, 'speak, tell me why you have come, because if you have come to-day rather than yesterday or to-morrow, it is because you have something to tell me.'

The faithful servant was hesitating.

'Mistress,' he said, 'has always been good to Maltar, good as the heavens which give him light, as the earth which gives him rest, and as the grain which gives him food, and Maltar is not ungrateful. He knows that his mistress is unhappy, and he does not believe that she deserves to be.'

He stopped a moment, as if expecting an answer, but Laura remained silent. Then he continued:

'Maltar has not come until now because he had hopes; he knew that master was unhappy also, and that, tired of this cruel torture, master and mistress would meet some day, when an explanation would easily take place, especially when young Mistress Paulette will be here.'

'My daughter!' cried Laura. 'Did you learn anything? Do you know when she will return?'

'No,' answered the Indian, shaking his head. 'Maltar knows nothing. He had hopes, that's all. Only——'

'Only?'

'Well, there are events preparing, and mistress must not wait any longer if she wishes to say——'

'What do you wish me to say?' replied the unhappy woman. 'You know very well I have confessed.'

'Yes, Maltar knows. But Maltar does not believe.'

The good fellow looked at Laura full in the face in speaking thus.

'I have told the truth, she said.' 'Do not insist any more. Your devotion and your love for me make you doubt my words. You are wrong. Tell me only the events you allude to.'

'Mistress,' asked the Indian, 'if the master were sick, if he were at the point of death—it is only a supposition—would not mistress go and see him? Would she not speak in his ear for a moment, and would not she reveal some secret which she has not revealed and which she refuses to tell to-day?'

'What can I tell you?' asked Laura, with sorrow. 'Once more, I have told the truth.'

Maltar shook his head. The good Indian had some secret intuition, which attested, in his mind, the innocence of his old mistress. He continued in his generous stubbornness:

' And if the master were on the eve of doing, through madness or sorrow, something which would be **worse** than death for him, would not mistress try to prevent him from rushing to destruction ? '

' But what is the terrible project which brings you **here, and** which threatens him ? ' asked Laura, with anguish.

' The master loves another woman,' slowly answered Maltar, ' or rather thinks he loves her, and he is going to marry her.'

' Marry her !' cried Laura, distracted. ' Ah ! it is impossible !

That, believing himself deceived, M de Moray had repudiated the guilty wife, it was his legitimate right, and Laura had felt a mortal sorrow. But she had the supreme consolation to believe, in her madness, that the man who had repulsed her from his heart and his house was suffering also. And she imagined that, thanks to this communion of sorrow, some mysterious tie would continue to bind them together. But, alas ! the announcement of his marriage destroyed her last illusion.

' No ! No ! it is impossible,' she was repeating, hoping that Maltar would tell her that he had been playing with her credulity.

But the gloomy silence of the Indian made her understand that he had told her the truth. Then she wanted to know who it was that Roger was to marry, undoubtedly to escape from his solitude. She passed in rapid review all the women of their relations, and could not see her among them. Suddenly she had an inspiration, and she felt sure she was not mistaken.

' She !' **she** cried in a shriek more painful than the first. ' It is she, is it not ? Oh ! the wretches ! the wretches !'

' Yes,' answered Maltar, who understood very well that she **was** alluding to the Duchess de San Lucca. ' It is she.'

A spasm of anger rushed to the brain of the unhappy woman, **and** forgetting the fault she believed herself to be guilty of, **the martyr** became a rebel.

' Ah !' she cried with indignation, ' it is low ; it is villainous ; it **is** infamous ! and still I should have expected this humiliation ; I have condemned myself. I have stupidly sharpened the knife which cuts my heart ! They were loving each other, and I saw it, I guessed it ; I told myself that it was not so ! I accused myself for the suspicions !

' Mistress !' muttered the Indian, trying to calm the fever of **her** anger.

' Why don't you say that I am lying ?' cried Laura, tearing her hair, with despair. ' You know as well as I do the guilty passion which attracted them towards each other, like an irresistible mag**net** ! Perhaps you know more than I do ! Ah ! It is not then only in the future, nor in the present, that I lose the love of Roger ! it is also in the past ! Now I understand why he was so quick to

accuse. 'It was because being traitor himself he could not belive in
the faithfulness of his wife, tried, however, by seventeen years of
loyal tenderness ! I understand also why he was so prompt in
killing ! the proud nobleman ! It was because room had to be made
for the mistress who was waiting ! And if I was not killed instead
of my accomplice, it was because the paramour would have hesitated, perhaps, to occupy the bed stained with blood by the murder
of the first wife ! Ah ! no ! it is too much ! too much ! '

And she walked furiously around the room.

'Mistress,' he tried a last time, 'if, however, you did not tell the
truth when you accused yourself, the master would repent and he
would not marry her !—— her !'

Her fury fell suddenly at these words. After trembling and hesitating for a second, Laura regained her usual coolness, and remembering suddenly her imaginary fault : 'It is justice!' she cried.
And she fell, stunned.

We will now tell the readers what has happened and give them
details which Maltar has not made known to Laura. While the
woman he had repudiated was hiding her shame and sorrow in a miserable lodging. M. de Moray continued to live in the house on de
Varennes street : but he was not alone in the old family mansion.
The Duchess de San Lucca and her brother still occupied the first
story. Since the murder of the supposed lover of the countess, and
during the divorce suit, the *rôle* of the two adventurers had been
necessarily thrown into the shade. At first, the old house wore a
mournful look. All motion had been suddenly stopped. Annibal
was very much affected by the funeral aspect of the great house,
and he advised his sister to move out.

'Let us go,' he said to his sister. 'Let us go at once. Since there
has been a man killed in this house, it seems to me that one can
feel death. Upon my word ! I always have a mind to take my hat
off when I enter.'

He was much embarrassed in saying these words. The duchess
noticed it and asked him what the matter was.

'Well ! little sister,' he said, scratching his ear with a familiar
gesture. 'I cannot help having remorse, whatever I may do, about
the poor devil the count has murdered. One thing is certain, if I
had not said a word, the unhappy fellow would still be living, and
undoubtedly very happily, with the money of Mme. de Moray.'

'You pity him !' answered Gorgon, shrugging her shoulders.

'Certainly ! I put myself in his place, and I declare that I would
have hated, on the point of dying, the indiscreet ones whose prattle
had been the cause of my mishap. After all he did nothing to us ;
we had no motive of hatred against him.'

'Eh !' said Gorgon, carelessly, 'have the soldiers who kill each
in battle motives of hatred ? life is an every day struggle and takes
a thousand forms. *Væ victis !* and the spoils to the victors !'

'Victors! victors!' said the Neapolitan, 'I do not see what we have gained so far. I should be inclined to think we are going backwards. We don't see a living thing in the house.'

'Wait another week only,' said Gorgon, 'and you will **see.** I guarantee that my drawing-room will not be deserted.'

The adventuress was not mistaken. After the first moment of public stupor, a great curiosity attracted a crowd to the house. People who hardly knew the Duchess de San Lucca, and who had been the most bitter opponents of her introduction into their exclusive society, were the first to come and see her. Every one knew **the** friendship and intimacy which existed between the duchess and **the** family of M. de Moray, and through her, they hoped to learn exact news, untold details concerning the drama which occupied the whole of Paris. To tell the truth, Gorgon found herself in a delicate situation, but she came out of it with honor. The public expressed an equal affection for the two heroes of the sinister adventure. But with the most hypocritical ability, she succeeded, without making her effort apparent to divert all sympathy which might have excused Mme. de Moray. Without saying anything against Laura, she praised with such an accent of sincerity the devotedness and the love of Roger for his wife that very soon the count was regarded as a hero and a martyr to conjugal faithfulness. She did not display less astuteness and judgement in the relations she was to have with M. de Moray after his divorce. The reader may judge from what will follow.

The very next day after Laura had left his house, M. de Moray had asked the favor of a moment's conversation with Mme. de San Lucca. The Count had acted and spoken like a man who obeys some unknown magnetic power. He resembled, in the disorder of his recovered liberty, a lost child who is frightened. He had knocked at a door which he thought **a** friendly hand **would** open. His heart was desirous of effusion, **of** confidence. **Now** that no **ties** united him to another woman, he was sure he would enter with the duchess into an intimacy of life which would fill the emptiness of his ruined affections. From the very first words, he understood that the upsetting of his existence had modified the dispositions of the duchess. He expressed his disappointment in very bitter **terms.**

'**Am** I not unhappy enough?' **he** asked. 'Why don't you consent to come to my help? **In** exchange for all the fulness of my heart, why don't you offer me the treasures which yours contains? And still I remember the time when, although I was not free, you offered me unconditionally the joys of love which I had no right to hope for or to accept. And now that we are both the masters of our destinies, when we can listen to the voice of our passion, **you seem to** have suddenly become of ice! What has happened?

Why are you so cold? Have I offended you unknowingly?'
The duchess made a negative sign.

'No,' she said, 'you have not offended me yet, but you would
soon do so if you should continue to speak as you do at this moment. In other days, you say, I was different from what I seem to
be to-day. You are mistaken. The passion you recall always exists,
and it is as powerful to-day as it was on that eventful day when I
almost dragged myself at your feet, forgetful of my dignity as a
woman?'

On saying these words a flash darted from her eyes, and M. de
Moray understood then that the old flame was still burning in her
veins. The duchess continued :

'Only the terrible spectacle of past events has revealed to me
truths with which I was not sufficiently acquainted. There is
no possible happiness except in the rigorous accomplishment of
duty. In other days I should have been foolish enough to consent to become your mistress. I even had the weakness to provoke
the avowal of your love. But to-day the fatal example of her who
had the happiness of being your wife ——'

'Never mention her name to me!' cried M. de Moray, with violence. 'May the name of that woman whom I hate and despise
never resound in my ears! May the remembrance of her never
come to my heart! I have nothing but disgust for her!'

'And it is exactly to avoid inspiring you with such a sentiment
for me,' said the artful Italian, 'that I would not yield, in my turn,
to a passion which would not be consecrated by legitimate ties.
Yes, I have the presentiment of it. The day would come when you
would be astonished at yourself for giving so much love to a woman
who would deserve so little!'

The reader will easily guess what the result of this conversation
would be. Placed between the necessity of renouncing an intimacy in which he had put all his hopes of happiness, or making it
still closer by a legitimate union, M. de Moray could not hesitate.

In this first interview a project of marriage was formed and promises exchanged. However, the duchess did not wish to appear
to yield too quickly, and she refused at first.

'Do not ask any engagement from me to-day,' she said. 'Do not
make any yourself. This thing is so serious that it must be
weighed carefully by both of us, separately, in order not to have
to reproach ourselves later with having yielded to a fugitive transport of passion.'

'Ah!' cried Roger, 'it is because you do not love me as much
as I thought, that you can speak with so much coolness?'

'You should say wisdom!'

'No, it is not wisdom which inspires you at this moment. True
wisdom is to be happy when one can and as much as he can. Ah!

I implore you ! Do not bargain so much over that *yes*, on which depend my last chances of happiness ! ' If you have loved me, if you love me still, accept now and promise to become my wife ! '

'You wish it earnestly ?' asked Gorgon, intoxicated with joy at her triumph, but seeming to struggle with herself.

'I beg on bended knees !' cried Roger, falling at the feet of the duchess, who for an answer made him rise and leaned her head against his breast.

M. de Moray was in good faith in attesting his love. But he experienced another feeling which he did not exactly understand. It was the unconscious desire to do everything he could to tear from his heart the last spark of tenderness he had for his unworthy companion of so many years. The sooner he would be married again, the sooner he would forget the wretch who was not satisfied with his powerful and loyal affection. And he was not only seeking forgetfulness, he also cherished a desire for revenge. He felt an ardent longing to see another woman bear his name ; it would be a supreme revenge which would reach Laura in her solitude.

'She will see,' he thought, 'that I can do without her, and that I can love others ! she will see that if I have killed her lover, it was not through a stupid jealousy, but to revenge my outraged honor ! '

Gorgon understood all this ; but what did she care now ? She had attained the end for which she had worked for the last six months. She would soon belong to Roger and possess him at the same time ; and this possession would be more complete than she had ever hoped for, since it was not only a lover, but a husband she was to have.

Three weeks after, **Gorgon became Countess** de Moray.

II.

Under the influence of the new countess, the aristocratic mansion had changed its tone of mourning to one of joyful life, and had almost become a palace. In the house pleasure reigned from morning until night, and very often from night until morning. This atmosphere of luxury was not new to M. de Moray, with whom it was an every day occurrence when he was governor of India. His large fortune also allowed him to surround Claudia with all that could flatter her pride, and she used it largely. By these means she had succeeded in entering the high world, and had taken a firm hold of the high society, which was the aim of her life and the height of her ambition.

One day, in March, the gay society which frequented the mansion had projected an excursion to Auteuil, when M. de Moray had announced his intention of remaining at home under the pretence of some important business that had to be attended to, and he had asked M. de Roquevaire to take his place. We are already acquainted with this gentleman, on whose advice Gorgon had gone to the Cape of Antibes. After promising to take M. de Moray's place, M. de. Roquevaire drew near the mistress of the house.

'I must tender you my sincere compliments,' he said.

'Why?'

'The morning papers speak of nothing but your success at the ball of the British Embassy, given on the occasion of the short sojourn of the Prince of Wales in Paris.'

'It was a brilliant affair.'

'And the prince was very amiable, they say.'

'In fact, his Royal Highness has even been so kind as to ask me if he would meet me at the races to-day.'

M. de Moray having heard these last words, she asked him, not without satisfied vanity:

'What do you say, Roger? Do I sustain your honor?'

'Certainly,' said the count, gallantly kissing the hand of his wife. 'Who has ever obtained as great a success as you? Every day you are the queen of some *fete* or other. You bear in triumph the splendor of your strange and marvellous beauty! Oh! yes, I am proud of you, Claudia, very proud!'

'And very happy also, I hope?' answered the young wife with a gay smile.

'You ask if I am very happy? Certainly, I am!' he said, although the question produced an uneasy feeling that he could not define. 'What more could I ask? I have a beautiful wife, a considerable fortune, and friends faithful and devoted!'

After their departure, M. de Moray, instead of attending to his business, fell to thinking.

'Happy!' he said to himself. 'Yes, they are right! I am perfectly happy! I am the happiest of men! And why should not I be? Is there, in the midst of this whirlwind of pleasures, any room left for regret? Is there even room for memories?'

He rose suddenly and commenced to walk about the room, passing his hands through his hair, which were becoming grey.

'And what should I remember, after all?' he continued. 'What and whom, chiefly? Her who has odiously betrayed me? It would be sheer madness! And when I think she has not had even one hour's repentance! With what pride she avowed herself guilty! But I took the means of breaking her insolent pride! How she must have suffered when she heard of my marriage! And my choice must have caused her more despair than any other! Ah! I hope she has suffered, so as to make **my** revenge more complete ! And to suffer, she has only to remember the happiness of the past ! Whilst I ! —— Well, what, I ! I remember also ! But it is to hate the wretched woman still more, and to curse her ! —— '

M. de Moray had just then a feeling of involuntary sincerity, and he cried out in a sudden burst of despair :

' But why is it that, in spite of her treachery and her infamy, my **thoughts** will turn towards her ? Why do I run away from all the **pleasures awaiting me,** and why **do** I remain alone to think **more freely of the cruel absent one** ? **Ah** ! it is because, though **I have driven her away from my house,** I cannot throw her **out of my heart !** '

And he fell **exhausted in** a chair. **At** this moment Maltar entered, and the count **raised** his head **at** the noise. The Indian was before him, **in** his **usual** humble attitude. However, M. de Moray noticed on his face an air of embarrassment which made him understand **that his** strange servant did not come only for the wants of his service.

' You have something to **tell me ?** he **said suddenly.**

Maltar bowed still lower.

' Well, speak ! What is it ? '

' The master will excuse me,' answered Maltar **in his sweet voice.** ' I have to tell him that I am going to quit his house.'

' Quit my house ! cried the count, stupefied. ' Are you mad ? '

' No, master, not yet,' said the Indian artlessly ; ' but I should soon become mad if I remained. **That's** why I prefer going away.'

' Ah ! your answer **is** beyond **joking and you** will explain—— '

' No. I beg master to ask **nothing.'**

' On the contrary, I want you **to speak.** You have belonged to me for five years, and I hope you **have not** forgotten the circumstances under which I befriended you, **for** you had endured enough **misery** to remember. I have taken you into **my** service with con**fidence,** I can say even with friendship.'

' **Yes.** The master has always been good to his unworthy slave.'

' **Lastly,** you have been judged worthy to accompany me here, **to** receive **the same** benefits and render **the same** services, and in spite of **all that, you** want to leave me. Would you do like most servants in this country ? Are you enticed away by some maniac attracted by your **queer** costume and your strange features ? '

' Oh ! master !' protested the Indian with an accent of sadness.

' Then if it is not so, once more, explain yourself, speak, **you** must.'

' If I must,' said the Indian, ' I will obey. **Since** certain events have happened in this house, all the old servants have been replaced by others. It is not fair that there should **be an** exception in my **favor.'**

H

'Oh!' said the count suddenly saddened by the memory evoked by the Indian of what he called, "certain events." 'You pretend that is the reason. Then you are more in the wrong than I supposed. It is exactly because you belonged to the old house, as you say, that I would regret a great deal to see you go away. Your departure would not be an ordinary departure, like all the others; it would be almost an abandonment.'

At this last word Maltar raised his head which he had kept bowed down until then. He had just taken the resolution to tell the truth, for, it can be presumed that the reason he had given was only a pretence.

'The master speaks of abandonment,' he said. 'Well, if I want to leave you, it is to give my services to another person who is truly abandoned.'

'Whom do you speak of?' haughtily asked the count, who understood very well.

'I speak of Mme. de Moray.'

'Ah! you don't know whereof you speak, then, for Mme. de Moray inhabits this house, where she is the sovereign mistress, even before me.'

'She is not the one I speak of, master, and you know it well.'

'There is none other, however. Only one woman in the world has a right to bear that name.'

'She who bore it so long was good to me, almost as much as you have been yourself. So, whatever name she bears to-day, it is her I will serve, since she is unhappy.'

'Ah!' said the count, 'it is a singular freak to devote yourself to the one who has committed the fault and who lives in shame.'

'Master!' retorted Maltar with firmness, 'I do not believe that Mme. Laura has committed any fault, and I believe that the shame she lives in is not deserved.'

M. de Moray was startled.

'You are mad!' he cried. 'You were there, however, when all that happened; you were a witness to my anger, to my revenge!'

'Yes, master. But I do not believe what you have believed. I do not believe what I have seen!'

'You were also at the trial. You heard the avowal she made to the judge and to the jurors. Your ears, like mine, heard the echo of her words when she was saying: The man killed by M. de Moray was my lover!'

'I heard and I remember. But I do not believe what I heard and what I remember. Let the master remember also. There was in Mme. Laura's voice a strange accent which I had never heard before that day. There was in her eyes the wandering of madness. And this terrible sound of her voice, this wandering of her eyes, I have found them again nearly two months ago when I told her whom I always consider as my mistress **that** you were going to marry another woman.'

'Ah ! you have seen her, then ?' **asked the** count, with avidity. 'You did not tell me!'

'It was of no use. At that time you would not have listened to me, even less than to-day.'

'And why did you bring her the news of my marriage ?'

'To prevent her learning it by chance, from wicked **or only in**-different persons,' said Maltar, with the dignity which every noble sentiment gives to the one who utters it. 'Well, **the** news of your marriage has finished the work which her sufferings had commenced. For many weeks, and until the last few days, Mme. Laura has been in peril of her life. As long as the danger lasted, I passed several hours each day, each night I should say, by the side of my dear mistress, nursing her while her only servant took a little rest. If she had died, I would have said nothing and I should have remained here to consecrate myself to the master, and perhaps to console him later on. But now Mme. Laura is saved. She tries to cling to life for the sake of her daughter. Just think, master ! I am the only being to whom she can speak of her daughter, since she is separated now from all those who loved the child with her ; since she has no husband, since her father and mother themselves have driven her away!'

The voice of the poor Indian broke in a pitiful sob. Big tears rolled down his cheeks. M. de Moray had to make a strong effort not to be carried away by the force of this emotion.

'Well, Maltar!' he said with more softness than he had exhibited since the beginning of the interview, 'it is in the very name of Paulette, in the name of my daughter, that I oppose myself to your departure.'

'In the name of Miss **Paulette?**' asked the **Indian,** who did **not** understand.

'Yes, my daughter will land shortly at Marseilles. I was expect-ing the arrival of the steamer to-day ; but since I have not received any despatch it is because the steamer has been delayed for **a** few days.'

'The young mistress **is coming !**' repeated the Indian, troubled by this unexpected news.

'She will be here in two **or** three days at the latest. The last letter of Aunt Basilique announced their departure by the follow-ing steamer. This abode, where my daughter has lived a few years of her childhood with her mother, will appear very empty to her. I will be the only one she will find of all those she has loved !'

'The young mistress will return !' repeated the Indian. 'Oh ! the poor child!'

'The poor child! you are right in speaking thus. An orphan would be less to be pitied than she. How she must suffer now, for Aunt Basilique has probably told her all.'

' What? Miss Paulette did not know?——'

'No. Although strong enough to undertake the voyage, she was yet too weak to hear this cruel truth. She must have learnt it only after landing, in time to prevent her entering into this house with a hope of seeing her mother which would be too suddenly deceived. It is only then that my sister must have told Paulette what it is necessary that she should know, and only to the extent which her chaste ignorance could make her understand!'

' It is only yesterday, perhaps only to-day, you say, master, that Miss Paulette knows that, on arriving here, she will find her mother's place empty! What am I saying? She knows, or she is going to know that this place is already occupied by another. Oh! master! master! What a terrible meeting that will be between your daughter and——'

The Indian did not dare to finish. After all, the new countess was the wife of his master, and she had a right to his respect.

' Yes, very terrible! in truth!' said the count sadly. 'And it is to render the first hours of her return less cruel ; it is to slowly console the poor orphan child that I depend upon your help, Maltar. It is to watch over her, to weep with her also, that I struggle against your departure. But since you want to leave me, since you wish to abandon my child, go, Maltar, go! I do not retain you!'

' No, master!' said the Indian with emotion. ' Now I will remain!'

M. de Moray gave his hand to the faithful servant who bowed and kissed it, weeping bitterly.

. . . .

The reader remembers that Gorgon had sworn to grant the first request her brother would formulate in exchange for the information he had given, and which led to the divorce and to her subsequent marriage. Annibal did not exactly know then what he would ask, but he had an idea, vague and indefinite, it is true, but which had eventually become a firm desire; and he held on to his determination with tenacity. He had not said anything to his sister about it yet. On the day after the races at Auteuil he called on the count.

' I have very bad news to give you about the Rio Negro gold mine ; as you are one of the directors, it will be a very serious matter. You have been the victim of knaves. The principal shareholders have acquired the proof that the nuggets which you and your co-directors have declared to have been extracted from the Rio Negro mine were taken from another mine.

' But it is an infamous robbery,' said the count.

'*Parbleu!* and what is worse, the shareholders declare that unless they are re-imbursed, they will prosecute the board criminally. Of course you are not accused of having wronged any one intentionally, but nevertheless they will prosecute the promoters of the enterprise. There are six directors on the board, and of that number three are filibusters. I told you to guard against them at the time you engaged yourself in that mine. So you are not six directors, but three: The General de Saint Rony, the Marquis de Sistenay, and yourself. The general and the marquis will pay one million each, and they hope you will do the same thing.'

M. de Moray wiped his forehead, on which could be seen **drops of** cold perspiration.

'Those gentlemen have done well to depend on me,' he said. 'But it is very happy that the amount is not larger, because I would have been unable to pay it.'

'I tell you honestly,' rejoined Annibal, trying to hide his disappointment, '**that** what you are telling me gives me great pleasure. Although **I do not** know the extent of your wealth, I was afraid that your **fortune** would not allow you to face such a great loss.'

'I have been very lucky in some enterprises I launched in in India. When I liquidated my liability at the time of the dissolution of my marriage, our settlement of accounts amounted to two millions. The mansion we are now in was estimated at four hundred thousand francs, so that there remained one million six hundred thousand francs in cash. I remitted at that time eight hundred thousand **francs** in French values **to the** first Mme. de Moray's notary. The surplus, that is to **say the** eight hundred thousand francs which constitute my portion, and which were **the** product of the sale of our properties in India, have remained in **the** Indo-Marseillaise bank, which has a branch in Pondichéry. So that, in two weeks at the latest, these funds will be at my disposition. I would easily console myself at that **loss** if the dowry of my daughter was not swallowed up with my fortune.'

'**It** only depends on you, my dear Roger,' said Annibal, ' to **assure** to Miss Paulette a larger fortune than the one you so nobly sacrifice.'

'What **do** you mean ?'

'The simplest thing in the world. Remember, my dear count, that when you solicited my assent to the marriage of my sister with you, although she was perfectly free, by right of widowhood, you would not hear of her bringing a dowry.'

'It could not be otherwise,' said M. **de Moray.** 'The painful circumstances under which I recovered my liberty, and which allowed **me to marry** your sister, imposed upon **me an** exceptional reserve in money matters. I could not, without dishonor, be suspected of making a bargain in marrying a wealthy woman.'

'Very well ! Let me, in my turn, I pray you, do what you have done. It is equally without a dowry that I have the honor to ask you for the hand of your daughter.'

Roger took a step backwards, altogether suffocated by what he had just heard, and unable to believe his ears.

'You !' he said at last, 'you, the husband of Paulette ! you who are the brother of —— '

'As he stopped, Palmeri continued :

'I, the brother of your new wife. That's what you mean, is it not ? Eh ! I am very well aware of the prejudice which this title will create in the mind of Miss Paulette. But leave that to my sister and myself. Claudia will give her back, through her affection, the happiness she undoubtedly fears she has lost in learning that she is to be separated from her mother. As to the rest, with time and the fortune which I am happy to place this very moment at the feet of Mme. Palmeri, I will succeed in winning her love !'

'You ask me for the hand of Paulette,' said M. de Moray, 'and yet you don't know that child.'

'Pardon me,' said Annibal, smiling, 'I know her and, if I must say so, I love her ! Oh ! I have never seen her ! it is true !' he added, on noticing the astonishment of the count. 'But I have as guarantee of her charms the tenderness which you have for her, the great affection of all those who have lived with her, and the respectful devotedness which some of your servants have for her ; I am speaking of Maltar. As to her beauty —— '

The Italian took a photograph which was on M. de Moray's desk.

'As to her beauty, this portrait is my answer. I have often contemplated it unknown to you, and, upon my word, it has inspired me with a sincere admiration for her whose image it is. Once more, my dear count, I love Miss Paulette and I ask you to give me her hand.'

'But it is madness !' said M. de Moray, who was convinced at last of the sincerity of his brother-in-law.

'It is madness, perhaps,' said Palmeri, 'but it can be explained very easily in a man of my character and of my country. Come, my dear count, it is yes, is it not ?'

M. de Moray answered evasively.

'Well,' he said, 'since you insist so much, with a generosity for which I am very grateful under the present circumstances, I do not repulse, deliberately, the proposition you have made. But I do not accept it either. Paulette will be here, as you know, in a few days. I shall leave it to her decision.'

'That's all I ask,' answered the handsome Italian. 'You will allow me to plead my cause and I am confident of success.'

The two men shook hands and separated. Instead of going to his rooms, Annibal went to the apartment of his sister. On hearing of his intention, Claudia repeated the words of M. de Moray.

'It is madness!' she cried.

'Did I tell you it was madness when you acquainted me with the passion you entertained for M. de Moray, and when you told me you would willingly give millions to become his wife?'

She shrugged her shoulders.

'It is not the same thing at all,' she said. 'I adored Roger, and, whatever you may say, you cannot love a sixteen-year old child whom you never saw.'

'I will admit that I do not love this little girl in your way, that is to say with fever, with rage; but I am very certain that I will love her when she is my wife, and this is sufficient for the time being. You have married M. de Moray through passion; I want to marry Mlle. de Moray through reason. My dream is to have a home very quiet, surrounded by the people we know and who know us, and who will have no temptation to make an inquiry into our past life, because, in spite of our good luck so far, I very often tremble. Paulette is just the thing. She must be a timid young girl who knows nothing of the world, who has seen nothing, heard nothing, who loves nobody, and consequently will be very glad to love the first handsome fellow who will pay his attentions to her. Add to this a father whom we have got hold of, who is your husband, who swears only by you, and who, by a happy accident, finds himself ruined at the very moment it is useful to us that he should require our services to pay his debts.'

'So that story of a mine that you spoke about is confirmed?'

'Nothing can be truer. Ah! if we were not here, your poor devil of a husband would be in a sad plight. And even with our help, I don't know how he will get out of that scrape.'

'It is very simple,' said Claudia. 'Roger will pay. All his fortune will be swallowed up.'

'He will pay! what with?'

'With the funds he has in the Indo-Marseillaise bank.'

'Well, he need not depend on that, because according to this morning's despatches, the bank has failed, and will be a total wreck.'

'In that case Roger is ruined, and he will be criminally prosecuted, dishonored!'

'Exactly. Unless he resigns himself to the sweet necessity of having recourse to the purse of his son-in-law; you must admit that your Count de Moray has been very lucky to meet us.'

And the adventurer bust out laughing. His sister sent him away and made ready for her visits.

. . . .

About an hour after this conversation, a young girl was entering
on tiptoe the drawing-room of the apartments of M. de Moray,
dragging by the hand a middle-aged man.

'This way, Mr. Drack,' she was saying to her companion who resisted, 'this way. We are in mother's drawing-room.'

It was Paulette.

III.

We must now explain how it happens that Paulette arrives thus
unexpectedly in Paris, when her father does not even know that she
has landed in Marseilles; and how it is that she drags behind her a
character unknown to us, whom she calls Mr. Drack, and who hesi-
tates to enter a house where he is not expected. To give all these
explanations, we will have to return to India. The day after the
scene of the murder, M. and Mme. de Moray had decided to keep
on writing to their daughter, without giving even a hint of the terrible drama which had been enacted. Aunt Basilique, on the contrary, was to be informed of all the particulars, and she would make
the revelation to the child at the moment she would judge oppor-
tune. It had been done as agreed. On the arrival of the first
steamer, all the colony had heard of the sinister adventure. Paulette alone knew nothing. Aunt Basilique and the doctor had
managed so cleverly that not a word had transpired. The doctor
was afraid that the child, in her state of health, could not bear such
a revelation.

'When Paulette is in Paris,' he had said, 'it will be better. She
will see her father and mother; she will weep with both, each in
his turn, and perhaps, who knows? her sweet influence will bring
those two beings together again, because there cannot be anything
but a misunderstanding between them.'

They had not yet heard in India, as can be seen by these words,
of the divorce and new marriage of the count. When this news
arrived the doctor trembled. It seemed very difficult to keep the
secret from Paulette now, and he resolved to send her away as soon
as possible. This decision had caused a great sorrow to a certain
young man, with whom our readers are already acquainted. We
are speaking of M. Gaston de Vallières, the lover of Paulette. Even
before M. and Mme. de Moray had left the colony, M. de Vallières
loved their daughter. He was waiting for her to attain her six-
teenth year, before declaring himself. Under these conditions, M.
de Vallières felt a great sorrow in learning of her earlier departure.

'Do not be uneasy, my dear Gaston,' Aunt Basilique had said to console him. 'When we will be in Paris, I shall plead your cause and I will win it.'

So they started. Aunt Basilique was perplexed. The deep affection she bore to her brother made her desire to see him as soon as possible, to share his sorrows. But the maternal tenderness she felt towards Paulette caused her to fear the fatal moment when she would have to reveal everything : the murder of a man by M. de Moray, the separation, and finally the divorce of her parents, both of whom Paulette loved equally. As the steamer was speeding on its way, the anxiety of Aunt Basilique increased. The truth must necessarily be told before their arrival in Marseilles. Moreover, she was afraid that the indiscretion of some passenger might reveal these events too suddenly to the young girl and cause a relapse, and she took the following means to prevent such an occurence. She addressed herself, on the very first day of the voyage, to a passenger whose physiognomy and social situation were such as to give her confidence. He was an Englishman, who had been a trader in India for thirty years, and who was going back to his country to rest at his ease, he said, and have no trouble, which would be easy for him, since his fortune was made, and there was not a single living being in the world in whom he took any interest, except himself. Sir Elias Drack, that was his name, was consular agent at Calcutta, of we know not what European power. This last qualification was one of the great reasons which had attracted M. de Moray's sister's attention to Mr. Drack. Aunt Basilique met him squarely ; when she had been presented to him by the captain she asked him to come to her aid in establishing a conspiracy of silence among the passengers. Mr. Drack was a regular character, as we say to-day ; at the first words of Aunt Basilique, he cried out against her proposal.

'I return to Europe that I may have no more cares,' he said. 'I did not marry so as to have neither wife nor children, that is to say no cause of anxiety or trouble, and you imagine that I am going to turn conspirator !—I, Elias Drack, conspirator! great heavens! for the sake of a little girl who is a total stranger to me, whom I saw this morning for the first time! No, never!'

After this first resistance of egotism, Mr. Drack promised Aunt Basilique everything she asked and commenced to fulfil his mission on the very same day. It is well known that we get attached to those to whom we devote ourselves, however little it may be. Mr. Drack could not escape the common law. So twenty-four hours after he had received the confidence of Aunt Basilique, he felt more involuntary sympathy for Paulette than he had ever experienced for anyone in his life. But what was amusing in this case is that he was angry at himself for this weakness which he denied, and sometimes he even assumed surly airs, as if asserting the independence of his heart. Only he could not deceive anyone for a long time, and Aunt Basilique and Paulette soon found out the real kindness which was hidden under his rough exterior.

At last the land was sighted. They were reaching Marseilles. When they neared the coast, a terrible accident occurred. A hurricane rose suddenly, and the magnificent steamer was tossed like a nutshell on immense waves. There was no danger, however. Nevertheless, most of the passengers had gone below. There remained on deck only a few travellers who wished to witness the grand spectacle afforded by the storm.

Since the time they had heard that they were approaching Marseilles, Paulette had been a prey to a violent emotion. Marseilles! that is to say her native soil, the land where her parents were expecting her. Something told her that her father and mother were there, at the very end of the wharf, exposed to the fury of the storm, to witness the entrance in port of the steamer bearing their child. Yes, certainly, they were there, huddled together, much affected, getting ready to seek her with their eyes, to make signs of welcome, to send her their love in their far-off kisses.

We have said that the hurricane had forced nearly all the passengers to go down. As the coast was not yet quite near, Paulette had resigned herself to this general measure of safety without grumbling. But as they were getting nearer to the land, as the city appeared more distinctly through the thick glasses of the cabin, she felt a terrible agitation. She asked her aunt permission to go on deck. However prudent she was, the good old lady had not the courage to oppose her will.

'We will be wet to the skin in less than a minute,' she thought, 'but then we will have only to change our clothes. Moreover, the first deception which Paulette will experience at not seeing her parents, as she hopes, will be a sort of preparation for the painful confidence I am obliged now to make.'

They were ready to go on deck at the moment the steamer was entering port.

'Are you coming with us, Mr. Drack?' asked Paulette in a joyful tone.

The Englishman was reading the *British Magazine*, when she called him. He raised his head without dropping his book.

'Where?' he asked with astonishment.

'On deck. Don't you remember? I told you that, no matter what sort of weather it would be, I would go on deck on arriving.'

'Yes! yes!' grumbled the old consul, 'I remember now. You said that. But it does not stand to reason, because you have said you would do a foolish thing, that you should do it. And it is downright foolishness to go and get drenched by the waves which are sweeping the deck at this moment.'

'Come, come! aunty has given permission; do not be wicked, but come and get drenched with us.'

'If the waves only wetted people,' retorted the Englishman, 'it would be nothing. But they also wash them overboard.'

'Bah! I shall take good care of myself,' said the young girl, pulling him by the arm.

Once on deck, Aunt Basilique, seated on a bench, had asked to have a rope passed around her body, so as to prevent her being thrown down by the motion of the steamer. Paulette, would not submit to this measure of precaution. She wanted to be free in her movements, in order to be in the best part of the steamer to see her parents sooner. As to Mr. Drack, he was, in spite of his age, a vigorous man. Like most of his countrymen he had travelled a great deal, and did not want any advice. The steamer was entering the port itself, and in less than a minute would be in calm waters, when a wave larger than any they had yet encountered broke itself on the side of the steamer. A mountain of water fell on the deck and swept it. In the midst of the noise of this unexpected cataract, a loud cry was heard, a heart-rending cry, and then silence. When the deck was clear, Aunt Basilique and Mr. Drack found themselves alone. The same exclamation of despair escaped from their lips at the same time.

'Paulette! Paulette!'

It was only too easy to understand what had happened. The wave had thrown her down and carried her away, on retiring. The unhappy girl was lost.

'Paulette!' cried Aunt Basilique once more, struggling with the anguish of madness. 'Wait, I am going to your help!'

And the unhappy woman, who did not know how to swim, would certainly have thrown herself into the sea with the mad heroism of those who, without depending on their strength and on their science, obey the first movement of their heart. Luckily, she had been tied with a rope, as we have said, and she was unable to move. She attempted to undo the hard sailor's knot. She only hurt her fingers, but she could not succeed. All this time Mr. Drack had not remained inactive, and while storming against the mad imprudence of the young girl who, after all, he said, was only a stranger to him, he had mechanically taken off his heavier clothing. Then seeing a life-preserver at hand, he had thrown it overboard. After that, taking advantage of a new wave which was sweeping the deck, he was voluntarily carried by it.

'This way,' he thought, with ten feet of water over his head, 'there are chances that I will be pushed towards the little one.'

When he appeared at the surface, he looked around him. At first he could not see anything in the small radius his eyes could embrace. For one moment he thought he had undertaken a useless

task. But being lifted a few feet higher by a wave, he perceived a
shred of stuff.   It was the petticoat of Paulette, whose body was
sometimes floating and sometimes sinking, at the whim of the storm.
The courageous Englishman did not exhaust his strength in super-
fluous cries.   He swam a short distance, with the supreme effort
inspired by desperate situations, and he soon had the chance of
seizing the child by her beautiful hair, which was untied.

'Good !' he thought, with his usual phlegm, 'the most important part of the task is accomplished.

But he had hardly raised the head of the young girl above water
to allow her to breathe, then with the desperate instinct common to
all people who are drowning, she clung to him with such violence
that all his movements were paralyzed.

'If I do not tear myself away from her grasp,' he thought, 'we
will sink together, and we are lost.   Yes, but if I abandon her, if I
let her die, the image of the little one will come every night and
trouble me in my sleep ; and it will be very annoying.   Decidedly,
I will either go up there with her, or I will not go up at all !'

And, disengaging, by a supreme effort, his arms from those of the
young girl, he commenced to swim vigorously ; but it was not a
small affair to struggle against such a sea, chiefly with the weight
of the body of the poor child.   Luckily, the life preserver he had
thrown overboard passed near him.   He grasped it and was able to
find a little rest.

'Provided,' he said to himself, 'that somebody has noticed our
disappearance, because we cannot depend much upon Aunt Basilique.   The poor lady must have lost her head altogether.'

He looked towards the land and saw that he was about four or
five hundred feet from the coast.

'It wouldn't be the devil of a job, if I was alone.   But for the
two it will be harder !   And then there must be breakers on that
coast, and perhaps I will not be able to prevent the head of the
little one from being broken !'

But after all, feeling that his strength was getting exhausted in
spite of the help of the life preserver, he had almost resolved to
abandon this transient support, and try to reach the shore with his
precious burden, when a boat appeared.   The accident had been
signalled on board, and four courageous sailors had reached the
scene.   One minute after they were carrying Paulette unconscious,
but still living, to the arms of Aunt Basilique, who had also fainted,
As soon as the two women, so rudely shaken, had regained consci-
ousness, and when they had embraced each other, with the joy of
people who had lost all hopes of seeing each other again, Paulette
asked to go on shore at once.

'Let us quit the ship as soon as possible,' she asked.   'Let us
go on shore.   My father and mother must be in a terrible state.

Poor dear parents ! If they have witnessed the accident, they must certainly be mad with fright !'

'Yes,' answered her aunt. **'Let us go** at once. We will go to the hotel and rest a little.'

And we will find father and mother !' insisted **Paulette.**

'Probably,' answered the old lady with embarrassment. Now less than ever had she the courage to tell the poor young girl of the threatening evil.

As they were leaving **the** steamer, **they met** Mr. Drack. **Paulette** had just been told it was he who had saved her life. **She** threw herself on the breast of the good Englishman. He repulsed her with a little roughness, perhaps to hide his emotion, although he pretended not to know what that word meant.

'Be careful, I pray you, Mlle. Paulette,' he said. 'This is **the** second time to-day that you have rumpled my linen in kissing me so hard !'

'You did not think of your linen when you jumped into the sea a few minutes ago,' looking at him with eyes full of gratitude. 'I owe you my life, Mr. Drack ! Oh ! how my father and my mother will love you when I tell them what you have done for me ! How they will thank you !'

'I defy them to do so ! On coming out of the steamer I take the first train to Paris, and thence to England !'

'Oh ! you will not do that ! It **is** impossible ! My parents **must** see you, they must know you !'

'Dear Mr. Drack,' added Aunt Basilique, 'I pray you, come with **us to** the hotel, your presence will perhaps **be** very necessary there also !'

The old consul bowed and obeyed, saying to himself at the same time that it was not worth while to be unmarried, if he was to be the prey of the first woman who required his services. Arrived at the hotel Aunt Basilique found herself very unwell ; not only the shock had been too violent for her nerves, when she had seen her niece disappear, but she also felt physical suffering. The wet clothes she had kept on too long had given her a severe cold.

Paulette had to give up the hope of seeing her parents. **But** how was it that they had not **come** to meet her ?

'It is quite natural,' answered Mr. Drack, to soothe her, ' our steamer is **a** splendid sailer and we have arrived two days ahead **of** our time.'

'Well,' said Paulette, 'since they could **not** come on **time I will** go to them myself, without losing even an hour.'

'Listen,' said Aunt Basilique, who was **in** bed and shivering, 'I will go if you desire it, but I assure you I am **very** unwell. I want two days' rest.'

'Two days !'

Paulette repeated the word with such an accent of despair that
the old lady took pity on her. It was the good Mr. Drack, who,
annoyed at being obliged to remain in Marseilles all the time Paulette wished to keep him there, came to the rescue.

' Let us see,' he said to the child, ' we must come to a conclu-
sion. Will you let me take you to your father in Paris ? Your
aunt will remain here a few days to rest herself.'

The proposition, transmitted to Aunt Basilique, had been accepted with enthusiasm, the more so that this combination threw
on the ex-consul the heavy task of telling Paulette how matters
stood between her parents whilst they were speeding on to Paris.
M. de Moray's sister had given to the good man all the instructions
necessary. He had promised to reveal to the young girl all that
was necessary for her to know on the way. He had promised, true
enough, but he had not dared, so that Paulette when she arrived at
the house, happy and confiding, had only one thought, that of
clasping her father and her mother in her arms.

When Paulette entered the drawing-room, dragging after her
Mr. Elias Drack, who was in sore distress, Maltar was coming in
by another door. A large screen hid him from the young girl.
Her voice startled him.

' Mlle. Paulette,' thought the Indian. ' How does it happen
that she has arrived to-day, unknown to her father ? And who is
the man accompanying her ? '

The faithful servant thought he should find his young mistress
in deep sorrow. The poor child must have felt a painful sensation
in seeing the house where a stranger had taken the place of her
beloved mother. And as he hesitated to show himself, he was
astonished to h hear Paulette cry out in joyful tones :

' Come, come, Mr. Drack, why do you argue with that porter?
I do not know him. Do you suppose I want any one to show me
my way through my father's house ? '

' But this man asks——' answered the good Englishman, who
was very much embarrassed.

' Well, let him ask, and come in with me. What is more natural
after all ? We disembark on Varennes street, where nobody expects either of us; and as for you, you are completely unknown.
We meet the porter, and the following conversation takes place :

' M. and Mme. de Moray, if you please ? '

' They are both out, miss.'

' Both of them ? '

' Both of them.'

' That is annoying. M. and Mme. de la Marche are there ? '

' The admiral and Mme. de la Marche do not live here, now,
miss.'

' Is that so ? When did they leave ? '

' About two months ago.'

'That is strange. What does it mean? However, it shall be explained by-and-by. And as I come into the house, although the masters are out.'

'Where are you going, miss?' says the porter, in no gracious mood. 'I have told you that the Count and Countess de Moray were out.'

'Well, I say, I shall wait for them,' laughing at the ruffled look of that Cerberus. 'When they come in, tell M. and Mme. de Moray that Miss Paulette de Moray has arrived, and wishes to see them at once.'

'And then I take your hand, to the great amazement of the porter, and lead you into this drawing-room, where I must tell you my joy and my happiness, cost what it will.'

'But, my dear child,' says Mr. Drack, trying to stop her prattle.

'Yes, yes,' she said, quickly, 'I know what you are going to say. What odds is it to you that I am happy? That is none of your business. You will take the first train to England, where there is no little girl to throw herself in your way, and whom you shall not be obliged to save from drowning at the risk of your life. And there you will be egotistical at your ease. And you will think of yourself, only of yourself; you will be the happiest man in the world. That's understood. But remain here one short hour before you enter on that beautiful life. Wait until I meet my father and mother. Witness once in your life people who love each other dearly, and who, on account of that love, are still happier than you, no matter what you may say to the contrary, for their own happiness is increased tenfold by the happiness of those whom they love!'

Upon hearing this flood of words, Maltar understood. His young mistress knew nothing of the events which had transpired in the house. He shuddered. An involuntary motion and the noise he made in striking a piece of furniture, revealed his presence. He then showed himself.

'Ah! Maltar!' cried Paulette, joyously 'It is you, Maltar! How happy I am to see you! Seeing you is like seeing a member of the family.'

The Indian, much moved, respectfully kissed the hand of the child.

'Mistress!' he stammered.

'Do you understand this, Maltar?' said Paulette, 'the porter would not let me come in, under the pretence that M. and Mme. de Moray are out!'

'He wanted to know who we were,' observed Mr. Drack, who was afraid, if Maltar spoke he would say too much, 'and the man was right, since, not finding your parents in Marseilles, you would not allow me to advise them by despatch of your early arrival in Paris.'

'No, no,' said the young girl, 'I wanted to surprise my dear father and my beloved mother, in throwing myself suddenly into their arms, and offering them all my heart on my lips.'

'Her mother!' sighed Maltar.

Mr. Drack made an energetic gesture behind Paulette. He put his first finger on his lips, and opened his eyes so wide that they nearly jumped out of their sockets. Maltar gave a nod that he understood.

'Well, well, Maltar!' joyfully cried the unhappy child, 'speak to me of my father and mother. How are they? Both well, undoubtedly, since they are out!'

While talking, Paulette had commenced to take off her travelling dress.

'You do not even ask news of Aunt Basilique,' said she in a tone of reproach to the Indian. 'I have left her in Marseilles, a little unwell, but it will be nothing. Only that is the reason why Mr. Drack has been kind enough to come with me. What was I saying? Oh, yes! Since my father and mother were not there to receive us, we will receive them, that's all. In the first place, Maltar, see that no one advises them of my arrival.'

'Yes, mistress, at once.'

And the faithful servant went out of the drawing-room. He wanted to be alone to relieve his heart, which was overflowing with tears. Mr. Drack, also wanted to go away. He was not much flattered with the mission which Aunt Basilique had confided to him to impart to the young girl the painful knowledge of her unhappiness; at first, he had hesitated a good deal on the way between Marseilles and Lyons, and had resolved to speak beyond the latter place. But between Lyons and Paris, he had taken, as we have seen, a resolution altogether contrary to the instructions he had received, and he had made himself believe that nobody could break the news to the poor child more prudently than her father. That was the reason why he had brought her to Varennes street without having spoken.

And now that his charge was out of all danger, under the care of her family, the good man had a fixed idea : he wanted to go away, very far, at once ; he did not wish to be present when the necessary explanation between father and daughter would take place. He made a move towards his hat, which he had placed on a table on entering. Paulette noticed it, and stopped him short.

'Well,' she said, 'what are you doing?'

'You see, dear child, I —— but no, nothing! I am doing nothing!'

'Nevertheless,' said the young girl, laughing, 'if I had not turned around in time, you would have fled like a thief. But I have caught you in the very act, and you deny it in vain.'

'Well, it is true,' said Mr. Drack, 'I confess. I wanted to go away.'

'After having taken care of me during the whole passage, after having saved me from drowning at the risk of your own life, after having brought me, all alone, by ourselves, all the way from Marseilles to Paris, **you want** to run away without receiving my parents' **thanks.**'

'My dear lady, you have nothing to thank me for. **I have done** that without enthusiasm, I can assure you.'

Paulette smiled. She was getting used now to the self-depreciation of that excellent man.

'And **now** that you **are at home,**' continued **the Englishman,** ' now that you **do** not require my services any longer, **I have** the honor to —— '

'No,' gently said Paulette, resting her little hand **on** the old gentleman's arm, and looking at him with sincere affection, 'no, you will not have the honor to —— You will remain. My parents must see the one with whom I have made this long trip, and I must tell them all your solicitude, the kindness you have displayed towards me, that they **may** thank you.'

'You think I must **see** your parents,' **asked the** ex-consul, scratching his nose, as a sign of hesitation.

'It is imperative. You must see them **all.**'

'**All !** even **your** grand-father, the admiral ? and your grandmother ?'

'Even my grand-mother and my grand-father.'

'Great heavens !' groaned Mr. Drack. 'People should **not be** allowed to have so many relations.'

'And how many have you got ?' asked Paulette, laughing.

'I ! none. I am my only relative, thank God !'

'Oh ! how I pity you !'

'You are very wrong. Being alone in the world, all the affection which I should divide, otherwise, among the different members of my family I have concentrated altogether on the only person who is dear to me.'

'And who is that person, dear sir ?'

'That person, miss, is myself.'

'What ! It is yourself that you love so tenderly ?' said Paulette, still laughing.

'Well,' said the selfish man, 'I know of no better means to have nothing to do with ungrateful people.'

'Still, it is a great pleasure to have **some one to** love,' cried the **young** girl, with **a** charming impulse.

I

'Who do you say that to!' said Mr. Drack. 'If you only knew the immense love I have for myself.'

'Say, Mr. Drack?'

'What?'

Paulette hesitated a little, and then recovered her courage.

'You have never loved a woman, then, since you are not married?'

'Well! that is preposterous!' energetically protested the old trader.

'Well! I—I have not told you yet, but I have no secret from you. I love a young man.'

The poor girl blushed as she said this, and hastily continued,

'And we will be married soon, M. Gaston de Vallières and I; for, luckily my parents are rich enough not to care for the wealth of the man of my choice, and in that matter they will have no will but mine.'

Mr. Drack trembled again. The conversation was getting on burning ground, and the good man would have given a great deal to see M. de Moray come in to relieve him. Happily, with the versatility of youth, the mind of Paulette took another direction.'

'By the way,' she said quickly, 'I was almost forgetting. It is very lucky I thought of it in time. I say, my dear Mr. Drack.'

'My dear lady?'

'Have you your likeness with you.'

'My likeness!' repeated the ex-consul, astonished and almost flattered.

'Yes, your portrait.'

'What, you want me to give you my portrait,' said he, modestly

'Oh! it is not for me. It is to send it to M. Gaston.'

'Who is M. Gaston?'

'M. de Vallières, the young man whom——'

'Oh! yes, the young man whose—— But what a queer idea to send my likeness to that young man. How can it interest him?'

'It is very simple. M. Gaston de Vallières will know some day that Aunt Basilique and I had a very assiduous companion on the boat. And what is more serious, he will also know that we have travelled all alone from Marseilles to Paris. So, I wish him to have your likeness, to be reassured. Because he might believe—— You understand, don't you?'

'Oh! oh!' said Mr. Drack, 'it is to reassure him that you wish me to give you my likeness. Well, truly, I must confess, it is the first time that a young lady has ever asked a man's photograph to reassure another.'

'What I ask you is very natural,' said Paulette.

'Ahem! and very flattering.'

'Why, certainly ! very flattering ! When he sees those eyes so good, so loyal, that face so open and so frank, M. Gaston de Vallières will understand what an honest man I had as a protector during that long voyage, and he shall love you as dearly as those I will find here will.'

'Well, well,' answered the old gentleman, grumbling, 'all these people will make a poor investment of their affection, because I must confess I could not pay the interest on their capital.'

'Well, now,' said Paulette, gaily, 'I am sure that is pure calumny on your part. You will see how good are all those I love ! you will see how you will be forced to love them, in spite of your-self ! and you shall also see the great happiness there is in this house, because love reigns supreme, because, say what you will, true happiness is in affection and love. Ah ! the dear house ! ' she kept on with a delicious impulse, ' this cradle of my childhood, this beloved abode which I have not seen for at least eight years ! But, nevertheless, although I have not seen it for such a long time, I remember it quite well. Here, see for yourself. There, at the right, is a little parlor that I recall to my mind as if I had been there yesterday. It is mamma's boudoir, the room she liked best. The hangings are rose-colored. Go and see it.'

Mr. Drack opened the door she showed him.

'Yes,' he said, ' it is a little parlor in truth ; only your little rose parlor is blue.'

'Blue ! oh ! I am so sorry. I liked it so much as it was in other days.'

'Well, the hangings have been changed. This is done very often, and you need not fret over it. Hangings get old and they are re-placed by others. It is very simple.'

'Certainly, yes, it is simple. Well, no matter, let us keep on. You will see that this time I am not mistaken. In the little par-lor, on the right side of the door, there is a wall, and on that wall, you will see a large portrait.'

'A large portrait ?'

'Yes. A beautiful young woman with a white satin dress on, a ball dress. That beautiful lady is mamma, you know.'

This time the old gentleman was again embarrassed. However, he was obliged to tell the truth.

'No, my dear child , no. You are mistaken.'

'What ! is not there a wall on which hangs a portrait ?'

'The wall, oh, yes ! the wall is still there, but no portrait is there.'

'But it is impossible !' cried Paulette, rushing to the door of the little parlor, which Mr. Drack had kept open. 'It is so,' she continued ; ' my mother's portrait is not there. What have they done with it ?'

The occasion to make the terrible declaration was good, but the old gentleman did not improve it.

'Undoubtedly,' he said, 'the portrait has been damaged during your long absence, and it is being repaired.'

'Yes,' repeated Paulette, already comforted by this declaration; 'it must be getting repaired. Or perhaps my father had it transferred to his own private room, so as to have it always under his eyes. Yes, it must be so. Oh! here!'

And saying this the young girl seized a little picture frame which was on the mantelpiece of the drawing-room.

'See, here is my own portrait. A miniature they have always with them, and which they have brought all the way from Pondichéry. I was very young when this photograph was taken. It was during my last voyage to Paris, eight years ago. Oh! look!'

'Where?'

'There, on the glass.'

'Well, what?'

'You see nothing?'

'Nothing at all.'

'Well, I —— I see marks of kisses,' cried Paulette, much moved.

She pressed her lips to the miniature with infinite tenderness.

'Ah!' she said, 'it is not my resemblance I am kissing. Dear mother, I am gathering your own kisses.'

Had Mr. Drack caught a cold? He had hardly coughed as yet. But this time it was too much for him. He coughed loudly and blew his nose with violence. Paulette noticed the emotion of the good man.

'You see,' she said, 'that you are kind-hearted. It touches you when I speak of my mother.'

'I,' protested the old consul, vainly trying to look like a crocodile. 'What odds is that to me? Is it any of my business? I do not even know your mother.'

Paulette kept on without paying any heed to this affected indifference and callousness which she was now used to.

'Oh!' she said joyfully, 'here is the stand on which mother puts her favorite books, and her fancy work. Why, there are no books to-day.'

'There is no work, either,' answered Mr. Drack.

'No, no books! no work!' cried the child with a joyful cry, 'but a handkerchief which mother has forgotten. Oh! mamma! mamma!'

Saying this, the dear girl put the handkerchief to her lips, but soon dropped it.

'It is singular,' she said, softly, 'this handkerchief is perfumed, but it is not my mother's favorite perfume. Certainly, this handkerchief is not **hers.** However, here is the crown and the inter-woven initials. **But** no, these initials are not hers ; before the M there is a C, instead of an L. How is **that** ? '

She remained silent for a few minutes, and then she cried with anxiety in her voice.

' Oh ! my God ! I do not know what I feel. All **these** changes in **our** house where I remember nothing, where **I** am like a stranger. My mother's portrait which is not in its usual place. The cipher which is changed on **a** handkerchief which belongs **to** her, which must belong to her. All that irritates and disturbs **me.** I must know ! '

And she turned towards another door leading in an opposite **di-**rection.

' Where are you going ? ' asked the old consul.

' Into my mother's room,' answered the child quickly. ' There, at least, I shall find things which will speak to me of her. Wait for me, Mr. Drack ; wait for me.'

She hastily withdrew from the drawing-room.

' Poor thing ! ' thought the good Englishman when he was alone, but without losing his usual placidity. ' She is very nervous, very excited. It is **too** bad. I **am** very glad, indeed, not to have any children. **In** the first place, it means usually that we have not, **or** that we never had a wife ; and when one loves a calm and peace-able life, it is already a serious chance of happiness.'

He was thus philosophically soliloquizing, when Paulette re-entered the room. The poor child looked excited, worse than that,— terrified. She was staggering, and was obliged to lean **on** the fur-niture to save herself from falling.

' Mr. Drack ! Mr. Drack ! ' she cried with **a** strangled voice.

' What is the matter, my dear ? ' asked her companion, more and more annoyed to be mixed **up** with **a** venture which began so tragically.

' The matter is that I am frightened,' **she** said.

And she shuddered as she leaned **on his** arm.

' **It** is true, you are trembling. Come, my dear child, it is not **at** all reasonable to put yourself into such a state.'

' You know,' she said, ' I went into my mother's room, thinking that there, at **least,** there would be no change, **as** in the little parlor.'

' Well ? '

' Well, there, as here, I found nothing belonging to my mother. Everything is changed. Every piece of furniture my mother liked so much has been removed. Already annoyed by this change, moved in spite of myself, I opened **the** door of my mother's dress-ing room, where she always makes her toilet. A strange sight met my eyes. In other days **my** mother **was** simplicity itself in her

dress, and there I saw, thrown on dummies, dresses of great luxury,
so much so, indeed, that I asked myself if I was dreaming.'

The good Englishman was very much embarrassed and pained to
see Paulette in such a state of excitement, and would willingly have
done something to soothe her, although the effort demanded more
sensibility than he credited himself with.   But, on the other hand,
since in a few minutes the poor child would necessarily learn the
cruel truth, why not let her get used to the pain by her first suspicions, however vague they were ?

'Come,' he said, ' there is no use in tormenting yourself.   Your
mother was very simple in her tastes, you say ?   Well, she has
changed since her arrival in Paris.   She has become worldly, elegant.'

'No, no,' she cried, ' it is impossible.   Those dresses which I
have seen, and which shock my sight and my modesty, would
never be worn by my mother.   But I have not told you all ! Attracted by the noise I made in entering the room, the maid came in.   It
is not the same one my mother had with her in India, and whom
she brought back with her.'

" What are you doing here ? " sharply demanded the girl.   " Who
are you ? "

' I told her my name, and she looked at me with a sneer in her
eyes, which made me ashamed.   Then, she said, ironically I
would swear :—

" Ah ! you are the daughter of M. de Moray.   Then I beg your
pardon."

' M. de Moray's daughter !   Why did she speak thus ?   I had a
mind to ask her if I was not Mme. de Moray's daughter as well as
M. de Moray's, I did not do so, because I was wounded too deeply
by her chaffing looks.   I merely took a last glance around me, and I
felt that I was not in my mother's room.   I lost my senses.   I
yelled aloud, I think, and I fled towards you, hardly knowing what
I was doing, and groping my way, as my eyesight was dimmed by
tears.'

The poor child sobbed bitterly.   She had arrived in Paris full
of happiness at the thought of seeing her mother, and in less than
half an hour she had been thrown from the highest hopes to the
direst misery.   Poor Mr. Drack was nearly demented.   He could
only repeat the same common phrases.

' Now ! now ! dear child ! be calm ! I beg of you !'

Be calm ! the only words of people who have no good reason to
give.

' But,' said Paulette, ' if everything here is so different from what
it was, my mother must also have changed.   Great heavens ! if
her heart should not be the same as of yore, and if her eyes did not
know me !'

This time the consul thought he could protest without danger, and he did it in a humorous way, which he thought was the height of amiability.

'What you say is foolish,' he said with generous indignation. 'In truth these little French women are capable of all sorts of absurd things. The devil! my dear child, your mother may have changed the hangings and the carpets of the house, her dresses and her jewels. She might even have taken another husband (this was **the** phrase he thought so clever), but she has not ceased to love you. The love of a mother never changes.'

'You are right,' said Paulette, laughing through her tears, '**and I am** foolish, as you say. I will soon see **my** mother, and then—— But, hark! I hear the noise of **a carriage in** the yard. Here **is** mother. I——'

She rushed to the window **to see** Mme. de Moray.

'No,' she said, 'it is not her. It is my father. Ah! my dear Mr. Drack! Now, I will await mother's return without anxiety, since I shall be in my father's arms.'

She went towards the door **on** saying these words. A few moments later a man rushed **in**. It **was** the Count de Moray.

'Paulette! my child!' **cried** Roger, pressing his daughter to his heart.

'Oh! father! dear father!' cried the dear girl, answering his deep tenderness by endless kisses.

'At last!' thought **Mr.** Drack, who had turned aside not **to** hinder the out-pourings of their love. 'At last my little companion is under the care of her **father.** **My task** is ended. am not at all sorry.'

'My daughter! my beloved daughter!' the count was repeating **between** kisses. 'Yes, kiss me! kiss me again!'

And their caresses commenced anew. Mr. Drack was the first one tired. It is true he was only a spectator.

'Mr. de Moray,' he said, 'I have the honor to bid you goodbye!'

M. de Moray turned around. He had not yet seen the stranger. As to Paulette, she had altogether forgotten that there were Englishmen at all in the world, although there was one right there who had escorted, protected, and even saved her at the risk of his life within two months. The sound of his voice brought her back to a sentiment of gratitude.

'Father,' she said, 'I am very ungrateful. I have forgotten to introduce you to Mr. Drack, a friend **who** has been very good to Aunt Basilique and to myself, and **who** has accompanied me all alone from Marseilles.'

'Alone!' repeated the count, astonished, 'How is that?'

'Alone! Yes, M. de Moray,' answered the old gentleman. 'Drack, Elias Drack, ex-trader in British India, and ex-consul of Italy at Calcutta. I have resigned those functions, and I am retired from business. Your sister was unwell, and was obliged to stay over in Marseilles. She then placed Miss Paulette under my care—— But Miss Paulette will explain all that to you. I wish only to say a few words in private before I go.'

M. de Moray tore himself from his daughter's arms to listen to the private communication the Englishman wished to impart. When the two men were alone, the ex-consul said:

'Be careful, M. de Moray, how you tell your daughter what neither your sister nor I have had the courage to say. Miss Paulette knows nothing of what has happened between you and your wife.'

'Nothing!' cried M. de Moray, tottering. 'My God! I shall have to tell my daughter——'

'That you have killed a man, and obtained a divorce between her mother and yourself. Yes, M. de Moray, the task is not an easy one, and you must understand that I would rather let you undertake it.'

And turning to the young girl:

'Good-bye, my dear Miss Paulette. I am very happy to have made your acquaintance: to the pleasure of our next meeting.'

He took the hand of the child and shook it energetically, English fashion.

'You are going already,' asked Paulette, 'before my mother's return?'

'I must go, my dear child. I have an appointment at the hotel. Besides, your father has a great many things to tell you, things which do not concern me.'

'But you will come again.'

'I do not know; I must leave for London soon.'

'Oh! I wish to see you again. I want to make you acquainted with mamma. Promise me that you will come.'

'Well, since you wish it, I promise.'

Having gained his liberty by this promise, Mr. Drack obtained permission to go. Only, coming down the stairs he said to himself:

'I have promised to come back, it is true, but I have not said *when*; and I shall certainly wait until everything is quiet in this house. May the devil take me! I do not want to catch heart-disease.'

Let us leave the good man on the way to his hotel, and remain in the house where a heart-rending scene awaits the reader. M. de Moray must now summon all his courage to tell his daughter, if not the whole truth, at least enough to let her understand how it has happened that her parents must thereafter be strangers to each other.

After Mr. Drack's departure, M. de Moray fell in an arm-chair. His daughter seated herself on a stool, her arm leaning on her father's knees, and her head resting on his breast.

'Father, dear! how happy I am!' she said. 'You have done well to come back. Do you see, I could not bear to remain any longer in this deserted house without you! It is true! I assure you, I was losing my head! I fancied all sorts of foolish things, without even understanding the nightmares I formed. But now you are here; I am in your arms; I fear nothing, and can await my mother's return without that horrible anxiety which was grasping my whole being.'

'Your mother!' repeated M. de Moray, in sore distress.

'Yes, my mother! oh! you will not be jealous, will you, if I tell you how ardently I long to see her! No! You cannot imagine the joy that fills my heart, when I think that we shall be together, all three of us!'

'All three of us!' again repeated M. de Moray, covering his face with his hands.

'But, my dear father, what ails you?' cried Paulette, terrified. 'What is the matter? you weep! and you turn from me! Oh, my God! What evil can reach me now?'

Paulette, hearing the sobs of her father, had separated his hands, with which he had covered his face to hide the anguish of his mind.

'You weep, father, you weep! and you refuse to tell me the cause of your tears. But, don't you know, however terrible may be the secret, which you dare not tell, its revelation will be less painful than your silence, which kills me!'

And she had knelt before him, begging a look, a word only.

'Paulette, my darling,' at last said M. de Moray, in despair. 'You must gather all your strength, all your courage.'

'My courage! I trust I shall need much, if I judge of that by the courage you want. And still I ask myself what evil can reach me, when I am here, near you, and that in a very few moments I shall see my mother.'

'Your mother!' answered the count, dolefully. 'Alas! you will not see her again!'

'What? She is out? She will not come in until late to-night; perhaps not till to-morrow? No—— You do not answer? Not even to-morrow?'

'Not even to-morrow; no!'

'My God! I understand that she may have absented herself to-day for I do not know what reason you will not tell me, since, in my joy, I did not let you know the precise moment of my ar-

rival. But you knew, both of you, that I should be here within
a couple of days. If it was not to-day it would be to-morrow,
or the day after, at the latest. She cannot be absent very long.
What! you are silent! Oh! cruel father! It will not even be in
two days! Ah! I understand! since you do not answer, it is because my mother is sick, in danger of death, dead, perhaps!'

She cried with distress at these last words, and nearly fainted.

'No, no!' cried M. de Moray, supporting her, 'be calm, your
mother lives!'

'Ah!' said the child, 'I thought I was going to die!'

'Listen, my beloved,' said the unhappy man, who was forced at
last to make the avowal he had put off such a long time. 'A serious
dissension has arisen between your mother and myself since we arrived in Paris, and we have resolved to live separated from each
other.'

'Separated?' cried Paulette, with fright. 'But it is impossible!'

'Still, it is so. Your mother does not live in this house, now.'

The child got up, threw her hair backwards, with the gesture of
a maniac who tries to understand what is told him, and does not
succeed.

'Let us see,' she said. 'I must recall what you have just said:
a serious dissension—a separation; that's what you said. You,
who loved each other so much, who lived for each other, and thus
united, lived for me. No! it is impossible! Tell me it is only a
trial!'

A smile of hope flitted across her features, but did not last long
at the sight of her father's darkened face.

'Alas?' he said, 'it is only too true, Paulette!'

'Ah! why was not I here when that dissension arose? such a
thing never would have happened, I am sure. But now I have
come back,' she said, with confidence, 'and thanks to my presence,
the past will be wiped off, the abyss lying between you will be
filled. My mother will return and I shall press and yourself in
my arms at the same time.'

'Never!' said the count. 'What you say is impossible. There
is a wall between us which no human power can overthrow.'

'Ah! do not say that, no, do not say that!' repeated Paulette,
with vehemence, 'if you do not want me to doubt my reason or the
love you had for me in the happier days. Ah! I see very well that
I am speaking to a father, not to a mother. If my mother were
there instead of you, she would not struggle as you are doing, and
whatever motives of rancor she might have against you, she would
soon forget them, leaving to my love the task of obliterating them.'

Just then Maltar appeared, much troubled.

'Master,' he said, 'Mme. de Moray is coming here.'

Paulette cried with triumph.

'Ah! now, did you tell me the truth?—— It was only a **trial,** my mother, here she comes—— I shall see her at last? Dear mother?'

Through the heavy draperies could be heard a woman's voice, yet indistinct, giving orders to a servant, and her footsteps were plainly audible.

'Do you hear?' said Paulette. 'It is mother! **Here she is** coming!'

'Paulette,' again **said** M. de Moray, trying to **stop her.**

But it was in vain. The young girl rushed **to the door, and at** the same time the heavy curtains were put **aside and a woman** entered. This woman, whom Paulette did not know, was the person announced. It was the Countess de Moray. Only it was not the daughter of the Admiral Firmin de la Marche; it was Claudia Palmeri, duchess of San Lucca, or rather, it was Gorgon.

'Ah!' said Paulette, stopping short. 'I beg your pardon, Madam, I did not know—— I misunderstood—— I thought——'

Then turning to Maltar, who was terrified, she spoke to him with reproach, almost with anger.

'What were you thinking about?' she asked. '**You** said : Mme. de Moray is coming **in.**'

The Indian remained silent. The person who had just come in, advanced a few steps and answered :

'You are, I suppose, Mlle. de Moray?'

Paulette nodded. Claudia coolly continued :

'Well, miss, you are wrong in abusing Maltar for what he said. I am the Countess de Moray.'

'The Countess de Moray!' repeated Paulette, who did **not** understand, and thought she was some distant relative she **was not** acquainted with. Claudia noticed her mistake.

'Yes,' she continued. 'I am the Countess de **Moray, your** father's wife.'

'You! you! my father's wife!'

The cry of Paulette was a shriek of revolt and stupefaction. The child threw herself forward as if to snatch from that woman the name she seemed to dishonor. But she stopped short, terrified.

'Ah!' she cried, as recoiling from danger. 'A lunatic? she is mad. Take care, father, she is mad!'

She rushed into her father's arms, seeking a refuge where no danger could reach her.

'Roger,' coolly said the countess, 'if you have not yet told the truth to your child, it is now time to do so. Tell her that I am really your wife, so that I shall not have to bear her insults.'

'Father,' shrieked Paulette, 'you hear! she dares say that she **is the** Countess de Moray and that you are her husband! why don't you silence her?'

M. de Moray bowed his head and did not attempt to justify himself.

'That lady spoke the truth, Paulette,' he said in a low voice. 'She is the Countess de Moray ; she is my wife.'

'Your wife! and my mother then! what is she?' cried the child with an angry gesture.

The truth could not be concealed any longer, and each word struck like a dagger.

'Your mother!' repeated the count. 'I have told you already that we are separated. Divorce has torn asunder the ties which united us, and when those bonds were broken, I married this lady. Once more I repeat it, she is the Countess de Moray, my wife!'

This thunderbolt, instead of breaking Paulette's spirits, gave her new strength, at least for a moment.

'Divorce!' she said with an indignant gesture. 'What offence have you been guilty of that she should thus desert your roof and reject your name?'

Not one moment did the child hesitate, with the instinct of love, with the just knowledge of her heart, she had judged that her mother was stainless, and in thus taking her defence, she logically became her father's accuser. M. de Moray understood the divine law which dictated the words aimed at him by his daughter. He would have been ashamed to fight against her noble sentiments, although he thought he was the victim, while really he was the executioner, and he thought to himself.

'She accuses and condemns me without knowing!'

But the new Countess de Moray did not possess that supreme delicacy of sentiment.

'Why don't you ask,' she said to Paulette with arrogance, 'what fault your mother has been guilty of to be repudiated by her husband?'

'Repudiated! you say!' shrieked Paulette, indignantly. 'My mother guilty! It is a lie! Madam! it is a lie!'

'Ah! it is thus you insult me!' said Gorgon, wounded in her pride. 'I was prepared to receive you with the consideration, even with the affection I owe to my husband's daughter, and the sincerity of my welcome constitutes an offence. If it is thus, I shall tell you the truth which your father is too weak to confess. Know then——'

'Claudia!' interrupted M. de Moray. 'In heaven's name be silent!'

And drawing near his wife, he said in a low voice :

'I implore you! be silent! Even at the expense of my honor ; even if I am accused by my own daughter, I do not want to impose on her the sorrow of despising her mother!'

Paulette did not hear the last words of her father, but she guessed

them and her filial love revolted **against the pretended** pity which
the count was begging for her.

'Come now,' she said to the Italian, 'why don't you speak?
you must tell **me what** you accuse my mother **of** ! If, however,
you persist in your refusal to speak, it is because **your** accusations
are nothing but lies and cowardly calumnies !'

Gorgon, thus chastised, was preparing to say the words :

'Your mother had a lover whom her husband killed,' when M.
de Moray intervened, speaking with the authority that his double
title of father and husband gave him.

'And I exact that nothing more be said, neither by you, Paulette,
nor by you, Claudia. I order both of you to be silent !'

And turning to Paulette :

'Listen, my child. God knows that I deplore this painful scene.
I had the right to think that you were acquainted with the sad
events of the past. Then, prepared to learn the worst, you would
have understood the duties imposed on you by the new state of
things. Think of this, Paulette ! It is an impious daughter that
constitutes herself judge between her father and mother. She cannot
think one is innocent without condemning the other. Do not attempt to find out, and keep for the two beings who have loved you
so tenderly since your birth, the respect which God commands. So
then you will ask no questions, you will not accuse, and you will
not defend. I have your word, have I not ?'

The child hesitated a moment.

'**You have my** word,' she said at last, and she started to go.

'Where are you going ?' asked **M.** de Moray, astonished.

'To see my mother and live with her.'

'Stay,' said M. de Moray, 'that is impossible !'

There are in the battles of life moments when all notions of danger and the just extent of **his** weakness escape the combatant.
After a violent emotion, he does not compare his forces with those
of his adversary, and he fights for the sake of fighting, without hope
of gaining the battle, without fear of being defeated. Paulette felt
that sentiment. Her father's will was erecting a wall between herself and her mother. She rushed against that wall. For the first
time in her life she rebelled against paternal authority. M. de
Moray had forbidden her to go and see her mother, she would not
obey.

'Ah !' **she cried,** 'what you ask is cruel. **I must know** nothing
of the past, you say? You are right. And **now** I ask nothing.
But you have a new family. You **are** surrounded with love and
tender **cares,** while my mother is alone and doubtless dying slowly
with **grief.** Don't you see that I am right and that you cannot
prevent me from seeing my mother.'

She had spoken with anger. The child's voice usually so sweet,
was bitter and pricked the father's heart like a spur. He felt
wounded to the quick, and at the same time he wished to press the
courageous child to his heart, in saying to her : 'You are right !
you belong to the more unhappy' but if he had said the last words,
perhaps he would have added, in spite of himself : 'It is for that
very reason that I beg of you to stay, because, now that I have
seen you, now that through you, the ghost of the past has appeared
before me, the most unhappy is the one who is not free to cry !'
He was prudent enough to remain on neutral grounds and to con-
sign himself to the cold facts.

'A superior authority,' he said, trying to be calm, 'has decided
on your fate. The law has entrusted the care of your honor to your
father.'

In her ignorance, Paulette did not understand the full meaning
of these words. If she had known the law, it would have been
clear to her mind that justice, in pronouncing the divorce, had
thrown all the guilt on the wife. And she would have suffered intensely. But this was spared to her. Happily she did not know.

'Justice,' she said, 'has entrusted you with the care of my honor.
It must be right. Being the man you are the stronger. But what
right has justice to dispose of my heart? Did it decide to whom I
shall give my love.'

This was the most cruel blow to M. de Moray.

'Cruel child !' he said. 'Since you ask me such a question, it
is because you have already answered it. You have made this division of your love, which the law dared not do, in a moment ; if we
can call division the abandonment of your whole heart to the profit
of one !'

Paulette took pity on him.

'No !' she said softly, 'do not accuse me of having lost my love
for you. It has not diminished. Only the tenderness I felt for my
mother has increased to the extent of her sufferings.'

The count listened to his daughter's words with rapture, but still
he could not yield to her demand.

'Listen, Paulette !' he said. 'I have already told you that I
could not tell you the cause of our separation, but I have told you
that the law has decided that you belong to me only. We must
respect the decision of the law, and I have neither the power nor
the will to change the decision. However, what I cannot do, others
may help you to accomplish. To-morrow you shall visit your grand-
parents, and the Admiral and Mme. de La Marche will decide
whether or not they can allow their grand-daughter to meet their
own daughter."

This promise soothed the brave girl. It was false, however,
for M. de Moray well knew that the merciless honor of the old sailor

had dug an abyss between his daughter and himself. But Paulette was not aware of this increase of misery heaped on her mother, and she thanked her father with a kiss.

Perhaps the reader has forgotten that during this emotional scene, a third person was in the room. We speak of the Countess de Moray. After the first explanation between Paulette and herself, she had said nothing, because she understood that any intervention on her part would only spur the young girl on in her desperate resistance, and she admired her bravery. However, she wanted to see the end of the debate, and she silently sat down in the chimney corner. In their animation the count and his daughter had forgotten her presence. M. de Moray had just remembered it, and felt much embarrassed when a fourth person brought him unexpected help. It was Annibal Palmeri. Having bowed to Paulette, of whose arrival he was aware, the Neapolitan moved towards his sister and shook her hand.

'She is his daughter,' she **said in a low** voice. 'What do you think of her.'

'She is a thousand times more charming than the cold image I have seen.'

'Take care ! she is already an enemy !'

'Bast ! don't bother. I don't know if she will ever be a friend, but she mu t become an ally, when she will be my wife.'

'Always that folly, then ?"

'Now more than ever.'

During their colloquy the count had explained to his daughter that they were brother and sister.

'The situation cannot be changed,' he said in a low **voice, 'and** any attempt to create strife in this house would force **me to take** back the promise I have just made. Whoever I may present to you, be courageous and strong.'

'I will be,' she answered firmly, 'since it is at that price that I can hope to see my mother again.'

'My dear Palmeri,' said the count.

Annibal drew near.

'Paulette,' continued M. de Moray, **'this gentloman is M.** Annibal Palmeri, the brother of my —— '

He did not dare to say—my wife.

'The brother of Mme. de Moray. And **to you, M.** Palmeri, I present my daughter.'

The Italian saluted Paulette, who bowed to him as she would have done to a stranger she was not going to see again. Still there **was an** effort of good-will in that action for which her father was grateful. Nothing more would have happened had not Claudia been willingly imprudent. The pride of the beautiful woman was not satisfied with the semblance of submission which **the count** had obtained from Paulette, and she wanted at the very outset, to have all the persons who were to live together in this great house put in their proper places. She said to her brother: ·

'M. de Moray has said his daughter. If Miss Paulette consents, I shall say *our* daughter.'

A motion of revolt met these words. Even if her mother had been dead. Even if her father had married again, Paulette would never have allowed any woman to take the sweet name which M. de Moray's first wife would have carried with her to her grave. But this was worse. Her mother was living, and she was suffering, and she was weeping! And a woman, a stranger, dared to claim a title which was not vacant. It was worse than robbery, it was sacrilege! She would never be an accomplice through weakness.

'Your daughter!' she said. 'No, Madam, no! Never call me by that name, because I would not think you were speaking to me, and I would not answer.'

'Ah!' shrieked Claudia, pale with anger.

'I still have a mother, Madam,' continued the child, provocating and disdainful, 'and I keep for her all my respect, all my tenderness, and I have none for anybody else!'

'M. de Moray,' said the countess to her husband, 'will you allow your wife to be thus insulted, when the only fault she has committed was to open her heart too large to the child you love?'

Mme. de Moray was in the right, and the count could not deny her his protection. However, his daughter's words had moved him to his very heart.

'There must be an end to this painful debate,' he said with a firmness he did not feel. 'I shall judge of your affection by the care each of you will take not to provoke such scenes again. Claudia, you shall be respected, but unfortunately I can only promise my daughter's respect, I cannot dispose of her affection. As to you, Paulette, go to your room and await my orders.'

Paulette stepped backwards, and without bidding her father the tender farewell he seemed to expect, swept out of the room. Mme. de Moray went to her room, still irritated by the wound she had received. Before going, Palmeri negligently handed a letter to the count.

'Ah!' he said, 'I was forgetting to give this letter.'

M. de Moray looked at the envelope. It was from Marseilles. He tore the letter open, and nearly fainted.

'Ah!' he said.

'What is the matter?'

'Read for yourself. The Indo-Marseillaise Bank has suspended its payments. Its assets amount to nothing. The funds I depended upon to pay the shareholders of the mine of the Rio-Negro were deposited there! I am lost!'

IV

Annibal Palmeri knew what he was doing in handing that letter to M. de Moray. It contained the confirmation of a telegram he had read the day before. It advised the count of the failure of the Indo-Marseillaise, and the news fell upon him like a thunderbolt.

'Yes, I am lost!' he repeated, walking to and fro.

He stopped in front of Palmeri, who seemed to **be** much surprised and affected by the news he had learnt the evening before.

'You remember,' the count said, 'that a few hours ago I met the General de Saint Rony and the Marquis de Sistenay, and we agreed to reimburse the shareholders of the Rio-Negro. For my part I depended upon the Indo-Marseillaise, and, as the bank has failed, I am dishonored.'

'I beg your pardon,' said Annibal. '**You** forget what I was telling you this morning. You forget that I asked the hand of your daughter. I had not then seen Miss Paulette. **Now** that I have had the pleasure of meeting her, the feeling I experienced towards her has been intensified, and I could hardly renounce her hand.

'But this marriage, which would give my daughter a large fortune, would not give me my honor.'

'You do not understand,' said the Italian, or rather you do not wish to understand. In marrying Miss Paulette, I would become your son-in-law, and you could not prevent me from **offering you** the help you need in this crisis, and this name of son, **I repeat, I** should be happy and proud to wear.'

M. de Moray was deeply moved by his insistance.

'Thank you,' he said giving his hand to Annibal. 'Whatever comes, I shall never forget the words you have just spoken. But even admitting that I had the desire to accept these unexpected propositions, what has happened in your presence must convince you that your dream cannot be realized.'

'Why?'

'You have been a witness of the revolt of Paulette at the presence of another woman than her mother in this house. I had foreseen the existence of this sentiment this morning, but it has exceeded my fears. It is not only a feeling of antipathy which **Pau**lette experiences for those who live in this house ———'

'It is one of hatred,' said Annibal. 'But when your daughter becomes acquainted with the offer I have just made, when she knows that in giving me her hand, she will spare her father the shame of a judgment, her consent will be assured, and provided the marriage takes place within one month, that is to say, before the general meeting of the Rio-Negro, all the shareholders will be

J

indemnified by your notary, to whom I shall give, on signing the contract, the sum necessary to save your honor.'

'Very well!' said M. de Moray, 'I accept the bargain which you propose, but I will not bind myself, however, to use coercion towards my daughter. I shall not do violence to her wishes.'

'It is agreed,' said Annibal.

The two men shook hands and parted. We have already said, that the Neapolitan adventurer was not a bad man at the bottom, so it was with entire good faith that he said to himself, on his way to his room:

'It is lucky for the great lord, who calls himself the Count de Moray, that a mean Italian civil service employee, the son of a ballet girl, has had the idea to personate this Annibal Palmeri. Without me the count had no other resource than to blow out his brains.'

On the same day, about six o'clock in the evening, Maltar went to the Hotel du Louvre and asked at the office the number of the room occupied by a traveller who had arrived in the afternoon, and whose name was Mr. Drack. Every day people of all nations can be seen at the hotel, but the peculiar costume of the Indian provoked the curiosity of the servants. They even mistook him for some rajah's son, and led him, with deep marks of respect, to the room occupied by the English traveller. Maltar saw the error, but said nothing, saying to himself that if he had given his right title he might have been told that Mr. Drack was out.

'His Excellency Prince Maltar wishes to see you, sir,' said the porter, who had followed the Indian to the third story.

'There is a prince wishing to see me?' answered the traveller, very much astonished. 'And you say his name is?'

'Maltar.'

'Maltar! I have a vague idea that I have heard that name before, but the devil take me, if I can remember where.'

'His Excellency wears an Indian costume.'

'Oh, all right!' said Mr. Drack, smiling, who knew then who the prince was. 'Well show his excellency in, since he is an excellency.'

A moment later Maltar and Mr. Drack were alone. The Indian, with his arms crossed, lowered his head, waiting to be allowed to speak. Seeing him so humble Mr. Drack understood that if the good fellow suffered himself to be called a prince, it was with a good intention.

'So you are Maltar?' said the Englishman, 'and you are one of the Count de Moray's servants? I remember you now. You received me this morning on Varennes street. Have you something to tell me?'

'Yes, master' softly answered Maltar.

'Has Miss Paulette sent you? Is she sick?'

'Sick? No.'

'Oh ! so much the better,' said Mr. Drack with a sigh of relief.

And he added, as if ashamed of this kindly feeling.

'Indeed ! I do not know why I asked you that question. I hardly know Miss Paulette. She is neither my sister nor my daughter. If a fellow were to trouble himself about every little girl who may be thrown on his care, under the pretence that she has crossed the ocean with him, or because he happened to fish her out of the sea, as any one else would have done, there would be no end to the bother. So, then, everything passed off smoothly at the count's house after my departure ?' continued the good man, unable to conceal any longer his kind feelings under the mask of egotism. 'Well ! it is very kind of Miss Paulette to let me know of it, because I must tell you that I was somewhat anxious.'

'Miss Paulette did not send me,' said the Indian.

'But then ——'

'And everything did not pass off smothly at the house.

'The devil ! Then explain what brings you here, and tell me who sends you, because I cannot guess.'

Maltar narrated the scenes which had been enacted at the Count de Moray's house. He had been present at some ; others he had guessed, and finally his young mistress, still vibrating with anger and despair, had repeated to him the offers of friendship which had been made to her by the new wife of her father.

'The young mistress is very unhappy,' continued the Indian, 'but she is not the only one to suffer, and there is a person who is still more unhappy than her.

'By jove! I should think so!' cried Mr. Drack with a comical anger, turning around to dry a big tear which Maltar's story had brought to his eyes, 'and that person is myself. Did you ever ? — the idea !—to invade a traveller's room when he is busy unpacking his traps, and tell him stories about all kinds of people he does not care for, but which irritate his nerves. If it happens again, you confounded counterfeit prince, I shall have you kicked out. You know —— somebody more unhappy than poor little Paulette,' he kept on muttering between his teeth ; 'the person you speak of must be devilish wretched. And you say that person is ?'

'The mother of the young mistress,' said the Indian, who had kept still during all this time, waiting for a return of the kindly feelings of the old gentleman, 'the first wife of the Count de Moray. She is not aware of her daughter's arrival, sir, and she does not know that her husband will not allow Miss Paulette to see her.'

'What !' cried Mr. Drack. 'You say that Paulette will not be allowed to see her mother ? But that is atrocious !'

'Yes, it is atrocious !' continued Maltar. 'That poor mother awaits her child's arrival every day, every hour, and she has gathered all her love, all her tenderness, for their first meeting. Poor woman ! What will become of her when I tell her that she will not see her daughter ? She might die with sorrow !'

'Die ! twenty-four hours' delay will not kill her ! If she does not see her to-day, she will see her to-morrow.'

'No, neither to-day nor to-morrow ! Never !'

'How do you know ?'

'After one hour's rest, which she needed badly, the young mistress sent me to her father with a letter, asking him permission to visit her grandfather, M. Firmin de la Marche, where she thought she would meet her mother. Perhaps M. de Moray would have consented, but the new countess, who was then with him, would not allow it.'

'By what right ?' asked Mr. Drack, with indignation, 'and why ?'

'Mme. de Moray said Miss Paulette should not be allowed to see her mother, and even then only very seldom, until she had repented of what she had said, and when she would consent to exhibit to her the respect and the appearances of affection which she owed to the wife of her father.'

'Ah, ah ! This would seem to me exceedingly ridiculous, if I cared at all about all these things,' growled Mr. Drack, upsetting all his toilet articles, which he had just put in order with great care, 'and you have repeated that to the child ? You have been barbarous enough to do that, and you pretend to love Paulette ?'

'I had to. It was the master's order.'

'And what did she say. I will wager that she started to cry.'

'No ! on the contrary.'

'What ! she laughed ?'

'Yes ! But then her laugh was strange and almost threatening. "Then I would rather never see my mother again," she cried, "If I have to pay each one of her kisses with a cowardice and baseness. Do not trouble yourself about me, Maltar. A day will come, sooner than you think, when my mother will be allowed to come and kiss me. It will be the day when she will press her lips to the forehead of her dead daughter !"'

'But, by the heavens ! why do you tell me all this ?' said Mr. Drack, with a gesture of sorrow. 'Can I do anything ? Is there any sense in tormenting one with such stories which do not concern me at all ?'

'I have come to tell you all this,' softly answered the Indian, 'because you must come with me.'

'I ? with you ? where ? To Paulette's ?'

'No, to her mother's.'

The Englishman jumped up.

'Never !' he said. 'I have enough of this family of M. de Moray ! What am I saying ? Enough ! Forsooth ! I have too much of it. I would rather be quartered than be mixed any more with all these stories. And what do you want me to go there for ? If I follow you, I must know, at least, what to say.'

As usual, after having raged and stormed, the excellent man was ready to do anything.

'You will acquaint the mother of the young mistress with what I have told you.'

'Couldn't you do it yourself, by chance ?'

'Yes ; but I cannot tell her anything about the voyage you have made with Miss Paulette ; I could not repeat to her what the young mistress has told you during the journey. Listen ! I am quite sure she was always talking of her mother.'

'Indeed ! she talked of nothing else.'

'She told you of the joy she felt at the idea of meeting her, and how surprised she would be.'

'It was a fixed idea with her.'

'And she made you the confident of all her projects ; of all her hopes.'

'Why she even told me all about a nice young man she expects to marry, and whom she loves dearly.'

'Great heavens !' cried the Indian, astounded. 'Miss Paulette loves a young man ? You are quite certain of that ?'

'More so than I am of my existence which, I commence to think, is very much compromised by the emotions caused by all this confounded business. But what difference does it make that Miss Paulette should love somebody in Pondichéry ?'

'Because, if I understood a few words I heard between my master and another person, M. de Moray has already disposed of the hand of his daughter.'

'Well, that beats all. And in whose favor has he disposed of his daughter's hand without consulting her ?'

'In favor of M. Palmeri, the brother of his new wife.'

'Palmeri ?' said the Englishman. 'Where the devil did I hear that name ? Bah, no matter ! Well, since you must have it so, let us go and see the Countess de Moray.'

While Mr. Drack was methodically closing his toilet-case, Maltar seized the skirt of his coat and was kissing it as a token of gratitude. The two conspirators, because they were nothing else, took a carriage on the street to go to Mme. de Moray's house. Maltar, out of respect, wanted to sit beside the driver, but Mr. Drack pushed him inside the coupe, feigning to offer him the most humble attentions.

'You forget that you are a princely excellency,' observed the Englishman. 'Be careful not to lose your prestige.'

The distance seemed short to them. Absorbed in the emotions which they expected to arise out of their interview with the unhappy woman, they were at her door before they had thought of it.

'Go up first and announce me,' said Mr. Drack.

'No. Come up with me. Only you will wait in the ante-chamber, and I will call you when it is time.'

The servant girl who answered the ring of the bell, welcomed the Indian. He was, in fact, the only human being Mme. de Moray had seen since she lived in that house, like a recluse. Maltar visited her frequently, unknown to M. de Moray. He had tried everything which the generosity of his heart could invent to relieve the sufferings of his mistress. He had even the courage to present himself at the house of Admiral Firmin de la Marche to acquaint him with the gravity of the state of his daughter, and to supplicate him to be less severe toward his daughter, at least for a few days. The old sailor had stopped him as soon as he understood the object of his errand. In his prodigious stubbornness with regard to his honor, M. de la Marche could have seen his own daughter exposed to the most cruel and imminent danger without lifting a finger to help her out of it. Shocked by this inexorable severity, Maltar was constantly near his mistress ; he not only visited her house now and then, but he had passed every night there as long as there was danger. After he had finished his service at M. de Moray's, he would come and do the work of a nurse, or rather of a sister of charity, at the bed-side of the unhappy woman, who had at least, in her delirious dreams, the illusion of thinking herself still at Pondichéry, in the happy time when loving affections surrounded her. During Maltar's watch the servant rested and gathered strength for the next day's work. When the poor martyr felt better, the Indian came less often, because M. de Moray might learn of his visits and forbid them. But he soon discovered that his presence was the only relief to the sufferings of her whom he had never looked upon as guilty : even if he had thought so, he would have pitied her and cared for her with the same devotion. This was the reason which had led him two or three days before to leave the house of the Count de Moray, in order to devote himself entirely to the service of his benefactress.

The reader will remember the scene when M. de Moray asked the faithful servant to remain in the old house on Varennes street, invoking him to remain in the name of Paulette, who was to arrive shortly, and who would want to find some one near her to whom she could speak of her mother. Between the two duties thus presented to him, Maltar had chosen the one he thought most sacred. The young mistress would suffer so much among these strangers ! She would find herself so far from any sincere affection ! and then she was not used to sorrow, while her mother was. He had promised M. de Moray that he would remain at his post. But he had not made this promise without restrictions. He would always be

at liberty to change his decision, **if** Paulette should become resigned
to her new situation. Then, breaking every tie, he would devote
his whole life to her **who** would not and could not be comforted.
The proud **revolt** of Paulette when she heard the terrible revelations
which she should **have** known before, proved to the Indian the prudence of his conduct, and he congratulated himself **on** the choice he
had made between the two duties which **we** have **just** mentioned.

As it had been decided, Maltar went to Mme. **de Moray's** room
alone. We still give her that name, as the Indian does, **in** spite of
the sorrowful protestations of Laura. It **was** night, **and a wax**
candle lighted the parlor. The poor martyr, seated in an **arm-chair,**
remained inactive; she had nothing to occupy her mind, except **to**
recall the remembrances of the past. When she heard the voice of
her friend, that was the name she gave him, and it filled him with
deep gratitude, she lifted her head.

' I did not think **I** would **see you to-day,' she** said. 'I had understood that **you had announced your visit** only for to-morrow
night.'

She gave him her hand, which **he pressed to** his lips.

' What brings you, then ? Alas ! **I need not** ask ! because **you** '
cannot but bring tales of sorrow.'

' Mistress,' Maltar said, slowly, because he understood the necessity of not jarring the nerves of the poor lady, ' to-day we had
news from the young mistress.'

Laura got up, as if moved by a spring. She placed her **hand**
upon her heart, which was beating as if it was going to break.

' Ah ! ' she said, with a faltering voice. ' Paulette, where is she ?
When will she arrive ? Tell me, oh, tell me. Don't you see you **are**
killing me ? '

' The vessel has arrived in Marseilles.'

' To-day ? '

' Oh, no. Two days ago.'

' Two days ! but then she will soon **be in** Paris, to-morrow, this
evening ? Perhaps she is here **now.** You do not answer ! Oh, I un-
derstand your silence ; you want to spare me the emotion of her
return ! My daughter has arrived already, I shall see her in an **hour**
—in a moment, ah, she is there ! My heart tells me she is **behind**
that door, **and** she awaits one word from **me** to rush into **my arms**
—but why don't you come, Paulette ? Hurry and come **into your**
mother's arms and rest upon the heart which beats for you **only.'**

The poor woman had raised her voice, **so** that her words **might**
cross the thickness of the door to reach her daughter's ears. With arms
outstretched, panting, and with fixed eyes she looked at that door,
which was **so** long opening, and Maltar **was** trying to calm her,
when **a noise in** the antechamber doubled **her fever.**

'Don't you hear me, Paulette?' cried the poor mother, desperately. 'Still I hear you.'

Rushing towards the hall, before Maltar could prevent her, she violently pushed open the door which seemed to her the only obstacle between her kisses and those of her darling child. A small lamp shed a shadowy light through the room. Instead of the beloved girl she expected to seize in her arms, Laura saw a man standing up, a man whom she did not know. A shriek of shattered hope and fright escaped from her lips.

'Ah!' she cried, drawing back as if she had seen a spectre. 'There! there! Who is there?'

And as Mr. Drack followed her she shrieked:

'Maltar! a man! a man!'

The Indian caught her in his arms as she was falling.

'Take courage, mistress,' he said with his usual softness which always soothed her. 'The man who is there is a friend, and he has come to speak to you of the young mistress, whose friend, and only friend he is, with Maltar.'

'Ah!' said the mother, suddenly mellowed, 'you are a friend of my daughter, and you have come to speak of her to me. Perhaps you will take me to her. Then, be blessed! a thousand times. Thank you! thank you!' muttered the poor woman, pressing the hands of Paulette's friend, and bathing them with her tears.

This time we give up all idea of describing the state of mind Mr. Drack was in. The feeling uppermost in him was anger. He was literally furious. Furious at feeling so much emotion. Furious because he was thus upsetting the principles of his whole life. He had worked himself up to that pitch of anger while waiting in the antechamber, where he was making bitter reflections on his actual situation. At first, egotism had prompted him to run away before the Indian would call him, as agreed between them, but a second thought, a thought of good and generous charity, had forced him to sit down and wait. It was at that moment that he had involuntarily moved a chair, and the noise had caused Laura to believe that her daughter was there, near her. Now the good Mr. Drack found himself caught in the cogs of the wheel, and since he had been so unwise as to put his fingers into them, he must pass through it bodily. As it annoyed him to see the poor woman crying, he seated her in an arm-chair, took a handkerchief which was on a table and dried her tears.

'There! there!' he said, like a father who is trying to smother the last spasms of despair of his child. 'It will be all right, dear madam! your daughter is not lost! you will see her again!'

By again and again repeating this promise, in which he did not believe much himself, after what the Indian had told him, Mr. Drack succeeded in soothing Laura to a certain extent.

'Pardon me,' said the unhappy woman to the new friend who was entering into her life so suddenly, 'I am ungrateful towards you, who come to speak to me of my beloved child, but you cannot know how wretched and unhappy I am !'

'Yes !' said the Englishman, trying to repair the disorder of his dress, ' yes, I know all. The prince——No, Maltar, I mean to say —Maltar has told me everything.'

'He has told you only what he knew, with all the kindness of his boundless devotion,' said the wretched woman, smothering a sigh. 'But I am still more unhappy than Maltar could have told you, and than I could have imagined myself, since the very sight of my child is denied to me on the day of her arrival. As for you, sir, may God bless you for your kindness in speaking to me of my dear child.'

A long conversation followed, incessantly interrupted by the endless questions of the anxious mother, who wished to hear everything all at once. The Englishman had to narrate, with the minutest details, the long ocean voyage, the arrival at Marseilles, the sickness of Aunt Basilique, and at last the arrival of Paulette at the old house of her father. And as he was furious at his own devotedness to the young girl he carefully omitted the recital of the storm before entering the port, the falling of Paulette into the sea, and her rescue by him, Sir Elias Drack.

'And you say,' asked Laura, shivering, 'that the darling knew nothing on her arrival at Paris ? That neither her aunt nor yourself dared to forwarn her ! Then her father had the terrible task of telling her everything. However cruel M. de Moray may have shown himself towards me in his merciless revenge, I pity him,' she continued with an involuntary shiver. 'In his place I do not think I should have had the courage to reveal to my daughter the extent of her unhappiness ! Oh ! the dear and wretched child, how she must have suffered and how I pity her ! But you do not tell me how Paulette has borne the ordeal ?'

'How could I tell you,' answered Mr. Drack. 'I left Varennes street just at the moment when, thank God, my mission was ended by leaving the child with her father. Maltar alone can tell you the rest.'

It was the Indian's turn to be interrogated. The martyr wanted to know with a precision and an astonishing minuteness of details how Paulette was ; if she had regained all her health, and if she had borne with courage the terrible knowledge of the sad event which had made her almost an orphan. The poor woman was divided between two contrary wishes equally well known to the heart of a mother, namely, that the child could not bear to be separated from her mother, and that, however, her suffering was not above her strength. Suddenly, just as she was going to ask the

Indian a new question, Laura became ashy pale. A horrible doubt, an uneasiness which had not occured to her mind as yet, was being intensely felt by her now. And this time, it was with a feeling of fear that she interrogated Maltar.

'What did my daughter say,' she asked softly, 'when she learned the cause assigned by her father to obtain a judgment of divorce between himself and me? How did she judge her mother? Did she accept without a protest the accusation of the crime I did not deny in the presence of my judges?'

'The young mistress knows nothing of the events which have preceded or accompanied the judgment of divorce,' said Maltar, happy to have this consolation to offer to the unhappy woman. 'M. de Moray has told her nothing. He only spoke of grave dissensions which had arisen between you and him.'

'God be blessed!' cried Laura, joining her hands in an action of gratitude, 'at least my daughter will not be ashamed of her mother. But alas! her ignorance cannot last long. A very legitimate and ardent desire to know all will seize upon her mind. And if she does not find out by chance, there are now in the house where Paulette will live people who hate me, and who will acquaint her with what she should not know. That woman, oh! that woman who wears my name and who occupies my place near my husband, near my child, that woman is my mortal enemy.'

Time had passed very rapidly during this interview, in which so much suffering had been revealed to the noble martyr. She had been spared only the knowledge of two things, and these would only be revealed to her when there was no longer any reason for silence.

In the first place, she was not told positively that she would not see Paulette, and indeed a contrary expression was left on her mind. The prohibition of M. de Moray was talked of as only a transitory measure, and Mr. Drack said nothing of the project of the marriage which was to throw her daughter into the arms of Annibal Palmeri, the brother of the second Countess de Moray. Then what was the use of uselessly tormenting the poor mother, who had already enough sufferings to bear? Be that as it may, Mr. Drack, who had secretly sworn to have nothing more to do with that confounded family, as he expressed himself, promised to Laura that he would come and see her again before his departure from Paris.

'And when do you expect to go away?' asked Maltar, anxiously.

'To-morrow,' answered the Englishman firmly.

'To-morrow,' said Laura, afflicted at the thought of losing that new friend, who was so kind to her.

'Yes, madam,' and meeting her eyes full of tears, 'to-morrow a

week, or two weeks —— or ——. Do I know when ? I shall depart
when you and our dear little Paulette tell me : '' We do not require
your services any longer, Sir Elias Drack, go away ! '' '

V.

Let us now return to M. Firmin de la Marche's house. The reader
will remember that after the murder of the young man who remained unknown, and whom everybody designated as the lover of
the first Countess de Moray, the admiral had left the house on
Varennes street, to go and take up a residence in the neighbourhood
of the Trocadero. It was there, on Longchamp street, that the old
and loyal sailor was hiding the stain which he thought the pretended
adultery of his daughter had cast on his spotless honor. There
Laura had come, like a mendicant, to implore her father not to be
so severe, and having been mercilessly driven away, she had remained several hours, depressed and heart-sore, on the stairway, at
the door of her father's house.

The reader knows what tenderness Mme. de la Marche bore to
Laura. It had been very painful to her to obey the will of her
husband and to leave her daughter in such a complete state of abandonment, denied all affection and all pity. Very often the wretched
mother had prayed to her husband, supplicating to be allowed to go
and see her daughter, or at least to be allowed to write to her. The
admiral had shown himself inflexible. If she did not rebel against
that iron will, if she humbly bowed her head, it was because the
dark mystery of her past life imposed upon her a resignation without limit to the orders of her husband. The guilty woman she had
been in her youth could not have in her old age the right to enter
into open rebellion against the outraged authority of the husband.
Only the more she submitted to the impassive judge of her daughter,
the more bitter were the sufferings she endured herself. She suffered
at the same time by her own sorrows, and by those which her
silence imposed on Laura. One day, while alone in her room, she
opened the Holy Scriptures, as she used to do very often, and she

d the words which suited too well her gloomy thoughts : ' The
children of adulterers,' the Book of Wisdom said, ' shall not come
to perfection, and the seed of the unlawful bed shall be rooted
out.'

' Alas ! ' thought the poor woman, ' how cruel these words are,
and still they are beneath the truth, for in my case it is not only the

child of my own adultery who has been punished ; even the legitimate offspring bears the weight of my fault.'

She continued : ' And if they live long,' said the book, ' their last
old age shall be without honor, and if they die quickly they shall
have no hope nor speech of comfort in the day of trial.'

The tears which filled her eyes prevented her from reading any
more.

' What has become of the child of my shame ?' she thought. ' Is
he already dead without hope, or is he living without honor and
without consolation ? I know nothing, nothing of him. But I can
easily guess to what trials he has been subjected by the sufferings
which have been heaped on the daughter who was not sullied by
any original fault.'

Then she cried in despair :

' Laura ! my poor Laura ! my beloved daughter ! what a long
time has elapsed since I have been permitted to see you ? what
bitter tears you must have shed ! '

Her maternal love revolted against the harshness of the Book of
Wisdom.

' Let her, who was guilty,' she cried, ' be punished ! My God, it
is only just, and I submit. But to prevent the guilty mother to
suffer with her daughter and console her is too hard, yes, too hard ! '

As she was drying her tears, M. de la Marche entered the room.
He said to her, harshly :

' You are still crying ? '

' Alas ! ' humbly answered Mme. de la Marche, ' to obey you my
face shows the appearance of a firmness which my heart belies. But
to-day my courage gave way ; just think, it is three months since I
have seen my daughter.'

' Your daughter ! ' cried the admiral. ' I have forbidden you to
pronounce that name. The woman who bore it is dead to us.'

' Then, give me the liberty of crying. Was there ever a mother
forbidden the right to cry over her dead child ? '

' Suppose, then, if you prefer, that she has never existed.'

' How can you believe that I will suppose that, when I know that
she is within hearing, that her sobs come through these walls, and
when, for the past three months she lives in a horrible solitude, a
divorced wife, an accursed daughter !! '

The admiral, however strong was his will over himself and over
others was startled.

' I forbade you,' he said, ' ever to mention her name.'

Mme. de la Marche had more courage than at other times, and
she dared to insist.

' However guilty Laura may have been,' she continued, ' she is
your daughter ! Remember the love you have felt for her ! '

The old man had regained his self-possession, and he answered in
an implacable tone :

'The tenderer my love was when I believed her worthy of it, the more merciless is my anger to-day. For the last time, I forbid you to speak of her.'

'Well, if you refuse all pity to your child,' said Mme. de la Marche, joining her hands, 'at least show mercy towards me : Believe me, I have neither your strength nor your courage. I am only a **woman**! I am only a mother! I pray **to you on** bended knees! allow me to see my daughter!'

'No! she will never enter this house. Never!'

'Oh! my God! not here, since you do not **wish it ; but at her** home, secretly.'

'**No**! I tell you ; do not ask **that.** The punishment **of the fault** committed without **excuse** must be merciless.'

'Without excuse, **you affirm**! **Who** knows if there is not **one she** could invoke ?'

'There is no excuse for the treason of a wife!'

Mme. de la Marche felt deeply wounded. In condemning her daughter, the husband was pronouncing her own sentence. So, in pleading the cause of her daughter, she was defending her own.

'Ah!' she said, '**since** you show yourself so merciless, it is because you do not know what fatal circumstances might surround a woman and cause her **to** fall. A feeling of love, undoubtedly criminal, but unconscious, **at** first creeps into her heart unknown to herself. Who knows that afterwards she did not struggle vigorously against that **love.** Perhaps she has called to her help the husband who was absent. Who knows that the betrayer has not contrived a plot into which the unfortunate **woman has** fallen, despairing and affrighted ? What can a woman **do in such** a case, then ? She resists, she fights, she implores!'

'No!' said the admiral. 'She dies.'

'And if at the time she is to strike the **fatal blow, she remem**bers she has a child, a daughter whom she adores ?'

'She dies for that child,' repeated the old man with the same en**ergy.** 'She dies! so that her fault **may** not sully the daughter as **it** sullies the husband and the father.'

Mme. de la Marche was silenced, overwhelmed and vanquished at last. We have said that in the desperate attempt she had made on behalf of Laura, she was pleading her own cause. She had done it with so much sincerity and animation that for a few moments she had forgotten the fault and the punishment of her daughter in thinking only of the fault committed by herself, and which, unknown **to her** husband, had not been punished by him.

'Ah!' she answered at last,' you are right. It would have been better to have died!' and she was speaking about herself.

We have not told our readers that Paulette had made a visit to **M.** and Mme. **de** la Marche. It was eight days since their grand-daughter had visited them when the above conversation took place. M. de Moray had advised them by letter that Miss de Moray, who had just arrived, would present her **respects** to her grand-parents during the day. The interview had been very short, and if we may be allowed to use the word, very embarrassing. On the lips of the grand-mother, and on those of the grand-daughter, was a word, a name, which was burning them, and which both were wishing to repeat amid their tears. But M. de Moray had allowed his daughter to visit her grand-parents only on condition that that very name would not be mentioned. On the other hand, the admiral would not allow Mme. de la Marche to receive **Paulette** unless no allusion whatever was made to the one who, although her mother, had not the right to be called by the same name as her daughter. Under these circumstances, what words could be freely exchanged between the grand-mother and the child. The remembrance of the absent one had stopped every other, **as they** would have thought of committing an impiety by holding a common-place conversation. These two women, placed at the two extremes of age, and still united by sorrow, had embraced each other, mingling their tears, and that was all. Paulette had gone, saying she would **come a** week after, on the same day.

The day indicated had arrived, and one hour only was wanting for the time of that second interview, when the servant brought in a card which he gave to the admiral.

'Sir Elias Drack,' he said, trying to remember. '**That** name is not unknown to me. What may that gentleman have to tell me? Well, we shall know.'

While waiting for the stranger, M. de la Marche prevailed upon his wife to suppress her tears. She had hardly done so when Paulette's companion entered the room.

'Be welcome, sir,' said the admiral, '**and please sit down.**'

In showing him to a seat, the admiral looked at his visitor, and the Englishman's face recalled an indistinct **recollection.**

'I do not know, sir, if I am mistaken,' said he, hesitating, 'but it seems to me this is not the first time we meet.'

'Faith! admiral!' answered Mr. Drack,' I was just thinking about the same thing. And I remember now. It was in Calcutta, where, although I was only an English merchant, I occupied the post of consul of Italy.'

'Exactly so,' said M. de la Marche. 'I remember also. It was at a banquet given by the clubs of that city to **the** officers of my squadron, during **the** few days **we** passed there.'

'**I was** one of **the** organizers of that banquet, and as I speak French pretty well, I was charged to welcome the brave sailors placed under your orders. Between you and me, 1 was annoyed and flattered both by the proceeding. I am a quiet man, and anything changed in my every-day habits upsets me. And the idea of making a speech, I who had never spoken in public, was more than I could bear.'

' But you did much better than many professional speakers, politely said the admiral.' I have a pleasant recollection of that banquet, and also of the speech you made. And you have given up trade ?'

' And the consulate **at the same** time, yes, admiral.'

' And definitely ?'

' Oh, yes, definitely. I do not deny that I thought **of** asking **my** government the favor of entering into the diplomatic service.'

' It is a difficult career for those who do not enter it very **young.**'

' In olden times, Admiral, you would have been right, but **it is** much simplified now-a-days.'

' How is that ?'

' Undoubtedly. All the science of our political men consists of two very simple ideas. The first is, naturally, to get into power.'

' And the second ?'

' When they get there, it is to stay **in.**'

' Then, decidedly, you shall serve your country **again,**' said the admiral, smiling at this whim.

' No, Admiral. **I** have decided to abandon public **affairs to de-**vote myself entirely——'

' To your own ?'

' To rest only. Rest will become the sole occupation **of my life** after I have acquitted myself of a mission, which is **all the more** delicate as I am not at all personally interested in it.'

' A mission ? From whom ?'

' From Mlle. de Moray, Admiral.'

Until then Mme. de la Marche had taken no part in the conversation, but the name of her grand-daughter awakened her interest.

' Paulette has sent you ?' she said. ' You know **my** grand-daughter ?'

' I had the pleasure to cross the ocean with her and to escort her to Paris, because her aunt **was** unable to continue the journey.'

' Doubtless you know,' **said** the admiral, ' that Miss Basilique, the Count de Moray's sister, **has** died at Marseilles ?'

' I heard it this morning. Miss Paulette, who was very much affected by this bad news, told me of it.'

' You have seen my grand-daughter this morning ?' said Mme. de la Marche, surprised at the intimacy existing between a stranger and M. **de** Moray's daughter, ' and she has entrusted you with a mission ?'

' Well, Madam,' answered the Englishman with a good-natured smile, ' under **the** pretence that I have **had** occasion to be useful to her once, Miss Paulette thinks I am bound to humor all her fan-

cies. As I am not strong-minded, I do not resist, and in this way
I avoid discussions which would trouble my rest, and I have become her factotum.'

'And she sends you, undoubtedly, to tell us she would not pay
us a visit to-day?'

'I beg your pardon. That is not exactly what I came for. I must
even acknowledge that I have somewhat altered the truth in saying
that Miss Paulette has sent me. I have taken upon myself to do
what I am doing now. I have borrowed Miss Paulette's name only
to engage your attention.'

'Then why do you come, sir,' asked the admiral, who was getting annoyed.

'To speak to you of Miss Paulette's mother, Admiral, of Mme.
de Moray.

It was really too bad that Sir Elias Drack had abandoned the
diplomatic career. He would have rendered great services to his
country, if we may judge of his talent by the ability he had displayed in pronouncing Mme. de Moray's name in the admiral's
house. Anybody else, in trying other means. would have been put
out. But M. de la Marche had been caught unawares, and he could
only protest feebly.

'You come to speak to me of Paulette's mother?' he asked,
irresolutely, not knowing what to do or say.

'Of Laura! of our daughter!' whispered Mme. de la Marche.

'Yes, sir,—yes, Madam,' answered Sir Elias Drack, in the most
artless way, 'of your daughter. You are probably not aware that
M. de Moray has forbidden his daughter to see her mother,
which is an action exceedingly cruel and odious.'

'You think so,' said the admiral, severely. 'For my part, I believe M. de Moray's action to be perfectly just and legitimate.'

'That is what I was saying,' continued the Englishman. 'Just,
but cruel; legitimate, but odious. We are exactly of the same
opinion. It is exactly the same thing as if you forbade the baroness
here present, to see her daughter.'

'But I do forbid her, sir, and I do not understand that you
should take the liberty——'

'Nor I either, admiral, I do not understand it,' answered Sir
Elias Drack. 'It surprises me to find myself interfering in family
affairs I care nothing about. But I do as people do who have a dislike
of cold water and who fall in the river, I must swim to get out of it.
So, I was telling you that Miss Paulette not being allowed to see
her mother, I went myself to the home of Mme. Laura, whom I was
not acquainted with, to give her notice of her child's return to Paris.
A beautiful woman, sir, is Mme. Laura, but she looks very unwell,
I must tell you.'

'Sir!' said the admiral, getting angry.

But the **more angry** M. **de la Marche** was getting, the cooler **Sir** Elias became.

'Well, imagine **that I** have been subjected **to** a very trying ordeal, I, who have **not** your strong-minded character, Admiral, when I saw Miss Paulette's mother pass successively from extreme joy to extreme despair. Happy at the thought of knowing that **her** daughter was **so** near, after such a long absence, she nearly **fainted** in my arms on hearing of the hard-heartedness **of the Count de** Moray, who would not allow his daughter to receive **her mother's kisses.**'

'Oh! unhappy woman,' whispered Mme **de la** Marche.

'I had thought,' continued Sir Elias **Drack,** coolly, '**that time** would appease these emotions. Not at all, sir, they are growing **worse;** and now, each of them, Miss Paulette and Mme. Laura, **seem to** have an understanding to die **of** sorrow. Then I had an idea **(I** have ideas sometimes), and **I** said to myself : Since M. de Moray will **not** allow Miss Paulette to go to her mother, there is only one way **of** fixing this **matter.** See how very simple it is. I said this morning to Mme. Laura : "Your daughter will **go** to-day to her grand-father's, why **not** go yourself? And there, **on** neutral ground, you shall see and kiss your child **at** your ease."'

The admiral **cut** him short.

'But I **again tell you,** sir,' he cried, with the thundering voice he used to have **on board** his vessel, 'that **I** will not see the person you speak of.'

'I know that, admiral. I perfectly understand. But this is **where my** idea becomes altogether clever. **Did** you notice the fine **weather we** have to-day, admiral? Just the kind of weather to crowd all sails, and run eleven knots an hour, before the wind. You **are** near the Bois de Boulogne. Go and take a walk and **during** that time the baroness will receive **her** daughter and her **grand-daughter.**'

'I have told you also that I forbid **Mme.** de la Marche **to see the** person you speak of,' brutally said **the** admiral.

'Bravo! better and better,' said **the** Englishman. 'Mme. de **la Marche** will **go** with you. You will take a walk around the lake, arm in arm, **and Mme** Laura and Miss Paulette will meet here during that time. **You** readily understand how happy you will make these **poor** women, this mother and this daughter, who have not seen each other for **a year,** and who have so many things to tell each other.'

The admiral exploded at this insistance, **so** cutting in its artless impudence. He even forgot **in** his **anger, that** he had forbidden his own lips ever to pronounce **the name of** his daughter.

'Laura shall not come here,' **he cried** with an oath, 'she knows **she must not** come here.'

'**I beg your** pardon, but she will **come.**'

K

'She would dare ! after I drove her out of my house.'

'She will dare, Admiral. Because I told her to do so, and I promised to obtain your permission.'

'You have not done that ?'

'I beg your pardon, but I have. Mme. Laura will come to your door, to await your decision, and to tell the truth she is there now.'

'At my door ?'

'In the street, under your window, hid in a cab, waiting for a signal which will give her the greatest joy, or throw her into the depths of despair.'

'A signal.'

'Very ingenious. On arriving, Mme. Laura showed me your apartment and told me :—"Behind that window are my father and mother." And I answered : "I will try to soften the heart of your father. If I succeed, I will open the window and you will come up. If I fail I will let the curtain drop, in which case you will return to your lonely abode."'

The ex-consul had hardly finished speaking when the admiral almost tore the curtain which was to acquaint Laura that the efforts of Sir Elias Drack had failed.

'Ah ! what are you doing ?' cried Mme, de la Marche, trying to stop her husband.

The Englishman prevented her.

'Let him go !' he said in a low voice.

After a few seconds of a deep silence, the diplomat uttered an exclamation of surprise.

'By Jove !' he cried. 'What have I done ?'

'What do you mean ?' asked the admiral.

'I have made a mistake.'

'How ?'

'In my trouble, in my emotion, I made a mistake, I tell you. It was in case you would consent to let Mme. Laura come in that I was to drop the curtain.'

'Oh ! my God !' cried Mme. de la Marche, understanding the clever comedy just played.

'So that now ?' asked the admiral, at the same time furious to have been the dupe of a pious treachery, and moved to the innermost of his soul at the thought that his daughter, answering the signal, would appear before him.

'So that now,' said Sir Elias, speaking slowly to give time for Laura to arrive, 'thanks to my blunder, Mme. Laura has entered the house, she has climbed the stairs, her heart trembling with gratitude and emotion, she has knocked at your door, and—and—here, admiral, here she is.'

Just as the Englishman spoke these last words, Laura opened the door of her mother's room, and remained a moment on the threshold, hardly breathing. She was so pale, so changed, so different from her old self, that even her friends would hardly have known her. But the heart of a mother could only see in the distress of her child one more motive to love and pity her. However rigorous might have been the orders of the admiral, Mme. de la Marche could not resist the sentiment which overcame her.

'Laura!' she cried, 'My daughter!'

And for the first time in three months the two women found themselves closely clasped together.

'Well! well!' thought Sir Elias Drack, rubbing his hands with modest triumph,' decidedly, I think I could have entered diplomacy! I would not have been more clumsy than others.'

Surprised himself, and laboring under an insuperable emotion, the admiral stood as if paralyzed. A little more, and he would have rushed to his daughter's arms, like his wife. But his anger getting the better of him, he tore his wife from her child. Then he said to Laura :

'By error or treachery you have thought yourself authorized to cross the threshold of the door which I kept closed to you until now. Sir Elias Drack, in his quality of occasional diplomat, has been guilty of a lie!——'

'An error, admiral!' he said humbly. 'A simple error for which I alone am responsible.'

Laura joined her hands and looked at her father through the tears which blinded her eyes.

'The most unhappy,' she said, 'have access to your house, my father ; and I swear to you that of all those who come here, there is not one whose fate is more worthy of pity than mine!'

'Undoubtedly,' cried the admiral, 'because there is not one who is as guilty as you are!'

Sir Elias Drack was then near Mme. de la Marche.

'Have courage,' he said in a low voice to the noble old mother, who was violently trembling, 'since he listens to his daughter, he will forgive.'

'Alas!' answered the poor woman, 'you do not know the merciless will of my husband. My daughter has come here only to return still more unhappy than before.'

What followed seemed to prove the fears of Mme. de la Marche. The admiral showed the door to his daughter.

'Go,' he said coolly, 'and may the remembrance of your crime prevent you from again entering this house!'

Laura made a last effort.

'If my crime deserved such a chastisement,' she said with touching tenderness, 'it belonged to another, to my husband, not to you, my father, to inflict it, and he has very cruelly struck me.

'M. de Moray has spared your life, and you say you have been cruelly struck?' interrupted the admiral.

'I have been driven away and repudiated. Death, if the man whom the law constituted my judge had given it, would have been a punishment less severe. And still,' she said in a mysterious and involuntary protest, 'it seems to me that now, since I plead the cause of my daughter and mine, that a sentiment of rebellion springs up in my heart, and that sentiment tells me that I have been more cruelly punished than I deserved.'

And while she was saying these words her voice had acquired new energy, and her dazzling look seemed to burst the shadows which darkened her reason. The cold and severe voice of the admiral brought her back to herself, or rather plunged her anew into her painful mania.

'Others than M. de Moray would have been still more merciless,' said the admiral. 'I, yes, I who speak, if I had been your husband, I would have taken a more terrible revenge, and then I should have died of despair and shame.'

'It is true,' said Laura indistinctly, 'I could have been deprived of my life as well as of my happiness. It is for that reason I submitted without protesting or resisting to the will of my—of the man who was my husband. But towards you, my father, I have been guilty of no offence. I have always been to you and my mother a dutiful and devoted daughter. And I entreat you, in remembrance of that devotion, to take pity on me.'

There was an immense despair in this heart-rending prayer. Although it was none of his business, and he was sure nothing which did not touch him personally could move him, Sir Elias Drack was biting his lips to smother a sob which was rising in his throat, he knew not why.

'Here, admiral,' he said, 'that is true. Unless you are a cannibal, you will have pity.'

M. de la Marche, without even hearing him, answered his daughter.

'Your only hope is that age and sorrow will drown my memory. As long as I remember, I can do nothing for you.'

'Oh! what can I say to convince you?' cried Laura once more. 'Can one fault erase the remembrances of a whole life? Remember! Was it not you whom I cherished more than anything in the world, when a little child, I escaped from my mother's arms to run into yours? Later, as a young girl, I was so proud to lean on your arm? Remember, father! oh, remember!'

'The more I remember,' said the old man, whose anger seemed to be still increasing, the greater abhorrence I feel for her who has poisoned the sweet remembrances you evoke! Go! accursed daughter!

and hope that I may forget the tenderness and love I had for you, to be able to forget your crime at the same time.'

This time Laura felt vanquished. At these words : Accursed daughter, at the remembrance of that terrible malediction, which had contributed to drive her mad, she had started, her blood had been frozen in her veins. She resigned herself.

'Very well !' she said, 'be merciless, my father, and may God have pity on you. I shall not implore your forgiveness or your pity for myself. I shall speak to you now in the name of another. It is for her sake that my exile must cease. It is to save her life that I must be free to enter this house at will.'

'You must !' said the admiral, astonished at this new departure. 'And why *must you*, as you say ?'

'Because my daughter has returned, whom I have not seen for almost one year, and that she may be enabled to visit me. Heed not the sorrows of the guilty woman, since that is your will. But do not inflict the same punishment on the poor child, so pure and innocent ! Do not deprive her of her mother's caresses ; and if she does not meet me here, where can I see her ? M. de Moray's house is a paradise closed to me forever. You are also aware that Paulette is forbidden to enter the house of a condemned woman.'

'That is true,' thought the admiral, moved at last. 'Poor Paulette !'

Laura continued to plead with more force. She was gathering strength, as the struggle went on, like all mothers fighting for their children.

'But think of it,' she said again. 'You must allow my daughter to come and see me, to kiss me, to cry with me, and right here. It is not into the heart of the second wife her father has taken that she will pour her confidence and her sorrows. And then, if it is not in M. de Moray's house, or in mine, that we are able to meet, *it must* be in yours. Because, at last, if you throw me out, I shall be obliged, to meet my daughter, to stand at the corner of the streets and to beg one of her looks, to ask for her kisses as a charity. Do not require that from me, father, because, indeed, it is too much, yes, too much.'

'Oh ! unhappy child !' thought the admiral, hesitating and fighting against his heart.

'Don't you see what she suffers !' said Mme. de la Marche to her husband.

By a strange phenomenon, Laura's mother was not crying any more. All of a sudden she had transformed herself, as if she had taken a grave resolution. Elias Drack, who was then looking at her, was stupefied at the change in her face.

'Decidedly, I begin to find all this very amusing,' he thought, trying to stifle his feelings.

On hearing his wife asking him if he did not notice Laura's sufferings, the admiral betrayed himself.

'And don't you see the sufferings I endure,' he cried. 'Do you not understand that my own heart is torn as much as hers. All my being urges me to open my heart and my arms to her. And still I must not; I cannot, and I will not!' he ended, striking the floor with rage. 'She must go!'

Laura held up her head, which she had hitherto kept lowered.

'Your will shall be done, my father, I am going away. But I pray to the Almighty that, on the day of his judgment he may be less severe towards you than you have been towards your child. Farewell!'

She started to go away, but her strength failed her, and she staggered. Mme. de la Marche ran to help her and caught her in her arms.

'Laura, my child!' she cried.

'Mother dear!' answered the poor woman. 'At least I have never doubted your love. It would be sweet for me to die now, resting on your loving heart, as I used to in happier days, and gathering the dew of your tears on my face.'

'Unhappy child! you wish to die!'

'Oh! yes,' answered the martyr, with a celestial smile, 'I wish to die in your arms, mother, and in my beloved daughter's arms. Give me another kiss, dear mother, and now that I have received it, let me go. If I remained here longer, I would not have the strength to leave, and I should fall there, despairing, dead! Farewell! mother! farewell!'

'No,' cried Mme. de la Marche, 'I cannot leave you thus. Listen,' turning towards the inflexible admiral.

'What do you wish?'

'I want to tell you that this struggle against your own heart cannot last any longer; that repentance calls for forgiveness, and that tears deserve pity! You will not repulse your child who prostrates herself at your feet!'

The admiral was like one of those lunatics who hear nothing, and are always trying to break their heads against the walls of their cells.

'No! no! no!' he cried vehemently.

Mme. de la Marche raised Laura, who was on her knees.

'Then, get up, Laura,' she said firmly, 'we shall go together!'

'Ah! my mother!' cried Laura distracted.

'What are you doing?' asked the admiral.

'My duty,' nobly answered Mme. de la Marche, 'I quit the house from which my child is banished to go and weep with her.'

'You wish to leave me, your husband! the old man whose name is above reproach.

'To follow my repented child, yes!'

'Go, then!' said the admiral. 'And I hope that with your departure, the remembrance of forty years of devotion and affection may be wiped out for **you** and for me. I had thought that death alone could part us; and now I shall wait for **it** anxiously. Farewell! then, farewell!'

And he made **a** gesture to drive away **from** his house the only beings he had loved, his wife and his daughter, but his heart broke and he fell into an arm-chair, sobbing bitterly. Sir Elias Drack, at the sight of his tears, began to cough loudly. He took **out a** handkerchief which he feigned to put to his mouth, but in **reality**, it **was** to dry his eyes. Laura, hearing her mother say she **was going to** leave her husband's house to weep with her, felt **an** immense **joy in** the midst of her sorrow. But the **despair of the old man shattered** the sudden hope which had **sprung** up **in her heart.**

'Mother,' she said softly, '**look** at **my father.** He weeps; he **who was not** moved by the storms of the ocean, or in **the midst of battles. He** weeps, and you would leave him! No, no, remain with him, mother! I do not wish him to know the anguish of loneliness and abandonment. I have been already, through the fault I am expiating, a cause of sorrow to my father, and I do not want to add anything to **the** burden of his woes. Remain with him, mother, and keep my heart between yourselves.'

Saying this, she gave a parting embrace **to** the mother whom **her** self-denial repulsed and started away. Mme. de la Marche, with **her** hands clasped, seemed to call upon her daughter the consolations which her love could not give, and which she could expect only **from heaven.** This time, the admiral was vanquished. His iron **will was** broken to pieces. The generosity of his daughter con**quered him** quicker than her tears and her supplications.

'Laura!' he **cried,** 'Laura? **I** am vanquished. Come **to my** heart!'

The poor woman looked at her father, and her **eyes seemed to** ask if his words were true.

'Yes, come!' repeated the **old man.** '**I** could **not have** survived the abandonment of her who was the companion of **all** my life, and still I would not have said a word to retain her, **since** she preferred going with **you.** But you forgot that I had been merciless My daughter, **my** beloved child! You know **not** how wretched I felt when I forced **my lips to** condemn you to exile, **and** I closed **my** arms, which were tempted to clasp you to my heart. **Now** that your devotion has made me another man, it seems that **a ray** of hope glitters in the future, and that we may yet have happiness. Come then, dear Laura! come to my heart and let us try to forget.'

'Oh! father! dear father!' cried Laura. And she rushed into her father's arms. Mme. de la Marche leaned towards them, and those three beings who had been **so sorely** tried, found infinite hap-

piness in mingling their tears. As to Sir Elias Drack, this touching scene had impressed him so much, in spite of himself, that he
rushed to the admiral, and unable to utter a sound he seized his
hands and shook them energetically. Feeling that his tears would
betray him, he rushed out of the house and started towards his hotel
on foot. On his way, he was making a very judicious observation,
this false and stoic philosopher.

'What this old admiral has done is well, it is even very well.
Why, an English admiral could hardly have done better, my word
of honor ! But didn't he say he had been conquered by his daughter's devotion ? Zounds ! he should have said victorious. This de-
feat does him more credit than his most glorious victories. For if
it is a success to conquer others, it is a greater one to conquer one-
self.'

Having uttered this last aphorism, Sir Elias Drack entered the
hotel, and called at the office to see if there was a letter or despatch,
when the porter came up to him :

'Sir,' he said, 'the prince is here and has been waiting for you
for nearly an hour.'

'The prince ? what prince ? asked the Englishman with astonishment.

'His excellency the Indian prince.'

'Oh ! yes,' said Mr. Drack, smiling, 'I was forgetting——'

The porter admired this traveller, who must have a terrible lot
of fine acquaintances since he did not know who he was talking
about when he said the prince.

'His excellency is in your apartments,' said the porter. 'Strangers
are not generally allowed in the travellers' rooms, but we thought
we might let his excellency——'

'That's all right,' said Mr. Drack. 'That animal will be very expensive,' he thought to himself. 'A man, who, like me, knows an
Indian prince, is obliged to give enormous gratuities to the servants, a thing altogether contrary to the principles of the children
of such a great country as England.'

On entering his room the good man looked for Maltar, and could
not see him at first. The Indian had seated himself on the floor in
a corner and was fast asleep. However he awoke at the noise and
jumped up suddenly, excusing himself for the liberty he had taken
to go to sleep.

'You are forgiven,' said the Englishman. 'I know too well where
you have spent your nights during the last month, not to understand that you have a good deal of lost sleep to catch up. Now tell me
what brings your excellency to my humble room.'

'I have come,' said Maltar, 'to tell you of a very serious danger
which threatens my young mistress.'

And the **Indian** told him, that, listening at **the** doors, he had that very morning overheard a conversation between his master and M. Palmeri, during which the latter had called upon M. de Moray to fulfil **the** promise he had made **to** give him **the** hand of his daughter. The count, it seems, had asked a few **days' respite,** which the merciless creditor had flatly refused.

'**Ah ! sir,**' said Maltar, '**find** some means **to** prevent this marriage. It would **be** a crime to sacrifice the **young** mistress to this M. Palmeri.'

'The more so that she **loves another, as I have already told you,** rejoined the Englishman.

And the good man thought to himself :

'Palmeri ! Palmeri ! where did I hear that name ?'

VI.

After Mr. Drack's departure, a few moments of delicious emotion were experienced by the admiral, his wife and Laura. A servant interupted them suddenly.

'Mlle. de Moray is in the drawing-room,' said this man, 'and she wishes to know if M. and Mme de la Marche can receive her ?'

'Paulette !' cried Laura, pressing her hands to her heart, which was ready to burst. The beloved daughter she had not seen for a year was there and her head was bowed with shame at the thought of seeing her. This thought filled her soul with trouble. The deep emotion she felt a moment before, while speaking of her child, **was** still more intense. Unknown to her, it was a decisive trial. **Would** her reason, already shaken come out victorious, or founder entirely ? ——Paulette appeared at last. At the sight of the child she had left sick and suffering, and who had become a woman full **of** life and radiant with beauty, an immense joy filled her heart, and all her fears disappeared. At the same time, by a phenomenon similar to the one by which she had lost her reason, the truth flashed on her mind, and **the spectre** of her imaginary shame vanished. **She** was proud **of that splendid creature and** she felt herself **worthy of** being her mother. **Unable to utter** a word, her lips were **silently** calling her.

'Paulette ! my beloved !' **she** whispered at **last.**

'Mother ! dear mother !' cried Paulette, and she rushed into her arms. And their kisses mingled with their tears. And each of her child's caresses tore away a shred of the veil which darkened the poor mother's intellect. The darkness brought **on by** suffering had been dispelled by maternal love. In one moment, the past unfolded itself before her eyes. The burnt letters, Robert's death, the undeserved accusation brought against her and accepted by her : and then her abandonment, the divorce, she remembered everything. And when Paulette became indignant because her father would not allow their meeting.

'Ah !' she cried, 'it is because he believes me guilty.'

'It is because *he believes* you guilty ! ' repeated M. and Mme. de la Marche, 'what do you mean ?'

They asked for an explanation, and she had made up her mind to tell everything, her innocence and her unhappiness, when she remembered the threatening words of the admiral : ' I would have taken a more terrible revenge, and then I should have died with despair and shame ! ' Then she turned her eyes full of tears towards her mother, and she bowed her head, as if confessing her guilt anew. But, again, she well knew that she was innocent, and she felt that to let Paulette suspect and despise her mother would be a crime, a sacrilege. She prayed to be left alone with her. Her prayer being granted, the mother sat down, while Paulette leaned on her knees, the same as she used to, when, a little child, she was saying her prayers, morning and evening.

'Let me look at you again !' said Laura, 'how beautiful you have become, my Paulette ! How I love you !'

'And how I love you also !' repeated Paulette with the faithful accent of a mysterious echo. ' But, alas ! how you have changed ! How you seem to have suffered. Your features bear the stamp of sorrow, and your eyes the traces of bitter tears ! Your hair has become white. Oh, mother ! mother ! you must have endured terrible sufferings since such a change has been made in you, who are so young yet ?'

'You cannot imagine,' said Laura with a bitter smile, ' the sufferings I have borne.'

She started up. Without knowing exactly how far she would be taken into her confidence, she felt that a certain explanation was necessary between them, and that the time had come.

'Answer me,' she said. 'What did they tell you ? On your arrival, when you did not find me there to receive you, when you saw another woman bearing my name, you enquired, you questioned ? What answer did you receive ?'

'They said nothing,' answered Paulette, letting her eyes full of her pure innocence rest on her mother. ' Nothing. They have told me nothing.'

'Why,' cried Laura, ' you did not wish to know! '

'No ! I have merely suffered. I remember, however, that when, trembling with despair, I asked my father what he could have done to cause you to leave his house and break the ties which united you ; this woman you speak of, who bears your name, and who had almost the audacity to wish me to call her *mother !——* '

' Oh, the wretch !' thought Laura with indignation.

'This woman, I say, commenced I know not what revelation in which I easily understood from the first words, that she was throwing on you the responsibility of all that had happened.'

' Oh, the impious woman !' thought Laura. ' Denounce a mother to her own daughter !'

' My father bade her to be silent,' continued Paulette, 'and since that day they told me nothing. Moreover, I would have refused to listen to anything.'

Laura was thoughtful for a moment. She was thankful to Roger not to have allowed his second wife to dishonor the memory of the first before her own daughter. However, it was impossible that Paulette should remain any longer in complete ignorance. She would be too much exposed to the sufferings that an indiscretion, even involuntary, might bring on.

' Listen, my child,' she said. ' It is not your father, as your tenderness for me made you suppose, who is the cause of our separation.'

' Ah !' feebly said Paulette, with an aching heart.

' Terrible charges have been brought against me. I did not deny them ; neither to your father, nor my own parents—nor even to justice itself.'

' Why ? Since those charges were not true !'

' Dear soul !' said Laura with emotion, ' blessed be you, who affirm my innocence without even knowing the fault I have been accused of ! No, I did not deny those cruel charges. I did not wish to, and I could not then. But to-day the situation is changed : I cannot consent to see my child tempted to condemn or even suspect me. Listen to me, then, with all your soul's faith. Recall the sweet memories and the pious thoughts of your childhood !'

' Mother, I am listening.'

' Remember what I have been to you during sixteen years. Remember the cares I lavished on you, the happiness I enjoyed in loving you, the immense tenderness I surrounded you with, and of which we alone mysteriously kept the secret, as if afraid others would be jealous.'

' Mother, I remember all that.'

' Remember my solicitude in guiding your soul towards good, in forming your heart to virtue, in unfolding before your eyes, and in engraving in your mind the sacred sentiment of duty.'

' Yes, mother, I remember, and I venerate and admire you as much as I adore you !'

' Well, remembering all that I have recalled, can you suppose that such a mother could become a criminal wife ?'

'A criminal wife!' repeated Paulette. 'Never! never! You only accuse yourself to force me to answer? No, it is not true; you calumniate yourself! Do you wish to know my whole mind? Well, it must be by virtue. It was in obedience to some sublime devotion that an angel such as you could accuse herself!'

'Ah! pure and saintly child!' said Laura, moved to tears. 'Your heart understands, and the cry of your soul has redeemed all my past sufferings! Yes, it is an imperious duty, a sacred duty, which has kept me silent. You have said it, my child. When I accused myself, I was lying!'

'But why?'

'I was lying to prevent a danger a hundred times more terrible than the one which threatened me!'

'And you have taken upon yourself alone the weight of a fault you were innocent of?'

'No! Another one accused himself with me of the same crime?'

'And this other, where is he?'

'Alas! the devotion which I paid with my honor has cost him his life!'

Paulette turned horribly pale. Until then the pure child did not have a just notion of what had happened. These words of fault and crime did not offer a precise sense to her ear. She had vaguely supposed it meant some sins like those she would have accused herself of at confession. But now the words of her mother overwhelmed her. A human being had paid with his life his pretended complicity in a crime avowed, but not actually committed.

'Another! Killed! Great God! But who?'

'The name you ask is a secret I share with God alone. Even your father has never known it.'

'But for whose sake, at least, did you bring upon your head the evil which was to make two victims?'

'I cannot tell you that either. My duty was to reveal the whole secret to M. de Moray. To him alone belonged the right to decide what was expedient to suppress and to divulge, in the interest of his honor. I was ready to fulfil that duty as soon as I found myself alone with him; but when the first accusation fell upon me, the anger of my husband exploded so violently, so terribly, the curse of my father was so withering that what remained in me of strength, of energy, and of courage was suddenly annihilated; I lost my head; yes, I understand now, I lost my reason; I was mad!'

'What do you say?'

'Yes, mad! and I remained in that state until I saw you again; until the moment your looks, your kisses and caresses redeemed me.

'And you can justify youself, now?'

'Yes, I could justify myself; that is to say, inflict on M. de Moray the remorse of having killed an innocent man, the remorse of having shamefully repudiated me, of having driven me away from his house to give my place at the conjugal hearth to a stranger ; I could do all that. But none of these evils, none of these faults, can be repaired. It is for ever that an impious law has condemned me, and I would perhaps lose, alas ! those I wish to **save,** without dragging myself out of the abyss in which I have fallen ! You, my daughter, you must forget this secret. In the eyes of all I must remain what I seem to **be : a guilty** wife justly disgraced !'

'However ! ——'

'It is my will ! Do not cause me to regret the confidence I **have had** in you in destroying with a single word the work I have **accomplished.** To you also I should have kept silent. But **I am a** mother, and I must have your respect as well as your love. Undoubtedly, you said I was incapable of doing wrong, but that **was** not sufficient. I must have all the confidence as well as the tenderness of your heart, without trouble, regret, or afterthought. Since I am always your mother, you must know how to defend me, in your heart, if ever you hear it said that I have avowed the crime. It is for that reason, and **that** only, that I have told you that my avowal was a lie. But, **once** more, keep preciously the secret I have confided to nobody, not even to my judge. You promise, don't you ?'

'Mother !' said the child, with solemn gravity, 'I shall keep your secret piously. I shall keep it without understanding what you ask, **except** that you are not only a saint, but that you are also a martyr.'

'Yes, a **martyr!'** murmured **Laura,** 'a martyr to a sacred duty.'

Paulette suddenly had a generous impulse of indignation.

'And my father,' she cried, could not discover the truth ? **He** has believed this avowal of a fault which did not exist. Alas! to cherish you still more than I do, must I learn to love him less ?'

Laura had the loyalty to defend the man who had caused her to endure such sufferings, and who had forgotten her so quickly in the arms of another.

'Do not accuse your father,' she simply said ; 'he has done nothing which exceeded his rights. The care of his honor has dictated his conduct.'

The conversation had lasted **for** a long **time. The** young soul of Paulette was not enough tempered yet to support without danger the terrible emotions of which her mother had given her the presentiment, without, however, revealing them altogether. Laura noticed the paleness of her face, and the trembling of her whole frame. She then wished to engage in a sweeter conversation, which would cause the spring flower to regain her brightness, as if the sun's brilliant rays were succeeding to a violent storm.

'Come,' she said, trying to smile, 'let us speak of yourself, now. Tell me everything that has happened since I saw you on the day I deserted you to save your father's life, leaving you to the care of Aunt Basilique——'

'Aunt Basilique!' interrupted the child, whose eyes filled with tears. 'You know, mother?'

'Yes, I have heard of her death on reaching port. Alas! poor Aunt Basilique! she loved you well, and I wept over her as if she had still been my sister. But speak to me of the beautiful country where we were happy. Speak to me of the kind friends we left behind us.'

A crimson blush suffused the cheeks of the child, and she commenced an adorable confession, the confession of a pure love for a young man who had been so good, so tenderly affectionate and devoted when she had found herself alone in Pondichéry. Although the chaste young girl had blushed on thinking of Gaston de Vallières, she felt no embarrassment in telling her mother of the sentiments of sweet tenderness for him which filled her heart. The purity of her love expressed itself without fear, with a serene confidence.

'Do you see, mother,' she said, with a beautiful smile, 'I love him so much that I would rather die than become the wife of another.'

Laura pressed her child to her heart.

'Reassure yourself,' she said, 'M. de Vallières will be your husband. I know no one who is so worthy of you and to whom I would be so glad to confide your happiness.'

A short time after these two beings, who loved each other so well, separated, and Paulette returned to her father's house.

We will also return to M. de Moray's, where we have not been for a long time. Many events have happened since the previous week. Roger had seen his honor compromised by the failure of the Indo-Marseillaise bank. We are acquainted with most of of them. They have been told us incidentally, thanks to the intervention of Maltar.

The Indian had informed M. de la Marche of the death of Aunt Basilique. M. de Moray had been with his sister at her last moments, having been called to Marseilles by the care of his interests through the failure of the bank. The Indian had also informed Sir Elias Drack of the project in view against Paulette, which threatened to give to Annibal Palmeri a heart already disposed of in favor of M. de Vallières. Maltar had learned this project through eaves-dropping. This was undoubtedly a grave violation of professional duty, but Maltar was conscious that he was not betraying M. de Moray in trying to discover the intrigues which surrounded him.

His instinct had told him that the master was the prey of infamous characters, and he was spying them to discover the means to open the eyes of the count. The known suppleness and cunning of the people of his race made this spying very easy. Every Indian covers an acrobat. For those people there is no difficulty in entering rooms and in closing and opening doors without being seen or heard. Maltar, then, had heard the whole conversation between M. de Moray and Palmeri, and he had told the principal parts of it to Mr. Drack. This conversation had been very painful to M. de Moray. He had returned from Marseilles very much affected by the emotions of his trip. The death of his sister, and the confirmation of his total ruin, had completely demoralized him. Another cause of anxiety, the future of Paulette, had increased the trouble of his mind. A few moments before dying, Aunt Basilique had exchanged supreme confidences with her brother. In the midst of the heart-rendings of their separation, the poor woman had told him that she had at least the consolation of being able to depend on the happiness of Paulette. And with the authority which the approach of death gives to the words of those who leave us, Aunt Basilique had entreated M. de Moray to entrust, as soon as possible, the fate of his daughter to an honest and loyal young man who would love her.

' I cannot judge,' she had said, ' how far you were right to replace so quickly the guilty woman you have just repudiated. But, knowing the tenderness of Paulette for her mother, I can easily guess the numberless causes of suffering which await her under your roof, where a stranger rules. Then give her soon the husband she will desire and love. Every minute of delay you cause to this union means an increase of sorrow which you would impose upon her.'

She did not say any more. She would not betray the secret of Paulette's heart, reserving to the young girl the sweet confidence of her love. On his side, not to trouble the last moments of his sister, M. de Moray did not acquaint her with the engagement he had made three or four days before, concerning Paulette, with Annibal Palmeri. He let her die in the false confidence of the near realization of the project she had already formed months before. Nevertheless this advice *in extremis* made him understand the gravity of the situation. Certainly the project of a marriage between his daughter and Annibal had not been accepted by him without a struggle. Everything that was revolting in such an union had been apparent to his mind the very first moment Palmeri had made his intentions known. But the reader will remember under what circumstances this project had been proposed. His life, his honor itself was condemned. Between two evils he had chosen the one which then appeared the least. Furthermore, he had not disposed of the hand of Paulette without restriction, and if he had known that she had disposed of herself, his weakness would have appeared to him like a crime.

He was very much embarrassed when on the morning of his return, Annibal came to remind him of his promise. He took up the question of his marriage with Paulette squarely, and wished her father to make the overture to her on that very day.

'Not to-day,' answered Roger, tired out, 'I pray you, not to-day. Give me at least a few days.'

'My dear sir,' coolly said the Italian, 'when you had to be saved from ruin, I asked you neither a few days nor a few hours ; I came to you open-handed and I said : Here is salvation, and here is the condition on which I offer it ; you have accepted, then it is well understood. You will speak, this very day, to Miss Paulette.'

'I have given you my word,' answered the count, broken-hearted,' and since you desire it, I shall keep it.'

Such was the conversation which Maltar had overheard and transmitted to Sir Elias Drack ; but what the Indian did not know, since he had started almost at once for the hotel du Louvre, was that M. de Moray had asked his wife to obtain from Annibal the delay of a few days which he had vainly solicited. To his astonishment and to his deep regret Claudia refused point-blank. The triumphant pride of the adventuress had received a terrible wound at the hands of her husband's daughter The disdain, the hatred which the child had shown, and which nothing could curb, had re-kindled in the breast of the Neapolitan the bitterness hardly extinguished yet of her painful beginnings in Paris. If she could not bend Paulette before her, Gorgon would break her.

Thus the attempt made by M. de Moray to obtain the intervention of his wife unfortunately resulted contrary to what he expected. The more the unhappy father defended his daughter, the more he injured her. It was exactly because a hasty union imposed on Paulette on the morrow of the day she had learned the disaster of her mother would be cruel to the child that the countess was rejoicing to see the celebration of the marriage hastened. And it was also because it was odious to impose her own brother as a husband upon the unfortunate child that she imperiously invoked the realization of the word given to Annibal. M. de Moray, seeing the uselessness of his efforts, retired with sadness. An unexpected encounter, as he was coming out of the apartment of the countess, caused him a great emotion. He was crossing the parlor when he found himself face to face with Paulette, who was returning from her visit to her grandfather's. He thought it was chance that had brought her into his presence, and that he must acquaint her at once with her fate. Putting his arm affectionately round her waist, he brought her to his room.

'Come with me,' he said ; 'I have something to say to you.'

Paulette had not yet taken **her** bonnet off, when the count spoke to her :

'You have been out with your maid ?'

'Yes, father ; but ——'

'This girl is not the companion you want, I know ; but it is only for a short time. You will soon have a governess. But you did not tell me where you have been ?'

'I went to grandfather's.'

'Ah ! you went to see your grand-parents ?'

'Yes. You do not forbid me to go there, do you ?'

In asking this question Paulette's voice was full of anxiety. It was not only her grand-parents she could not see, if she had been forbidden to go, it was also her mother. Happily M. de Moray re-assured her.

'Oh ! no,' he said quickly. 'It would cause you too much pain. You will go and see them as often as you like ; even to-morrow, if you wish.'

Paulette threw her arms around her father's neck **in** a sincere burst of gratitude. Roger kept his daughter close to him and looked **at** her with a mixture of love and deep pity. It seemed cruel to him to choose exactly the moment she was more loving than usual to acquaint her with the terrible news.

'I love you when you are like your old self,' he said with tenderness. 'It is the first time in eight days that I find in your eyes a little of your old love.'

'It is because this is the first time we find **ourselves alone together**, as of old.'

Paulette thought she was saying the **whole truth to her** father in reproaching him indirectly with never having dared to seek to see her alone. But she was mistaken. It was because she had had during the day the supreme joy of seeing her mother again that her soul was more open to sentiments of love. Such was the sweetness of their interview that M. de Moray had not the courage to end it by a thunderbolt. On the other hand he felt a sort of conscious shame, which made him blush at the mere thought of the words he would **use to** make Paulette acquainted with the name of the husband he intended to give her.

'No,' he said to himself at last, 'I shall never be able, and I will leave to others the task of telling the cruel necessities to which I have to submit, and they will reveal the truth to Paulette. I shall go to the admiral's to-morrow, and ask him to speak to my daughter for me.'

This idea of making M. and Mme. de la Marche the missionaries of the painful revelation he did dare to make, eased the mind of M. de Moray. He knew, too well, the rigid principles of the admiral concerning honor, not to be certain that the old soldier would ap-

L

prove of his sacrificing everything to the glory of his name. And then the public approval which M. de la Marche would give to the marriage of his grand-daughter with M. Annibal Palmeri would have a good effect. It would be a great moral support for the divorced husband, whom many people would be disposed to blame at seeing the child of the first wife enter his new family. The combination appeared excellent in every way, and the next day Roger went out on his errand. The admiral had just gone out. As Roger appeared to be very much annoyed at this mishap, the servant asked him if he would not come in, and await the return of his master.

'Very well,' said the count, 'I shall wait.'

'Shall I tell Madam ?' asked the servant with a little embarrassment.

'Yes,' answered M. de Moray, who had a great veneration for the admiral's wife. 'See if she will receive me.'

A mistake had just been made. In the servant's mind, the word : *Madam* had a sense which M. de Moray could not understand. It was only the day before that Laura had succeeded in vanquishing the merciless severity of her father. The joy of the poor woman in finding herself amid those surroundings of love and honor, was so great that she had not strength enough to tear herself away. She took possession of a vacant room in the house, and such is the force of illusion, that on the night which followed her return, her imagination carried her twenty years backwards, when a happy young girl, she was dreaming of the husband, for whom to-day she was wearing a mourning more cruel than that of death.

Be it as it may, on seeing at a few hours' interval his master's daughter, and the man who had been her husband so long, the servant had established a connection easily explained between the return of the one and the visit of the other. So, in saying : 'Shall I tell Madam ?' he meant Laura. It was not possible, however, that the count should understand the phrase as it had been pronounced. *Madam*, in the house of Mme. de la Marche, could only be Mme. de la Marche herself. Moreover, Roger knew that the admiral had mercilessly closed his door against his guilty daughter, and he had not learnt the incidents which had caused that door to be opened. The reader may judge of his sudden emotion on seeing before him Laura. Yes, Laura herself! At the sight of the woman he had in turn so ardently loved and so deeply hated, Roger felt a sort of trembling agitation of all his nerves. He thought he was going to fall.

'You !' he cried, throwing his arms forward, as if to repulse a threatening vision. 'You ! you ! in this house !'

We have shown the emotion felt by M. de Moray at this meeting, but we have not had occasion to speak of the wondrous power of will which Laura had to appeal to, in order to meet her husband. The servant was very much troubled himself when he came to her and told her :

'Madam, M. de Moray asks if Madam is willing to receive him.'

Laura had been very much astonished at the request brought by the servant, and in spite of all, she had hesitated. To see as a stranger the man she had loved so much, the man she loved yet, seemed an ordeal beyond her strength. However, since he asked to see her, he must have very grave reasons. Then how could she refuse to grant a necessary interview ? Perhaps it was on account of her daughter ? She was thus deceiving herself ; but in reality she said to herself, at the bottom of her heart, that Roger was there ; Roger through whom she had known her greatest joys and her greatest sorrows ; Roger, lastly, the father of her child. There stood only the thickness of a door between them. She opened it at last. She was coming to this interview, thinking she had been called to it. The first words of M. de Moray undeceived her and she understood that a mistake had occurred.

'You !' cried Roger with terror depicted in his face. 'What are you doing in this house ?'

This *you* which Roger had said with such terror was like the stroke of a whip lashing her across the face. There was everything in that exclamation : fright, anger, threats, contempt. There was everything but peace, pardon, and, chiefly, repentance. Struck to the heart, she stopped short. Was it thus that she was to see him for the first time ? But she had suffered so much and so long already, that she was used to sufferings. She submitted.

'You have driven me away from your own house,' she said with a sadness full of dignity. 'Have you come here to-day yourself to reproach my father and my mother because they have opened theirs to me ? If it is so, and if you exact, for the satisfaction of your anger, that my solitude should be eternal, I will obey and I will return to my abandonment. What must I do ? What do you command ?'

This voluntary submission to a master who had freed her from all duty to himself by breaking all the ties which united them to each other, touched M. de Moray more deeply than he cared to acknowledge.

'I have not the right,' he said with en effort at rudeness, 'to regulate your life now. But if I had known that you were here, I would not have sent my daughter, and I would not have come myself.

'Alas !' answered Laura in a low voice, '*your* daughter ! She is mine also as much as yours, but I do not think of disputing for her with you. It is doubtless a fatal mistake which has placed us in each other's presence. You will perhaps take advantage of this

error to deny me the right to see Paulette again for a long time !
Well, you must be satisfied, and having nothing else to impose to
make me suffer still more, you will allow me retire.'

She made a motion to retire. In spite of himself, and as if
carried away by an invincible force, M. de Moray stopped her with
a word.

'Stay !' he said.

'You wish me to stay !' she said astonished. 'Why ? What can
be common between us hereafter ? The divorce is the abyss which
divides us. The sight of me alone is, I know, an outrage to you,
as the sight of your face is an ordeal beyond my strength ! Let me
go away !'

'No. Stay ! if only for an instant. Since chance has placed us in
each other's presence, we might as well take advantage of our meeting to settle, once for all, the only question which can interest both
of us hereafter, our daughter.'

'What more can you say than I have said myself ?' painfully
asked Laura. 'Your anger is still bitter enough to impose upon me,
as a sort of posthumous chastisement, the order not to see my
daughter again. I have told you that I would submit to this excess
of severity, not through loss of love for my child, God knows ! but
to spare Paulette even the temptation of a struggle with your will !
I ask you again what more do you want ?'

'I want you to thoroughly understand,' said M. de Moray with
agitation, 'that it is not through a barbarous feeling of anger that I
am acting, as you seem to think at this moment. The judgment
which has pronounced an eternal separation between us, has decided
also that the guardianship of Paulette, as well as the conduct of
her life, should belong to me alone. This judgment has decided
thus to protect against yourself, against the attraction of your love
for your daughter, against the attraction of my own weakness, perhaps, the future and the honor of a child whom the infection of
your tarnished honor would compromise for ever !'

'Oh !' thought Laura struck to the heart. 'I had not thought
of this heaping ignominy, that my contact could ever appear a threat
of corruption and a cause of shame to my daughter !'

'And then to conclude,' continued Roger, getting more and more
angry, although he was not being contradicted, 'the judgment has
decided thus, in order that the betrayed husband, every time he
shall put his lips on his child's forehead, may not find there the
trace of the kisses of the guilty wife !'

'Guilty ! The *mother* at least was not, if the wife was !' Laura
could not help saying,

'You were her mother only because you were my wife,' answered
Roger. It is impossible to punish the one without striking the other.
So much the worse for you !'

'Ah !' said Laura, trembling under his cruelty, ' what sort of a man have you become ?'

'I have become the man you have made me.

'I! how ?' asked the martyr with anxiety.

'Yes, you ! The deeper my affection and my respect have been for you, the greater the anger they have awakened in me ! Do not try to implore my pity ; it would be useless ! '

Nothing could increase the sufferings inflicted upon the martyr in the present, but the violence of M. de Moray reflected on the past. A cry of protestation escaped from her lips.

'And you !' she cried, 'do not speak of the love you pretend to have felt for me ! The man who persecutes me in the way you are doing after having inflicted so much evil, this man, I say, has never loved me ! '

At these words, Roger forgot everything else to remember only one thing that was true ; it was that for many long years, he had borne to Laura a boundless love. He uttered a heart-rending laugh.

'She dares to say that I did not love her !' he cried, ' she dares to say that !'

He raised his arms as if to call heaven to witness the injustice of such an accusation.

'She dares to say that ' he repeated. 'I ! I who had given her all my life ! I whose love and respect repulsed from my heart all temptations and attractions ! For it is true. I had subdued everything, conquered every passion, while she was betraying me basely, not thinking that I might die of her treachery !'

The words of M. de Moray could not convince Laura. The brutality of the facts gave them the lie in her eyes.

'Die of my treachery,' she said with a painful smile. 'You consoled yourself too quickly ; the danger was not great.'

M. de Moray drew near her, with his teeth set, hissing his words rather than pronouncing them.

'I have married the other too quickly ! That's what you mean, is it not ? But who tells you that in my haste there was not more desire for revenge and a challenge thrown at my own sorrow ?'

'Nonsense !' cried Laura, drawing nearer to Roger, as he had done himself. 'You loved that woman before you thought you had any cause of revenge against me.'

'Even admitting that I had loved her,' answered the count, 'I swear before God who hears me, I swear that I had victoriously resisted all the attractions which were dragging me to her. But no !' he cried, striking the floor with his foot as if to better attest the truth of his word, 'it is false ! I did not love her. I understood my error too well by the terrible sufferings I endured at the discovery of your crime.'

A feeling of egotistical joy filled the heart of Laura.

'Ah!' she said almost fainting, 'is it very true that you have suffered so much?'

Roger seized her roughly by the wrist.

'Ah!' he answered, 'do you think that I could, without despair and without weeping tear from my heart the roots of a love which had grown for eighteen years?'

Laura was drinking his words. They entered her ears like a delicious music. In living over again the love of the past, it almost seemed to her a new love. She insisted, abandoning her arm to the hand which clasped it as a vice, enjoying this physical suffering better than a caress.

'Is it very true also that you have wept so much?' she muttered.

Roger stepped back a little, placing himself in the light afforded by the window.

'Look at me!' he said in a low voice. 'Look at my emaciated face, at my sunken eyes, at my hair—white, but not by age—and do not ask any more if I have suffered. The wreck you are looking on is the work of one day. In a few hours you have made me an old man. Ah! yes, I must have loved you to suffer so much!'

'And now?' asked Laura, panting, 'instead of that love?——'

'Instead of that love,' cried Roger with violence, throwing from him the arm he had bruised. 'Instead of that love, it is hatred which fills my heart. Yes! I hate you with all the strength of my lost happiness, of my profaned memories, of my broken hopes! I hate you! do you hear me! I hate you!'

Laura could not be mistaken, and her joy exploded in a burst which she could not have withheld even at the cost of her life.

'You hate me!' she cried; 'you hate me! Ah! repeat those words again, which resound in my heart like the sweetest accents of love. I thought I was indifferent to you, and it was killing me. But now I can live, your anger and your threats have revived my courage. Ah! if you did not love me, you would not hate me so much.'

Roger staggered a few steps backwards. He did not have the strength to protest.

'I—I—' he said stammering, 'I would be cowardly enough.'

'Yes! she retorted, walking towards him, 'yes, you love me always. We are still tied to each other by this love which you command, but which does not obey. Do now what you will. Everything that will come from you will be good and sweet, even your anger, even your rigor, even your acts of violence!'

'Be quiet!' cried Roger, distracted, 'in the name of heaven, be quiet!'

But Laura had suffered too much not to abandon herself entirely to the joys of this unexpected, unhoped-for victory.

'That I should be silent!' she **said,** raising her head with **a** gesture of triumph. 'Whatever you may do now, you belong to me by that love which you vainly attempt to deny, and which your whole being proclaims. Do what you will, I tell you, it matters not. Tear your daughter away from my arms, keep her for yourself alone! It is my features you will see when your eyes rest upon her ; it will be my kisses which you will find on her lips, and you will return them to me in giving her yours.'

M. de Moray was trying to run away, leaning **on** the **furniture,** against the walls, beating the air with his arms, and **sustaining** against himself a struggle still more desperate than the **one he was** fighting with Laura.

'Be silent!' he implored **once more.** '**Don't** you **see that I am** becoming mad.'

'I will be silent,' **said Laura,** 'on one condition. **Dare to tell me you** do not love **me!**'

He tried to **lie a last time.**

'I do not——'

But **his** strength failed him ; he could not finish the perjury.

'Yes! yes!' he said, falling on his knees. 'Yes! in spite of your treachery, in spite of myself, in spite of my shame, and in spite of the revolt of my honor, I must make the avowal. It is mean and cowardly, but since you force me to it, hear then the words which you tear from my heart after having broken it : "I love you! I love you always!"'

For a moment Laura felt a mad temptation to accord **a true avowal of a** lover, the confidence she had refused to **the rage of the** outraged husband. **It** was sufficient for her to **cry out :** '**Yes, love** me! You have a right **to** do so! I did not betray you!' **and he** would have believed her. But what good would it do to-day? **This** cry of her innocence would remain without effect since the husband who had spoken with such a powerful passion had contracted new engagements. And the danger remained the same for the honor of her mother. So she resigned herself once **more, but** this time, it **was** with a deep and tender sweetness.

'We can leave each other,' she said, 'and even we may not meet again ; I shall keep mysteriously, like a treasure, the secret of your own heart. Perhaps we shall not see each other again in this world. But no matter how long the separation of life may be, it is but a second in comparison to the eternity when our **two** souls will be forever united. Farewell, Roger! you love me, **and** I adore you!'

The noise of steps separated them. The admiral and his wife were entering the room. On his arrival the old sailor had been told by a servant of the presence of M. de Moray in the parlor. Astonished and even troubled on hearing **that an** interview was taking place between their daughter and **the man** they used to call their son-in-law, the old couple had resolved not to interfere. But as time passed, their anxiety had increased and they decided to go to the help of Laura, whose situation must be very painful, face to face with the man who had repudiated her. To rejoin their daughter they even left alone a person who was in their room. On entering they saw both Laura and Roger standing a few steps from each other, evidently a prey to great emotion, but silent.

'You have asked to see us, M. de Moray?' said the admiral. 'Mme. de la Marche and myself are at your orders.'

The appearance of the new-comers had caused the excitement of Laura and Roger to fall suddenly. But, although M. de Moray usually had a great mastery over himself, he was in need of a few seconds to recover the balance of his mind. What a change it was thus to re-enter the immediate reality of his life! How rapidly he had been recalled from the heaven where his meeting with the woman he still loved passionately had made him ascend! He was so troubled that he had forgotten why he had come to see the admiral ; but his memory soon returned, and he shuddered.

'Yes, yes, I wanted to see you, he muttered. 'I—it is a thing which——'

His lips opened and closed in uttering inarticulate sounds.

'Pardon me,' he said, succeeding in restraining himself. 'The unexpected presence of a woman I never thought of seeing again has thrown me into a great state of trouble. I believe I have been mad. Once more, I pray you, forgive me and hear me.'

'We are listening,' said the admiral, motioning to everyone to sit down.

M. de Moray turned towards Laura.

'The communication I have to make,' he said, 'was to be addressed only to the admiral and his wife ; but after the interview we have had, Madam, I have not the right to exclude you.'

Laura bowed her head softly as a sign of compliance, and Roger continued, preparing himself to climb a painful calvary.

'The terrible events which have divided our two families,' he said, after a moment's silence, 'have not been able to alter either my sentiments of respect for you, Admiral, or my feelings of veneration for you, Mme. de la Marche. This being the case, even had I not wished to invoke your assistance in a project I have formed, I should have felt it as a duty to acquaint you to-day with a determination I have come to.'

'A project?' asked Mme de la Marche.

'A determination?' said the admiral.

'Yes, I have resolved to marry my daughter.'

'Marry Paulette!' cried Laura, with fear, interfering for the first time.

' Our family dissensions,' continued M. de Moray, ' imposed upon me the duty to put an end as quickly as possible to the very embarrassing situation in which my daughter was placed in my own house. But having decided on marrying her promptly, I had not chosen the husband she was to have, until a fatal event has forced on me the choice of that husband, and I will tell you his name. It is ——,'

' It is ?——' asked Laura with anguish.

' It is M. Annibal Palmeri,' answered Roger with an effort, and speaking in a low voice, as if ashamed to hear himself making this revelation.

' Annibal Palmeri!' repeated everyone with the same cry of revolt.

' The brother of the woman who has usurped my place!' cried Laura, with intense indignation. ' Why, you are mad! Even if I had deserved a chastisement a hundred times more severe than the one you have inflicted ; even if I was the lowest specimen of the lost, Paulette is nevertheless my daughter, and on account of that title alone, she cannot love the brother of the woman who bears the old name of her mother!'

' Who speaks of love ?' asked M. de Moray, sadly. ' Moreover,' he continued, with bitterness, ' are you quite sure, madam, that a marriage of love always realizes the happiness it promises ?'

A leaden silence weighed on these four persons, separated by manifold interests, but who, certainly, met on the same thought : the happiness of Paulette. For a moment they remained motionless, silent. Laura was the first to find enough strength to speak. Mothers are capable of all the energies when the happiness of their child is in jeopardy.

' Let us see !' she said, passing her hand across her forehead, as if to drive away a horrible dream. ' There is in all this something which you do not say, and which alone can dictate the monstrous words we have just heard. Listen ! do not interrupt me yet. A few minutes ago, I might have suspected in you some evil thought which would have led you to destroy my child's happiness, after having contributed, I would have sworn, to the destruction of mine. But now, without wishing to recall anything of what has happened when we were alone together ; now, I cannot accuse you of such a weakness, of such a crime, I may say. There is something you do not tell, a necessity which pushes you in spite of yourself. Well, it is that something you must tell, that mystery you must reveal. You must understand that you cannot tell me that you are sacrificing my daughter, without also telling me what merciless law you are obeying. Come, speak out, I am listening !'

One would have said that the rôles were changed now. After having so rudely exercised his power, M. de Moray was forced to lower his head. His victim was his judge, in her turn.

'Yes,' added the admiral, ' we must know.'

'I have come to tell you all,' said the count, sadly. 'Perhaps when you are better informed, you will judge me less harshly. Know, then, that after the evil which struck me in my love, another affliction befel me. After the honor of the husband, the honor of the man has been threatened, compromised.'

'Great heaven !'

'In two words, the facts are these, and, as you have said, here is the law imposed upon my will. Certain circumstances which it would be too long to tell, and which it is useless to mention, have compromised my name and my honor in such a terrible manner, that even to-day I am threatened with a criminal prosecution before the tribunals, where I will be condemned. But I hope you will not suspect my good faith ; I can be accused only of a guilty imprudence. Be that as it may, when the peril was revealed to me, I felt lost, condemned in advance. I had before me the expectation of the felon's cell, or the bullet of the honest man prosecuted for a fault involuntarily committed.'

'You wanted to kill yourself ?' cried Laura.

'It was the only thing I could do,' coolly said the count. 'And, believe me, M. de la Marche would not have blamed me. I was almost touching the fatal minute when I was to strike the blow, when a man came to me and offered me a chance of salvation.'

'And that man was ?'

'The man I named just now, M. Annibal Palmeri. He offered to save me from disaster. But he made a bargain, and the price of this bargain was the hand of Paulette. I accepted.'

'I should have died !' cried Laura, with the inspired accent of voluntary sacrifice. 'Yes, rather than sacrifice my child, I should have struck myself with my own hand !'

'Do you think I was not tempted to do so ?' asked the count, painfully. 'And I believe that God would have shown Himself more merciful in His judgment of the crime I should have committed in taking the life He had given me. But had I the right to prefer death ? I did not judge so,'

'And you are right,' said the admiral. 'The death to which you would have condemned yourself would have only weakly glossed your shame ; it could not have obliterated it. You had to accept everything, to consent to everything, to redeem your honor, no matter how cruel were the conditions imposed. Once more, I say it, you have done your duty.'

'Even at the cost of his daughter's happiness ?' cried Laura, desperately.

'Even at that cost !' confirmed the admiral, without hesitation.

'No, it shall not be !' cried the loving mother, who saw only the evil, perhaps **the** death of her child. ' You have promised, it is true, but you could only engage yourself, and ——'

. . . .

'And Paulette will redeem the word of her father !' said the poor girl, pale and shuddering, pushing open a door behind which she had been **a silent** spectator of this dramatic interview, and entering the room. ' I am ready to marry M. Palmeri, father !' **re**peated Paulette, because it was she who had just entered.

The day previous M. de Moray had told his daughter that she could visit her grand-parents as often as she wished. Taking advantage of this permission, the young girl had returned to the admiral's on the next day. She had met her grand-father **on** the threshhold of the door, and had learnt at the same time the presence **of** her father in the house. She had been told that he was having **a** private interview with her mother, and lastly, she had seen her grand-parents going, with deep emotion, tc join the two beings to whom she owed her life, and between whom she shared her love equally. When she found herself alone an invincible presentiment told her that she was the cause of this strange meeting, and she wanted to know ; and had she been told that death was awaiting her behind that door, she would have gone there to listen. It was death, in fact, but a death more slow, more cruel, than would have been the stroke of a dagger through her heart. So she had listened, standing up **at** first, then as the terrible truth was being gradually revealed to her through the thin boards, her strength becoming exhausted, she had fallen on her knees. It was in this attitude of prayer she had heard her sentence. It was a condemnation which tore away from her heart the word given to M. de Vallières, the absent friend so dearly loved, to impose respect to the promise made by M. de Moray. She did not hesitate, even for a second, having drawn from the blood of her mother the courage of sacrifice. In one moment she immolated her happiness to satisfy the honor of her father. And when she **had** heard her mother, who had also sacrificed herself, she knew **it,** rebelling in her maternal instinct, she had risen, she had made the sign of the cross, like the soldier on the eve of engaging in battle, or the missionary preparing himself to die at the stake, and she had opened the door. It was then that she uttered these simple words of devotedness and heroism ; ' Paulette will redeem the word of her father !' Only having added: ' I am ready to marry M. Palmeri !' she felt **an in**voluntary weakness and would have fallen if **her** mother had not caught her **in** her arms.

' Paulette ! Paulette, my child !' cried Laura. ' Forget these words. Think of it, my beloved. It is your life, it is your happiness you are giving.'

'It is his honor I am redeeming,' retorted the generous child, in a supreme effort. Then turning to Mme. de Moray, 'You were right in not doubting your child, father. What you have done is well done.'

After these words she leaned her head on Laura's shoulder, and told her in a voice so low that nobody else could hear her;

'It seems to me, do you see, that something is broken in my heart. I do not know what I feel; I do not suffer, and still I am not conscious. Oh! mother, one must feel so on the point of death.'

Her limbs trembled and sank under her. Her blood rushed to her heart and to her brain; as pale as a corpse, she uttered a dull moan; her eyes closed.

'Farewell, mother,' she muttered, 'Fare——'

She could not finish the word. She fell, slipping, from the arms of Laura, who could only lessen the force of her unexpected fall. All this scene had been enacted in a few seconds. Laura uttered a heart-rending shriek.

'Ah,' she cried, 'Dead! she is dead!'

Then throwing herself down beside the child, she raised her, and took her in her arms. Mad with sorrow, she rocked the big girl to and fro in her arms, as she used to do long ago when she took the little child out of her cradle. M. de Moray and the admiral, frightened by the despair of the mother, almost as much as by the fainting of the daughter, finally succeeded in taking her from Laura's arms and placed her on a sofa, where Mme. de la Marche bathed her temples with water.

'Ah,' suddenly cried Laura, who saw signs of life on her child's lips, 'she has moved, she has moved, I tell you. She lives, she lives, great God!'

And passing from extreme terror to extreme joy, the unhappy woman burst into sobs, bathing the face of her daughter with her tears.

'Ah, sir,' said the admiral to Roger, 'if you have been cruelly offended, you are now cruelly revenged.'

M. de Moray lowered his head, and wept bitterly in his turn. They had the charity to leave the two women alone. Laura sat down by her child, whose hands she held in her own. She was silent, thinking that she would soon go to sleep. But Paulette pressed her mother's hand to call her attention, and spoke to her in a low voice:

'Mother,' she said, 'I have reflected a great deal within the last few minutes. Do you see, it is our common fate to suffer, although neither you nor I have anything to reproach ourselves with. We love each other so much, dearest, that sorrow could not create any jealousy between us. You and I are sisters now, sisters in tears and sorrows. Since it is so, and in order that we may fulfill our destinies without flinching, **we** need great courage, and the first thing we must do is to resign ourselves not to see each other again.'

'Not see each other again!' **cried Laura.** 'Is that the means **you have** found to keep up your courage?'

'**Yes,**' answered Paulette, with grave firmness. 'I remember my childhood; if **I** fell and hurt myself, I would get up with courage, and **start to** run again, certain that you had not seen me. But if, pale with fright, you would raise me up, and **ask if I was** wounded, tears would come to my eyes, because I **felt at the same** time both your pain and mine. Well, it would be the same **thing** for the terrible fall which awaits me: the fall of all my dreams, **of** all my hopes! I must become insensible to everything, and it **is** only in thinking of myself that I can attain that end.'

Laura had leaned her face on the sofa, smothering the murmurs of her maternal revolt. She rose to **answer:**

'You will do what your strength will allow,' **she** said. '**You will** go, on the road **to** your calvary, as far as your feet will be **able to** carry you, and as long as your shoulders will be **able to** bear your cross. I shall walk by your side in thought only, since you are afraid that my real presence would be a cause of weakness. But if, after all, you felt that you are going to fall before reaching the end will you refuse me the right to attempt **a** last effort to save you?'

'What could you do?' asked the child with a gesture of despair. 'However, be quiet! If I feel that the task is beyond my strength, I will write to you.'

'You promise?'

'I promise!'

The **hour** of their separation had **come.**

'Farewell, mother!' said Paulette.

'Farewell!' repeated Laura, clasping the hand of her **child, and** pressing it on her heart.

Paulette, accompanied by her father, returned **to the old** mansion, and soon after the usual guests of the house sat down to dinner Paulette was by the side of Annibal Palmeri, and, except that she was a little paler than usual, nothing in her demeanor recalled the murderous emotions of the day. After dinner Paulette approached Annibal.

'I shall be grateful to you,' she said, '**if you** will lead me into the garden. I have a few words to speak **to** you in private.'

Palmeri bowed without answering, and gave her his arm. We must say, to the honor of the Neapolitan that his heart was beating faster at that moment than he thought it was capable of. The virginal charms of Paulette had made a deep impression on that bandit born at the foot of Vesuvius. Even so, that he was trembling

like a young man who goes to his first rendezvous. They were
hardly seated when Paulette said to Annibal that her father had
told her of the obligations he owed to the brother of his second
wife, and of the engagements he had taken in exchange. These
engagements, whose execution depended upon herself alone, she
was ready to keep. She would become M. Palmeri's wife to release
her father from his debts. But it was her duty to tell him, that she
could dispose only of her person, her heart having been already
given to another.

'I hope, Miss,' said the Italian, with a smile full of conceit, 'I
hope to be able to make you forget the whim of a young girl. At
your age, the imagination is easily carried away.'

'At my age,' Paulette answered coolly, 'a young girl such as I
am does not take back the heart she has once given. Be that as it
may, sir, do you still insist upon your demand, after what I have
told you?'

'More than ever, Miss.'

'Then I shall be your wife, and redeem my father's promise!'
She bowed and walked away.

VII.

Two or three days after the events we have just narrated, the
servant of Sir Elias Drack at the hotel of the Louvre, told him that
the prince wished to see him.

'Still the Indian,' grunted the good man, visibly anxious, and
trying to disguise his anxiety with an air of bad humor. 'The
prince is commencing to annoy me. But it makes no difference.
Show his excellency in. Ah, here you are,' said Mr. Drack to the
faithful Indian when they were left alone. 'I was in hopes of
being able to take the train for Calais this evening without hearing
from you or your masters. They are well, those people, eh?'

'Not, not well! But is it true that you are going away!' asked
Maltar, in his turn.

'If it is true! This evening, by express! I leave for England.'

'You return to your family!'

'Eh! I have very little family.'

'Among your friends?'

'I think that I have less of them than of a family.'

'To your country then?'

'My country! my country! You mean the country where I was
born, and where I have lived until I was seven or eight months old.
Later, my parents sent me around the world.'

'Well, if it is so,' continued Maltar, 'why are you thinking of leaving Paris, where I know somebody who wants you.'

'That's another reason why I should go,' growled the Englishman. 'Wants me! and who is it that wants me?'

'The young mistress.'

'Paulette! What can I do for her, even if I consent to inconvenience myself? She has her father!'

'Unhappily, yes,' answered Maltar, in a low voice.

'She has her mother.'

'Unhappily, no!' added Maltar, a little louder.

'What are you saying no for? Has not Mme. Laura, thanks to me, been reinstated into the good graces of the old seal?'

'The old seal?' asked Maltar, opening his eyes.

'The old admiral, if you prefer the term, and will not Paulette, who is allowed to visit her grand-parents, see her mother as much as she wants?'

'Oh!' said the devoted servant, 'there has been a great change within forty-eight hours.'

'A change?' asked Mr. Drack, stopping in his preparations for his departure. 'And what is that change?'

'I went to see the Countess de Moray last night.'

'Which countess? Because one loses himself among all these people.'

'There is only one Countess de Moray for me,' answered the Indian, his eyes flashing with anger. 'I mean Mme. Laura. My old mistress has told me, crying bitterly, that her daughter could not come and see her any more, on account of her going to be married.'

With this Palmeri you have spoken about. The project is not abandoned.

'Alas! no.'

'And Mme. Laura consents to it?'

'What can she do to prevent it? Nobody can do anything. She, no more than the others!'

'Nobody, nobody!' repeated Mr. Drack, 'It is not yet written that nobody can do anything. Perhaps there would be one way of which I have already thought.'

'One way?' asked Maltar. 'One way to prevent this marriage which will kill Miss Paulette. Yes, Mr. Drack, it will kill my young mistress, I am sure.'

'Kill her!' said the Englishman with agitation. 'Tell me, do you think Miss Paulette would consent to receive me, if I went and proposed one way to put this Annibal out of the way?'

'Oh! yes, sir,' answered Maltar, who knew very well that all the bad humor of good Mr. Drack would end in a proposition of that

kind. ' And I am sure the young mistress would be very happy to
see you.'

' Well, return to the mansion, and tell her of my visit. Ah ! one
word yet. Do you think I could enter the house without meeting
her father. You know, your master irritates me. He is the cause
of all this annoyance. I could not help telling him that he has
neither heart nor soul, which would make me angry and it might
injure my health.'

' I shall expect you, Mr. Drack,' said the Indian retiring, ' and
you will enter without anybody seeing you.'

An hour later the good Englishman was introduced into Paulette's room. The young girl greeted him with a tender caress, as
if feeling that he was her best friend.

' How good of you ! ' said Paulette, with tears in her eyes. ' How
I thank you ! '

' Oh ! you are welcome,' answered Mr. Drack. ' As I had nothing
to do this morning, I came this way, by chance. Then what Maltar has told me is true, they are marrying you ? '

Paulette looked at him and answered firmly :

' Maltar makes a mistake. They do not marry me ; I consent to
the marriage myself.'

' Hum ! ' said the old consul, ' the result is about the same. But
then, if you get married what will become of poor M. de Vallières ? '

' Gaston ! ' cried the child.

' Yes, Gaston ! that young man so good, so charming, from what
you have told me, at least, because I don't know him myself.'

' Gaston ! ' repeated Paulette. ' Ah ! if I only dared ! '

' What ? '

' Nothing ! A foolish idea ! '

' Say it, anyhow.'

' Well, if some day soon, you should return to India —— ! '

' Never in my life, thank you. Return to India ! there is no
danger. If it did happen, however, what do you want me to do ? '

' You will go and see M. de Vallières and tell him all you have
heard since you came to Paris, all you have witnessed until the
moment of your departure. You will tell him that she who was
wedded was not a happy and smiling bride, but a victim to an imperious, to a sacred duty, and you will so make him understand my
story that he shall not think of accusing me, who will never cease
to love him, until my last —— ! '

' Your last what ? ' asked the Englishman with the same phlegm,
when she stopped for the second time.

' Until the time when this necessary marriage has made me the
wife of another ! ' said the child with heroic courage.

' Poor unhappy child ! ' the good man could not help saying, at
the same time grumbling at himself for being so weak and sensi-

tive. 'Certainly, if what you say **should** happen, I would probably have business which would call **me to** India, and I would have time to deliver your message **to** M. Gaston de Vallières. But as I **was** telling Maltar this morning, there is a very simple means to prevent this confounded marriage, and you **have** only to say the word. I have never **told you** that I have acquired many physical accomplishments ; **I am as** clever as **a** monkey.'

'I am **aware that you** swim well !' **said the young girl, with a look** of **affection** and gratitude.

'Eh ! I swim, **I swim**,' he answered modestly, ' say that **I swim a** little. But there are lots **of** things I can do infinitely better. I am as good a swordsman as a fencing-master, and with **a pistol I** hit the mark at thirty feet **every** time. I have never **had the** chance to utilize those little **talents**, and I believe I have **a good** occasion to-day to pass from **theory to** practice. This M. **Palmeri** of yours, whom I **never saw, annoys** me ; disturbs me ; he **upsets** all my combinations. **Come, would** it cause you great **sorrow if I tried** my skill upon him ?'

'No, no, said Paulette **quickly**, 'I have nothing against M. Palmeri, whose conduct **towards my** father has been generous, and he has my word. **I must, do you hear,** I must become his wife !'

'As you will,' **said Mr. Drack, who** appeared disappointed. 'I shall make experiments **on** someone else. But I would have preferred ——. After all, **my** child, it is your business. And when is the wedding to take place ?'

'As soon as possible,' answered Paulette. '**Since this** marriage is necessary, I am in a hurry **to see** it celebrated. **I have** asked my father to shorten the delays. It **will** be **in** fifteen days perhaps.'

'Good !' thought the honest Englishman. '**In** fifteen days one can do many things, and **we** have time to **turn around**.'

While Paulette was extending her hand **to her old friend, to say** farewell, the door opened and the maid **appeared, asking if M.** Palmeri could be received.

'Certainly,' said Mr. Drack, **without** waiting **Paulette's answer.** 'Introduce him.'

Then **turning to** Paulette.

'I **beg your pardon if** I answered for you, my dear child,' he said, '**but it affords me great** pleasure indeed to see this excellent M. Annibal, **your future** husband.'

The presence of **Sir** Elias Drack **on** that **day** spared Paulette **a** painful annoyance which she had to suffer since the previous day, and which would come every day until the wedding. This annoyance, or rather this downright torture **was** the necessity the young girl had to submit to, of receiving the **visit** of her affianced lover. This **visit** was very painful to Paulette, **for the** man who sat by her and **tried to** conquer, if not her love, **at** least her indifference, this

M

man appeared, in her eyes, to be an executioner. And was he not one, in reality? For our readers have understood that Paulette had resolved to die. M. de Moray had pronounced her sentence of death in taking in her name the engagement to make her the wife of the brother of Claudia. He had doubly pronounced that sentence when he had disposed, without her consent, of a heart she had given, and which she would never take back. And the man who was to execute the sentence, the man who was to be thereafter, we repeat the word, the executioner of Paulette, this man was the very one designated to lead her to the altar. It was Annibal Palmeri. More than once, she had made a comparison between herself, the innocent, and the wretch awaiting with anguish, in his cell, the terrible morning of the last toilet. This last toilet ! for her, the bride whom everyone would envy, it would be made of flowers and silk ! It would be the virginal dress with which every young girl adorns herself one day in her life, to go and meet the expected husband. But, no matter how beautiful, it would be her last toilet, the one which precedes death. And there was one thing which rendered the approach of the torture still more acute to Paulette than to ordinary criminals : it was the obligation she was under, in order to hide her project, to make her own preparations, and to weave, so to speak, the wedding veil which was to be her shroud. There are voluntary deaths to which those who are resigned rush with nervous enthusiasm. It seems then that life has been so hard to those who resolve to quit it that it is a burden they are in a hurry to be rid of. But it was far from being so in the case of Paulette. Hardly one month before her existence was full of beautiful promises. The joys of her childhood held out still greater happiness for the future. One month, nay, fifteen days ago she was landing from the steamer at Marseilles, knowing nothing of the drama which had filled the old family mansion with blood ; of the divorce which had separated her parents, of the financial disaster which was threatening the honor of her father, and lastly of the engagement which bound her to a man she abhorred. In such a short time, what a revolution in and around her. The visits of Palmeri awakened all these sad ideas in her heart, and it is no wonder that they were a downright torture. On that day the presence of Sir Elias Drack made the visit less painful. She presented the two gentlemen to each other, and shortly after she retired, leaving them together. Annibal, who was annoyed by the incident, tried nevertheless to be amiable.

' I believe it was you,' he said, ' who escorted Miss de Moray on her voyage ? '

' My own self ! ' answered Mr. Drack, whose eyes, piercing like daggers, were searching to the very bottom of his interlocutor's brains, trying to discover his secrets. ' And it is you who are going to marry my young companion ? '

' Yes, sir, I have this great happiness ! '

' It is a great happiness, as you say, and I congratulate you sincerely. But this marriage was decided on very quickly, it seems to me ? '

' It has been sufficient to me to see Miss Paulette, to become suddenly smitten with her beauty, her charms, and her grace. Does not that seem natural to you ? '

' Quite natural. And I doubt not that at your first interview, my young friend has experienced the same feeling as yourself. Reciprocated and instantaneous love ! A thunderbolt, double pressure, as we say in France, I believe.'

Annibal who was an ass at times, but who still was nothing of an imbecile, felt the irony of the remark, and experienced a feeling of anger. At the very moment he was giving way to his passion, the adventurer felt that he would make himself ridiculous, and he pretended not to have understood. This was the more easy to him as M. Drack had a good-natured air, and appeared convinced of what he said.

' The thunderbolt, sir, as you say,' he replied.

' So that,' rejoined the ex-consul, ' the daughter—of the wife —of the husband—of Madam, your sister—it is that, is it not ? is made perfectly happy by this sudden union ? '

Mr. Drack had wound the chaplet of relations we have just written with a very comical accent, as if seeking his words. But the Neapolitan had made up his mind not to be offended or astonished at anything.

' Happy!' he replied. ' Certainly Miss Paulette is very happy, and I doubt not she will be still more so after her marriage, when she will have appreciated the sincerity of my sentiments. But I see with the greatest satisfaction, sir,' he added, setting his teeth in an involuntary movementy of humor, ' that you feel a great deal of interest in Miss de Moray.'

' A great deal, dear sir, indeed! I even offered her my services a minute ago for a favor to which, by the way, you were not indifferent.'

' A favor! And what was it ? Tell me, I pray.'

' Oh, nonsense! Since Miss Paulette has refused to take advantage of certain talents which I put at her entire disposal, it is quite useless——'

' Ah! she has refused ? '

' Yes, unluckily. I regret it for her sake, and for mine also, to tell you the truth ; because it would have been a great satisfaction to me if I——'

Mr. Drack did not go any further in his confidence, as the reader will easily understand, when he will remember the nature of his little talents and the favor he alluded to. Annibal, although filled with mistrust, felt obliged to answer a few polite words.

'Whatever may be the favor you speak of, sir, I am very grateful for the intention.'

'You are quite welcome, I assure you, my dear Mr. Palmeri. Ah! do me a favor in your turn.'

'If it is in my power.'

'Oh! the simplest thing in the world for you, but which is giving me a great deal of bother. I have just called you my dear Mr. Palmeri, and every time I pronounce your name, it seems to me I have heard it before. Please tell me where I have met you.'

Annibal, as it happened every time someone enquired about his personality, felt a cold shiver, to use a familiar expression. Nevertheless, it could not be noticed.

'It is not very surprising,' he said, 'that my name should be known to you. M. Palmeri, my uncle, who was in the banking business, made a great fortune, which we inherited, my sister and I. It is undoubtedly my uncle whom you have heard spoken of.'

'It is probable,' answered the Englishman, apparently satisfied. 'And you say you have inherited; recently, is it not?'

'About a year ago.'

'A year, in truth! it is very recent yet. And you are Italian, are you not?'

'Yes, by origin, but I was born in India.'

'Ah! in India, I begin to understand.'

'What?'

'It must have been in India I heard your family spoken of. Ah! my dear Mr. Palmeri, there is another thing I have forgotten to tell you, and which I hope will not annoy you. I have consented to be one of the witnesses of your bride.'

'She could not make a choice more agreeable to me,' politely said Annibal, who had a good mind to send his bride's friend to the devil.

'I am very happy that it is so agreeable to you,' rejoined Mr. Drack, giving Annibal one of those shakes of the hand of which one is never sure whether its aim is not to pull off one's arm. 'Inasmuch as my quality of witness will afford me an opportunity, I hope, of getting better acquainted with your charming family. I have not had occasion to be presented to Madam your sister yet.'

'She will be at home to-morrow night,' politely answered Annibal. 'She receives every Friday. You will be welcome.'

'One cannot be more courteous. I will have the honor to come and pay her my respects, with your kind permission. Good-bye, dear Mr. Palmeri, until to-morrow. Ah! a last word. When you see your amiable betrothed, please tell her on my part that if she changes her mind about that little favor, she will always find me ready.'

' Depend on me,' said Annibal, ' **I shall not fail.**'

' Thank you. Good-bye.'

Saying these words, Mr. Drack went away.

' The confounded prattler,' thought Annibal, I fancied he would never go away.' Then, reflecting : ' What might be the nature of the little favor he is always speaking of ? I should not be sorry to know **what** he **is** alluding **to.**'

Our intention is **not to dwell at length upon the** events of the fifteen days which were to **elapse before** the **marriage** of Mlle. de Moray. We are too anxious **to arrive** at the grave **changes** which are preparing. Moreover, the situation was such, **between the** different actors of our drama, that it could **not** be materially altered. Mr. Drack was the only **one** to modify his manner of life. He made himself altogether at home, affecting the keenest sympathy for his hosts, and becoming a great friend of the new countess and her brother, at least as much as **of** Paulette. This transformation grieved Paulette greatly at first, **because** she had thought she had lost her only protector. But she **had been** reassured very quickly by Maltar, who went to her one **day, and** told her that the conduct of Mr. Drack was only a **deceit.**

' **Mr.** Drack has charged me **to tell** young mistress,' rapidly said the **Indian** in a low voice, ' **not to** believe that he is forgetting her.'

' **So** you have seen him ?' **asked** Paulette surprised.

' **Yes** ; Maltar goes almost **every** morning, secretly, **to the hotel,** where they let the prince come **in.**'

' What prince?'

' **No** matter, **don't** mind !' answered the good servant with a silent laugh. ' **And** when he arrives, Maltar always sees Mr. Drack working with **a** fencing-master. One, **two.** One, two. He is a good swordsman, Mr. Drack.'

' Poor old friend,' thought **Paulette with a** grateful heart. ' He has always the same foolish idea.'

Then addressing herself again **to her** humble and faithful **servant,** she lowered her voice still **more and** said :

' And my mother, Maltar ? **Did you** see her yesterday ? How is she ?'

' Well,' answered the Indian ; it is always the same thing at **the** admiral's. Everybody weeps. But they are all glad of being together again. Mme. Laura hopes that when the young mistress will be married, **she** will see her again. Until then she entreats her to keep up her courage.'

' Yes, yes,' said Paulette quickly. ' **Tell** my mother that I have courage, a great deal of courage. Tell **her** that my evils will soon end — and that — when I will be — '

Her voice fell in a moment of weakness, **but was soon firm again** as she continued :

'Tell her that when I will be — married, I will be by her side always. I will watch over her. I will console her. — Go, now, go.'

When she was alone, the poor child burst into sobs.

'Yes, beloved mother,' she thought, crying, 'I will be near you. I will console you. My soul, delivered from its chains, will fly to you. My breath will heal the wounds of your heart. And, knowing then the mysteries of your life, I will share the weight of the sufferings of the saintly and heroic martyr.'

While his daughter was preparing for her funeral wedding, M. de Moray was beginning to undergo the just punishment of the attraction which had dragged him in his new life, as if he had been suddenly attacked with madness. His interview with Laura at the admiral's had dissipated a portion of the clouds which darkened his heart. He looked at himself now with a sort of instinctive horror. Moreover, the emotions which he owed to his financial disasters and to the imperious necessity of marrying Paulette against her wish had weakened his will and his courage. He was living after a mechanical fashion, and was avoiding thought as much as possible. He was seeking the numerous gatherings ; noise, movement, and, in a word, everything which could divert his thoughts from him. Only one thing had survived in the ruin of this high personality : the sentiment of honor.

Gorgon was enjoying her triumph. The marriage of Paulette was the crowning of her success. There was nothing left of the scruples, the disdains, and the jealousies of which she had been the object. Her will had passed through everything like the scythe which cuts, and the harrow which levels. Her harvest was made, and she was getting the ground ready for the seeding of new successes. Annibal, also was frankly happy. The heart of such a man did not want, to be satisfied, the love of the woman he was going to marry. He was asking from Paulette only the gift of her beauty, and that he felt sure to have.

Let us return once more to Paulette and her mother. The reader will remember that the noble young girl, after her unexpected presence at the interview at the admiral's, in which her fate was settled, had implored her mother to cease all relations between them until the day her sacrifice would be consummated. Paulette had said that she must be free from all causes of emotion to be able to attain the end she had in view. It had been agreed that they would neither meet nor write to each other. They had news of each other through a few words hastily exchanged with Maltar. One day as Laura was expressing her surprise at not receiving the visit of the ex-consul, the Indian had told her that Sir Elias Drack hardly ever left the old mansion.

'Ah!' Laura had cried with discouragement, 'that one is also tired of being the companion of the unhappy ! He courts the rising sun, and wants his share of the pleasures, having found too much bitterness in the tears.'

'No, mistress,' answered Maltar, shaking his head. 'I do not know what Mr. Drack's projects are, but I am certain that he has not abandoned his unhappy friends, and moreover, he is quite changed, Mr. Drack is ! he does not say, as a month ago, that this confounded house of de Moray does not concern him. He does not speak of his broken rest. He does not threaten to leave every morning. Do you see, mistress, I am quite sure he has an idea, and he hopes in something.'

'What can he hope for ?' asked Laura, 'think of it, Maltar ! It is to-morrow, to-morrow ! that the crime will be perpetrated ! To-morrow my daughter will become almost the sister of the woman who occupies my place in my own house ! It is to-morrow that Paulette, burying her own love for M. Gaston de Vallières, will become the wife of one Annibal Palmeri !'

'I don't know, mistress ! I know nothing !' repeated Maltar. 'But I believe Mr. Drack has a project and a hope he does not speak of.'

. . . .

We are now on the morning of the day fixed for the marriage. The ceremony is to take place at two o'clock. It is nine o'clock. Then only five hour separate Paulette from the moment when everything will end for her. And when she counts the minutes she says the day will have no morrow. When she will have redeemed the promise of her father, she will have regained her freedom. She will die then ! At times she touches in her pocket a thin little dagger she has brought with her fron India. The wound of the weapon is mortal. The point of it has been charged with a subtle poison, known to the negroes only. A single touch of the dagger, and in a few minutes the work of destruction will deliver her from the work of profanation. This is how she came into possession of this dangerous arm : after her long illness, during her convalescence, M. de Vallières had told her one day, while showing her the dagger :

'If you had died, Paulette, this would have delivered me from this life, and I should have rejoined you where our souls, at least, could be united for eternity !'

Paulette, frightened, had taken away the weapon from his hands. She had kept it religiously ever since, and to-day she was saying to herself : 'It is with this dagger he would have killed himself if he had been obliged to renounce me ; it is by this dagger I will die, sooner than belong to another.' All these things whirl in her head, and she is hardly conscious of the fleeting hours. Nevertheless, she hears the clock strike ten, and she remembers that on the previous day she has said to Mr. Drack : 'Come to-morrow at ten o'clock. I have something to entrust to your care.' It is even in anticipation of this visit, and to prepare what she was to remit to her faithful friend that she was up writing the greater part of the night.

'Quarter past ten already !' she says to herself with nervous impatience. 'Has he forgotten his promise ; still I must speak to him !'

At the same moment, the old consul arrived, much agitated. He excused himself.

'Pardon me, my dear child, if I am a little late ; but I was expecting some important despatches.'

'Despatches !' answered Paulette, inattentively. 'What despatches ?'

'Oh ! nothing that concerns you,' hastily rectified Sir Elias Drack. 'Moreover, when you will have informed me what you called me for, I will return to the hotel to remain until the hour of your sacrifice. Tell me at once what you want.'

'I wish you to do me a favor,' said Paulette, 'and I hope you will not refuse me.'

To claim a favor with so much insistance on the morning of the day of her marriage, Paulette must have attached a particular importance to it. Sir Elias Drack understood that, and he did not hesitate to answer.

'I am entirely at your orders,' he said, eagerly. 'Did you think, at the last minute, to have recourse to the little talents I have spoken of ?'

'It is not that,' answered Paulette, with an icy smile. 'I do not desire the death of anybody. It is simply this : You know that my mother will not be present at the ceremony of the marriage. She knows that I want all my courage, and she understands that her presence would provoke in me emotions which would annihilate my strength. So it has been decided between my mother and myself that we would not see each other to-day.'

'Well, you will allow me to tell you that this combination of yours is not very clever. It is heart-rending for your mother, and threatening to you. Yes, I say *threatening*, and I maintain the word. I should not wonder if it was a cause of misfortune.'

'Perhaps so,' said Paulette, with the same enigmatical smile, which did not escape the attention of her old friend, 'it may be possible that it will be a cause of misfortune, even very soon. But it must be so. Well, if I must not see my mother, I should like very much that a letter should be handed to her this very day, one hour, minute for minute, after the time we have left the mayor's office. Here is the letter. Will you be kind enough to deliver it under the conditions I have told you ?'

'Very willingly,' said Mr. Drack, with a good-natured air. 'It is understood, I shall do your errand at once, before returning to the hotel. I have all the time necessary. Give it to me.'

The young girl who was on the point of giving her letter to the Englishman, withdrew her hand suddenly.

' No, no,' she said, quickly. ' It is this evening, through the day. I mean, one hour after my husband and I shall have returned. It is only one hour after that the letter must be handed to my mother. Can I depend on your punctuality ? '

' Perfectly,' retorted the good Mr. Drack, with the same affectionate frankness. ' You know very well that I do only what you wish.'

' You give me your word ? '

' I give it to you.'

' You swear on your honor as a gentleman, and on your faith as a Christian, to hand this letter to my mother only one hour after the accomplishment of my marriage ; but you swear also not to deliver it later ? '

' Must I swear by Styx ?' laughingly asked the consul.

' Do not laugh,' said Paulette, with gravity. ' Otherwise, seeing that I could not confide in you, I would think of somebody else.'

Saying these words, the noble child turned towards Maltar, who had just entered the room to attend to his duties, and who, taking advantage of the great freedom he was enjoying in exchange for his immense devotion, was listening to their conversation. That one, at least, she was sure, would not argue ; he would execute her orders faithfully.

' No, no,' cried Mr. Drack, with a sober air, ' I am not laughing. Don't you see that I am not thinking of laughing. On my faith as a Christian, on my honor as a gentleman, I swear that this letter shall be placed in the hands of your mother one hour only after your marriage.'

' Very well, my friend. I thank you, and I have confidence in you.'

The young girl gave her little hand to the Englishman, who squeezed it affectionately between his own.

' Now,' she added, making an effort to smile, ' I am going to survey the last preparations of my toilet, because I must be a beautiful bride.'

She did not wait for an answer, because she was afraid to yield to her sorrow in the presence of the only two friends she had. The poor child was hardly out of the room when Sir Elias Drack turned towards the Indian :

' Maltar,' he said, ' do not lose a minute ! Take this letter to Paulette's mother at once, this very moment ! '

' But you have promised the young mistress to remit it only one hour after the ceremo —— '

' Why don't you start !' retorted Mr. Drack, with anger, not allowing him to end the word. ' Go, as I would go myself if I was not obliged to return to the hotel for these confounded despatches, which may arrive at any minute. Don't you understand that it would be the farewell of a corpse I would take to Mme. Laura if I waited until the middle of the day to send this message. You don't wish then that Mme. Laura should be warned in time to prevent her daughter killing herself ? '

In spite of his violent words, Maltar was not quite decided.

' Sir,' he said, hesitating, 'you have taken an oath, a solemn oath. Can one break an oath ? '

' Certainly not ! ' cried Mr. Drack, with comical energy. ' But all oaths are equally sacred ; and long before I took this one for the poor young girl, there was one I solemnly made to myself : I have sworn always to act according to my conscience. And my conscience tells me that neither my conscience nor my faith will be compromised because I will have saved this dear child who wants to kill herself. Moreover, this is an affair between heaven and myself, and it does not concern you, you wretched idolator ! '

Maltar did not insist any more, but he revenged himself in his own way for this outrage to his faith.

' Very well,' he said, ' I fly to Mme. Laura's, and I will tell her : Madam, this is sent by the English gentleman who never bothers about anything that does not concern him, who hates emotion, and who thinks only of himself.'

' Yes,' grumbled Sir Elias Drack, ' laugh at me, old buffer, that's your right. Only hurry up, because the minutes are counted, do you see. And if you should arrive too late on account of your confounded prattle, I think I should strangle you with these fingers.'

' And the master would be right,' humbly said the Indian, leaning towards the threatening hand of Mr. Drack to kiss it. ' The master loves Mme. Laura and Mlle. Paulette almost as much as I love them myself, and I would die for him, at once, if he desired it.'

On these words they separated.

We will let them pursue their work of devotion, and we will remain in the mansion, where the preparations for the ceremony are being actively pushed. The servants have put on their most gorgeous livery. In the yard the coachmen throw a last look at the carriages ; in the kitchen the cooks are already preparing the banquet to which will be invited only the most intimate friends of the family. There is only one poor wretch in this magnificent mansion : the one to whom it belongs, whose name it bears, the one who seems to command as master, the Count de Moray. He must be very poor, indeed ! this one, most horribly ruined, not to be able, by sacrificing all he possesses to redeem the life of his daughter ! On this eventful morning this thought preyed on his mind still more than usual. At the moment the sacrifice was to be consummated without hopes of ever turning back, he was **perceiving** with greater lucidity than on the previous days the immense responsibility **he** was incurring for the whole future. Nevertheless, worldly honor obliged him to let these things be done. If he were to die, if Paulette herself were **to** be condemned to inconsolable sorrow, the mar**riage** must take **place,** since there was no means to avoid criminal proceedings but **to take** refuge in suicide, **or** to accept salvation at the sacrifice of **his** daughter. It was eleven o'clock when M. de Moray was thinking thus. **At** the same time, with a brazen effrontery, the new Countess de Moray, accompanied by her **brother,** sent **a** servant to Paulette to ask her if **she** would receive **them.** She wanted to be the first to kiss the **dear** child on the day **of her** marriage ! Paulette, the courageous girl, had made answer **that she** would rejoin the countess in the drawing-room as soon as she **was** ready. Annibal and his sister, **full** of joy at their triumph, **had** been waiting **for a few** minutes, **when** the door was opened **with a** crash.

'I **will enter** ! I **tell** you ! I will enter !' cried an angry voice.

The **Italian turned** around suddenly, and recognized Laura. The **two** Countesses de Moray were facing each other. It was a fatal law which made these two women meet, so that one would crush the other. All that remains to be known are **the** conditions and the issue of this duel in which **is resumed** all the morality of this story ; all that remains to be known **is, w**ho will be definitely and logically winner, either virtue **disarmed or** vice defended and protected by all the seductions of beauty, youth, and **fortune.**

On seeing the first wife of her husband, the **second Mme. de** Moray had the presentiment that something definit**e would be done.** She accordingly accepted the battle without hesitation, **like a** valiant wrestler. But this time, as the reader will see, she had **to** contend against a powerful enemy. Her adversary was not, **as a few** months before, a daughter who **sacrificed** herself for the honor of her mother, a wife who resigned **herself to** the abandonment of her husband. It was a mother **who wanted to** save the life of her child, and who would fight with **tooth and nail,** until she would be out of the hands of her executioners.

'I will enter !' had cried Laura, **dashing by sheer strength** into the drawing-room.

'**You** ! you in **my house** !' answered another shriek, uttered by **the** Italian.

'I do **not** know where **I am or in** whose house I am !' said Laura, with force. 'I know only one **thing** ! it is that my daughter is going to die, and I have come to **prevent** her killing herself.'

'Die !' repeated Palmeri and **his sister,** with the same accent.

'Yes, die ! rather than be the **wife of the one she** had accepted.'

'You are mad!' retorted the beautiful Claudia, with disdain.
'So, your insults do not reach us. Only is it not customary to
keep mad people in a house, you will go out, do you hear!'

'I will not go out! at least not without seeing my daughter and
taking her away with me. Come! make room! madam! I must
see my daughter!'

The adventuress had placed herself near the door of Paulette's
room, and to get to that door, Laura made a gesture to push her
aside. Annibal rushed to the help of his sister, and placed himself
by her side. But Claudia refused his aid.

'There is only one person,' she said proudly, 'whose help I am
willing to accept against this woman; and that is my husband. Call
M. de Moray, Annibal. He will judge between us.'

Palmeri hesitated before he obeyed, not knowing what would happen during the few minutes he would be away. But Laura reassured him.

'Yes,' she said, 'your sister is right, sir. Call M. de Moray. Go
without fear. I will await his decision.'

Annibal bowed and went away. During the few minutes they
remained alone, the two rivals were silent.

At last the count, sent by Palmeri, entered the room.

'Come, come quickly, sir,' said the Italian, again becoming insolent, with the certainty of victory brought by the arrival of her
husband. 'Put a stop, I pray, to the insults and threats of
Madam!'

On hearing from Annibal of the unexpected presence of Laura in
his daughter's apartment, M. de Moray felt troubled to the bottom
of his soul. But the legal exigencies of the situation imposed upon
him the duty of taking the part of her who had become his wife
against her who had been repudiated. Firmly resolved to fulfil
this duty, he approached Laura and said coolly:

'Have you calculated, Madam, before crossing the threshold of
this house, the consequences of such a proceeding?'

Laura answered as coolly.

'I have not come,' she said, 'to engage in a discussion with you.
I only wished to see my daughter. Your appearance gives me the
occasion to say some things I did not intend to say. I shall do and
say what I know is my duty, which is a sacred one. It is placed
higher than all your social conventions, higher than all your laws.
For a mother the care of the life of her child is the first of
duties.'

'The life of Paulette?' asked M. de Moray with anxiety.

'This marriage, if it is accomplished, is the death warrant of
your child.'

'What do you say?'

'I say that Paulette will kill herself if you persist in imposing
this marriage upon her.'

' You are strangely mistaken,' said the count. ' Remember that
Paulette herself has accepted the husband I destined for her, but
which I would not have imposed, neither this one nor any other. If
what you affirm is true, she would not have accepted this union, or
having accepted it presuming too much on her strength, she would
have renounced it since.'

' I have said,' affirmed Laura in despair, 'that this marriage will
kill Paulette. Here is the proof. You see this letter ? It is her
eternal farewell which she has sent me. It was to be given to me
only at the very moment she was to strike the fatal blow, one hour
after her marriage. Happily, the friend to whom she had entrusted
it guessed her project, and betrayed her confidence. If I had received it only at the hour appointed, this night your daughter
would be no more. My mother and I have read it. It is wet with
our tears yet. But read it, sir, read it in your turn, and you will
not doubt, after, that this marriage was going to kill your daughter.'

M. de Moray took the pages which Laura was handing him, and
read them rapidly. In an instant he learned the love of Paulette
for Gaston de Vallières and her invincible hatred for the man
whose sister had been the cause of her mother's unhappiness.
Henceforth his mind was made up.

' Be reassured, Madam,' he said with great emotion. ' Paulette
shall live. This marriage will not take place, since, thank God, it
is time yet.'

A cry of joy escaped from the lips of Laura. In truth, God owed
her this moment of happiness. But the Italian claimed the rights
of Annibal Palmeri.

' Ah!' she said with sovereign contempt, ' my brother and I
should have expected this. The nobleman I have married thinks
very little of his honor!'

' You are mistaken, Madam,' said M. de Moray. ' I forget nothing of what I owe either to you or M. Palmeri. Only, instead of
sacrificing my daughter to pay my debt, I will acquit it myself before
this evening ; depend upon it, the honor of the gentleman will soon
be redeemed.'

' You want to die! you!' cried Laura, stupefied. ' Why ?'

' Did not you hear ?' asked Roger with a painful smile. ' The
honor of a nobleman is engaged. I must, within twenty-four hours,
pay a considerable sum of money. This money, which I have not,
the marriage of Paulette with M Palmeri put at my disposal. But
since this marriage will not take place, I will have to pay with my
blood what I cannot pay with my money.'

Laura stopped him with a shriek.

' So,' she said, ' you were going to sacrifice your daughter for the
sake of money, and it is for the sake of money that you want to

kill yourself.   In that case it will soon be settled.   I will save both
of you!'
    'You?' cried the Italian.
    'Save us? and how can you do it?' asked the count.
    'When the tribunal pronounced our divorce,' answered Laura
with animation, 'you remitted to my notary about eight hundred
thousand francs, which formed my dowry ; take that money, Roger,
it is yours!'
    'If that is the only means you have to offer,' said M. de Moray,
'I cannot accept it!'
    'But why? why?' cried Laura stupefied.
    'Certainly,' ironically said Claudia, 'who can prevent you re-
deeming your honor with the money of the woman who has dishonored you?'
    'Yes, the world would pronounce the same judgment as my con-
science.   Once more I repeat : I do not accept!'
    'But it is impossible,' cried Laura, 'I cannot be placed between
those two torments :   Either to see my daughter die, or to see my
husband die!'
    'Your husband!' protested Claudia with a threatening laugh.
    'No! yours!' answered Laura, distracted.   'Yours! But let
him live, and live without condemning his child.   Roger, in the
name of the past! in the name of our daughter! do not repulse the
offer I make, and which you would accept from anybody else!'
    The count was strangely moved by this generous struggle for his
life.
    'Alas!' he repeated, 'don't you understand that you are exactly
the only person in the world from whom I cannot accept any help?'
    'But this money is not even mine ; just think!   It is the result
of the long services and privations of my father.   And since I am
an unworthy woman, a guilty woman, a dishonored woman, it is
only just that this fortune honorably gained should pass from the
glorious hands of the grand-father to the pure and innocent hands
of his grand-daughter.   It is not I, Roger, it is she!   It is your
daughter who offers you her ransom and yours! and since it is so,
you will accept this money, Roger ; you cannot refuse it!'
    'It is your dowry! I will not accept it!'
    'So the child, or the husband will be sacrificed, because the
mother——'
    'Because the mother has been guilty!   Yes,' cried M. de Moray
with force ; 'it is the chastisement inflicted on the guilty wife!'
    This was too much.   Laura rebelled at last.
    'Well, no!' she cried ; 'it will not be! I have suffered every
shame, every evil, every despair!   But before this one my heart
rebels!   I will not, and I raise my head!'
    'What do you mean?' cried the count.

At this moment Mme. de la Marche entered the room. The reader will remember what Laura had said : Paulette's letter, sent by Mr. Drack, had been read by her mother and by herself at the same time. Laura had fled without losing a minute, and now the arrival of Mme. de la Marche brought a powerful auxiliary to her daughter.

' Come, mother !' said Laura, ' Come !'

' Well ?' asked Mme. de la Marche, ' our poor Paulette ?'

' They deny me the right to save her !' cried Laura with distraction.

' What do you say ?'

' I say that pride leads M. de Moray either to a criminal suicide or to the murder of his child !'

' Is that true ?' asked Mme. de la Marche, turning towards the count.

' Since your daughter appeals to you, madam,' answered M. de Moray, ' you whom I respect and deeply honor, I will also accept you as judge in this question of honor and dignity !'

' I ?' she answered, hesitating.

' You will decide between us,' repeated the count.

' And you will accept her decision ?' asked Laura.

' I will accept it.'

' And you swear to submit to it ?'

' I swear.'

' Very well ! please let me alone with my mother.'

' Madam,' said the count to Mme. de la Marche, ' it is more than my life I entrust you with, it is my honor.'

' It is in good hands, Roger !' she answered. ' Go without fear. Leave us !'

The count bowed and left the room, taking his wife with him. The mother and daughter were alone.

' Speak, now !' said Mme. de la Marche.

' Mother, you know that it is to redeem his honor that M. de Moray wishes to marry Paulette to this Palmeri ?'

' I know that : Go on.'

' You know that this marriage would cause the death of Paulette. Well, to save those who are dearest to me, I offered my dowry to M. de Moray.'

' What did he answer ?'

' He has refused this money ?'

' He has done well,' said the noble woman. ' Roger cannot accept anything from you.'

' But think of it. It is the condemnation of my daughter which you are pronouncing. Paulette will save her father at any price, and she will die, since the death of one of the two is necessary to redeem his honor !'

' Ah ! it is the merciless justice of heaven ! It strikes the guilty
mothers even through their children ! '

' Then you recognize that if I was not guilty, M. de Moray could
accept the money which I have offered ? Well, know it then.   I
have been unjustly accused, and I have been unjustly condemned ! '

' What do you say ? ' cried Mme. de la Marche.   ' Ah ! I understand,' she added, ' the falsehood you would not utter so as to
escape the punishment which was threatening you, you would utter
now to redeem Paulette.   Alas ! however pious it may be, it will
be a useless falsehood ! '

' But it is not a falsehood ! ' said Laura with force.   ' I tell you,
mother, that I was not guilty ! '

This time, there was in her voice such a ring of truth, that Mme.
de la Marche was astonished.

' You were not guilty ? ' she repeated, her eyes full of anxiety.

' No, mother ! no ; I was not guilty ! And without asking any
other proof, you must affirm to Roger that he can accept without
shame the money belonging to me.'

' I will not say that ! ' said Mme. de la Marche, with discouragement.

' Mother ! '

' I will not say that ! For if I do not obtain from you the proof
of this innocence which you refuse to give even to me, your mother,
the trouble of my look, the hesitation of my lips, the blush on my
forehead will contradict my words ! '

' And still you have the right to swear for me ; for, before God,
and on the salvation of my soul, I swear, mother, that I was
innocent ! '

Laura had risen and had pronounced this protestation in a sort
of mystic ecstasy, as if she had been at the foot of the altar.

' So,' asked Mme. de la Marche, more and more divided between
doubt and faith, ' you swear that you have not betrayed your duty
as a wife ? '

' I swear it ! '

' That you have not dishonored the name of your husband ? '

' I swear it ! I swear that I have never loved but Roger, and that
I never belonged to anybody else ! I swear it ! '

' But you must not only swear, you must also give proofs ! '

' Proofs ! oh ! no ! no ! Do not ask that, mother ! '

' You must, Laura ! For the sake of your daughter ! you must ! '

' Well ! Since you order me to ! '

' Yes, I order you to ! speak ! speak, then ! unhappy child ! '

' Then, I shall tell you all ! But, alas ! I am trembling more at
the moment I am justifying myself than I was on the day I bowed
my head under undeserved shame ! '

' Undeserved shame ! ' said Mme. de la Marche, still doubting.

' Did I not see your accomplice expiring under my eyes ? '

' My accomplice ! he ! he !' muttered Laura, invoking **heaven as** witness.

' **Did I not hear his** avowal, which was in accordance with yours ? **Did I not see the** unhappy man die rather than give up those letters, proof of **your** crime ?'

'Those letters !' cried the generous woman painfully, vanquished at last in her last struggles, ' those letters contained only the cruel secret of his birth. They truly belonged to him whom you call my accomplice, but it was his mother, not I, **who** would have been lost if he had consented **to have them read** !

' His mother !' **cried Mme. de la Marche, not yet understanding,** but instinctively pained, however.

Laura was silent as if unable to continue.

' Go on !' cried Mme. de la Marche. 'Those letters would have ruined his mother, you say ?'

' Yes his mother ! A saintly and noble woman ! A beloved **angel,** guilty only of a moment of weakness, or perhaps the victim **of an** odious plot !'

' A moment of weakness ! A plot !'

' It must have been **so,**' cried Laura, **wringing her** hands, ' if this **one** has succumbed !

' But what did this victim and this plot matter to you ?' ask Mme. **de la** Marche, panting. 'Why did you hide the secret of this man, **even at** the cost of your honor ?'

' He was hiding it, **even at** the cost of his life.'

' But he !' cried Mme. **de la** Marche, with violence, ' **he was** protecting his mother !'

' Alas ! I was also protecting **mine, !' muttered Laura, hiding her** face in her hands.

Mme. de la Marche **uttered a shriek of** despair. **She rose and** walked about the room, striking her heaving breast.

' For me !' muttered at last the noble woman in **the midst of** abundant tears. ' You have sacrificed yourself for me ! **You have** suffered all these shames and all these sorrows for my sake !'

' Oh ! mother ! beloved mother !' repeated Laura.

' And he—he was my son ! But how is it that, when he was dying for my **sake, my** heart did not cry out : It is your child !'

Then **the mother wept** bitterly over the son lost as soon as he had **been** born, **and whose fate** she had never known, and whom she had seen only once **to lose him** in a terrible tragedy.

' Mother !' said **the** poor Martyr whose courage seemed **to** be broken, now that her long sacrifice had become useless, ' mother ! pardon me if I had not the strength of keeping this secret any longer. Forgive me your despair and your tears. But I could not keep silent any more. Remember ! you have said it yourself. It was to save Paulette, **and** I had not the right to keep silent **any**

N

longer. To save you I sacrificed myself without hesitation, as you
have seen, but to save my daughter, I would sacrifice the world !'
   'And you would do your duty,' answered Mme. de la Marche.
' You would do your duty as I am going to do mine.'
   'What do you mean ?'
   Mme. de la Marche walked to the door which opened on the
boudoir to which M. de Moray and the Italian had retired. She
invited Roger to come into the drawing-room. Claudia and her
brother Annibal who had joined her, wanted to come in also, but
Mme. de la Marche stopped them.
   'No,' she said, ' M. de Moray alone. In a moment I shall call
you.'
   However anxious Claudia might have been to be present at the
interview, and whatever right she had to know everything which
happened in her house, she did not dare to insist. The high dignity
of character and the age of the admiral's wife commanded her respect. Then Roger, Laura and her mother were alone. Mme de
la Marche was the first to speak.
   'Dear Roger,' she said, ' the one we gave you for a wife, the
Admiral de la Marche and myself, was the image itself of virtue ;
she was an angel of God !'
   ' And I have adored her,' loyally answered M. de Moray, ' as we
adore God in his purest works until that fatal day when——'
   'Until the day when the saint, taking upon herself the fault of
another, has become a Martyr.'
   'What do you mean ?' cried Roger.
   'Mother !' interupted the imploring voice of Laura.
   Mme de la Marche turned to her daughter.
   'To save your child, you have said, you would sacrifice the world.
I only sacrifice a culprit. Let me speak.'
   'No, no, not another word !' implored Laura, with clasped
hands.
   Mme. de la Marche did not even answer.
   ' Roger,' she said, ' it is through a sublime devotion that the one
who was your wife has borne the consequences of an unjust sus-
picion, of an infamous accusation. The man you found with her
was not her lover.'
   'What do you mean ?'
   'The letters this man threw in the fire were not hers.'
   'But then whose were they ?'
   'They were mine !'
   'Yours !' said Roger, not understanding the extent of the reve-
lation. 'What means —— '
   ' Be silent, mother !' cried Laura, ' For God's sake, be silent.'
   'The man you killed,' continued the noble woman, humiliating
the honor of her old age, ' that man was not her lover ! He was my
son.'

'Your son !' cried M. de Moray, stupefied.

'Do not listen to her, Roger,' cried Laura, distracted. 'Do not believe her !'

'On the life of Laura,' answered Mme. de la Marche, impassible, 'I swear that what I have just said is the truth. Dare you, then, Laura, take on the life of Paulette, to give me the lie, the oath I have just taken on your head to accuse myself. Swear ! swear at once !'

Laura did not dare to add perjury to the false avowals she had already made. She bent her head and remained silent. M. de Moray awoke at last from the torpor into which his mind had fallen for the last few minutes.

'Ah ! all that is true !' he cried with force, 'all that is very true ! I believe it ! I feel it ! I swear it in my turn. And I, wretched insensate that I was, I saw nothing, guessed nothing, and in my blind anger, in my criminal jealousy, I forgot everything.'

He was walking about the room as if mad, and in a rage against himself. However, a flash of reason crossed this violent storm.

'Happily,' he cried, 'it is time yet, and I can repair at least a part of the evil I was the cause of.'

He rushed to the door of his daughter's room.

'Paulette !' he cried, 'Paulette ! Come ! come quickly to kiss your mother.'

Paulette entered the room, already dressed and ready for the sacrifice.

'My mother !' cried the child, who, drowned in her own sorrow, had heard nothing of the solemn interview which had just taken place in the drawing-room. 'My mother ! you here ! what has happened that I should see you once more ?'

'Yes,' said M. de Moray, panting. 'Your mother ! that is to say, honor, modesty, and virtue itself ! Throw yourself at her feet and ask her to forgive me. I dare not do it myself. I cannot implore for pardon because I have been too cruelly unjust towards her.'

And in saying these words the unhappy man hid his face in his hands and wept bitterly. If he doubted that the woman he had so mercilessly tortured would forgive him, it was because M. de Moray did not yet know her well.

'Roger !' cried Laura, opening her arms to him, 'forget everything. I remember only your love of old, and as of old, also, I love you.'

M. de Moray held her to his heart for a long time, supporting her with one arm, whilst with the other he drew Paulette to him, and she shared his kisses with her mother.

At this moment the door of the boudoir was opened, and Annibal and Claudia entered. The Italian had not heard anything of what had been said in the drawing-room. The thick hangings used as door curtains had deadened the noise of the voices, and only vague sounds had reached her ears. Exasperated because she could not hear what was said so near her, and strong besides in her rights as mistress of the house, she had not had the patience to wait until Mme. de la Marche should call her in, as she had promised ; she had suddenly rushed, as we have seen, into the room she was banished from.

'Ah !' she cried, with rage, addressing Laura, ' you were telling the truth, madam. One word has been sufficient to bring back to your feet the noble and loyal Count de Moray.'

Palmeri thought it was his duty to come to the help of his sister.

' What has happened, M. de Moray,' he asked, ' that such an outrage should be inflicted on my sister ? And how is it that this woman ——'

'This woman,' cried Roger, fiercely, pressing Laura to his heart, ' this woman has a right to all your admiration and your respect. To yours, sir ; to yours, also, madam, as well as to mine.'

' She may go somewhere else to receive the homage she deserves,' answered Claudia, brutally. ' But she will go out of here ! This house is mine, and I will have her thrown out of it.'

And the Italian went towards the chimney. She was going to ring for the servants when she found herself face to face with a personage who stopped her, by placing himself before her and making a bow so very profound that it exceeded the bounds of politeness and reached those of irony. It was Sir Elias Drack.

' Madam,' said the Englishman, with the greatest civility, ' if I heard aright, you have just said that you would have the mother of Miss Paulette put out by the servants. I shall be very grateful if you will tell me by what right and under what title you act so rudely towards such an honorable person ? '

' By what right and under what title I want to be the mistress of my house and keep my husband ? '

' Your husband ? I beg your pardon. Whom do you speak of ? '

' Whom do I speak of ? but of the Count de Moray, here ! '

' Let us agree, beautiful lady ! M. de Moray can only be the husband of a living person, I suppose, and if you have forgotten it, I have the regret to remind you that you are dead ! '

At this word they all looked at him. Was Sir Elias Drack becoming insane ? However, Annibal had started ; he had drawn little by little nearer the door, and was trying to slip off without making any noise. Sir Elias Drack stopped him with a word.

' I beg your pardon, dear M. Palmeri, do not run so quickly. He who has two feet in his grave needs to walk very carefully.'

' Two feet in his grave !' mechanically repeated Annibal, stupefied and mad with fright.

' Undoubtedly ! Born on the 9th June, 1851, you fell sick on the 22nd July, 1856. The next day, 23rd, your life was despaired of. On the morning of the 24th you died in the flower of your age, and a few hours after you were buried without further delay, for fear of epidemic infection. Your unfortunate sister, madam here present, attacked by the same disease, shared, alas! your demise and your funeral!'

'You are mad, sir!' cried Annibal, who was livid.

'The proof of what you advance? Give us the proof!' said Claudia, with effrontery.

'The proof! here it is!'

The Englishman then pulled out of his pocket a bundle of those yellow sheets used for telegraphic despatches.

'We have here,' he said, 'an official copy, giving word for word, the deeds of the civil status of M. Annibal and Miss Claudia Palmeri. A complete copy which proves, my dear madam, that you are neither Countess de Moray, nor Duchess de San Lucca, nor Claudia Palmeri, and that your two marriages, contracted under a false name, are null and void.'

'Who am I, then?' asked the young woman, with the arrogance of despair.

Sir Elias Drack, more and more gentlemanly, answered with exquisite grace:

'You are, pretty one, a splendid girl, the glory of the suburbs of Naples, called by her right name Gorgon! You are both surprised, undoubtedly, to find me so well informed. It is quite natural, however. When I heard this name of Palmeri, I remembered that I had something to do with people of that name, and that I had to legalise, in my quality of Italian consul at Calcutta, certain deeds concerning them. To make sure of it, I telegraphed to my successor in India, I telegraphed to the authorities at Naples, and I have gathered all the information I have just had the honor to acquaint you with.'

'So we have been the victims of low intriguers!' said M. de Moray.

'The law will punish them,' answered Elias Drack, 'and I am going ——'

'Roger,' said Laura, softly, 'this woman has been called the Countess de Moray. Let that name, although unduly borne, be the safeguard of the one it was entrusted to.'

'What! you wish it! But think it was she who made me doubt you?'

'If I meddled with other people's business, which I have never done and never will do,' said Mr. Drack, with modesty, 'I would take the liberty to urge you, my dear count, to follow the advice of the countess. It being well understood,' he continued, passing his arm through that of the Neapolitan, in order to prevent all desire of flight, if by chance he had any, 'it being well understood

that before their departure these two nice young people will settle
certain little accounts with me.'

'Certain accounts?' asked Annibal and Claudia together.

'A mere nothing,' said the consul. 'A simple formality. **M.**
Annibal will give up the millions of M. Palmeri.'

'The millions! I! never!'

'Unless he prefers going to gaol,' continued Sir Elias Drack, with
his usual calmness. 'These millions belong to the state, and they
will return to it. As to this interesting girl, she will recognize by
a deed already prepared to that effect, and which I have here, the
false quality she has used to sign her two deeds of marriage,
and thanks to her avowal, the two marriages will be made void
without scandal. Come, sign and be quick!' insisted for the last
time the mischievous old man, handing to Gorgon a pen which was
on the table.

The Italian took the pen; but before signing her own condemnation, she looked at M. de Moray. At this moment Roger was holding Laura's hands, and did not seem to remember that another
woman had ever crossed his life. Gorgon did not hesitate any
longer.

'And if I sign this,' she asked of Sir Elias Drack, 'will you let
me go?'

'With ten thousand francs to pay your expenses,' answered the
old consul graciously.

She leaned on the table and wrote a single word at the bottom of
the paper: Gorgon, simply. Then, without adding a word she
went out of the house, and on that evening she left for Italy with
Annibal, hardly wealthier than on the day they had come. But
they were free, and very happy to be so.

.   .   .   .

The false Annibal and the false Claudia had hardly left the mansion, in company with Sir Elias Drack, to settle the famous little
accounts, when M. de Moray went towards the room where a few
friends had gathered. They were to be the witnesses of the marriage
of poor Paulette with the Italian.

'Come, gentlemen, come all!' cried Roger, 'I have solemn and
happy things to tell you.'

Ten or twelve persons answered his appeal. At the same moment
appeared also the admiral, who, having learnt of the presence of his
wife and daughter at the mansion, had hurried thither. The reader
can judge of the astonishment produced by the sight of **Laura**, her
face radiant, leaning on the arm of M. de Moray.

'What does this mean?' asked the old sailor, stupefied.

Roger answered gravely, and deeply moved.

'M. de la Marche, and you, gentlemen,' he said, 'I am glad of
your presence, which allows me to publicly make a great act of

reparation. She who is by my side, and whom I repudiated unjustly, has never ceased to be a model of honor and virtue. I render this homage to her before you all, and I accuse myself before her and before you of the injurious suspicions of which I have been guilty. I had been led to suspicion, even to murder, by wretched adventurers. I went so far as to give to an unworthy woman the name and place of her who deserves my veneration and yours. Happily, the marriage I have contracted with the intriguer is null and void. A judgment will declare it so in a few days. So I will regain my freedom again. Thanks to the new law, divorced couples are allowed to contract between themselves a new marriage. Gentlemen, be all witnesses of the repentance I feel for the evil I have caused ; be witnesses to my sorrow and remorse ! '

Then turning to Laura, who was listening to his words, her eyes full of tears, he bended the knee.

' Laura,' he asked, ' will you allow me to redeem, by a whole life of devotion and love, the tortures I have inflicted on you ? '

For an answer the generous woman opened her arms.

' But to rehabilitate my daughter thus,' said in a low voice the old admiral to M. de Moray, ' what proof have you of her innocence ? '

At these words, Laura, trembling with fright, looked at her mother. Mme. de la Marche was livid. The noble Martyr devoted herself once more.

' Father,' she murmured, ' what proof could I give, alas ! The generous compassion of my husband rehabilitates me in the eyes of the world ; but in reality he does not justify me ; he forgives me ! '

Once more she had saved her mother and the old admiral.

.   .   .   .

Some time after, M. de Moray, invested anew with the high situation he used to occupy, and accompanied by all his family, was returning to India, where M. Gaston de Vallières married Paulette. On the very morning of the celebration of the marriage, a man recently disembarked appeared in the uniform of a consul before Paulette.

' Sir Elias Drack ! ' she cried, filled with joy and surprise.

' Myself,' he answered.

' But how does it come ? '

' Had not I promised I would be one of the witnesses of your marriage, Miss Paulette ? '

' That's true. But then you will stay here some time, with us ? '

' Some time, no, miss, no.'

' How ? '

' I have had the appointment of British Consul at Pondichéry, and I will remain here—always.'

At the cathedral where was celebrated, a few minutes after, the marriage of Paulette, a woman was praying by her side, her soul intoxicated with happiness. It was Laura. Even while living she had received the palms of Martyrdom, and God permitted her to know on this earth, between the mother, the husband, and the daughter she adored, the secret of celestial joys.

THE END.